THE
NAMESAKE

THE
NAMESAKE

JHUMPA LAHIRI

WHEELER
PUBLISHING

32.00
104

Published in 2003 by arrangement with Houghton Mifflin Company.

Wheeler Large Print Hardcover.

The text of this Large Print edition is unabridged.
Other aspects of the book may vary from the original edition.

Set in 16 pt. Plantin by Ramona Watson.

Printed in the United States on permanent paper.

Library of Congress Cataloging-in-Publication Data

Lahiri, Jhumpa.
 The namesake / Jhumpa Lahiri.
  p. cm.
  ISBN 1-58724-516-7 (lg. print : hc : alk. paper)
  1. Young men — Fiction. 2. Massachusetts — Fiction.
3. East Indian Americans — Fiction. 4. Children of immigrants — Fiction. 5. Assimilation (Sociology) — Fiction. 6. Alienation (Social psychology) — Fiction.
7. Gogolş' Nikolaæ Vasilş'vich, 1809–1852 — Appreciation — Fiction. 8. Large type books. I. Title.
PS3562.A316N36 2003
 813′.54—dc22   2003058056

For Alberto and Octavio,
whom I call by other names

As the Founder/CEO of NAVH, the only national health agency solely devoted to those who, although not totally blind, have an eye disease which could lead to serious visual impairment, I am pleased to recognize Thorndike Press* as one of the leading publishers in the large print field.

Founded in 1954 in San Francisco to prepare large print textbooks for partially seeing children, NAVH became the pioneer and standard setting agency in the preparation of large type.

Today, those publishers who meet our standards carry the prestigious "Seal of Approval" indicating high quality large print. We are delighted that Thorndike Press is one of the publishers whose titles meet these standards. We are also pleased to recognize the significant contribution Thorndike Press is making in this important and growing field.

Lorraine H. Marchi, L.H.D.
Founder/CEO
NAVH

* Thorndike Press encompasses the following imprints: Thorndike, Wheeler, Walker and Large Print Press.

The reader should realize himself that it could not have happened otherwise, and that to give him any other name was quite out of the question.

— NIKOLAI GOGOL, "The Overcoat"

Acknowledgments

I wish to thank the John Simon Guggenheim Foundation for its generous support. My deepest thanks also go to Susan Choi, Carin Clevidence, Gita Daneshjoo, Samantha Gillison, Daphne Kalotay, Cressida Leyshon, Heidi Pitlor, Janet Silver, Eric Simonoff, and Jayne Yaffe Kemp.

I am indebted to the following books: *Nikolai Gogol*, by Vladimir Nabokov, and *Divided Soul: The Life of Gogol*, by Henri Troyat. Quotations from "The Overcoat" are from David Magarshack's translation.

1.

1968

On a sticky August evening two weeks before her due date, Ashima Ganguli stands in the kitchen of a Central Square apartment, combining Rice Krispies and Planters peanuts and chopped red onion in a bowl. She adds salt, lemon juice, thin slices of green chili pepper, wishing there were mustard oil to pour into the mix. Ashima has been consuming this concoction throughout her pregnancy, a humble approximation of the snack sold for pennies on Calcutta sidewalks and on railway platforms throughout India, spilling from newspaper cones. Even now that there is barely space inside her, it is the one thing she craves. Tasting from a cupped palm, she frowns; as usual, there's something missing. She stares blankly at the pegboard behind the countertop where her cooking utensils hang, all slightly coated with grease. She wipes sweat from her face with the free end of her sari. Her swollen feet ache against speckled gray linoleum. Her pelvis aches from the baby's weight. She opens a cupboard, the shelves lined with a grimy

9

yellow-and-white-checkered paper she's been meaning to replace, and reaches for another onion, frowning again as she pulls at its crisp magenta skin. A curious warmth floods her abdomen, followed by a tightening so severe she doubles over, gasping without sound, dropping the onion with a thud on the floor.

The sensation passes, only to be followed by a more enduring spasm of discomfort. In the bathroom she discovers, on her underpants, a solid streak of brownish blood. She calls out to her husband, Ashoke, a doctoral candidate in electrical engineering at MIT, who is studying in the bedroom. He leans over a card table; the edge of their bed, two twin mattresses pushed together under a red and purple batik spread, serves as his chair. When she calls out to Ashoke, she doesn't say his name. Ashima never thinks of her husband's name when she thinks of her husband, even though she knows perfectly well what it is. She has adopted his surname but refuses, for propriety's sake, to utter his first. It's not the type of thing Bengali wives do. Like a kiss or caress in a Hindi movie, a husband's name is something intimate and therefore unspoken, cleverly patched over. And so, instead of saying Ashoke's name, she utters the interrogative that has come to replace it, which translates roughly as "Are you listening to me?"

★ ★ ★

At dawn a taxi is called to ferry them through deserted Cambridge streets, up Massachusetts Avenue and past Harvard Yard, to Mount Auburn Hospital. Ashima registers, answering questions about the frequency and duration of the contractions, as Ashoke fills out the forms. She is seated in a wheelchair and pushed through the shining, brightly lit corridors, whisked into an elevator more spacious than her kitchen. On the maternity floor she is assigned to a bed by a window, in a room at the end of the hall. She is asked to remove her Murshidabad silk sari in favor of a flowered cotton gown that, to her mild embarrassment, only reaches her knees. A nurse offers to fold up the sari but, exasperated by the six slippery yards, ends up stuffing the material into Ashima's slate blue suitcase. Her obstetrician, Dr. Ashley, gauntly handsome in a Lord Mountbatten sort of way, with fine sand-colored hair swept back from his temples, arrives to examine her progress. The baby's head is in the proper position, has already begun its descent. She is told that she is still in early labor, three centimeters dilated, beginning to efface. "What does it mean, dilated?" she asks, and Dr. Ashley holds up two fingers side by side, then draws them apart, explaining the unimaginable thing her body must do in order for the baby to pass. The process will take

11

some time, Dr. Ashley tells her; given that this is her first pregnancy, labor can take twenty-four hours, sometimes more. She searches for Ashoke's face, but he has stepped behind the curtain the doctor has drawn. "I'll be back," Ashoke says to her in Bengali, and then a nurse adds: "Don't you worry, Mr. Ganguli. She's got a long ways to go. We can take over from here."

Now she is alone, cut off by curtains from the three other women in the room. One woman's name, she gathers from bits of conversation, is Beverly. Another is Lois. Carol lies to her left. "Goddamnit, goddamn you, this is hell," she hears one of them say. And then a man's voice: "I love you, sweetheart." Words Ashima has neither heard nor expects to hear from her own husband; this is not how they are. It is the first time in her life she has slept alone, surrounded by strangers; all her life she has slept either in a room with her parents, or with Ashoke at her side. She wishes the curtains were open, so that she could talk to the American women. Perhaps one of them has given birth before, can tell her what to expect. But she has gathered that Americans, in spite of their public declarations of affection, in spite of their miniskirts and bikinis, in spite of their hand-holding on the street and lying on top of each other on the Cambridge Common, prefer their privacy. She spreads her fingers over the taut, enormous drum her middle has become, wondering where the baby's feet and hands are at this moment. The child is no longer restless; for the past few days, apart from the occasional flutter, she has not felt it punch or kick or press against her ribs. She wonders if she is the only Indian person in the hospital, but a gentle twitch from the baby reminds her that she is, technically speaking, not alone. Ashima thinks it's strange that her child will be born in a place most people enter either to suffer or to die. There is nothing to comfort her in the off-white tiles of the floor, the off-white panels of the ceiling, the white sheets tucked tightly into the bed. In India, she thinks to herself, women go home to their parents to give birth, away from husbands and in-laws and household cares, retreating briefly to child-hood when the baby arrives.

Another contraction begins, more violent than the last. She cries out, pressing her head against the pillow. Her fingers grip the chilly rails of the bed. No one hears her, no nurse rushes to her side. She has been instructed to time the duration of the contractions and so she consults her watch, a bon voyage gift from her parents, slipped over her wrist the last time she saw them, amid airport confusion and tears. It wasn't until she was on the plane, flying for the first time in her life on a BOAC VC-10 whose deafening ascent twenty-six members of her family had watched from the balcony at Dum Dum Airport, as she was drifting over parts of India she'd never set foot in, and then even farther, outside India itself, that she'd noticed the watch among the cavalcade of matrimonial bracelets on both her arms: iron, gold, coral, conch. Now, in addition, she wears a plastic bracelet with a typed label identifying her as a patient of the hospital. She keeps the watch face turned to the inside of her wrist. On the back, surrounded by the words *waterproof, antimagnetic,* and *shock-protected,* her married initials, *A.G.,* are inscribed.

American seconds tick on top of her pulse point. For half a minute, a band of pain wraps around her stomach, radiating toward her back and shooting down her legs. And then, again, relief. She calculates the Indian time on her hands. The tip of her thumb strikes each rung of the brown ladders etched onto the backs of her fingers, then stops at the middle of the third: it is nine and a half hours ahead in Calcutta, already evening, half past eight. In the kitchen of her parents' flat on Amherst Street, at this very moment, a servant is pouring after-dinner tea into steaming glasses, arranging Marie biscuits on a tray. Her mother, very soon to be a grandmother, is standing at the mirror of her dressing table, untangling waist-length hair, still more black than gray, with her fingers.

Her father hunches over his slanted ink-stained table by the window, sketching, smoking, listening to the Voice of America. Her younger brother, Rana, studies for a physics exam on the bed. She pictures clearly the gray cement floor of her parents' sitting room, feels its solid chill underfoot even on the hottest days. An enormous black-and-white photograph of her deceased paternal grandfather looms at one end against the pink plaster wall; opposite, an alcove shielded by clouded panes of glass is stuffed with books and papers and her father's watercolor tins. For an instant the weight of the baby vanishes, replaced by the scene that passes before her eyes, only to be replaced once more by a blue strip of the Charles River, thick green treetops, cars gliding up and down Memorial Drive.

In Cambridge it is eleven in the morning, already lunchtime in the hospital's acceler-ated day. A tray holding warm apple juice, Jell-O, ice cream, and cold baked chicken is brought to her side. Patty, the friendly nurse with the diamond engagement ring and a fringe of reddish hair beneath her cap, tells Ashima to consume only the Jell-O and the apple juice. It's just as well. Ashima would not have touched the chicken, even if per-mitted; Americans eat their chicken in its skin, though Ashima has recently found a kind butcher on Prospect Street willing to pull it off for her. Patty comes to fluff the pillows, tidy the bed. Dr. Ashley pokes in his head from time to time. "No need to worry," he chirps, putting a stethoscope to Ashima's belly, patting her hand, admiring her various bracelets. "Everything is looking perfectly normal. We are expecting a perfectly normal delivery, Mrs. Ganguli."

But nothing feels normal to Ashima. For the past eighteen months, ever since she's arrived in Cambridge, nothing has felt normal at all. It's not so much the pain, which she knows, somehow, she will survive. It's the consequence: motherhood in a foreign land. For it was one thing to be pregnant, to suffer the queasy mornings in bed, the sleepless nights, the dull throbbing in her back, the countless visits to the bathroom. Throughout the experience, in spite of her growing discomfort, she'd been astonished by her body's ability to make life, exactly as her mother and grandmother and all her great-grandmothers had done. That it was happening so far from home, unmonitored and unobserved by those she loved, had made it more miraculous still. But she is terrified to raise a child in a country where she is related to no one, where she knows so little, where life seems so tentative and spare.

"How about a little walk? It might do you good," Patty asks when she comes to clear the lunch tray.

Ashima looks up from a tattered copy of *Desh* magazine that she'd brought to read on her plane ride to Boston and still cannot bring herself to throw away. The printed pages of Bengali type, slightly rough to the touch, are a perpetual comfort to her. She's read each of the short stories and poems and articles a dozen times. There is a pen-and-ink drawing on page eleven by her father, an illustrator for the magazine: a view of the North Calcutta skyline sketched from the roof of their flat one foggy January morning. She had stood behind her father as he'd drawn it, watching as he crouched over his easel, a cigarette dangling from his lips, his shoulders wrapped in a black Kashmiri shawl.

"Yes, all right," Ashima says.

Patty helps Ashima out of bed, tucks her feet one by one into slippers, drapes a second nightgown around her shoulders. "Just think," Patty says as Ashima struggles to stand. "In a day or two you'll be half the size." She takes Ashima's arm as they step out of the room, into the hallway. After a few feet Ashima stops, her legs trembling as another wave of pain surges through her body. She shakes her head, her eyes filling with tears. "I cannot."

"You can. Squeeze my hand. Squeeze as tight as you like."

After a minute they continue on, toward

the nurses' station. "Hoping for a boy or a girl?" Patty asks.

"As long as there are ten finger and ten toe," Ashima replies. For these anatomical details, these particular signs of life, are the ones she has the most difficulty picturing when she imagines the baby in her arms.

Patty smiles, a little too widely, and suddenly Ashima realizes her error, knows she should have said "fingers" and "toes." This error pains her almost as much as her last contraction. English had been her subject. In Calcutta, before she was married, she was working toward a college degree. She used to tutor neighborhood schoolchildren in their homes, on their verandas and beds, helping them to memorize Tennyson and Wordsworth, to pronounce words like *sign* and *cough,* to understand the difference between Aristotelian and Shakespearean tragedy. But in Bengali, a finger can also mean fingers, a toe toes.

It had been after tutoring one day that Ashima's mother had met her at the door, told her to go straight to the bedroom and prepare herself; a man was waiting to see her. He was the third in as many months. The first had been a widower with four children. The second, a newspaper cartoonist who knew her father, had been hit by a bus in Esplanade and lost his left arm. To her great relief they had both rejected her. She was

18

nineteen, in the middle of her studies, in no rush to be a bride. And so, obediently but without expectation, she had untangled and rebraided her hair, wiped away the kohl that had smudged below her eyes, patted some Cuticura powder from a velvet puff onto her skin. The sheer parrot green sari she pleated and tucked into her petticoat had been laid out for her on the bed by her mother. Before entering the sitting room, Ashima had paused in the corridor. She could hear her mother saying, "She is fond of cooking, and she can knit extremely well. Within a week she finished this cardigan I am wearing."

Ashima smiled, amused by her mother's salesmanship; it had taken her the better part of a year to finish the cardigan, and still her mother had had to do the sleeves. Glancing at the floor where visitors customarily removed their slippers, she noticed, beside two sets of chappals, a pair of men's shoes that were not like any she'd ever seen on the streets and trams and buses of Calcutta, or even in the windows of Bata. They were brown shoes with black heels and off-white laces and stitching. There was a band of lentil-sized holes embossed on either side of each shoe, and at the tips was a pretty pattern pricked into the leather as if with a needle. Looking more closely, she saw the shoemaker's name written on the insides, in gold lettering that had all but faded: something and sons, it said. She saw the size, eight and a half, and the initials U.S.A. And as her mother continued to sing her praises, Ashima, unable to resist a sudden and over-whelming urge, stepped into the shoes at her feet. Lingering sweat from the owner's feet mingled with hers, causing her heart to race; it was the closest thing she had ever experi-enced to the touch of a man. The leather was creased, heavy, and still warm. On the left shoe she had noticed that one of the crisscrossing laces had missed a hole, and this oversight set her at ease.

She extracted her feet, entered the room. The man was sitting in a rattan chair, his parents perched on the edge of the twin bed where her brother slept at night. He was slightly plump, scholarly-looking but still youthful, with black thick-framed glasses and a sharp, prominent nose. A neatly trimmed mustache connected to a beard that covered only his chin lent him an elegant, vaguely aristocratic air. He wore brown socks and brown trousers and a green-and-white-striped shirt and was staring glumly at his knees.

He did not look up when she appeared. Though she was aware of his gaze as she crossed the room, by the time she managed to steal another look at him he was once again indifferent, focused on his knees. He cleared his throat as if to speak but then said nothing. Instead it was his father who did the talking, saying that the man had gone to St. Xavier's, and then B.E. College, graduating first-class-first from both institutions. Ashima took her seat and smoothed the pleats of her sari. She sensed the mother eyeing her with approval. Ashima was five feet four inches, tall for a Bengali woman, ninety-nine pounds. Her complexion was on the dark side of fair, but she had been compared on more than one occasion to the actress Madhabi Mukherjee. Her nails were admirably long, her fingers, like her father's, artistically slim. They inquired after her studies and she was asked to recite a few stanzas from "The Daffodils." The man's family lived in Alipore. The father was a labor officer for the customs department of a shipping company. "My son has been living abroad for two years," the man's father said, "earning a Ph.D. in Boston, researching in the field of fiber optics." Ashima had never heard of Boston, or of fiber optics. She was asked whether she was willing to fly on a plane and then if she was capable of living in a city characterized by severe, snowy winters, alone.

"Won't he be there?" she'd asked, pointing to the man whose shoes she'd briefly occupied, but who had yet to say a word to her.

It was only after the betrothal that she'd learned his name. One week later the invitations were printed, and two weeks after that she was adorned and adjusted by countless aunts, countless cousins hovering around her. These were her last moments as Ashima Bhaduri, before becoming Ashima Ganguli. Her lips were darkened, her brow and cheeks dotted with sandalwood paste, her hair wound up, bound with flowers, held in place by a hundred wire pins that would take an hour to remove once the wedding was finally over. Her head was draped with scarlet netting. The air was damp, and in spite of the pins Ashima's hair, thickest of all the cousins', would not lie flat. She wore all the necklaces and chokers and bracelets that were destined to live most of their lives in an extra-large safety deposit box in a bank vault in New England. At the designated hour she was seated on a piri that her father had decorated, hoisted five feet off the ground, carried out to meet the groom. She had hidden her face with a heart-shaped betel leaf, kept her head bent low until she had circled him seven times.

Eight thousand miles away in Cambridge, she has come to know him. In the evenings she cooks for him, hoping to please, with the unrationed, remarkably unblemished sugar, flour, rice, and salt she had written about to her mother in her very first letter home. By now she has learned that her husband likes his food on the salty side, that his favorite thing about lamb curry is the potatoes, and that he likes to finish his dinner with a small final helping of rice and dal. At night, lying beside her in bed, he listens to her describe the events of her day: her walks along Massachusetts Avenue, the shops she visits, the Hare Krishnas who pester her with their leaflets, the pistachio ice cream cones she treats herself to in Harvard Square. In spite of his meager graduate student wages he sets aside money to send every few months to his father to help put an extension on his parents' house. He is fastidious about his clothing; their first argument had been over a sweater she'd shrunk in the washing machine. As soon as he comes home from the university the first thing he does is hang up his shirt and trousers, donning a pair of drawstring pajamas and a pullover if it's cold. On Sundays he spends an hour occupied with his tins of shoe polishes and his three pairs of shoes, two black and one brown. The brown ones are the ones he'd been wearing when he'd first come to see her. The sight of him cross-legged on newspapers spread on the floor, intently whisking a brush over the leather, always reminds her of her indiscretion in her parents' corridor. It is a moment that shocks her still, and that she prefers, in spite of all she tells him at night about the life they now share, to keep to herself.

On another floor of the hospital, in a waiting room, Ashoke hunches over a *Boston*

Globe from a month ago, abandoned on a neighboring chair. He reads about the riots that took place during the Democratic National Convention in Chicago and about Dr. Benjamin Spock, the baby doctor, being sentenced to two years in jail for threatening to counsel draft evaders. The Favre Leuba strapped to his wrist is running six minutes ahead of the large gray-faced clock on the wall. It is four-thirty in the morning. An hour before, Ashoke had been fast asleep, at home, Ashima's side of the bed covered with exams he'd been grading late at night, when the telephone rang. Ashima was fully dilated and being taken to the delivery room, the person on the other end had said. Upon arrival at the hospital he was told that she was pushing, that it could be any minute now. Any minute. And yet it seemed only the other day, one steel-colored winter's morning when the windows of the house were being pelted with hail, that she had spit out her tea, accusing him of mistaking the salt for sugar. To prove himself right he had taken a sip of the sweet liquid from her cup, but she had insisted on its bitterness, and poured it down the sink. That was the first thing that had caused her to suspect, and then the doctor had confirmed it, and then he would wake to the sounds, every morning when she went to brush her teeth, of her retching. Before he left for the university he would leave a cup of tea by the side of the bed, where she lay listless and silent. Often, returning in the evenings, he would find her still lying there, the tea untouched.

He now desperately needs a cup of tea for himself, not having managed to make one before leaving the house. But the machine in the corridor dispenses only coffee, tepid at best, in paper cups. He takes off his thick-rimmed glasses, fitted by a Calcutta optometrist, polishes the lenses with the cotton handkerchief he always keeps in his pocket, *A* for *Ashoke* embroidered by his mother in light blue thread. His black hair, normally combed back neatly from his forehead, is disheveled, sections of it on end. He stands and begins pacing as the other expectant fathers do. So far, the door to the waiting room has opened twice, and a nurse has announced that one of them has a boy or a girl. There are handshakes all around, pats on the back, before the father is escorted away. The men wait with cigars, flowers, address books, bottles of champagne. They smoke cigarettes, ashing onto the floor. Ashoke is indifferent to such indulgences. He neither smokes nor drinks alcohol of any kind. Ashima is the one who keeps all their addresses, in a small notebook she carries in her purse. It has never occurred to him to buy his wife flowers.

He returns to the *Globe*, still pacing as he

25

reads. A slight limp causes Ashoke's right foot to drag almost imperceptibly with each step. Since childhood he has had the habit and the ability to read while walking, holding a book in one hand on his way to school, from room to room in his parents' three-story house in Alipore, and up and down the red clay stairs. Nothing roused him. Nothing distracted him. Nothing caused him to stumble. As a teenager he had gone through all of Dickens. He read newer authors as well, Graham Greene and Somerset Maugham, all purchased from his favorite stall on College Street with pujo money. But most of all he loved the Russians. His paternal grandfather, a former professor of European literature at Calcutta University, had read from them aloud in English translations when Ashoke was a boy. Each day at tea time, as his brothers and sisters played kabadi and cricket outside, Ashoke would go to his grandfather's room, and for an hour his grandfather would read supine on the bed, his ankles crossed and the book propped open on his chest, Ashoke curled at his side. For that hour Ashoke was deaf and blind to the world around him. He did not hear his brothers and sisters laughing on the rooftop, or see the tiny, dusty, cluttered room in which his grandfather read. "Read all the Russians, and then reread them," his grandfather had said. "They will never fail you." When Ashoke's

English was good enough, he began to read the books himself. It was while walking on some of the world's noisiest, busiest streets, on Chowringhee and Gariahat Road, that he had read pages of *The Brothers Karamazov*, and *Anna Karenina*, and *Fathers and Sons*. Once, a younger cousin who had tried to imitate him had fallen down the red clay staircase in Ashoke's house and broken an arm. Ashoke's mother was always convinced that her eldest son would be hit by a bus or a tram, his nose deep into *War and Peace*. That he would be reading a book the moment he died.

One day, in the earliest hours of October 20, 1961, this nearly happened. Ashoke was twenty-two, a student at B.E. College. He was traveling on the 83 Up Howrah–Ranchi Express to visit his grandparents for the holidays; they had moved from Calcutta to Jamshedpur upon his grandfather's retirement from the university. Ashoke had never spent the holidays away from his family. But his grandfather had recently gone blind, and he had requested Ashoke's company specifically, to read him *The Statesman* in the morning, Dostoyevsky and Tolstoy in the afternoon. Ashoke accepted the invitation eagerly. He carried two suitcases, the first one containing clothes and gifts, the second empty. For it would be on this visit, his grandfather had said, that the books in his glass-fronted case, collected over a lifetime and preserved under lock and key, would be given to Ashoke. The books had been promised to Ashoke throughout his childhood, and for as long as he could remember he had coveted them more than anything else in the world. He had already received a few in recent years, given to him on birthdays and other special occasions. But now that the day had come to inherit the rest, a day his grandfather could no longer read the books himself, Ashoke was saddened, and as he placed the empty suitcase under his seat, he was disconcerted by its weightlessness, regretful of the circumstances that would cause it, upon his return, to be full.

He carried a single volume for the journey, a hardbound collection of short stories by Nikolai Gogol, which his grandfather had given him when he'd graduated from class twelve. On the title page, beneath his grandfather's signature, Ashoke had written his own. Because of Ashoke's passion for this particular book, the spine had recently split, threatening to divide the pages into two sections. His favorite story in the book was the last, "The Overcoat," and that was the one Ashoke had begun to reread as the train pulled out of Howrah Station late in the evening with a prolonged and deafening shriek, away from his parents and his six younger brothers and sisters, all of whom had come to see him off and had huddled until the last moment by the window, waving to him from the long dusky platform. He had read "The Overcoat" too many times to count, certain sentences and phrases embedded in his memory. Each time he was captivated by the absurd, tragic, yet oddly inspiring story of Akaky Akakyevich, the impoverished main character who spends his life meekly copying documents written by others and suffering the ridicule of absolutely everyone. His heart went out to poor Akaky, a humble clerk just as Ashoke's father had been at the start of his career. Each time, reading the account of Akaky's christening, and the series of queer names his mother had rejected, Ashoke laughed aloud. He shuddered at the description of the tailor Petrovich's big toe, "with its deformed nail as thick and hard as the shell of a tortoise." His mouth watered at the cold veal and cream pastries and champagne Akaky consumed the night his precious coat was stolen, in spite of the fact that Ashoke had never tasted these things himself. Ashoke was always devastated when Akaky was robbed in "a square that looked to him like a dreadful desert," leaving him cold and vulnerable, and Akaky's death, some pages later, never failed to bring tears to his eyes. In some ways the story made less sense each time he read it, the scenes he pictured so vividly, and absorbed so fully, growing more elusive and profound. Just as Akaky's ghost haunted the final pages, so did it haunt a place deep in Ashoke's soul, shedding light on all that was irrational, all that was inevitable about the world.

Outside the view turned quickly black, the scattered lights of Howrah giving way to nothing at all. He had a second-class sleeper in the seventh bogie, behind the air-conditioned coach. Because of the season, the train was especially crowded, especially raucous, filled with families on holiday. Small children were wearing their best clothing, the girls with brightly colored ribbons in their hair. Though he had had his dinner before leaving for the station, a four-layer tiffin carrier packed by his mother sat at his feet, in the event that hunger should attack him in the night. He shared his compartment with three others. There was a middle-aged Bihari couple who, he gathered from overhearing their conversation, had just married off their eldest daughter, and a friendly, potbellied, middle-aged Bengali businessman wearing a suit and tie, by the name of Ghosh. Ghosh told Ashoke that he had recently returned to India after spending two years in England on a job voucher, but that he had come back home because his wife was inconsolably miserable abroad. Ghosh spoke reverently of England. The sparkling, empty streets, the polished black cars, the rows of gleaming white houses, he said, were like a dream. Trains departed and arrived according to schedule, Ghosh said. No one spat on the sidewalks. It was in a British hospital that his son had been born.

"Seen much of this world?" Ghosh asked Ashoke, untying his shoes and settling himself cross-legged on the berth. He pulled a packet of Dunhill cigarettes from his jacket pocket, offering them around the compartment before lighting one for himself.

"Once to Delhi," Ashoke replied. "And lately once a year to Jamshedpur."

Ghosh extended his arm out the window, flicking the glowing tip of his cigarette into the night. "Not this world," he said, glancing disappointedly about the interior of the train. He tilted his head toward the window. "England. America," he said, as if the nameless villages they passed had been replaced by those countries. "Have you considered going there?"

"My professors mention it from time to time. But I have a family," Ashoke said.

Ghosh frowned. "Already married?"

"No. A mother and father and six siblings. I am the eldest."

"And in a few years you will be married and living in your parents' house," Ghosh speculated.

"I suppose."

Ghosh shook his head. "You are still

young. Free," he said, spreading his hands apart for emphasis. "Do yourself a favor. Before it's too late, without thinking too much about it first, pack a pillow and a blanket and see as much of the world as you can. You will not regret it. One day it will be too late."

"My grandfather always says that's what books are for," Ashoke said, using the opportunity to open the volume in his hands. "To travel without moving an inch."

"To each his own," Ghosh said. He tipped his head politely to one side, letting the last of the cigarette drop from his fingertips. He reached into a bag by his feet and took out his diary, turning to the twentieth of October. The page was blank and on it, with a fountain pen whose cap he ceremoniously unscrewed, he wrote his name and address. He ripped out the page and handed it to Ashoke. "If you ever change your mind and need contacts, let me know. I live in Tollygunge, just behind the tram depot."

"Thank you," Ashoke said, folding up the information and putting it at the back of his book.

"How about a game of cards?" Ghosh suggested. He pulled out a well-worn deck from his suit pocket, with Big Ben's image on the back. But Ashoke politely declined, for he knew no card games, and besides which, he preferred to read. One by one the passengers brushed their teeth in the vestibule, changed into their pajamas, fastened the curtain around their compartments, and went to sleep. Ghosh offered to take the upper berth, climbing barefoot up the ladder, his suit carefully folded away, so that Ashoke had the window to himself. The Bihari couple shared some sweets from a box and drank water from the same cup without either of them putting their lips to the rim, then settled into their berths as well, switching off the lights and turning their heads to the wall.

Only Ashoke continued to read, still seated, still dressed. A single small bulb glowed dimly over his head. From time to time he looked through the open window at the inky Bengal night, at the vague shapes of palm trees and the simplest of homes. Carefully he turned the soft yellow pages of his book, a few delicately tunneled by worms. The steam engine puffed reassuringly, powerfully. Deep in his chest he felt the rough jostle of the wheels. Sparks from the smokestack passed by his window. A fine layer of sticky soot dotted one side of his face, his eyelid, his arm, his neck; his grandmother would insist that he scrub himself with a cake of Margo soap as soon as he arrived. Immersed in the sartorial plight of Akaky Akakyevich, lost in the wide, snow-white, windy avenues of St. Petersburg, unaware that one day he was to dwell in a snowy place himself, Ashoke was still reading at two-thirty in the morning, one of the few passengers on the train who was awake, when the locomotive engine and seven bogies derailed from the broad-gauge line. The sound was like a bomb exploding. The first four bogies capsized into a depression alongside the track. The fifth and sixth, containing the first-class and air-conditioned passengers, telescoped into each other, killing the passengers in their sleep. The seventh, where Ashoke was sitting, capsized as well, flung by the speed of the crash farther into the field. The accident occurred 209 kilometers from Calcutta, between the Ghatshila and Dhalbumgarh stations. The train guard's portable phone would not work; it was only after the guard ran nearly five kilometers from the site of the accident, to Ghatshila, that he was able to transmit the first message for help. Over an hour passed before the rescuers arrived, bearing lanterns and shovels and axes to pry bodies from the cars.

Ashoke can still remember their shouts, asking if anyone was alive. He remembers trying to shout back, unsuccessfully, his mouth emitting nothing but the faintest rasp. He remembers the sound of people half-dead around him, moaning and tapping on the walls of the train, whispering hoarsely for help, words that only those who were also trapped and injured could possibly hear.

Blood drenched his chest and the right arm of his shirt. He had been thrust partway out the window. He remembers being unable to see anything at all; for the first hours he thought that perhaps, like his grandfather whom he was on his way to visit, he'd gone blind. He remembers the acrid odor of flames, the buzzing of flies, children crying, the taste of dust and blood on his tongue. They were nowhere, somewhere in a field. Milling about them were villagers, police inspectors, a few doctors. He remembers believing that he was dying, that perhaps he was already dead. He could not feel the lower half of his body, and so was unaware that the mangled limbs of Ghosh were draped over his legs. Eventually he saw the cold, unfriendly blue of earliest morning, the moon and a few stars still lingering in the sky. The pages of his book, which had been tossed from his hand, fluttered in two sections a few feet away from the train. The glare from a search lantern briefly caught the pages, momentarily distracting one of the rescuers. "Nothing here," Ashoke heard someone say. "Let's keep going."

But the lantern's light lingered, just long enough for Ashoke to raise his hand, a gesture that he believed would consume the small fragment of life left in him. He was still clutching a single page of "The Overcoat," crumpled tightly in his fist, and when he raised his hand the wad of paper dropped from his fingers. "Wait!" he heard a voice cry out. "The fellow by that book. I saw him move."

He was pulled from the wreckage, placed on a stretcher, transported on another train to a hospital in Tatanagar. He had broken his pelvis, his right femur, and three of his ribs on the right side. For the next year of his life he lay flat on his back, ordered to keep as still as possible as the bones of his body healed. There was a risk that his right leg might be permanently paralyzed. He was transferred to Calcutta Medical College, where two screws were put into his hips. By December he had returned to his parents' house in Alipore, carried through the courtyard and up the red clay stairs like a corpse, hoisted on the shoulders of his four brothers. Three times a day he was spoon-fed. He urinated and defecated into a tin pan. Doctors and visitors came and went. Even his blind grandfather from Jamshedpur paid a visit. His family had saved the newspaper accounts. In a photograph, he observed the train smashed to shards, piled jaggedly against the sky, security guards sitting on the unclaimed belongings. He learned that fishplates and bolts had been found several feet from the main track, giving rise to the suspicion, never subsequently confirmed, of sabotage. That bodies had been mutilated beyond recogni-

36

tion. "Holiday-Makers' Tryst with Death," the *Times of India* had written.

In the beginning, for most of the day, he had stared at his bedroom ceiling, at the three beige blades of the fan churning at its center, their edges grimy. He could hear the top edge of a calendar scraping against the wall behind him when the fan was on. If he moved his neck to the right he had a view of a window with a dusty bottle of Dettol on its ledge and, if the shutters were open, the concrete of the wall that surrounded the house, the pale brown geckos that scampered there. He listened to the constant parade of sounds outside, footsteps, bicycle bells, the incessant squawking of crows and of the horns of cycle rickshaws in the lane so narrow that taxis could not fit. He heard the tube well at the corner being pumped into urns. Every evening at dusk he heard a conch shell being blown in the house next door to signal the hour for prayer. He could smell but not see the shimmering green sludge that collected in the open sewer. Life within the house continued. His father came and went from work, his brothers and sisters from school. His mother worked in the kitchen, checking in on him periodically, her lap stained with turmeric. Twice daily the maid twisted rags into buckets of water and wiped the floors.

During the day he was groggy from pain-killers. At night he dreamed either that he was still trapped inside the train or, worse, that the accident had never happened, that he was walking down a street, taking a bath, sitting cross-legged on the floor and eating a plate of food. And then he would wake up, coated in sweat, tears streaming down his face, convinced that he would never live to do such things again. Eventually, in an attempt to avoid his nightmares, he began to read, late at night, which was when his motionless body felt most restless, his mind agile and clear. Yet he refused to read the Russians his grandfather had brought to his bedside, or any novels, for that matter. Those books, set in countries he had never seen, reminded him only of his confinement. Instead he read his engineering books, trying his best to keep up with his courses, solving equations by flashlight. In those silent hours, he thought often of Ghosh. "Pack a pillow and a blanket," he heard Ghosh say. He remembered the address Ghosh had written on a page of his diary, somewhere behind the tram depot in Tollygunge. Now it was the home of a widow, a fatherless son. Each day, to bolster his spirits, his family reminded him of the future, the day he would stand unassisted, walk across the room. It was for this, each day, that his father and mother prayed. For this that his mother gave up meat on Wednesdays. But as the months passed, Ashoke began to envision another sort of future. He imagined not only walking, but walking away, as far as he could from the place in which he was born and in which he had nearly died. The following year, with the aid of a cane, he returned to college and graduated, and without telling his parents he applied to continue his engineering studies abroad. Only after he'd been accepted with a full fellowship, a newly issued passport in hand, did he inform them of his plans. "But we already nearly lost you once," his bewildered father had protested. His siblings had pleaded and wept. His mother, speechless, had refused food for three days. In spite of all that, he'd gone.

Seven years later, there are still certain images that wipe him flat. They lurk around a corner as he rushes through the engineering department at MIT, checks his campus mail. They hover by his shoulder as he leans over a plate of rice at dinnertime or nestles against Ashima's limbs at night. At every turning point in his life — at his wedding when he stood behind Ashima, encircling her waist and peering over her shoulder as they poured puffed rice into a fire, or during his first hours in America, seeing a small gray city caked with snow — he has tried but failed to push these images away: the twisted, battered, capsized bogies of the train, his body twisted below it, the terrible crunching sound he had heard but not comprehended, his bones crushed as fine as flour. It is not the memory of pain that haunts him; he has no memory of that. It is the memory of waiting before he was rescued, and the persistent fear, rising up in his throat, that he might not have been rescued at all. To this day he is claustrophobic, holding his breath in elevators, feels pent-up in cars unless the windows are open on both sides. On planes he requests the bulkhead seat. At times the wailing of children fills him with deepest dread. At times he still presses his ribs to make sure they are solid.

He presses them now, in the hospital, shaking his head in relief, disbelief. Although it is Ashima who carries the child, he, too, feels heavy, with the thought of life, of his life and the life about to come from it. He was raised without running water, nearly killed at twenty-two. Again he tastes the dust on his tongue, sees the twisted train, the giant overturned iron wheels. None of this was supposed to happen. But no, he had survived it. He was born twice in India, and then a third time, in America. Three lives by thirty. For this he thanks his parents, and their parents, and the parents of their parents. He does not thank God; he openly reveres Marx and quietly refuses religion. But there is one more dead soul he has to thank. He cannot thank the book; the book has perished, as he nearly did, in scattered pieces, in the earliest hours of an October day, in a field 209 kilometers from Calcutta. Instead of thanking God he thanks Gogol, the Russian writer who had saved his life, when Patty enters the waiting room.

2.

The baby, a boy, is born at five past five in the morning. He measures twenty inches long, weighs seven pounds nine ounces. Ashima's initial glimpse, before the cord is clipped and they carry him away, is of a creature coated with a thick white paste, and streaks of blood, her blood, on the shoulders, feet, and head. A needle placed in the small of her back has removed all sensation from her waist to her knees, and given her a blistering headache in the final stages of the delivery. When it is all over she begins to shiver profoundly, as if beset with an acute fever. For half an hour she trembles, in a daze, covered by a blanket, her insides empty, her outside still misshapen. She is unable to speak, to allow the nurses to help exchange her blood-soaked gown for a fresh one. In spite of endless glasses of water, her throat is parched. She is told to sit on a toilet, to squirt warm water from a bottle between her legs. Eventually she is sponged clean, put into a new gown, wheeled into yet another room. The lights are soothingly dim, and there is only one other bed next to hers, empty for the time being. When Ashoke arrives, Patty is taking Ashima's blood pressure, and Ashima is reclining against a pile of pillows, the child wrapped like an oblong white parcel in her arms. Beside the bed is a bassinet, labeled with a card that says BABY BOY GANGULI.

"He's here," she says quietly, looking up at Ashoke with a weak smile. Her skin is faintly yellow, the color missing from her lips. She has circles beneath her eyes, and her hair, spilling from its braid, looks as though it has not been combed for days. Her voice is hoarse, as if she'd caught a cold. He pulls up a chair by the side of the bed and Patty helps to transfer the child from mother's to father's arms. In the process, the child pierces the silence in the room with a short-lived cry. His parents react with mutual alarm, but Patty laughs approvingly. "You see," Patty says to Ashima, "he's already getting to know you."

Ashoke does as Patty tells him, stretching out his arms, putting one hand below the neck, another below the bottom.

"Go on," Patty urges. "He wants to be held tightly. He's stronger than you think."

Ashoke lifts the minuscule parcel higher, closer to his chest. "Like this?"

"There you go," Patty says. "I'll leave you three alone for a while."

At first Ashoke is more perplexed than moved, by the pointiness of the head, the puffiness of the lids, the small white spots on the cheeks, the fleshy upper lip that droops prominently over the lower one. The skin is paler than either Ashima's or his own, translucent enough to show slim green veins at the temples. The scalp is covered by a mass of wispy black hair. He attempts to count the eyelashes. He feels gently through the flannel for the hands and feet.

"It's all there," Ashima says, watching her husband. "I already checked."

"What are the eyes like? Why won't he open them? Has he opened them?"

She nods.

"What can he see? Can he see us?"

"I think so. But not very clearly. And not in full color. Not yet."

They sit in silence, the three of them as still as stones. "How are you feeling? Was it all right?" he asks Ashima.

But there is no answer, and when Ashoke lifts his gaze from his son's face he sees that she, too, is sleeping.

When he looks back to the child, the eyes are open, staring up at him, unblinking, as dark as the hair on its head. The face is transformed; Ashoke has never seen a more perfect thing. He imagines himself as a dark, grainy, blurry presence. As a father to his son. Again he thinks of the night he was nearly killed, the memory of those hours that have forever marked him flickering and fading in his mind. Being rescued from that shattered train had been the first miracle of his life. But here, now, reposing in his arms, weighing next to nothing but changing everything, is the second.

Apart from his father, the baby has three visitors, all Bengali — Maya and Dilip Nandi, a young married couple in Cambridge whom Ashima and Ashoke met a few months ago in the Purity Supreme, and Dr. Gupta, a mathematics postdoc from Dehradun, a bachelor in his fifties, whom Ashoke has befriended in the corridors of MIT. At feeding times the gentlemen, including Ashoke, step out into the hall. Maya and Dilip give the boy a rattle and a baby book, with places for his parents to commemorate every possible aspect of his infancy. There is even a circle in which to paste a few strands from his first haircut. Dr. Gupta gives the boy a handsome illustrated copy of Mother Goose rhymes. "Lucky boy," Ashoke remarks, turning the beautifully sewn pages. "Only hours old and already the owner of books." What a difference, he thinks, from the childhood he has known.

Ashima thinks the same, though for different reasons. For as grateful as she feels for the company of the Nandis and Dr. Gupta, these acquaintances are only substitutes for the people who really ought to be surrounding them. Without a single grandparent or parent or uncle or aunt at her side, the baby's birth, like most everything else in America, feels somehow haphazard, only half true. As she strokes and suckles and studies her son, she can't help but pity him. She has never known of a person entering the world so alone, so deprived.

Because neither set of grandparents has a working telephone, their only link to home is by telegram, which Ashoke has sent to both sides in Calcutta: "With your blessings, boy and mother fine." As for a name, they have decided to let Ashima's grandmother, who is past eighty now, who has named each of her other six great-grandchildren in the world, do the honors. When her grandmother learned of Ashima's pregnancy, she was particularly thrilled at the prospect of naming the family's first sahib. And so Ashima and Ashoke have agreed to put off the decision of what to name the baby until a letter comes, ignoring the forms from the hospital about filing for a birth certificate. Ashima's grandmother has mailed the letter herself, walking with her cane to the post office, her first trip out of the house in a decade. The letter contains one name for a girl, one for a boy. Ashima's grandmother has revealed them to no one.

Though the letter was sent a month ago, in July, it has yet to arrive. Ashima and Ashoke are not terribly concerned. After all, they both know, an infant doesn't really need a name. He needs to be fed and blessed, to be given some gold and silver, to be patted on the back after feedings and held carefully behind the neck. Names can wait. In India parents take their time. It wasn't unusual for years to pass before the right name, the best possible name, was determined. Ashima and Ashoke can both cite examples of cousins who were not officially named until they were registered, at six or seven, in school. The Nandis and Dr. Gupta understand perfectly. Of course you must wait, they agree, wait for the name in his great-grandmother's letter.

Besides, there are always pet names to tide one over: a practice of Bengali nomenclature grants, to every single person, two names. In Bengali the word for pet name is *daknam*, meaning, literally, the name by which one is called, by friends, family, and other intimates, at home and in other private, unguarded moments. Pet names are a persistent remnant of childhood, a reminder that life is not always so serious, so formal, so complicated. They are a reminder, too, that one is not all things to all people. They all have pet names. Ashima's pet name is Monu, Ashoke's is Mithu, and even as adults, these are the names by which they are known in their respective families, the names by which they are adored and scolded and missed and loved.

Every pet name is paired with a good name, a *bhalonam,* for identification in the outside world. Consequently, good names appear on envelopes, on diplomas, in telephone directories, and in all other public places. (For this reason, letters from Ashima's mother say "Ashima" on the outside, "Monu" on the inside.) Good names tend to represent dignified and enlightened qualities. Ashima means "she who is limitless, without borders." Ashoke, the name of an emperor, means "he who transcends grief." Pet names have no such aspirations. Pet names are never recorded officially, only uttered and remembered. Unlike good names, pet names are frequently meaningless, deliberately silly, ironic, even onomatopoetic. Often in one's infancy, one answers unwittingly to dozens of pet names, until one eventually sticks.

And so at one point, when the baby screws up his rosy, wrinkled face and regards his small circle of admirers, Mr. Nandi leans over and calls the baby "Buro," the Bengali word for "old man."

"What's his name? Buro?" Patty inquires brightly, bearing another tray of baked chicken for Ashima. Ashoke lifts the lid and polishes off the chicken; Ashima is now officially referred to by the maternity nurses as the Jell-O-and-Ice-Cream Lady.

"No, no, that is not a name," Ashima explains. "We haven't chosen. My grandmother is choosing."

Patty nods. "Will she be here soon?"

Ashima laughs, her first genuine laugh after giving birth. The thought of her grandmother, born in the previous century, a shrunken woman in widow's white and with tawny skin that refuses to wrinkle, boarding a plane and flying to Cambridge, is inconceivable to her, a thought that, no matter how welcome, how desirable, feels entirely impossible, absurd. "No. But a letter will."

That evening Ashoke goes home to the apartment, checks for the letter. Three days come and go. Ashima is shown by the nursing staff how to change diapers and how to clean the umbilical stub. She is given hot saltwater baths to soothe her bruises and stitches. She is given a list of pediatricians, and countless brochures on breast-feeding, and bonding, and immunizing, and samples of baby shampoos and Q-Tips and creams. The fourth day there is good news and bad news. The good news is that Ashima and the baby are to be discharged the following morning. The bad news is that they are told by Mr. Wilcox, compiler of hospital birth certificates, that they must choose a name for their son. For they learn that in America, a baby cannot be released from the hospital without a birth certificate. And that a birth certificate needs a name.

"But, sir," Ashima protests, "we can't possibly name him ourselves."

Mr. Wilcox, slight, bald, unamused, glances at the couple, both visibly distressed, then glances at the nameless child. "I see," he says. "The reason being?"

"We are waiting for a letter," Ashoke says, explaining the situation in detail.

"I see," Mr. Wilcox says again. "That is unfortunate. I'm afraid your only alternative is to have the certificate read 'Baby Boy Ganguli.' You will, of course, be required to amend the permanent record when a name is decided upon."

Ashima looks at Ashoke expectantly. "Is that what we should do?"

"I don't recommend it," Mr. Wilcox says. "You will have to appear before a judge, pay a fee. The red tape is endless."

"Oh dear," Ashoke says.

Mr. Wilcox nods, and silence ensues. "Don't you have any backups?" he asks.

Ashima frowns. "What does it mean, 'backup'?"

"Well, something in reserve, in case you didn't like what your grandmother has chosen."

Ashima and Ashoke shake their heads. It has never occurred to either of them to question Ashima's grandmother's selection, to disregard an elder's wishes in such a way.

"You can always name him after yourself,

or one of your ancestors," Mr. Wilcox suggests, admitting that he is actually Howard Wilcox III. "It's a fine tradition. The kings of France and England did it," he adds.

But this isn't possible, Ashima and Ashoke think to themselves. This tradition doesn't exist for Bengalis, naming a son after father or grandfather, a daughter after mother or grandmother. This sign of respect in America and Europe, this symbol of heritage and lineage, would be ridiculed in India. Within Benagli families, individual names are sacred, inviolable. They are not meant to be inherited or shared.

"Then what about naming him after another person? Someone you greatly admire?" Mr. Wilcox says, his eyebrows raised hopefully. He sighs. "Think about it. I'll be back in a few hours," he tells them, exiting the room.

The door shuts, which is when, with a slight quiver of recognition, as if he'd known it all along, the perfect pet name for his son occurs to Ashoke. He remembers the page crumpled tightly in his fingers, the sudden shock of the lantern's glare in his eyes. But for the first time he thinks of that moment not with terror, but with gratitude.

"Hello, Gogol," he whispers, leaning over his son's haughty face, his tightly bundled body. "Gogol," he repeats, satisfied. The baby turns his head with an expression of extreme

51

consternation and yawns.

Ashima approves, aware that the name stands not only for her son's life, but her husband's. She knows the story of the accident, a story she first heard with polite newlywed sympathy, but the thought of which now, now especially, makes her blood go cold. There are nights when she has been woken by her husband's muffled screams, times they have ridden the subway together and the rhythm of the wheels on the tracks makes him suddenly pensive, aloof. She has never read any Gogol herself, but she is willing to place him on a shelf in her mind, along with Tennyson and Wordsworth. Besides, it's only a pet name, not to be taken seriously, simply something to put on the certificate for now to release them from the hospital. When Mr. Wilcox returns with his typewriter, Ashoke spells out the name. Thus Gogol Ganguli is registered in the hospital's files. "Good-bye, Gogol," Patty says, planting a quiet kiss on his shoulder, and to Ashima, dressed once again in her wrinkled silk sari, "Good luck." A first photograph, somewhat overexposed, is taken by Dr. Gupta that broiling hot, late summer's day: Gogol, an indistinct blanketed mass, reposing in his weary mother's arms. She stands on the steps of the hospital, staring at the camera, her eyes squinting into the sun. Her husband looks on from one side, his wife's suitcase in his hand, smiling with his head lowered. "Gogol enters the world," his father will eventually write on the back in Bengali letters.

Gogol's first home is a fully furnished apartment ten minutes by foot to Harvard, twenty to MIT. The apartment is on the first floor of a three-story house, covered with salmon-colored shingles, surrounded by a waist-high chain-link fence. The gray of the roof, the gray of cigarette ashes, matches the pavement of the sidewalk and the street. A row of cars parked at meters perpetually lines one side of the curb. At the corner of the block there is a small used bookstore, which one enters by going down three steps from the sidewalk, and across from it a musty shop that sells the newspaper and cigarettes and eggs, and where, to Ashima's mild disgust, a furry black cat is permitted to sit as it pleases on the shelves. Other than these small businesses, there are more shingled houses, the same shape and size and in the same state of mild decrepitude, painted mint, or lilac, or powder blue. This is the house Ashoke had brought Ashima to eighteen months ago, late one February night after her arrival at Logan Airport. In the dark, through the windows of the taxi, wide awake from jet lag, she could barely make out a thing, apart from heaps of broken snow glowing like shattered, bluish white bricks on the ground. It

53

wasn't until morning, stepping briefly outside wearing a pair of Ashoke's socks under her thin-soled slippers, the frigid New England chill piercing her inner ears and jaw, that she'd had her first real glimpse of America: Leafless trees with ice-covered branches. Dog urine and excrement embedded in the snowbanks. Not a soul on the street.

The apartment consists of three rooms all in a row without a corridor. There is a living room at the front with a three-sided window overlooking the street, a pass-through bedroom in the middle, a kitchen at the back. It is not at all what she had expected. Not at all like the houses in *Gone With the Wind* or *The Seven-Year Itch*, movies she'd seen with her brother and cousins at the Lighthouse and the Metro. The apartment is drafty during winter, and in summer, intolerably hot. The thick glass windowpanes are covered by dreary dark brown curtains. There are even roaches in the bathroom, emerging at night from the cracks in the tiles. But she has complained of none of this. She has kept her disappointment to herself, not wanting to offend Ashoke, or worry her parents. Instead she writes, in her letters home, of the powerful cooking gas that flares up at any time of day or night from four burners on the stove, and the hot tap water fierce enough to scald her skin, and the cold water safe enough to drink.

The top two floors of the house are occupied by their landlords, the Montgomerys, a Harvard sociology professor and his wife. The Montgomerys have two children, both girls, Amber and Clover, aged seven and nine, whose waist-length hair is never braided, and who play on warm days for hours on a tire swing rigged to the only tree in the backyard. The professor, who has told Ashima and Ashoke to call him Alan, not Professor Montgomery as they had at first addressed him, has a wiry rust-colored beard that makes him look much older than he actually is. They see him walking to Harvard Yard in a pair of threadbare trousers, a fringed suede jacket, and rubber flip-flops. Rickshaw drivers dress better than professors here, Ashoke, who still attends meetings with his adviser in a jacket and tie, thinks frequently to himself. The Montgomerys have a dull green Volkswagen van covered with stickers: QUESTION AUTHORITY! GIVE A DAMN! BAN THE BRA! PEACE! They have a washing machine in the basement which Ashoke and Ashima are permitted to share, a television in their living room which Ashoke and Ashima can hear clearly through the ceiling. It had been through the ceiling one night in April, when Ashoke and Ashima were eating their dinner, that they'd heard about the assassination of Martin Luther King, Jr., and just recently, of Senator Robert Kennedy.

Sometimes Ashima and Alan's wife, Judy, stand side by side in the yard, clipping clothes to the line. Judy always wears blue jeans, torn up into shorts once summer comes, and a necklace of small seashells around her throat. A red cotton scarf over her stringy yellow hair, the same texture and shade as her daughters', is always tied at the back of her neck. She works for a women's health collective in Somerville a few days a week. When she learned of Ashima's pregnancy she approved of Ashima's decision to breast-feed but had been disappointed to learn that Ashima was going to put herself in the hands of the medical establishment for her child's delivery; Judy's daughters were born at home, with the help of midwives at the collective. Some nights Judy and Alan go out, leaving Amber and Clover unsupervised at home. Only once, when Clover had a cold, did they ask Ashima if she could check in on them. Ashima remembers their apartment with abiding horror — just beyond the ceiling yet so different from her own, piles everywhere, piles of books and papers, piles of dirty plates on the kitchen counter, ash-trays the size of serving platters heaped with crushed-out cigarettes. The girls slept to-gether on a bed piled with clothes. Sitting momentarily on the edge of Alan and Judy's mattress, she had cried out, falling clumsily backward, startled to discover that it was filled with water. Instead of cereal and tea bags, there were whiskey and wine bottles on top of the refrigerator, most of them nearly empty. Just standing there had made Ashima feel drunk.

They arrive home from the hospital courtesy of Dr. Gupta, who owns a car, and sit in the sweltering living room, in front of their only box fan, suddenly a family. Instead of a couch they have six chairs, all of them three-legged, with oval wooden backs and black triangular cushions. To her surprise, finding herself once again in the gloomy three-room apartment, Ashima misses the hustle-bustle of the hospital, and Patty, and the Jell-O and ice cream brought at regular intervals to her side. As she walks slowly through the rooms it irks her that there are dirty dishes stacked in the kitchen, that the bed has not been made. Until now Ashima has accepted that there is no one to sweep the floor, or do the dishes, or wash clothes, or shop for groceries, or prepare a meal on the days she is tired or homesick or cross. She has accepted that the very lack of such amenities is the American way. But now, with a baby crying in her arms, her breasts swollen with milk, her body coated with sweat, her groin still so sore she can scarcely sit, it is all suddenly unbearable.

"I can't do this," she tells Ashoke when he brings her a cup of tea, the only thing he can think to do for her, the last thing she feels like drinking.

"In a few days you'll get the hang of it," he says, hoping to encourage her, unsure of what else to do. He sets the cup beside her on the flaking windowsill. "I think he's falling asleep again," he adds, looking at Gogol, whose cheeks are working methodically at his wife's breast.

"I won't," she insists thickly, looking neither at the baby nor at him. She pulls back a bit of the curtain, then lets it fall. "Not here. Not like this."

"What are you saying, Ashima?"

"I'm saying hurry up and finish your degree." And then, impulsively, admitting it for the first time: "I'm saying I don't want to raise Gogol alone in this country. It's not right. I want to go back."

He looks at Ashima, her face leaner, the features sharper than they had been at their wedding, aware that her life in Cambridge, as his wife, has already taken a toll. On more than one occasion he has come home from the university to find her morose, in bed, rereading her parents' letters. Early mornings, when he senses that she is quietly crying, he puts an arm around her but can think of nothing to say, feeling that it is his fault, for marrying her, for bringing her here. He remembers suddenly about Ghosh, his companion on the train, who had returned from

England for his wife's sake. "It is my greatest regret, coming back," Ghosh had confessed to Ashoke, mere hours before he was killed.

A soft knock on the door interrupts them: Alan and Judy and Amber and Clover, all there to see the baby. Judy holds a dish covered with a checkered cloth in her hands, says she's made a broccoli quiche. Alan sets down a garbage bag full of Amber and Clover's old baby clothes, uncorks a bottle of cold champagne. The foaming liquid splashes onto the floor, is poured into mugs. They raise their mugs to Gogol, Ashima and Ashoke only pretending to take sips. Amber and Clover flank Ashima at either side, both delighted when Gogol wraps a hand around each of their fingers. Judy scoops the baby out of Ashima's lap. "Hello, handsome," she coos. "Oh, Alan," she says, "let's have another one of these." Alan offers to bring up the girls' crib from the basement, and together he and Ashoke assemble it in the space next to Ashima and Ashoke's bed. Ashoke goes out to the corner store, and a box of disposable diapers replaces the framed black-and-white pictures of Ashima's family on the dressing table. "Twenty minutes at three-fifty for the quiche," Judy says to Ashima. "Holler if you need anything," Alan adds before they disappear.

Three days later, Ashoke is back at MIT, Alan is back at Harvard, Amber and Clover are back at school. Judy is at work at the collective as usual, and Ashima, on her own with Gogol for the first time in the silent house, suffering from a sleep deprivation far worse than the worst of her jet lag, sits by the three-sided window in the living room on one of the triangular chairs and cries the whole day. She cries as she feeds him, and as she pats him to sleep, and as he cries between sleeping and feeding. She cries after the mailman's visit because there are no letters from Calcutta. She cries when she calls Ashoke at his department and he does not answer. One day she cries when she goes to the kitchen to make dinner and discovers that they've run out of rice. She goes upstairs and knocks on Alan and Judy's door. "Help yourself," Judy says, but the rice in Judy's canister is brown. To be polite, Ashima takes a cup, but downstairs she throws it away. She calls Ashoke at his department to ask him to pick up the rice on his way home. This time, when there is no answer, she gets up, washes her face and combs her hair. She changes and dresses Gogol and puts him into the navy blue, white-wheeled pram inherited from Alan and Judy. For the first time, she pushes him through the balmy streets of Cambridge, to Purity Supreme, to buy a bag of white long-grain rice. The errand takes longer than usual; for now she is repeatedly stopped on the street, and in the aisles of the supermarket, by perfect strangers, all Americans, suddenly taking notice of her, smiling, congratulating her for what she's done. They look curiously, appreciatively, into the pram. "How old?" they ask. "Boy or girl?" "What's his name?"

She begins to pride herself on doing it alone, in devising a routine. Like Ashoke, busy with his teaching and research and dissertation seven days a week, she, too, now has something to occupy her fully, to demand her utmost devotion, her last ounce of strength. Before Gogol's birth, her days had followed no visible pattern. She would spend hours in the apartment, napping, sulking, re-reading her same five Bengali novels on the bed. But now the days that had once dragged rush all too quickly toward evening — those same hours are consumed with Gogol, pacing the three rooms of the apartment with him in her arms. Now she wakes at six, pulling Gogol out of the crib for his first feeding, and then for half an hour she and Ashoke lie with the baby in bed between them, admiring the tiny person they've produced. Between eleven and one, while Gogol sleeps, she gets dinner out of the way, a habit she will maintain for decades to come. Every afternoon she takes him out, wandering up and down the streets, to pick up this or that, or to sit in Harvard Yard, sometimes meeting up with

Ashoke on a bench on the MIT campus, bringing him some homemade samosas and a fresh thermos of tea. At times, staring at the baby, she sees pieces of her family in his face — her mother's glossy eyes, her father's slim lips, her brother's lopsided smile. She discovers a yarn store and begins to knit for the coming winter, making Gogol sweaters, blankets, mittens, and caps. Every few days she gives Gogol a bath in the porcelain sink in the kitchen. Every week she carefully clips the nails of his ten fingers and toes. When she takes him in his pram for his immunizations at the pediatrician's, she stands outside the room and plugs up her ears. One day Ashoke arrives home with an Instamatic camera to take pictures of the baby, and when Gogol is napping she pastes the square, white-bordered prints behind plastic sheets in an album, captions written on pieces of masking tape. To put him to sleep, she sings him the Bengali songs her mother had sung to her. She drinks in the sweet, milky fragrance of his skin, the buttery scent of his breath. One day she lifts him high over her head, smiling at him with her mouth open, and a quick stream of undigested milk from his last feeding rises from his throat and pours into her own. For the rest of her life she will recall the shock of that warm, sour liquid, a taste that leaves her unable to swallow another thing for the rest of the day.

Letters arrive from her parents, from her husband's parents, from aunts and uncles and cousins and friends, from everyone, it seems, but Ashima's grandmother. The letters are filled with every possible blessing and good wish, composed in an alphabet they have seen all around them for most of their lives, on billboards and newspapers and awnings, but which they see now only in these precious, pale blue missives. Sometimes two letters arrive in a single week. One week there are three. As always Ashima keeps her ear trained, between the hours of twelve and two, for the sound of the postman's footsteps on the porch, followed by the soft click of the mail slot in the door. The margins of her parents' letters, always a block of her mother's hasty penmanship followed by her father's flourishing, elegant hand, are frequently decorated with drawings of animals done by Ashima's father, and Ashima tapes these on the wall over Gogol's crib. "We are dying to see him," her mother writes. "These are the most crucial months. Every hour there is a change. Remember it." Ashima writes back with careful descriptions of her son, reporting the circumstances of his first smile, the day he first rolls over, his first squeal of delight. She writes that they are saving money for a trip home the following December, after Gogol turns one. (She does not mention the pediatrician's concern about tropical diseases.

A trip to India will require a whole new set of immunizations, he has warned.)

In November, Gogol develops a mild ear infection. When Ashima and Ashoke see their son's pet name typed on the label of a prescription for antibiotics, when they see it at the top of his immunization record, it doesn't look right; pet names aren't meant to be made public in this way. But there is still no letter from Ashima's grandmother. They are forced to conclude that it is lost in the mail. Ashima decides to write to her grandmother, explaining the situation, asking her to send a second letter with the names. The very next day a letter arrives in Cambridge. Though it is from Ashima's father, no drawings for Gogol adorn the margins, no elephants or parrots or tigers. The letter is dated three weeks ago, and from it they learn that Ashima's grandmother has had a stroke, that her right side is permanently paralyzed, her mind dim. She can no longer chew, barely swallows, remembers and recognizes little of her eighty-odd years. "She is with us still, but to be honest we have already lost her," her father has written. "Prepare yourself, Ashima. Perhaps you may not see her again."

It is their first piece of bad news from home. Ashoke barely knows Ashima's grandmother, only vaguely recalls touching her feet at his wedding, but Ashima is inconsolable for days. She sits at home with Gogol as the leaves turn brown and drop from the trees, as the days begin to grow quickly, mercilessly dark, thinking of the last time she saw her grandmother, her dida, a few days before flying to Boston. Ashima had gone to visit her; for the occasion her grandmother had entered the kitchen after over a decade's retirement, to cook Ashima a light goat and potato stew. She had fed her sweets with her own hand. Unlike her parents, and her other relatives, her grandmother had not admonished Ashima not to eat beef or wear skirts or cut off her hair or forget her family the moment she landed in Boston. Her grandmother had not been fearful of such signs of betrayal; she was the only person to predict, rightly, that Ashima would never change. Before leaving, Ashima had stood, her head lowered, under her late grandfather's portrait, asking him to bless her journey. Then she bent down to touch the dust of her dida's feet to her head.

"Dida, I'm coming," Ashima had said. For this was the phrase Bengalis always used in place of good-bye.

"Enjoy it," her grandmother had bellowed in her thundering voice, helping Ashima to straighten. With trembling hands, her grandmother had pressed her thumbs to the tears streaming down Ashima's face, wiping them away. "Do what I will never do. It will all be for the best. Remember that. Now go."

★ ★ ★

As the baby grows, so, too, does their circle of Bengali acquaintances. Through the Nandis, now expecting a child of their own, Ashoke and Ashima meet the Mitras, and through the Mitras, the Banerjees. More than once, pushing Gogol in his stroller, Ashima has been approached on the streets of Cambridge by young Bengali bachelors, shyly inquiring after her origins. Like Ashoke, the bachelors fly back to Calcutta one by one, returning with wives. Every weekend, it seems, there is a new home to go to, a new couple or young family to meet. They all come from Calcutta, and for this reason alone they are friends. Most of them live within walking distance of one another in Cambridge. The husbands are teachers, researchers, doctors, engineers. The wives, homesick and bewildered, turn to Ashima for recipes and advice, and she tells them about the carp that's sold in Chinatown, that it's possible to make halwa from Cream of Wheat. The families drop by one another's homes on Sunday afternoons. They drink tea with sugar and evaporated milk and eat shrimp cutlets fried in saucepans. They sit in circles on the floor, singing songs by Nazrul and Tagore, passing a thick yellow cloth-bound book of lyrics among them as Dilip Nandi plays the harmonium. They argue riotously over the films of Ritwik Ghatak versus those of Satyajit Ray. The CPIM versus the Congress party. North Calcutta versus South. For hours they argue about the politics of America, a country in which none of them is eligible to vote.

By February, when Gogol is six months old, Ashima and Ashoke know enough people to entertain on a proper scale. The occasion: Gogol's annaprasan, his rice ceremony. There is no baptism for Bengali babies, no ritualistic naming in the eyes of God. Instead, the first formal ceremony of their lives centers around the consumption of solid food. They ask Dilip Nandi to play the part of Ashima's brother, to hold the child and feed him rice, the Bengali staff of life, for the very first time. Gogol is dressed as an infant Bengali groom, in a pale yellow pajama-punjabi from his grandmother in Calcutta. The fragrance of cumin seeds, sent in the package along with the pajamas, lingers in the weave. A headpiece that Ashima cut out of paper, decorated with pieces of aluminum foil, is tied around Gogol's head with string. He wears a thin fourteen-karat gold chain around his neck. His tiny forehead has been decorated with considerable struggle with sandalwood paste to form six miniature beige moons floating above his brows. His eyes have been darkened with a touch of kohl. He fidgets in the lap of his honorary uncle, who sits on a bedcover on the floor, surrounded by guests in front and behind and beside him. The food is arranged in ten separate bowls. Ashima regrets that the plate on which the rice is heaped is melamine, not silver or brass or at the very least stainless-steel. The final bowl contains payesh, a warm rice pudding Ashima will prepare for him to eat on each of his birthdays as a child, as an adult even, alongside a slice of bakery cake.

He is photographed by his father and friends, frowning, as he searches for his mother's face in the crowd. She is busy setting up the buffet. She wears a silvery sari, a wedding gift worn for the first time, the sleeves of her blouse reaching the crook of her elbow. His father wears a transparent white Punjabi top over bell-bottom trousers. Ashima sets out paper plates that have to be tripled to hold the weight of the biryani, the carp in yogurt sauce, the dal, the six different vegetable dishes she'd spent the past week preparing. The guests will eat standing, or sitting cross-legged on the floor. They've invited Alan and Judy from upstairs, who look as they always do, in jeans and thick sweaters because it is cold, leather sandals buckled over woolly socks. Judy eyes the buffet, bites into something that turns out to be a shrimp cutlet. "I thought Indians were supposed to be vegetarian," she whispers to Alan.

Gogol's feeding begins. It's all just a touch, a gesture. No one expects the boy to eat anything more than a grain of rice here, a drop of dal there — it is all meant to introduce him to a lifetime of consumption, a meal to inaugurate the tens of thousands of unremembered meals to come. A handful of women ululate as the proceedings begin. A conch shell is repeatedly tapped and passed around, but no one in the room is able to get it to emit a sound. Blades of grass and a pradeep's slim, steady flame are held to Gogol's head. The child is entranced, doesn't squirm or turn away, opens his mouth obediently for each and every course. He takes his payesh three times. Ashima's eyes fill with tears as Gogol's mouth eagerly invites the spoon. She can't help wishing her own brother were here to feed him, her own parents to bless him with their hands on his head. And then the grand finale, the moment they have all been waiting for. To predict his future path in life, Gogol is offered a plate holding a clump of cold Cambridge soil dug up from the backyard, a ballpoint pen, and a dollar bill, to see if he will be a landowner, scholar, or businessman. Most children will grab at one of them, sometimes all of them, but Gogol touches nothing. He shows no interest in the plate, instead turning away, briefly burying his face in his honorary uncle's shoulder.

"Put the money in his hand!" someone in the group calls out. "An American boy must be rich!"

"No!" his father protests. "The pen. Gogol, take the pen."

Gogol regards the plate doubtfully. Dozens of dark heads hover expectantly. The material of the Punjabi pajama set begins to scratch his skin.

"Go on, Gogol, take something," Dilip Nandi says, drawing the plate close. Gogol frowns, and his lower lip trembles. Only then, forced at six months to confront his destiny, does he begin to cry.

Another August. Gogol is one, grabbing, walking a little, repeating words in two languages. He calls his mother "Ma," his father "Baba." If a person in the room says "Gogol," he turns his head and smiles. He sleeps through the night and between noon and three each day. He has seven teeth. He constantly attempts to put the tiniest scraps of paper and lint and whatever else he finds on the floor into his mouth. Ashoke and Ashima are planning their first trip to Calcutta, in December, during Ashoke's winter break. The upcoming journey inspires them to try to come up with a good name for Gogol, so they can submit his passport application. They turn to their Bengali friends for suggestions. Long evenings are devoted to considering this name or that. But nothing appeals to them. By then they've given up on the letter from Ashima's grandmother.

They've given up on her grandmother remembering the name, for Ashima's grandmother, they are told, cannot even remember Ashima. Still, there is time. The trip to Calcutta is four months away. Ashima regrets that they can't go earlier, in time for Durga pujo, but it will be years before Ashoke is eligible for a sabbatical, and three weeks in December is all they can manage. "It is like going home a few months after your Christmas," Ashima explains to Judy one day over the clothesline. Judy replies that she and Alan are Buddhists.

At breakneck speed Ashima knits sweater-vests for her father, her father-in-law, her brother, her three favorite uncles. They are all the same, V-necked, pine green yarn, knit five, purl two, on number-nine needles. The exception is her father's, done in a double-seed stitch with two thick cables and buttons down the front; he prefers cardigans to pull-overs, and she remembers to put in pockets for the deck of cards he always carries with him, to play patience at a moment's notice. In addition to the sweater, she buys him three sable-haired paintbrushes from the Harvard Coop, sizes he's requested by mail. Though they are wildly expensive, more so than anything else she's ever bought in America, Ashoke says nothing when he sees the bill. One day Ashima goes shopping in downtown Boston, spending hours in the basement of Jordan Marsh as she pushes Gogol in his stroller, spending every last penny. She buys mismatched teaspoons, percale pillowcases, colored candles, soaps on ropes. In a drugstore she buys a Timex watch for her father-in-law, Bic pens for her cousins, embroidery thread and thimbles for her mother and her aunts. On the train home she is exhilarated, exhausted, nervous with anticipation of the trip. The train is crowded and at first she stands, struggling to hang on to all the bags and the stroller and the overhead strap, until a young girl asks if she'd like to sit down. Ashima thanks her, sinking gratefully into the seat, pushing the bags protectively behind her legs. She is tempted to sleep as Gogol does. She leans her head against the window and closes her eyes and thinks of home. She pictures the black iron bars in the windows of her parents' flat, and Gogol, in his American baby clothes and diapers, playing beneath the ceiling fan, on her parents' four-poster bed. She pictures her father missing a tooth, lost after a recent fall, her mother has written, on the stairs. She tries to imagine how it will feel when her grandmother doesn't recognize her.

When she opens her eyes she sees that the train is standing still, the doors open at her stop. She leaps up, her heart racing. "Excuse me, please," she says, pushing the stroller and herself through the tightly packed bodies.

"Ma'am," someone says as she struggles past, about to step onto the platform, "your things." The doors of the subway clamp shut as she realizes her mistake, and the train rolls slowly away. She stands there watching until the rear car disappears into the tunnel, until she and Gogol are the only people remaining on the platform. She pushes the stroller back down Massachusetts Avenue, weeping freely, knowing that she can't possibly afford to go back and buy it all again. For the rest of the afternoon she is furious with herself, humiliated at the prospect of arriving in Calcutta empty-handed apart from the sweaters and the paintbrushes. But when Ashoke comes home he calls the MBTA lost and found; the following day the bags are returned, not a teaspoon missing. Somehow, this small miracle causes Ashima to feel connected to Cambridge in a way she has not previously thought possible, affiliated with its exceptions as well as its rules. She has a story to tell at dinner parties. Friends listen, amazed at her luck. "Only in this country," Maya Nandi says.

One night not long after, they are fast asleep when the telephone rings. The sound rouses them instantly, their hearts hammering as if from the same frightening dream. Ashima knows even before Ashoke answers that it's a call from India. A few months ago, her family had asked in a letter for the

phone number in Cambridge, and she had
sent it reluctantly in her reply, aware that it
would only be a way for bad news to reach
her. As Ashoke sits up and takes the receiver,
answering in a weary, weakened voice,
Ashima prepares herself. She pushes down
the crib railing to comfort Gogol, who has
begun stirring as a result of the telephone's
rings, and reviews the facts in her head. Her
grandmother is in her eighties, bedridden, all
but senile, unable to eat or talk. The last few
months of her life, according to her parents'
most recent letter, have been painful, for her
grandmother, for those who know her. It was
no way to live. She pictures her mother
saying all this gently into the next-door
neighbors' phone, standing in the neighbors'
sitting room. Ashima prepares herself for the
news, to accept the fact that Gogol will never
meet his great-grandmother, the giver of his
lost name.

The room is unpleasantly cold. She picks
up Gogol and gets back into bed, under the
blanket. She presses the baby to her body for
strength, puts him to her breast. She thinks
of the cream-colored cardigan bought with
her grandmother in mind, sitting in a shopping bag in the closet. She hears Ashoke
speaking, saying soberly but loudly enough so
that she fears he will wake Alan and Judy
upstairs, "Yes, all right, I see. Don't worry,
yes, I will." For a while he is silent, listening.

"They want to talk to you," he says to Ashima, briefly putting a hand to her shoulder. In the dark, he hands her the phone, and after a moment's hesitation, he gets out of bed.

She takes the phone in order to hear the news for herself, to console her mother. She can't help but wonder who will console her the day her own mother dies, if that news will also come to her in this way, in the middle of the night, wresting her from dreams. In spite of her dread she feels a thrill; this will be the first time she's heard her mother's voice in nearly three years. The first time, since her departure from Dum Dum Airport, that she will be called Monu. Only it isn't her mother but her brother, Rana, on the other end. His voice sounds small, threaded into a wire, barely recognizable through the holes of the receiver. Ashima's first question is what time it is there. She has to repeat the question three times, shouting in order to be heard. Rana tells her it is lunchtime. "Are you still planning to visit in December?" he asks.

She feels her chest ache, moved after all this time to hear her brother call her Didi, his older sister, a term he alone in the world is entitled to use. At the same time she hears water running in the Cambridge kitchen, her husband opening a cupboard for a glass. "Of course we're coming," she says, unsettled when she hears her echo saying it faintly, less

75

convincingly, once again. "How is Dida? Has anything else happened to her?"

"Still alive," Rana says. "But still the same."

Ashima rests back on her pillow, limp with relief. She would see her grandmother, after all, even if for one last time. She kisses Gogol on the top of his head, presses her cheek to his. "Thank goodness. Put Ma on," she says, crossing her ankles. "Let me talk to her."

"She's not at home now," Rana says after a static-filled pause.

"And Baba?"

A patch of silence follows before his voice returns. "Not here."

"Oh." She remembers the time difference — her father must be at work already at the *Desh* offices, her mother at the market, a burlap bag in hand, buying vegetables and fish.

"How is little Gogol?" Rana asks her. "Does he only speak English?"

She laughs. "He doesn't speak much of anything, at the moment." She begins to tell Rana that she is teaching Gogol to say "Dida" and "Dadu" and "Mamu," to recognize his grandparents and his uncle from photographs. But another burst of static, longer this time, quiets her in midsentence.

"Rana? Can you hear me?"

"I can't hear you, Didi," Rana says, his

voice growing fainter. "Can't hear. Let's speak later."

"Yes," she says, "later. See you soon. Very soon. Write to me." She puts down the phone, invigorated by the sound of her brother's voice. An instant later she is confused and somewhat irritated. Why had he gone to the trouble of calling, only to ask an obvious question? Why call while both her parents were out?

Ashoke returns from the kitchen, a glass of water in his hand. He sets down the water and switches on the small lamp by the side of the bed.

"I'm awake," Ashoke says, though his voice is still small from fatigue.

"Me too."

"What about Gogol?"

"Asleep again." She gets up and puts him back in the crib, drawing the blanket to his shoulders, then returns to bed, shivering. "I don't understand it," she says, shaking her head at the rumpled sheet. "Why did Rana go to the trouble of calling just now? It's so expensive. It doesn't make sense." She turns to look at Ashoke. "What did he say to you, exactly?"

Ashoke shakes his head from side to side, his profile lowered.

"He told you something you're not telling me. Tell me, what did he say?"

He continues to shake his head, and then

he reaches across to her side of the bed and presses her hand so tightly that it is slightly painful. He presses her to the bed, lying on top of her, his face to one side, his body suddenly trembling. He holds her this way for so long that she begins to wonder if he is going to turn off the light and caress her. Instead he tells her what Rana told him a few minutes ago, what Rana couldn't bear to tell his sister, over the telephone, himself: that her father died yesterday evening, of a heart attack, playing patience on his bed.

They leave for India six days later, six weeks before they'd planned. Alan and Judy, waking the next morning to Ashima's sobs, then hearing the news from Ashoke, leave a vase filled with flowers by the door. In those six days, there is no time to think of a good name for Gogol. They get an express passport with "Gogol Ganguli" typed across the United States of America seal, Ashoke signing on his son's behalf. The day before leaving, Ashima puts Gogol in his stroller, puts the sweater she'd knit for her father and the paintbrushes in a shopping bag, and walks to Harvard Square, to the subway station. "Excuse me," she asks a gentleman on the street, "I must get on the train." The man helps her carry down the stroller, and Ashima waits on the platform. When the train comes she heads immediately back to

Central Square. This time she is wide awake. There are only a half-dozen people in the car, their faces hidden behind the *Globe*, or looking down at paperback books, or staring straight through her, at nothing. As the train slows to a halt she stands, ready to disembark. She does not turn back to look at the shopping bag, left purposely beneath her seat. "Hey, the Indian lady forgot her stuff," she hears as the doors shut, and as the train pulls away she hears a fist pounding on glass, but she keeps walking, pushing Gogol along the platform.

The following evening they board a Pan Am flight to London, where after a five-hour layover they will board a second flight to Calcutta, via Tehran and Bombay. On the runway in Boston, her seat belt buckled, Ashima looks at her watch and calculates the Indian time on her fingers. But this time no image of her family comes to mind. She refuses to picture what she shall see soon enough: her mother's vermilion erased from her part, her brother's thick hair shaved from his head in mourning. The wheels begin to move, causing the enormous metal wings to flap gently up and down. Ashima looks at Ashoke, who is double-checking to make sure their passports and green cards are in order. She watches him adjust his watch in anticipation of their arrival, the pale silver hands scissoring into place.

"I don't want to go," she says, turning toward the dark oval window. "I don't want to see them. I can't."

Ashoke puts his hand over hers as the plane begins to gather speed. And then Boston tilts away and they ascend effortlessly over a blackened Atlantic. The wheels retract and the cabin shakes as they struggle upward, through the first layer of clouds. Though Gogol's ears have been stuffed with cotton, he screams nevertheless in the arms of his grieving mother as they climb farther still, as he flies for the first time in his life across the world.

3.

1971

The Gangulis have moved to a university town outside Boston. As far as they know, they are the only Bengali residents. The town has a historic district, a brief strip of colonial architecture visited by tourists on summer weekends. There is a white steepled Congregational church, a stone courthouse with an adjoining jail, a cupolaed public library, a wooden well from which Paul Revere is rumored to have drunk. In winter, tapers burn in the windows of homes after dark. Ashoke has been hired as an assistant professor of electrical engineering at the university. In exchange for teaching five classes, he earns sixteen thousand dollars a year. He is given his own office, with his name etched onto a strip of black plastic by the door. He shares, along with the other members of his department, the services of an elderly secretary named Mrs. Jones, who often puts a plate of homemade banana bread by the coffee percolator in the staff room. Ashoke suspects that Mrs. Jones, whose husband used to teach in the English department until his death, is about his own mother's age. Mrs. Jones leads a life that Ashoke's mother would consider humiliating: eating alone, driving herself to work in snow and sleet, seeing her children and grandchildren, at most, three or four times a year.

The job is everything Ashoke has ever dreamed of. He has always hoped to teach in a university rather than work for a corporation. What a thrill, he thinks, to stand lecturing before a roomful of American students. What a sense of accomplishment it gives him to see his name printed under "Faculty" in the university directory. What joy each time Mrs. Jones says to him, "Professor Ganguli, your wife is on the phone." From his fourth-floor office he has a sweeping view of the quadrangle, surrounded by vine-covered brick buildings, and on pleasant days he takes his lunch on a bench, listening to the melody of bells chiming from the campus clock tower. On Fridays, after he has taught his last class, he visits the library, to read international newspapers on long wooden poles. He reads about U.S. planes bombing Vietcong supply routes in Cambodia, Naxalites being murdered on the streets of Calcutta, India and Pakistan going to war. At times he wanders up to the library's sun-filled, unpopulated top floor, where all the literature is shelved. He browses in the aisles, gravitating most often toward his beloved Russians, where he is particularly comforted, each time, by his son's name stamped in golden letters on the spines of a row of red and green and blue hardbound books.

For Ashima, migrating to the suburbs feels more drastic, more distressing than the move from Calcutta to Cambridge had been. She wishes Ashoke had accepted the position at Northeastern so that they could have stayed in the city. She is stunned that in this town there are no sidewalks to speak of, no streetlights, no public transportation, no stores for miles at a time. She has no interest in learning how to drive the new Toyota Corolla it is now necessary for them to own. Though no longer pregnant, she continues, at times, to mix Rice Krispies and peanuts and onions in a bowl. For being a foreigner, Ashima is beginning to realize, is a sort of lifelong pregnancy — a perpetual wait, a constant burden, a continuous feeling out of sorts. It is an ongoing responsibility, a parenthesis in what had once been ordinary life, only to discover that that previous life has vanished, replaced by something more complicated and demanding. Like pregnancy, being a foreigner, Ashima believes, is something that elicits the same curiosity from strangers, the same combination of pity and respect.

Her forays out of the apartment, while her husband is at work, are limited to the university within which they live, and to the historic district that flanks the campus on one edge. She wanders around with Gogol, letting him run across the quadrangle, or sitting with him on rainy days to watch television in the student lounge. Once a week she makes thirty samosas to sell at the international coffeehouse, for twenty-five cents each, next to the linzer squares baked by Mrs. Etzold, and baklava by Mrs. Cassolis. On Fridays she takes Gogol to the public library for children's story hour. After he turns four, she drops him off and fetches him from the university-run nursery school three mornings a week. For the hours that Gogol is at nursery school, finger-painting and learning the English alphabet, Ashima is despondent, unaccustomed, all over again, to being on her own. She misses her son's habit of always holding on to the free end of her sari as they walk together. She misses the sound of his sulky, high-pitched little-boy voice, telling her that he is hungry, or tired, or needs to go to the bathroom. To avoid being alone at home she sits in the reading room of the public library, in a cracked leather armchair, writing letters to her mother, or reading magazines or one of her Bengali books from home. The room is cheerful, filled with light, with a tomato-colored carpet on the floor and people reading the paper around a big, round wooden table with forsythias or cattails arranged at its center. When she misses Gogol especially, she wanders into the children's room; there, pinned to a bulletin board, is a picture of him in profile, sitting cross-legged on a cushion during story hour, listening to the children's librarian, Mrs. Aiken, reading *The Cat in the Hat.*

After two years in an overheated university-subsidized apartment, Ashima and Ashoke are ready to purchase a home. In the evenings, after dinner, they set out in their car, Gogol in the back seat, to look at houses for sale. They do not look in the historic district, where the chairman of Ashoke's department lives, in an eighteenth-century mansion to which he and Ashima and Gogol are invited once a year for Boxing Day tea. Instead they look on ordinary roads where plastic wading pools and baseball bats are left out on the lawns. All the houses belong to Americans. Shoes are worn inside, trays of cat litter are placed in the kitchens, dogs bark and jump when Ashima and Ashoke ring the bell. They learn the names of the different architectural styles: cape, saltbox, raised ranch, garrison. In the end they decide on a shingled two-story colonial in a recently built development, a house previously occupied by no one, erected on a quarter acre of land. This is the small patch of America to which they lay claim. Gogol accompanies his parents to banks, sits waiting as they sign the endless papers. The mortgage is approved and the move is scheduled for spring. Ashoke and Ashima are amazed, when moving by U-Haul to the new house, to discover how much they possess; each of them had come to America with a single suitcase, a few weeks' worth of clothes. Now there are enough old issues of the *Globe* stacked in the corners of the apartment to wrap all their plates and glasses. There are whole years of *Time* magazine to toss out.

The walls of the new house are painted, the driveway sealed with pitch, the shingles and sun deck weatherproofed and stained. Ashoke takes photographs of every room, Gogol standing somewhere in the frame, to send to relatives in India. There are pictures of Gogol opening up the refrigerator, pretending to talk on the phone. He is a sturdily built child, with full cheeks but already pensive features. When he poses for the camera he has to be coaxed into a smile. The house is fifteen minutes from the nearest supermarket, forty minutes from a mall. The address is 67 Pemberton Road. Their neighbors are the Johnsons, the Mertons, the Aspris, the Hills. There are four modest bedrooms, one and a half bathrooms, seven-foot ceilings, a one-car garage. In the living room is a brick fireplace and a bay window overlooking the yard. In the kitchen there are matching yellow appliances, a lazy Susan, linoleum made to look like tiles. A watercolor by

Ashima's father, of a caravan of camels in a desert in Rajasthan, is framed at the local print shop and hung on the living room wall. Gogol has a room of his own, a bed with a built-in drawer in its base, metal shelves that hold Tinkertoys, Lincoln Logs, a View-Master, an Etch-A-Sketch. Most of Gogol's toys come from yard sales, as does most of the furniture, and the curtains, and the toaster, and a set of pots and pans. At first Ashima is reluctant to introduce such items into her home, ashamed at the thought of buying what had originally belonged to strangers, American strangers at that. But Ashoke points out that even his chairman shops at yard sales, that in spite of living in a mansion an American is not above wearing a pair of secondhand pants, bought for fifty cents.

When they first move into the house, the grounds have yet to be landscaped. No trees grow on the property, no shrubs flank the front door, so that the cement of the foundation is clearly visible to the eye. And so for the first few months, four-year-old Gogol plays on an uneven, dirt-covered yard littered with stones and sticks, soiling his sneakers, leaving footprints in his path. It is among his earliest memories. For the rest of his life he will remember that cold, overcast spring, digging in the dirt, collecting rocks, discovering black and yellow salamanders beneath an overturned slab of slate. He will remember the sounds of the other children in the neighborhood, laughing and pedaling their Big Wheels down the road. He will remember the warm, bright summer's day when the topsoil was poured from the back of a truck, and stepping onto the sun deck a few weeks later with both of his parents to see thin blades of grass emerge from the bald black lawn.

In the beginning, in the evenings, his family goes for drives, exploring their new environs bit by bit: the neglected dirt lanes, the shaded back roads, the farms where one could pick pumpkins in autumn and buy berries sold in green cardboard boxes in July. The back seat of the car is sheathed with plastic, the ashtrays on the doors still sealed. They drive until it grows dark, without destination in mind, past hidden ponds and graveyards, culs-de-sac and dead ends. Sometimes they drive out of the town altogether, to one of the beaches along the North Shore. Even in summer, they never go to swim or to turn brown beneath the sun. Instead they go dressed in their ordinary clothes. By the time they arrive, the ticket collector's booth is empty, the crowds gone; there are only a handful of cars in the parking lot, and the only other visitors are people walking their dogs or watching the sun set or dragging metal detectors through the sand. Together, as the Gangulis drive, they anticipate the moment the thin blue line of ocean will come into view. On the beach Gogol collects rocks, digs tunnels in the sand. He and his father wander barefoot, their pant legs rolled halfway up their calves. He watches his father raise a kite within minutes into the wind, so high that Gogol must tip his head back in order to see, a rippling speck against the sky. The wind whips around their ears, turning their faces cold. Snowy gulls hover with wings spread, low enough to touch. Gogol darts in and out of the ocean, making faint, temporary footprints, soaking his rolled-up cuffs. His mother cries out, laughing, as she lifts her sari a few inches above her ankles, her slippers in one hand, and places her feet in foaming, ice-cold water. She reaches out to Gogol, takes his hand. "Not so far," she tells him. The waves retract, gathering force, the soft, dark sand seeming to shift away instantly beneath their feet, causing them to lose their balance. "I'm falling. It's pulling me in," she always says.

The August that Gogol turns five, Ashima discovers she is pregnant again. In the mornings she forces herself to eat a slice of toast, only because Ashoke makes it for her and watches her while she chews it in bed. Her head constantly spins. She spends her days lying down, a pink plastic wastepaper basket by her side, the shades drawn, her mouth and teeth coated with the taste of metal. She watches *The Price Is Right* and *Guiding Light* and *The $10,000 Pyramid* on the television Ashoke moves in from the living room to her side of the bed. Staggering out to the kitchen at lunchtime, to prepare a peanut butter and jelly sandwich for Gogol, she is revolted by the odor of the fridge, convinced that the contents of her vegetable drawers have been replaced with garbage, that meat is rotting on the shelves. Sometimes Gogol lies beside her in his parents' bedroom, reading a picture book, or coloring with crayons. "You're going to be an older brother," she tells him one day. "There'll be someone to call you Dada. Won't that be exciting?" Sometimes, if she is feeling energetic, she asks Gogol to go and get a photo album, and together they look at pictures of Gogol's grandparents, and his uncles and aunts and cousins, of whom, in spite of his one visit to Calcutta, he has no memory. She teaches him to memorize a four-line children's poem by Tagore, and the names of the deities adorning the ten-handed goddess Durga during pujo: Saraswati with her swan and Kartik with his peacock to her left, Lakshmi with her owl and Ganesh with his mouse to her right. Every afternoon Ashima sleeps, but before nodding off she switches the television to Channel 2, and tells Gogol to watch *Sesame Street* and *The Electric Company*, in order to keep up with the English he uses at nursery school.

In the evenings Gogol and his father eat together, alone, a week's worth of chicken curry and rice, which his father cooks in two battered Dutch ovens every Sunday. As the food reheats, his father tells Gogol to shut the bedroom door because his mother cannot tolerate the smell. It is odd to see his father presiding in the kitchen, standing in his mother's place at the stove. When they sit down at the table, the sound of his parents' conversation is missing, as is the sound of the television in the living room, playing the news. His father eats with his head bent over his plate, flipping through the latest issue of *Time*, occasionally glancing at Gogol to make sure he is eating as well. Though his father remembers to mix up the rice and curry for Gogol beforehand, he doesn't bother to shape it into individual balls the way his mother does, lining them around his plate like the numbers on a clockface. Gogol has already been taught to eat on his own with his fingers, not to let the food stain the skin of his palm. He has learned to suck the marrow from lamb, to extract the bones from fish. But without his mother at the table he does not feel like eating. He keeps wishing, every evening, that she would emerge from the bedroom and sit between him and his father, filling the air with her sari and cardigan smell. He grows bored of eating the same thing day after day, and one evening he discreetly pushes the remaining food to the side. With his index finger, in the traces of leftover sauce, he begins to draw on his plate. He plays tic-tac-toe.

"Finish," his father says, glancing up from his magazine. "Don't play with food that way."

"I'm full, Baba."

"There's still some food on your plate."

"Baba, I can't."

His father's plate is polished clean, the chicken bones denuded of cartilage and chewed to a pinkish pulp, the bay leaf and cinnamon stick as good as new. Ashoke shakes his head at Gogol, disapproving, unyielding. Each day Ashoke is pained by the half-eaten sandwiches people toss into garbage cans on campus, apples abandoned after one or two bites. "Finish it, Gogol. At your age I ate tin."

Because his mother tends to vomit the moment she finds herself in a moving car, she is unable to accompany her husband to take Gogol, in September of 1973, to his first day of kindergarten at the town's public elementary school. By the time Gogol starts, it is already the second week of the school year. But for the past week, Gogol has been in bed, just like his mother, listless, without appetite, claiming to have a stomachache, even vomiting one day into his mother's pink wastepaper basket. He doesn't want to go to kindergarten. He doesn't want to wear the new clothes his mother has bought him from Sears, hanging on a knob of his dresser, or carry his Charlie Brown lunch box, or board the yellow school bus that stops at the end of Pemberton Road. The school, unlike the nursery school, is several miles from the house, several miles from the university. On numerous occasions he's been driven to see the building, a low, long, brick structure with a perfectly flat roof and a flag that flaps at the top of a tall white pole planted on the lawn.

There is a reason Gogol doesn't want to go to kindergarten. His parents have told him that at school, instead of being called Gogol, he will be called by a new name, a good name, which his parents have finally decided on, just in time for him to begin his formal education. The name, Nikhil, is artfully connected to the old. Not only is it a perfectly respectable Bengali good name, meaning "he who is entire, encompassing all," but it also bears a satisfying resemblance to Nikolai, the first name of the Russian Gogol. Ashoke had thought of it recently, staring mindlessly at the Gogol spines in the library, and he had rushed back to the house to ask Ashima her opinion. He pointed out that it was relatively easy to pronounce, though there was the danger that Americans, obsessed with abbreviation, would truncate it to Nick. She told him she liked it well enough, though later, alone, she'd wept, thinking of her grandmother, who had died earlier in the year, and of the letter, forever hovering somewhere between India and America, containing the good name she'd chosen for Gogol. Ashima still dreams of the letter at times, discovering it after all these years in the mailbox on Pemberton Road, opening it up only to find it blank.

But Gogol doesn't want a new name. He can't understand why he has to answer to anything else. "Why do I have to have a new name?" he asks his parents, tears springing to his eyes. It would be one thing if his parents were to call him Nikhil, too. But they tell him that the new name will be used only by the teachers and children at school. He is afraid to be Nikhil, someone he doesn't know. Who doesn't know him. His parents tell him that they each have two names, too, as do all their Bengali friends in America, and all their relatives in Calcutta. It's a part of growing up, they tell him, part of being a Bengali. They write it for him on a sheet of paper, ask him to copy it over ten times. "Don't worry," his father says. "To me and your mother, you will never be anyone but Gogol."

At school, Ashoke and Gogol are greeted by the secretary, Mrs. McNab, who asks

Ashoke to fill out a registration form. He provides a copy of Gogol's birth certificate and immunization record, which Mrs. McNab puts in a folder along with the registration. "This way," Mrs. McNab says, leading them to the principal's office. CANDACE LAPIDUS, the name on the door says. Mrs. Lapidus assures Ashoke that missing the first week of kindergarten is not a problem, that things have yet to settle down. Mrs. Lapidus is a tall, slender woman with short white-blond hair. She wears frosted blue eye shadow and a lemon yellow suit. She shakes Ashoke's hand and tells him that there are two other Indian children at the school, Jayadev Modi in the third grade and Rekha Saxena in fifth. Perhaps the Gangulis know them? Ashoke tells Mrs. Lapidus that they do not. She looks at the registration form and smiles kindly at the boy, who is clutching his father's hand. Gogol is dressed in powder blue pants, red and white canvas sneakers, a striped turtleneck top.

"Welcome to elementary school, Nikhil. I am your principal, Mrs. Lapidus."

Gogol looks down at his sneakers. The way the principal pronounces his new name is different from the way his parents say it, the second part of it longer, sounding like "heel."

She bends down so that her face is level with his, and extends a hand to his shoulder. "Can you tell me how old you are, Nikhil?"

When the question is repeated and there is

95

still no response, Mrs. Lapidus asks, "Mr. Ganguli, does Nikhil follow English?"

"Of course he follows," Ashoke says. "My son is perfectly bilingual."

In order to prove that Gogol knows English, Ashoke does something he has never done before, and addresses his son in careful, accented English. "Go on, Gogol," he says, patting him on the head. "Tell Mrs. Lapidus how old you are."

"What was that?" Mrs. Lapidus says.

"I beg your pardon, madam?"

"That name you called him. Something with a *G*."

"Oh that, that is what we call him at home only. But his good name should be — is" — he nods his head firmly — "Nikhil."

Mrs. Lapidus frowns. "I'm afraid I don't understand. Good name?"

"Yes."

Mrs. Lapidus studies the registration form. She has not had to go through this confusion with the other two Indian children. She opens up the folder and examines the immunization record, the birth certificate. "There seems to be some confusion, Mr. Ganguli," she says. "According to these documents, your son's legal name is Gogol."

"That is correct. But please allow me to explain —"

"That you want us to call him Nikhil."

"That is correct."

Mrs. Lapidus nods. "The reason being?"

"That is our wish."

"I'm not sure I follow you, Mr. Ganguli. Do you mean that Nikhil is a middle name? Or a nickname? Many of the children go by nicknames here. On this form there is a space —"

"No, no, it's not a middle name," Ashoke says. He is beginning to lose patience. "He has no middle name. No nickname. The boy's good name, his school name, is Nikhil."

Mrs. Lapidus presses her lips together and smiles. "But clearly he doesn't respond."

"Please, Mrs. Lapidus," Ashoke says. "It is very common for a child to be confused at first. Please give it some time. I assure you he will grow accustomed."

He bends down and this time in Bengali, calmly and quietly, asks Gogol to please answer when Mrs. Lapidus asks a question. "Don't be scared, Gogol," he says, raising his son's chin with his finger. "You're a big boy now. No tears."

Though Mrs. Lapidus does not understand a word, she listens carefully, hears that name again. Gogol. Lightly, in pencil, she writes it down on the registration form.

Ashoke hands over the lunch box, a windbreaker in case it gets cold. He thanks Mrs. Lapidus. "Be good, Nikhil," he says in English. And then, after a moment's hesitation, he is gone.

When they are alone, Mrs. Lapidus asks, "Are you happy to be entering elementary school, Gogol?"

"My parents want me to have another name in school."

"And what about you, Gogol? Do you want to be called by another name?"

After a pause, he shakes his head.

"Is that a no?"

He nods. "Yes."

"Then it's settled. Can you write your name on this piece of paper?"

Gogol picks up a pencil, grips it tightly, and forms the letters of the only word he has learned thus far to write from memory, getting the "L" backward due to nerves. "What beautiful penmanship you have," Mrs. Lapidus says. She tears up the old registration form and asks Mrs. McNab to type up a new one. Then she takes Gogol by the hand, down a carpeted hallway with painted cement walls. She opens a door, and Gogol is introduced to his teacher, Miss Watkins, a woman with hair in two braids, wearing overalls and clogs. Inside the classroom it's a small universe of nicknames — Andrew is Andy, Alexandra Sandy, William Billy, Elizabeth Lizzy. It is nothing like the schooling Gogol's parents have known, fountain pens and polished black shoes and notebooks and good names and sir or madam at a tender age. Here the only official ritual is pledging allegiance first thing in the morning to the American flag. For the rest of the day, they sit at a communal round table, drinking punch and eating cookies, taking naps on little orange cushions on the floor. At the end of his first day he is sent home with a letter to his parents from Mrs. Lapidus, folded and stapled to a string around his neck, explaining that due to their son's preference he will be known as Gogol at school. What about the parents' preference? Ashima and Ashoke wonder, shaking their heads. But since neither of them feels comfortable pressing the issue, they have no choice but to give in.

And so Gogol's formal education begins. At the top of sheets of scratchy pale yellow paper he writes out his pet name again and again, and the alphabet in capitals and lowercase. He learns to add and subtract, and to spell his first words. In the front covers of the textbooks from which he is taught to read he leaves his legacy, writing his name in number-two pencil below a series of others. In art class, his favorite hour of the week, he carves his name with paper clips into the bottoms of clay cups and bowls. He pastes uncooked pasta to cardboard, and leaves his signature in fat brush strokes below paintings. Day after day he brings his creations home to Ashima, who hangs them proudly on the refrigerator door. "Gogol G," he signs his work in the lower right-hand corner, as if there were a need to distinguish him from any other Gogol in the school.

In May his sister is born. This time the labor happens quickly. They are thinking about going to a yard sale in the neighborhood one Saturday morning, playing Bengali songs on the stereo. Gogol is eating frozen waffles for breakfast, wishing his parents would turn off the music so that he could hear the cartoons he is watching, when his mother's water breaks. His father switches off the music and calls Dilip and Maya Nandi, who now live in a suburb twenty minutes away and have a little boy of their own. Then he calls the next-door neighbor, Mrs. Merton, who has offered to look after Gogol until the Nandis arrive. Though his parents have prepared him for the event, when Mrs. Merton shows up with her needlepoint he feels stranded, no longer in the mood for cartoons. He stands on the front step, watching his father help his mother into the car, waving as they pull away. To pass the time he draws a picture of himself and his parents and his new sibling, standing in a row in front of their house. He remembers to put a dot on his mother's forehead, glasses on his father's face, a lamppost by the flagstone path in front of the house. "Well, if that's not the spitting image," Mrs. Merton says, looking over his shoulder.

That evening Maya Nandi, whom he calls Maya Mashi, as if she were his own mother's sister, his own aunt, is heating up the dinner she's brought over, when his father calls to say the baby has arrived. The next day Gogol sees his mother sitting in an angled bed, a plastic bracelet around her wrist, her stomach no longer as hard and round. Through a big glass window, he sees his sister asleep, lying in a small glass bed, the only one of the babies in the nursery to have a thick head of black hair. He is introduced to his mother's nurses. He drinks the juice and eats the pudding off his mother's tray. Shyly he gives his mother the picture he's drawn. Underneath the figures he's written his own name, and Ma, and Baba. Only the space under the baby is blank. "I didn't know the baby's name," Gogol says, which is when his parents tell him. This time, Ashoke and Ashima are ready. They have the names lined up, for a boy or a girl. They've learned their lesson after Gogol. They've learned that schools in America will ignore parents' instructions and register a child under his pet name. The only way to avoid such confusion, they have concluded, is to do away with the pet name altogether, as many of their Bengali friends have already done. For their daughter, good name and pet name are one and the same: Sonali, meaning "she who is golden."

Two days later, coming back from school, Gogol finds his mother at home again, wearing a bathrobe instead of a sari, and sees his sister awake for the first time. She is dressed in pink pajamas that conceal her hands and feet, with a pink bonnet tied around her moon-shaped face. His father is home, too. His parents sit Gogol on the living room sofa and place Sonali in his lap, telling him to hold her against his chest, a hand cupped under her head, and his father takes pictures with a new Nikon 35-millimeter camera. The shutter advances softly, repeatedly; the room is bathed in rich afternoon light. "Hi, Sonali," Gogol says, sitting stiffly, looking down at her face, and then up at the lens. Though Sonali is the name on her birth certificate, the name she will carry officially through life, at home they begin to call her Sonu, then Sona, and finally Sonia. Sonia makes her a citizen of the world. It's a Russian link to her brother, it's European, South American. Eventually it will be the name of the Indian prime minister's Italian wife. At first Gogol is disappointed by the fact that he can't play with her, that all she does is sleep and soil her diapers and cry. But eventually she begins to respond to him, cackling when he tickles her stomach, or pushes her in a swing operated by a noisy crank, or when he cries out "Peekaboo." He helps his mother to bathe her, fetching the towel and the shampoo. He entertains her in the back seat of the car when they drive on the highway on Saturday evenings, on the way to dinner parties thrown by their parents' friends. For by now all the Cambridge Bengalis have moved to places like Dedham and Framingham and Lexington and Winchester, to houses with backyards and driveways. They have met so many Bengalis that there is rarely a Saturday free, so that for the rest of his life Gogol's childhood memories of Saturday evenings will consist of a single, repeated scene: thirty-odd people in a three-bedroom suburban house, the children watching television or playing board games in a basement, the parents eating and conversing in the Bengali their children don't speak among themselves. He will remember eating watered-down curry off paper plates, sometimes pizza or Chinese ordered specially for the kids. There are so many guests invited to Sonia's rice ceremony that Ashoke arranges to rent a building on campus, with twenty folding tables and an industrial stove. Unlike her compliant older brother, Sonia, seven months old, refuses all the food. She plays with the dirt they've dug up from the yard and threatens to put the dollar bill into her mouth. "This one," one of the guests remarks, "this one is the true American."

As their lives in New England swell with fellow Bengali friends, the members of that other, former life, those who know Ashima

103

and Ashoke not by their good names but as Monu and Mithu, slowly dwindle. More deaths come, more telephone calls startle them in the middle of the night, more letters arrive in the mailbox informing them of aunts and uncles no longer with them. The news of these deaths never gets lost in the mail as other letters do. Somehow, bad news, however ridden with static, however filled with echoes, always manages to be conveyed. Within a decade abroad, they are both orphaned; Ashoke's parents both dead from cancer, Ashima's mother from kidney disease. Gogol and Sonia are woken by these deaths in the early mornings, their parents screaming on the other side of thin bedroom walls. They stumble into their parents' room, uncomprehending, embarrassed at the sight of their parents' tears, feeling only slightly sad. In some senses Ashoke and Ashima live the lives of the extremely aged, those for whom everyone they once knew and loved is lost, those who survive and are consoled by memory alone. Even those family members who continue to live seem dead somehow, always invisible, impossible to touch. Voices on the phone, occasionally bearing news of births and weddings, send chills down their spines. How could it be, still alive, still talking? The sight of them when they visit Calcutta every few years feels stranger still, six or eight weeks passing like a dream. Once back on Pemberton Road, in the modest house that is suddenly mammoth, there is nothing to remind them; in spite of the hundred or so relatives they've just seen, they feel as if they are the only Gangulis in the world. The people they have grown up with will never see this life, of this they are certain. They will never breathe the air of a damp New England morning, see smoke rising from a neighbor's chimney, shiver in a car waiting for the glass to defrost and the engine to warm.

And yet to a casual observer, the Gangulis, apart from the name on their mailbox, apart from the issues of *India Abroad* and *Sangbad Bichitra* that are delivered there, appear no different from their neighbors. Their garage, like every other, contains shovels and pruning shears and a sled. They purchase a barbecue for tandoori on the porch in summer. Each step, each acquisition, no matter how small, involves deliberation, consultation with Bengali friends. Was there a difference between a plastic rake and a metal one? Which was preferable, a live Christmas tree or an artificial one? They learn to roast turkeys, albeit rubbed with garlic and cumin and cayenne, at Thanksgiving, to nail a wreath to their door in December, to wrap woolen scarves around snowmen, to color boiled eggs violet and pink at Easter and hide them around the house. For the sake of Gogol and Sonia they celebrate, with progressively increasing fan-fare, the birth of Christ, an event the children look forward to far more than the worship of Durga and Saraswati. During pujos, scheduled for convenience on two Saturdays a year, Gogol and Sonia are dragged off to a high school or a Knights of Columbus hall overtaken by Bengalis, where they are required to throw marigold petals at a cardboard effigy of a goddess and eat bland vegetarian food. It can't compare to Christmas, when they hang stockings on the fireplace mantel, and set out cookies and milk for Santa Claus, and receive heaps of presents, and stay home from school.

There are other ways in which Ashoke and Ashima give in. Though Ashima continues to wear nothing but saris and sandals from Bata, Ashoke, accustomed to wearing tailor-made pants and shirts all his life, learns to buy ready-made. He trades in fountain pens for ballpoints, Wilkinson blades and his boar-bristled shaving brush for Bic razors bought six to a pack. Though he is now a tenured full professor, he stops wearing jackets and ties to the university. Given that there is a clock everywhere he turns, at the side of his bed, over the stove where he prepares tea, in the car he drives to work, on the wall opposite his desk, he stops wearing a wristwatch, resigning his Favre Leuba to the depths of his sock drawer. In the supermarket they let

Gogol fill the cart with items that he and Sonia, but not they, consume: individually wrapped slices of cheese, mayonnaise, tuna fish, hot dogs. For Gogol's lunches they stand at the deli to buy cold cuts, and in the mornings Ashima makes sandwiches with bologna or roast beef. At his insistence, she concedes and makes him an American dinner once a week as a treat, Shake 'n Bake chicken or Hamburger Helper prepared with ground lamb.

Still, they do what they can. They make a point of driving into Cambridge with the children when the Apu Trilogy plays at the Orson Welles, or when there is a Kathakali dance performance or a sitar recital at Memorial Hall. When Gogol is in the third grade, they send him to Bengali language and culture lessons every other Saturday, held in the home of one of their friends. For when Ashima and Ashoke close their eyes it never fails to unsettle them, that their children sound just like Americans, expertly conversing in a language that still at times confounds them, in accents they are accustomed not to trust. In Bengali class, Gogol is taught to read and write his ancestral alphabet, which begins at the back of his throat with an unaspirated *K* and marches steadily across the roof of his mouth, ending with elusive vowels that hover outside his lips. He is taught to write letters that hang from a bar,

107

and eventually to cobble these intricate shapes into his name. They read handouts written in English about the Bengali Renaissance, and the revolutionary exploits of Subhas Chandra Bose. The children in the class study without interest, wishing they could be at ballet or softball practice instead. Gogol hates it because it keeps him from attending every other session of a Saturday-morning drawing class he's enrolled in, at the suggestion of his art teacher. The drawing class is held on the top floor of the public library; on nice days they are taken for walks through the historic district, carrying large sketchpads and pencils, and told to draw the facade of this building or that. In Bengali class they read from hand-sewn primers brought back by their teacher from Calcutta, intended for five-year-olds, printed, Gogol can't help noticing, on paper that resembles the folded toilet paper he uses at school.

As a young boy Gogol doesn't mind his name. He recognizes pieces of himself in road signs: GO LEFT, GO RIGHT, GO SLOW. For birthdays his mother orders a cake on which his name is piped across the white frosted surface in a bright blue sugary script. It all seems perfectly normal. It doesn't bother him that his name is never an option on key chains or metal pins or refrigerator magnets. He has been told that he was named after a famous Russian author, born in a previous century. That the author's name, and therefore his, is known throughout the world and will live on forever. One day his father takes him to the university library, and shows him, on a shelf well beyond his reach, a row of Gogol spines. When his father opens up one of the books to a random page, the print is far smaller than in the Hardy Boys series Gogol has begun recently to enjoy. "In a few years," his father tells him, "you'll be ready to read them." Though substitute teachers at school always pause, looking apologetic when they arrive at his name on the roster, forcing Gogol to call out, before even being summoned, "That's me," teachers in the school system know not to give it a second thought. After a year or two, the students no longer tease and say "Giggle" or "Gargle." In the programs of the school Christmas plays, the parents are accustomed to seeing his name among the cast. "Gogol is an outstanding student, curious and coopera-tive," his teachers write year after year on re-port cards. "Go, Gogol!" his classmates shout on golden autumn days as he runs the bases or sprints in a dash.

As for his last name, Ganguli, by the time he is ten he has been to Calcutta three more times, twice in summer and once during Durga pujo, and from the most recent trip he still remembers the sight of it etched respectably into the whitewashed exterior of his paternal grandparents' house. He remembers the astonishment of seeing six pages full of Gangulis, three columns to a page, in the Calcutta telephone directory. He'd wanted to rip out the page as a souvenir, but when he'd told this to one of his cousins, the cousin had laughed. On taxi rides through the city, going to visit the various homes of his relatives, his father had pointed out the name elsewhere, on the awnings of confectioners, and stationers, and opticians. He had told Gogol that Ganguli is a legacy of the British, an anglicized way of pronouncing his real surname, Gangopadhyay.

Back home on Pemberton Road, he helps his father paste individual golden letters bought from a rack in the hardware store, spelling out GANGULI on one side of their mailbox. One morning, the day after Halloween, Gogol discovers, on his way to the bus stop, that it has been shortened to GANG, with the word GREEN scrawled in pencil following it. His ears burn at the sight, and he runs back into the house, sickened, certain of the insult his father will feel. Though it is his last name, too, something tells Gogol that the desecration is intended for his parents more than Sonia and him. For by now he is aware, in stores, of cashiers smirking at his parents' accents, and of salesmen who prefer to direct their conversation to Gogol, as though his parents were either incompetent or deaf. But his father is unaffected at such moments, just as he is unaffected by the mailbox. "It's only boys having fun," he tells Gogol, flicking the matter away with the back of a hand, and that evening they drive back to the hardware store, to buy the missing letters again.

Then one day the peculiarity of his name becomes apparent. He is eleven years old, in the sixth grade, on a school field trip of some historical intent. They set off in their school bus, two classes, two teachers, two chaperones along for the ride, driving straight through the town and onto the highway. It is a chilly, spectacular November day, the blue sky cloudless, the trees shedding bright yellow leaves that blanket the ground. The children scream and sing and drink cans of soda wrapped in aluminum foil. First they visit a textile mill somewhere in Rhode Island. The next stop is a small unpainted wooden house with tiny windows, sitting on a large plot of land. Inside, after adjusting to the diminished light, they stare at a desk with an inkwell at its top, a soot-stained fireplace, a washtub, a short, narrow bed. It was once the home of a poet, they are told. All the furniture is roped off from the center of the room, with little signs telling them not to touch. The ceiling is so low that the teachers duck their heads as they walk from darkened room to room. They look at the kitchen, with its iron stove and stone sink, and file along a dirt path to look at the outhouse. The students shriek with disgust at the sight of a tin pan hanging from the bottom of a wooden chair. In the gift shop, Gogol buys a postcard of the house and a ballpoint pen disguised as a quill.

The final stop on the field trip, a short distance by bus from the poet's house, is a graveyard where the writer lies buried. They take a few minutes wandering from stone to stone, among thick and thin tablets, some leaning back as if pressed by a wind. The stones are square and arched, black and gray, more often plain than shiny, caked with lichen and moss. On many of the stones the inscriptions have faded. They find the stone that bears the poet's name. "Line up," the teachers say, "it's time for a project." The students are each given several sheets of newsprint and thick colored crayons whose labels have been peeled. Gogol can't help but feel a chill. He's never set foot in a graveyard before, only glimpsed them in passing, riding in cars. There is a large one on the outskirts of their town; once, stuck in traffic, he and his family had witnessed a burial from a distance, and ever since then, whenever they drive by, his mother always tells them to avert their eyes.

To Gogol's surprise they are told not to

draw the gravestones, but to rub their surfaces. A teacher crouches down, one hand holding the newsprint in place, and shows them how. The children begin to scamper between rows of the dead, over leathery leaves, looking for their own names, a handful triumphant when they are able to claim a grave they are related to. "Smith!" they holler. "Collins!" "Wood!" Gogol is old enough to know that there is no Ganguli here. He is old enough to know that he himself will be burned, not buried, that his body will occupy no plot of earth, that no stone in this country will bear his name beyond life. In Calcutta, from taxis and once from the roof of his grandparents' house, he has seen the dead bodies of strangers carried on people's shoulders through streets, decked with flowers, wrapped in sheets.

He walks over to a slim, blackened stone with a pleasing shape, rounded at the top before rising into a cross. He kneels on the grass and holds up the newsprint, then begins to rub gently with the side of his crayon. The sun is already sinking and his fingers are stiff with cold. The teachers and chaperones sit on the ground, legs extended, leaning back against the headstones, the aroma of their menthol cigarettes drifting through the air. At first nothing appears apart from a grainy, featureless wash of midnight blue. But then, suddenly, the crayon meets with slight resistance, and letters, one after another, emerge magically on the page: ABIJAH CRAVEN, 1701–45. Gogol has never met a person named Abijah, just as, he now realizes, he has never met another Gogol. He wonders how to pronounce Abijah, whether it's a man's or a woman's name. He walks to another tombstone, less than a foot tall, and presses another sheet of paper to its surface. This one says ANGUISH MATHER, A CHILD. He shudders, imagining bones no larger than his below the ground. Some of the other children in the class, already bored with the project, begin chasing one another around the stones, pushing and teasing and snapping gum. But Gogol goes from grave to grave with paper and crayon in hand, bringing to life one name after another. PEREGRINE WOTTON, D. 1699. EZEKIEL AND URIAH LOCKWOOD, BROTHERS, R.I.P. He likes these names, likes their oddness, their flamboyance. "Now those are some names you don't see very often these days," one of the chaperones, passing by and looking down at his rubbings, remarks. "Sort of like yours." Until now it has not occurred to Gogol that names die over time, that they perish just as people do. On the ride back to school the rubbings made by the other children are torn up, crumpled, tossed at one another's heads, abandoned below the dark green seats. But Gogol is silent, his rubbings rolled up carefully like parchment in his lap.

At home, his mother is horrified. What type of field trip was this? It was enough that they applied lipstick to their corpses and buried them in silk-lined boxes. Only in America (a phrase she has begun to resort to often these days), only in America are children taken to cemeteries in the name of art. What's next, she demands to know, a trip to the morgue? In Calcutta the burning ghats are the most forbidden of places, she tells Gogol, and though she tries her best not to, though she was here, not there, both times it happened, she sees her parents' bodies, swallowed by flames. "Death is not a pastime," she says, her voice rising unsteadily, "not a place to make paintings." She refuses to display the rubbings in the kitchen alongside his other creations, his charcoal drawings and his magazine collages, his pencil sketch of a Greek temple copied from an encyclopedia, his pastel image of the public library's facade, awarded first place in a contest sponsored by the library trustees. Never before has she rejected a piece of her son's art. The guilt she feels at Gogol's deflated expression is leavened by common sense. How can she be expected to cook dinner for her family with the names of dead people on the walls?

But Gogol is attached to them. For reasons he cannot explain or necessarily understand, these ancient Puritan spirits, these very first

115

immigrants to America, these bearers of unthinkable, obsolete names, have spoken to
him, so much so that in spite of his mother's
disgust he refuses to throw the rubbings
away. He rolls them up, takes them upstairs,
and puts them in his room, behind his chest
of drawers, where he knows his mother will
never bother to look, and where they will remain, ignored but protected, gathering dust
for years to come.

4.

Gogol's fourteenth birthday. Like most events in his life, it is another excuse for his parents to throw a party for their Bengali friends. His own friends from school were invited the previous day, a tame affair, with pizzas that his father picked up on his way home from work, a basketball game watched together on television, some Ping-Pong in the den. For the first time in his life he has said no to the frosted cake, the box of harlequin ice cream, the hot dogs in buns, the balloons and streamers taped to the walls. The other celebration, the Bengali one, is held on the closest Saturday to the actual date of his birth. As usual his mother cooks for days beforehand, cramming the refrigerator with stacks of foil-covered trays. She makes sure to prepare his favorite things: lamb curry with lots of potatoes, luchis, thick channa dal with swollen brown raisins, pineapple chutney, sandeshes molded out of saffron-tinted ricotta cheese. All this is less stressful to her than the task of feeding a handful of American children, half of whom always

117

claim they are allergic to milk, all of whom refuse to eat the crusts of their bread.

Close to forty guests come from three different states. Women are dressed in saris far more dazzling than the pants and polo shirts their husbands wear. A group of men sit in a circle on the floor and immediately start a game of poker. These are his mashis and meshos, his honorary aunts and uncles. They all bring their children; his parents' crowd does not believe in baby-sitters. As usual, Gogol is the oldest child in the group. He is too old to be playing hide-and-seek with eight-year-old Sonia and her ponytailed, gap-toothed friends, but not old enough to sit in the living room and discuss Reaganomics with his father and the rest of the husbands, or to sit around the dining room table, gossiping, with his mother and the wives. The closest person to him in age is a girl named Moushumi, whose family recently moved to Massachusetts from England, and whose thirteenth birthday was celebrated in a similar fashion a few months ago. But Gogol and Moushumi have nothing to say to each other. Moushumi sits cross-legged on the floor, in glasses with maroon plastic frames and a puffy polka-dotted headband holding back her thick, chin-length hair. In her lap is a kelly green Bermuda bag with pink piping and wooden handles; inside the bag is a tube of 7UP-flavored lip balm that she draws from time to time across her mouth. She is reading a well-thumbed paperback copy of *Pride and Prejudice* while the other children, Gogol included, watch *The Love Boat* and *Fantasy Island*, piled together on top and around the sides of his parents' bed. Occasionally one of the children asks Moushumi to say something, anything, in her English accent. Sonia asks if she's ever seen Princess Diana on the street. "I detest American television," Moushumi eventually declares to everyone's delight, then wanders into the hallway to continue her reading.

Presents are opened when the guests are gone. Gogol receives several dictionaries, several calculators, several Cross pen-and-pencil sets, several ugly sweaters. His parents give him an Instamatic camera, a new sketchbook, colored pencils and the mechanical pen he'd asked for, and twenty dollars to spend as he wishes. Sonia has made him a card with Magic Markers, on paper she's ripped out of one of his own sketchbooks, which says "Happy Birthday Goggles," the name she insists on calling him instead of Dada. His mother sets aside the things he doesn't like, which is most everything, to give to his cousins the next time they go to India. Later that night he is alone in his room, listening to side 3 of the White Album on his parents' cast-off RCA turntable. The album is a present from his American birthday party, given to him by one of his friends at school. Born when the band was near death, Gogol is a passionate devotee of John, Paul, George, and Ringo. In recent years he has collected nearly all their albums, and the only thing tacked to the bulletin board on the back of his door is Lennon's obituary, already yellow and brittle, clipped from the *Boston Globe*. He sits cross-legged on the bed, hunched over the lyrics, when he hears a knock on the door.

"Come in," he hollers, expecting it to be Sonia in her pajamas, asking if she can borrow his Magic 8 Ball or his Rubik's Cube. He is surprised to see his father, standing in stocking feet, a small potbelly visible beneath his oat-colored sweater vest, his mustache turning gray. Gogol is especially surprised to see a gift in his father's hands. His father has never given him birthday presents apart from whatever his mother buys, but this year, his father says, walking across the room to where Gogol is sitting, he has something special. The gift is covered in red-and-green-and-gold-striped paper left over from Christmas the year before, taped awkwardly at the seams. It is obviously a book, thick, hardcover, wrapped by his father's own hands. Gogol lifts the paper slowly, but in spite of this the tape leaves a scab. *The Short Stories of Nikolai Gogol*, the jacket says. Inside, the price has been snipped away on the diagonal.

"I ordered it from the bookstore, just for you," his father says, his voice raised in order to be heard over the music. "It's difficult to find in hardcover these days. It's a British publication, a very small press. It took four months to arrive. I hope you like it."

Gogol leans over toward the stereo to turn the volume down a bit. He would have preferred *The Hitchhiker's Guide to the Galaxy*, or even another copy of *The Hobbit* to replace the one he lost last summer in Calcutta, left on the rooftop of his father's house in Alipore and snatched away by crows. In spite of his father's occasional suggestions, he has never been inspired to read a word of Gogol, or any Russian writer, for that matter. He has never been told why he was really named Gogol, doesn't know about the accident that had nearly killed his father. He thinks his father's limp is the consequence of an injury playing soccer in his teens. He's been told only half the truth about Gogol: that his father is a fan.

"Thanks, Baba," Gogol says, eager to return to his lyrics. Lately he's been lazy, addressing his parents in English though they continue to speak to him in Bengali. Occasionally he wanders through the house with his running sneakers on. At dinner he sometimes uses a fork.

His father is still standing there in his room, watching expectantly, his hands clasped together behind his back, so Gogol flips through the book. A single picture at the front, on smoother paper than the rest of the pages, shows a pencil drawing of the author, sporting a velvet jacket, a billowy white shirt and cravat. The face is foxlike, with small, dark eyes, a thin, neat mustache, an extremely large pointy nose. Dark hair slants steeply across his forehead and is plastered to either side of his head, and there is a disturbing, vaguely supercilious smile set into long, narrow lips. Gogol Ganguli is relieved to see no resemblance. True, his nose is long but not so long, his hair dark but surely not so dark, his skin pale but certainly not so pale. The style of his own hair is altogether different — thick Beatle-like bangs that conceal his brows. Gogol Ganguli wears a Harvard sweatshirt and gray Levi's corduroys. He has worn a tie once in his life, to attend a friend's bar mitzvah. No, he concludes confidently, there is no resemblance at all.

For by now, he's come to hate questions pertaining to his name, hates having constantly to explain. He hates having to tell people that it doesn't mean anything "in Indian." He hates having to wear a nametag on his sweater at Model United Nations Day at school. He even hates signing his name at the bottom of his drawings in art class. He hates that his name is both absurd and obscure, that it has nothing to do with who he is, that it is neither Indian nor American but of all things Russian. He hates having to live with it, with a pet name turned good name, day after day, second after second. He hates seeing it on the brown paper sleeve of the *National Geographic* subscription his parents got him for his birthday the year before and perpetually listed in the honor roll printed in the town's newspaper. At times his name, an entity shapeless and weightless, manages nevertheless to distress him physically, like the scratchy tag of a shirt he has been forced permanently to wear. At times he wishes he could disguise it, shorten it somehow, the way the other Indian boy in his school, Jayadev, had gotten people to call him Jay. But Gogol, already short and catchy, resists mutation. Other boys his age have begun to court girls already, asking them to go to the movies or the pizza parlor, but he cannot imagine saying, "Hi, it's Gogol" under potentially romantic circumstances. He cannot imagine this at all.

From the little he knows about Russian writers, it dismays him that his parents chose the weirdest namesake. Leo or Anton, he could have lived with. Alexander, shortened to Alex, he would have greatly preferred. But Gogol sounds ludicrous to his ears, lacking dignity or gravity. What dismays him most is the irrelevance of it all. Gogol, he's been tempted to tell his father on more than one occasion, was his father's favorite author, not his. Then again, it's his own fault. He could have been known, at school at least, as Nikhil. That one day, that first day of kindergarten, which he no longer remembers, could have changed everything. He could have been Gogol only fifty percent of the time. Like his parents when they went to Calcutta, he could have had an alternative identity, a B-side to the self. "We tried," his parents explain to friends and relatives who ask why their son lacks a good name, "but he would only respond to Gogol. The school insisted." His parents would add, "We live in a country where a president is called Jimmy. Really, there was nothing we could do."

"Thanks again," Gogol tells his father now. He shuts the cover and swings his legs over the edge of the bed, to put the book away on his shelves. But his father takes the opportunity to sit beside him on the bed. For a moment he rests a hand on Gogol's shoulder. The boy's body, in recent months, has grown tall, nearly as tall as Ashoke's. The childhood pudginess has vanished from his face. The voice has begun to deepen, is slightly husky now. It occurs to Ashoke that he and his son probably wear the same size shoe. In the glow of the bedside lamp, Ashoke notices a scattered down emerging on his son's upper lip. An Adam's apple is prominent on his neck. The pale hands, like Ashima's, are long and thin. Ashoke wonders how closely Gogol resembles himself at this age. But there are no photographs to document Ashoke's childhood; not until his passport, not until his life in America, does visual documentation exist. On the night table Ashoke sees a can of deodorant, a tube of Clearasil. He lifts the book from where it lies on the bed between them, running a hand protectively over the cover. "I took the liberty of reading it first. It has been many years since I have read these stories. I hope you don't mind."

"No problem," Gogol says.

"I feel a special kinship with Gogol," Ashoke says, "more than with any other writer. Do you know why?"

"You like his stories."

"Apart from that. He spent most of his adult life outside his homeland. Like me."

Gogol nods. "Right."

"And there is another reason." The music ends and there is silence. But then Gogol flips the record, turning the volume up on "Revolution 1."

"What's that?" Gogol says, a bit impatiently.

Ashoke looks around the room. He notices the Lennon obituary pinned to the bulletin board, and then a cassette of classical Indian music he'd bought for Gogol months ago, after a concert at Kresge, still sealed in its wrapper. He sees the pile of birthday cards scattered on the carpet, and remembers a hot August day fourteen years ago in Cambridge when he held his son for the first time. Ever since that day, the day he became a father, the memory of his accident has receded, diminishing over the years. Though he will never forget that night, it no longer lurks persistently in his mind, stalking him in the same way. It no longer looms over his life, darkening it without warning as it used to do. Instead, it is affixed firmly to a distant time, to a place far from Pemberton Road. Today, his son's birthday, is a day to honor life, not brushes with death. And so, for now, Ashoke decides to keep the explanation of his son's name to himself.

"No other reason. Good night," he says to Gogol, getting up from the bed. At the door he pauses, turns around. "Do you know what Dostoyevsky once said?"

Gogol shakes his head.

" 'We all came out of Gogol's overcoat.' "

"What's that supposed to mean?"

"It will make sense to you one day. Many happy returns of the day."

Gogol gets up and shuts the door behind his father, who has the annoying habit of always leaving it partly open. He fastens the lock on the knob for good measure, then wedges the book on a high shelf between two volumes of the Hardy Boys. He settles down again with his lyrics on the bed when something occurs to him. This writer he is named after — Gogol isn't his first name. His first name is Nikolai. Not only does Gogol Ganguli have a pet name turned good name, but a last name turned first name. And so it occurs to him that no one he knows in the world, in Russia or India or America or anywhere, shares his name. Not even the source of his namesake.

The following year Ashoke is up for a sabbatical, and Gogol and Sonia are informed that they will all be going to Calcutta for eight months. When his parents tell him, one evening after dinner, Gogol thinks they're joking. But then they tell them that the tickets have already been booked, the plans already made. "Think of it as a long vacation," Ashoke and Ashima say to their crestfallen children. But Gogol knows that eight months is no vacation. He dreads the thought of eight months without a room of his own, without his records and his stereo, without friends. In Gogol's opinion, eight months in Calcutta is practically like moving there, a possibility that, until now, has never even remotely crossed his mind. Besides, he's a sophomore now. "What about school?" he points out. His parents remind him that in the past his teachers have never minded Gogol missing school now and again. They've given him math and language workbooks that

127

he's ignored, and when he returns, a month or two later, they praise him for keeping up with things. But Gogol's guidance counselor expresses concern when Gogol informs him that he will be missing the entire second half of the tenth grade. A meeting is called with Ashima and Ashoke to discuss the options. The guidance counselor asks if it's possible to enroll Gogol in an international school. But the nearest one is in Delhi, over eight hundred miles from Calcutta. The guidance counselor suggests that perhaps Gogol could join his parents later, after the school year ends, stay with a relative until June. "We have no relatives in this country," Ashima informs the guidance counselor. "That is why we are going to India in the first place."

And so after barely four months of tenth grade, after an early supper of rice and boiled potatoes and eggs that his mother insists they eat even though they will be served another supper on the plane, he is off, geometry and U.S. history books packed into his suitcase, which is locked, along with the others, with padlocks and bound with ropes, labeled with the address of his father's house in Alipore. Gogol always finds the labels unsettling, the sight of them making him feel that his family doesn't really live on Pemberton Road. They depart Christmas Day, driving with their massive collection of luggage to Logan when they should be home opening gifts. Sonia is morose, running a slight fever from her ty-phoid shot, still expecting, when she enters the living room in the morning, to see a tree trimmed with lights. But the only thing in the living room is debris: price tags from all the gifts they've packed for their relatives, plastic hangers, cardboard from shirts. They shiver as they leave the house, without coats or gloves; they won't need them where they're going, and it will be August by the time they return. The house has been rented to some American students his father has found through the university, an unmarried couple named Barbara and Steve. In the air-port Gogol stands in the check-in line with his father, who is dressed in a jacket and tie, clothes he still thinks to wear when riding on planes. "Four in the family," his father says when it is their turn, producing two U.S. passports and two Indian ones. "Two Hindu meals, please."

On the plane Gogol is seated several rows behind his parents and Sonia, in another sec-tion altogether. His parents are distressed by this, but Gogol is secretly pleased to be on his own. When the stewardess approaches with her cart of beverages he tries his luck and asks for a Bloody Mary, tasting the me-tallic bite of alcohol for the first time in his life. They fly first to London, and then to Calcutta via Dubai. When they fly over the Alps, his father gets out of his seat to take pictures of the snowcapped peaks through the window. On past trips, it used to thrill Gogol that they were flying over so many countries; again and again he would trace their itinerary on the map in the seat pocket below his tray and feel somehow adventurous. But this time it frustrates him that it is to Calcutta that they always go. Apart from visiting relatives there was nothing to do in Calcutta. He's already been to the planetarium and the Zoo Gardens and the Victoria Memorial a dozen times. They have never been to Disneyland or the Grand Canyon. Only once, when their connecting flight in London was delayed, did they leave Heathrow and take a double-decker bus tour of the city.

On the final leg of the trip there are only a few non-Indians left on the plane. Bengali conversation fills the cabin; his mother has already exchanged addresses with the family across the aisle. Before landing she slips into the bathroom and changes, miraculously in that minuscule space, into a fresh sari. A final meal is served, an herbed omelette topped with a slice of grilled tomato. Gogol savors each mouthful, aware that for the next eight months nothing will taste quite the same. Through the window he sees palm trees and banana trees, a damp, drab sky. The wheels touch the ground, the aircraft is sprayed with disinfectant, and then they descend onto the tarmac of Dum Dum Airport, breathing in the sour, stomach-turning, early morning air. They stop to wave back at the row of relatives waving madly from the observation deck, little cousins propped up on uncles' shoulders. As usual the Gangulis are relieved to learn that all their luggage has arrived, together and unmolested, and relieved further still when customs doesn't make a fuss. And then the frosted doors slide open and once again they are officially there, no longer in transit, swallowed by hugs and kisses and pinched cheeks and smiles. There are endless names Gogol and Sonia must remember to say, not aunt this and uncle that but terms far more specific: *mashi* and *pishi*, *mama* and *maima*, *kaku* and *jethu*, to signify whether they are related on their mother's or their father's side, by marriage or by blood. Ashima, now Monu, weeps with relief, and Ashoke, now Mithu, kisses his brothers on both cheeks, holds their heads in his hands. Gogol and Sonia know these people, but they do not feel close to them as their parents do. Within minutes, before their eyes Ashoke and Ashima slip into bolder, less complicated versions of themselves, their voices louder, their smiles wider, revealing a confidence Gogol and Sonia never see on Pemberton Road. "I'm scared, Goggles," Sonia whispers to her brother in English, seeking his hand and refusing to let go.

They are ushered into waiting taxis and

down VIP Road, past a colossal landfill and into the heart of North Calcutta. Gogol is accustomed to the scenery, yet he still stares, at the short, dark men pulling rickshaws and the crumbling buildings side by side with fretwork balconies, hammers and sickles painted on their facades. He stares at the commuters who cling precariously to trams and buses, threatening at any moment to spill onto the street, and at the families who boil rice and shampoo their hair on the sidewalk. At his mother's flat on Amherst Street, where his uncle's family lives now, neighbors look from their windows and roofs as Gogol and his family emerge from the taxi. They stand out in their bright, expensive sneakers, American haircuts, backpacks slung over one shoulder. Once inside, he and Sonia are given cups of Horlick's, plates of syrupy, spongy rossogollas for which they have no appetite but which they dutifully eat. They have their feet traced onto pieces of paper, and a servant is sent to Bata to bring back rubber slippers for them to wear indoors. The suitcases are unlocked and unbound and all the gifts are unearthed, admired, tried on for size.

In the days that follow they adjust once again to sleeping under a mosquito net, bathing by pouring tin cups of water over their heads. In the mornings Gogol watches his cousins put on their white and blue school uniforms and strap water bottles across their chests. His aunt, Uma Maima, presides in the kitchen all morning, harassing the servants as they squat by the drain scouring the dirty dishes with ash, or pound heaps of spices on slabs that resemble tombstones. At the Ganguli house in Alipore, he sees the room in which they would have lived had his parents remained in India, the ebony four-poster bed on which they would have slept all together, the armoire in which they would have stored their clothes.

Instead of renting an apartment of their own, they spend eight months with their various relatives, shuttling from home to home. They stay in Ballygunge, Tollygunge, Salt Lake, Budge Budge, ferried by endless bumpy taxi rides back and forth through the city. Every few weeks there is a different bed to sleep in, another family to live with, a new schedule to learn. Depending on where they are, they eat sitting on red clay or cement or terrazzo floors, or at marble-topped tables too cold to rest their elbows on. Their cousins and aunts and uncles ask them about life in America, about what they eat for breakfast, about their friends at school. They look at the pictures of their house on Pemberton Road. "Carpets in the bathroom," they say, "imagine that." His father keeps busy with his research, delivering lectures at Jadavpur University. His mother shops in

New Market and goes to movies and sees her old school friends. For eight months she does not set foot in a kitchen. She wanders freely around a city in which Gogol, in spite of his many visits, has no sense of direction. Within three months Sonia has read each of her Laura Ingalls Wilder books a dozen times. Gogol occasionally opens up one of his text-books, bloated from the heat. Though he's brought his sneakers with him, hoping to keep up with cross-country training, it is impossible, on these cracked, congested, chock-a-block streets, to run. The one day he tries, Uma Maima, watching from the rooftop, sends a servant to follow him so that Gogol doesn't get lost.

It's easier to surrender to confinement. On Amherst Street, Gogol sits at his grandfather's drawing table, poking through a tin full of dried-out nibs. He sketches what he sees through the iron window bars: the crooked skyline, the courtyards, the cobblestone square where he watches maids filling brass urns at the tube well, people passing under the soiled canopies of rickshaws, hurrying home with parcels in the rain. On the roof one day, with its view of Howrah Bridge in the distance, he smokes a bidi tightly rolled in olive green leaves with one of the servants. Of all the people who surround them at practically all times, Sonia is his only ally, the only person to speak and sit and see as he does. While the rest of the household sleeps, he and Sonia fight over the Walkman, over the melting collection of tapes Gogol recorded back in his room at home. From time to time, they privately admit to excruciating cravings, for hamburgers or a slice of pepperoni pizza or a cold glass of milk.

They are surprised, in the summer, to learn that their father has planned a trip for them, first to Delhi to visit an uncle, and then to Agra to see the Taj Mahal. It will be Gogol and Sonia's first journey outside of Calcutta, their first time on an Indian train. They depart from Howrah, that immense, soaring, echoing station, where barefoot coolies in red cotton shirts pile the Gangulis' Samsonite luggage on their heads, where entire families sleep, covered, in rows on the floor. Gogol is aware of the dangers involved: his cousins have told him about the bandits that lurk in Bihar, so that his father wears a special garment under his shirt, with hidden pockets to carry cash, and his mother and Sonia remove their gold jewels. On the platform they walk from compartment to compartment, looking for their four names on the passenger list pasted to the outside wall of the train. They settle onto their blue berths, the top two swinging down from the walls when it is time to sleep and held in place by sliding latches during the day. A conductor gives them their bedding, heavy white cotton sheets and thin woolen blankets. In the morning they look at the scenery through the tinted window of their air-conditioned car. As a result, the view, no matter how bright the day, is gloomy and gray.

They are unaccustomed, after all these months, to being just the four of them. For a few days, in Agra, which is as foreign to Ashima and Ashoke as it is to Gogol and Sonia, they are tourists, staying at a hotel with a swimming pool, sipping bottled water, eating in restaurants with forks and spoons, paying by credit card. Ashima and Ashoke speak in broken Hindi, and when young boys approach to sell postcards or marble trinkets Gogol and Sonia are forced to say, "English, please." Gogol notices in certain restaurants that they are the only Indians apart from the serving staff. For two days they wander around the marble mausoleum that glows gray and yellow and pink and orange depending on the light. They admire its perfect symmetry and pose for photographs beneath the minarets from which tourists used to leap to their deaths. "I want a picture here, just the two of us," Ashima says to Ashoke as they wander around the massive plinth, and so under the blinding Agra sun, overlooking the dried-up Yamuna, Ashoke teaches Gogol how to use the Nikon, how to focus and advance the film. A tour guide tells them that after the Taj was completed, each of the

136

builders, twenty-two thousand men, had his thumbs cut off so that the structure could never be built again. That night in the hotel Sonia wakes up screaming that her own thumbs are missing. "It's just legend," her parents tell her. But the idea of it haunts Gogol as well. No other building he's seen has affected him so powerfully. Their second day at the Taj he attempts to sketch the dome and a portion of the facade, but the building's grace eludes him and he throws the attempt away. Instead, he immerses himself in the guidebook, studying the history of Mughal architecture, learning the succession of emperors' names: Babur, Humayun, Akbar, Jahangir, Shah Jahan, Aurangzeb. At Agra Fort he and his family look through the window of the room where Shah Jahan was imprisoned by his own son. At Sikandra, Akbar's tomb, they gaze at gilded frescoes in the entryway, chipped, ransacked, burned, the gems gouged out with penknives, graffiti etched into the stone. At Fatehpur Sikri, Akbar's abandoned sandstone city, they wander among courtyards and cloisters as parrots and hawks fly overhead, and in Salim Chishti's tomb Ashima ties red threads for good luck to a marble lattice screen.

But bad luck trails them on the trip back to Calcutta. At Benares station, Sonia asks her father to buy her a slice of jackfruit, which makes her lips itch unbearably, then swell to three times their size. Somewhere in Bihar, in the middle of the night, a businessman in another compartment is stabbed in his sleep and robbed of three hundred thousand rupees, and the train stops for five hours while the local police investigate. The Gangulis learn the cause of the delay the following morning, as breakfast is being served, the passengers agitated and horrified, all speaking of the same thing. "Wake up. Some guy on the train got murdered," Gogol says to Sonia from his top berth to hers. No one is more horrified than Ashoke, who privately recalls that other train, on that other night, and that other field where he'd been stopped. This time he'd heard nothing. He'd slept through the whole thing.

Upon returning to Calcutta, Gogol and Sonia both get terribly ill. It is the air, the rice, the wind, their relatives casually remark; they were not made to survive in a poor country, they say. They have constipation followed by the opposite. Doctors come to the house in the evening with stethoscopes in black leather bags. They are given courses of Entroquinol, ajowan water that burns their throats. And once they've recovered it's time to go back: the day they were convinced would never come is just two weeks away. Kashmiri pencil cups are bought for Ashoke to give to his colleagues at the university. Gogol buys Indian comic books to give to his

American friends. On the evening of their departure he watches his parents standing in front of framed pictures of his dead grandparents on the walls, heads bowed, weeping like children. And then the caravan of taxis and Ambassadors comes to whisk them one last time across the city. Their flight is at dawn and so they must leave in darkness, driving through streets so empty they are unrecognizable, a tram with its small single headlight the only other thing that moves. At the airport the row of people who had greeted them, have hosted and fed and fawned over them for all these months, those with whom he shares a name if not his life, assemble once more on the balcony, to wave good-bye. Gogol knows that his relatives will stand there until the plane has drifted away, until the flashing lights are no longer visible in the sky. He knows that his mother will sit silently, staring at the clouds, as they journey back to Boston. But for Gogol, relief quickly replaces any lingering sadness. With relief he peels back the foil covering his breakfast, extracts the silverware from its sealed plastic packaging, asks the British Airways stewardess for a glass of orange juice. With relief he puts on his headset to watch *The Big Chill* and listen to top-forty songs all the way home.

Within twenty-four hours he and his family are back on Pemberton Road, the late August grass in need of trimming, a quart of milk and some bread left by their tenants in the refrigerator, four grocery bags on the staircase filled with mail. At first the Gangulis sleep most of the day and are wide awake at night, gorging themselves on toast at three in the morning, unpacking the suitcases one by one. Though they are home they are disconcerted by the space, by the uncompromising silence that surrounds them. They still feel somehow in transit, still disconnected from their lives, bound up in an alternate schedule, an intimacy only the four of them share. But by the end of the week, after his mother's friends come to admire her new gold and saris, after the eight suitcases have been aired out on the sun deck and put away, after the chanachur is poured into Tupperware and the smuggled mangoes eaten for breakfast with cereal and tea, it's as if they've never been gone. "How dark you've become," his parents' friends say regretfully to Gogol and Sonia. On this end, there is no effort involved. They retreat to their three rooms, to their three separate beds, to their thick mattresses and pillows and fitted sheets. After a single trip to the supermarket, the refrigerator and the cupboards fill with familiar labels: Skippy, Hood, Bumble Bee, Land O' Lakes. His mother enters the kitchen and prepares their meals once again; his father drives the car and mows the lawn and returns to the university. Gogol and Sonia sleep for as long as they want, watch television, make themselves peanut butter and jelly sandwiches at any time of day. Once again they are free to quarrel, to tease each other, to shout and holler and say shut up. They take hot showers, speak to each other in English, ride their bicycles around the neighborhood. They call up their American friends, who are happy enough to see them but ask them nothing about where they've been. And so the eight months are put behind them, quickly shed, quickly forgotten, like clothes worn for a special occasion, or for a season that has passed, suddenly cumbersome, irrelevant to their lives.

In September, Gogol returns to high school to begin his junior year: honors biology, honors U.S. history, advanced trigonometry, Spanish, honors English. In his English class he reads *Ethan Frome*, *The Great Gatsby*, *The Good Earth*, *The Red Badge of Courage*. He takes his turn at the podium and recites the "Tomorrow, and tomorrow, and tomorrow" speech from *Macbeth*, the only lines of poetry he will know by heart for the rest of his life. His teacher, Mr. Lawson, is a slight, wiry, shamelessly preppy man with a surprisingly deep voice, reddish blond hair, smallish but penetrating green eyes, horn-rimmed glasses. He is the subject of schoolwide speculation, and slight scandal, having once been married to Ms. Sagan, who teaches French. He wears khakis and Shetland sweaters in bright solid colors, kelly green and yellow and red, sips black coffee continually from the same chipped blue mug, cannot survive the fifty-minute class without excusing himself to go to the teachers' lounge for a cigarette. In spite of his diminutive stature he has a commanding, captivating presence in the room. His handwriting is famously illegible; student compositions are regularly returned stamped with tan rings of coffee, sometimes golden rings of Scotch. Every year he gives everyone either a D or an F on the first assignment, an analysis of Blake's "The Tiger." A number of girls in the class insist that Mr. Lawson is indescribably sexy and have raging crushes on him.

Mr. Lawson is the first of Gogol's teachers to know and to care about Gogol the author. The first day of class he had looked up from the podium when he came to Gogol's name on the roster, an expression of benign amazement on his face. Unlike other teachers he did not ask, Was that really his name, was that the last name, was it short for something else? He did not ask, as many foolishly did, "Wasn't he a writer?" Instead he called out the name in a perfectly reasonable way, without pause, without doubt, without a suppressed smile, just as he had called out Brian and Erica and Tom. And then: "Well, we're

142

going to have to read 'The Overcoat.' Either that or 'The Nose.' "

One January morning, the week after Christmas vacation, Gogol sits at his desk by the window and watches a thin, sugary snow fall inconsistently from the sky. "We're going to devote this quarter to the short story," Mr. Lawson announces, and instantly Gogol knows. With growing dread and a feeling of slight nausea, he watches as Mr. Lawson distributes the books piled on his desk, giving half a dozen well-worn copies of an anthology, *Short Story Classics*, to each of the students at the front of the rows. Gogol's copy is particularly battered, the corner blunted, the cover spotted as if by a whitish mold. He looks at the table of contents, sees Gogol listed after Faulkner, before Hemingway. The sight of it printed in capital letters on the crinkly page upsets him viscerally. It's as though the name were a particularly unflattering snapshot of himself that makes him want to say in his defense, "That's not really me." Gogol wants to excuse himself, to raise his hand and take a trip to the lavatory, but at the same time he wants to draw as little attention to himself as possible. And so he sits, avoiding eye contact with any of his classmates, and pages through the book. A number of the authors' names have been starred with penciled asterisks by previous readers, but there is no sign or mark by

Nikolai Gogol's name. A single story corresponds with each author's name. The one by Gogol is called "The Overcoat." But for the rest of the class, Mr. Lawson does not mention Gogol. Instead, to Gogol Ganguli's relief, they take turns reading aloud from "The Necklace," by Guy de Maupassant. Perhaps, Gogol begins to wonder hopefully, Mr. Lawson has no intention of assigning the Gogol story. Perhaps he's forgotten about it. But as the bell rings, and the students rise collectively from their desks, Mr. Lawson holds up a hand. "Read the Gogol for tomorrow," he hollers as they shuffle through the door.

The following day, Mr. Lawson writes "Nikolai Vasilievich Gogol" in capital letters on the board, draws a box around it, then writes the dates of the author's birth and death in parentheses. Gogol opens the binder on his desk, reluctantly copies the information down. He tells himself it isn't so strange; there is, after all, a William in the class, if not an Ernest. Mr. Lawson's left hand guides the chalk rapidly across the board, but Gogol's pen begins to lag. The loose-leaf pages remain blank as those of his classmates fill up with facts on which he will most likely soon be quizzed: Born 1809 in the province of Poltava to a family of Ukrainian Cossack gentry. Father a small landowner who also wrote plays, died when Gogol was sixteen.

144

Studied at the Lyceum of Nezhin, went to St. Petersburg in 1828 where he entered, in 1829, the civil service, in the Department of Public Works for the Ministry of the Interior. From 1830 to 1831, transferred to the Court Ministry in the Department of Royal Estates, after which time he became a teacher, lecturing on history at the Young Ladies' Institute, and later at the University of St. Petersburg. At the age of twenty-two, established a close friendship with Alexander Pushkin. In 1830, published his first short story. In 1836, a comic play, *The Government Inspector*, was produced in St. Petersburg. Dismayed by the play's mixed reception, left Russia. For the next twelve years lived abroad, in Paris, Rome, and elsewhere, composing the first volume of *Dead Souls*, the novel considered to be his finest work.

Mr. Lawson sits on the edge of his desk, crosses his legs, turns a few pages in a yellow legal pad covered with notes. Beside the legal pad is a biography of the author, a thick book called *Divided Soul*, the pages marked by numerous scraps of torn-up paper.

"Not your ordinary guy, Nikolai Gogol," Mr. Lawson says. "He is celebrated today as one of Russia's most brilliant writers. But during his life he was understood by no one, least of all himself. One might say he typified the phrase 'eccentric genius.' Gogol's life, in a nutshell, was a steady decline into madness.

The writer Ivan Turgenev described him as an intelligent, queer, and sickly creature. He was reputed to be a hypochondriac and a deeply paranoid, frustrated man. He was, in addition, by all accounts, morbidly melancholic, given to fits of severe depression. He had trouble making friends. He never married, fathered no children. It's commonly believed he died a virgin."

Warmth spreads from the back of Gogol's neck to his cheeks and his ears. Each time the name is uttered, he quietly winces. His parents have never told him any of this. He looks at his classmates, but they seem indifferent, obediently copying down the information as Mr. Lawson continues to speak, looking over one shoulder, his sloppy handwriting filling up the board. He feels angry at Mr. Lawson suddenly. Somehow he feels betrayed.

"Gogol's literary career spanned a period of about eleven years, after which he was more or less paralyzed by writer's block. The last years of his life were marked by physical deterioration and emotional torment," Mr. Lawson says. "Desperate to restore his health and creative inspiration, Gogol sought refuge in a series of spas and sanatoriums. In 1848 he made a pilgrimage to Palestine. Eventually he returned to Russia. In 1852, in Moscow, disillusioned and convinced of his failure as a writer, he renounced all literary activity and burned the manuscript to the second volume of *Dead Souls*. He then pronounced a death sentence on himself, and proceeded to commit slow suicide by starvation."

"Gross," someone says from the back of the classroom. "Why would someone want to do that to himself?"

A few people glance at Emily Gardener, rumored to have anorexia.

Mr. Lawson, holding up a finger, goes on. "In attempts to revive him on the day before his death, doctors immersed him in a bath of broth while ice water was poured over his head, and then affixed seven leeches to his nose. His hands were pinned down so that he could not tear the worms away."

The class, all but one, begins to moan in unison, so that Mr. Lawson has to raise his voice considerably in order to be heard. Gogol stares at his desk, seeing nothing. He is convinced that the entire school is listening to Mr. Lawson's lecture. That it's on the PA. He lowers his head over his desk, discreetly presses his hands against his ears. It's not enough to block out Mr. Lawson: "By the following evening he was no longer fully conscious, and so wasted that his spine could be felt through his stomach." Gogol shuts his eyes. Please, stop, he wishes he could say to Mr. Lawson. Please stop, he says, mouthing the words. And then, suddenly, there is silence. Gogol looks up, sees Mr. Lawson drop his chalk on the blackboard ledge.

"I'll be right back," he says, and disappears to have a cigarette. The students, accustomed to this routine, begin talking among themselves. They complain about the story, saying that it's too long. They complain that it was hard to get through. There is talk of the difficulty of Russian names, students confessing merely to skimming them. Gogol says nothing. He has not read the story himself. He has never touched the Gogol book his father gave him on his fourteenth birthday. And yesterday, after class, he'd shoved the short story anthology deep into his locker, refusing to bring it home. To read the story, he believes, would mean paying tribute to his namesake, accepting it somehow. Still, listening to his classmates complain, he feels perversely responsible, as if his own work were being attacked.

Mr. Lawson returns, sitting once more on his desk. Gogol hopes that perhaps the biographical portion of the lecture is over. What else could he possibly have left to say? But Mr. Lawson picks up *Divided Soul*. "Here is an account of his final moments," he says, and, turning toward the end of the book, he reads:

" 'His feet were icy. Tarasenkov slid a hot-water bottle into the bed, but it had no effect: he was shivering. Cold sweat covered his emaciated face. Blue circles appeared under his eyes. At midnight Dr. Klimentov relieved

Dr. Tarasenkov. To ease the dying man, he administered a dose of calomel and placed loaves of hot bread around his body. Gogol began to moan again. His mind wandered, quietly, all night long. "Go on!" he whispered. "Rise up, charge, charge the mill!" Then he became still weaker, his face hollowed and darkened, his breathing became imperceptible. He seemed to grow calm; at least he was no longer suffering. At eight in the morning of February 21, 1852, he breathed his last. He was not yet forty-three years old.' "

Gogol does not date anyone in high school. He suffers quiet crushes, which he admits to no one, on this girl or that girl with whom he is already friends. He does not attend dances or parties. He and his group of friends, Colin and Jason and Marc, prefer to listen to records together, to Dylan and Clapton and The Who, and read Nietzsche in their spare time. His parents do not find it strange that their son doesn't date, does not rent a tuxedo for his junior prom. They have never been on a date in their lives and therefore they see no reason to encourage Gogol, certainly not at his age. Instead they urge him to join the math team and maintain his A average. His father presses him to pursue engineering, perhaps at MIT. Assured by his grades and his apparent indifference to girls, his parents don't suspect Gogol of being, in his own fumbling way, an American teenager. They don't suspect him, for instance, of smoking pot, which he does from time to time when he and his friends get together to listen to records at one another's homes. They don't suspect him, when he goes to spend the night at a friend's house, of driving to a neighboring town to see *The Rocky Horror Picture Show*, or into Boston to see bands in Kenmore Square.

One Saturday, soon before he is scheduled to take the SAT, his family drives to Connecticut for the weekend, leaving Gogol at home alone overnight for the first time in his life. It never crosses his parents' minds that instead of taking timed pratice tests in his room, Gogol will drive with Colin and Jason and Marc to a party. They are invited by Colin's older brother, who is a freshman at the university where Gogol's father teaches. He dresses for the party as he normally does, in Levi's and boat shoes and a checkered flannel shirt. For all the times he's been to the campus, to visit his father at the engineering department or for swimming lessons or to run laps around the track, he has never been in a dorm before. They approach nervously, a bit giddy, afraid to be caught. "If anyone asks, my brother said to say we're freshmen at Amherst," Colin advises them in the car.

The party occupies an entire hallway, the doors of the individual rooms all open. They enter the first room they can manage to, crowded, dark, hot. No one notices as Gogol and his three friends make their way across the room to the keg. For a while, they stand in a circle, holding their plastic cups of beer, shouting over the music in order to be heard. But then Colin sees his brother in the hallway, and Jason needs to find a bathroom, and Marc needs another beer already. Gogol drifts into the hallway as well. Everyone seems to know everyone else, embroiled in conversations that are impossible to join. Music playing from the different rooms mingles unpleasantly in Gogol's ears. He feels too wholesome in this ripped jeans and T-shirt crowd, fears his hair was too recently washed and is too neatly combed. And yet it doesn't seem to matter, no one seems to care. At the end of the hallway, he climbs a set of stairs, and at the top there is another hallway, equally crowded and loud. In the corner he sees a couple kissing, pressed up against the wall. Instead of pushing his way through to the other end of the hallway, he decides to climb another set of stairs. This time the hallway is deserted, an expanse of dark blue carpeting and white wooden doors. The only presence in the space is the sound of muffled music and voices coming from below. He is about to turn back down the staircase when one of the doors opens and a girl emerges, a pretty, slender girl wearing a buttoned-up polka-dotted thrift store dress and scuffed Doc Martens. She has short, dark brown hair, curving in toward her cheeks and cut in a high fringe over her brows. Her face is heart-shaped, her lips painted a glamorous red.

"Sorry," Gogol says. "Am I not supposed to be up here?"

"Well, it's technically a girls' floor," the girl says. "But that's never stopped a guy before." She studies him thoughtfully, as no other girl has looked at him. "You don't go here, do you?"

"No," he says, his heart pounding. And then he remembers his surreptitious identity for the evening: "I'm a freshman at Amherst."

"That's cool," the girl says, walking toward him. "I'm Kim."

"Nice to meet you." He extends his hand, and Kim shakes it, a bit longer than necessary. For a moment she looks at him expectantly, then smiles, revealing two front teeth that are slightly overlapping.

"Come on," she says. "I can show you around." They walk together down the staircase. She leads him to a room where she gets herself a beer and he pours himself another. He stands awkwardly at her side as she pauses to say hello to friends. They work their way to a common area where there is a television, a Coke machine, a shabby sofa, and an assortment of chairs. They sit on the sofa, slouching, a considerable space between them. Kim notices a stray pack of cigarettes on the coffee table and lights one.

"Well?" she says, turning to look at him, somewhat suspiciously this time.

"What?"

"Aren't you going to introduce yourself to me?"

"Oh," he says. "Yeah." But he doesn't want to tell Kim his name. He doesn't want to endure her reaction, to watch her lovely blue eyes grow wide. He wishes there were another name he could use, just this once, to get him through the evening. It wouldn't be so terrible. He's lied to her already, about being at Amherst. He could introduce himself as Colin or Jason or Marc, as anybody at all, and their conversation could continue, and she would never know or care. There were a million names to choose from. But then he realizes there's no need to lie. Not technically. He remembers the other name that had once been chosen for him, the one that should have been.

"I'm Nikhil," he says for the first time in his life. He says it tentatively, his voice sounding strained to his ears, the statement turning without his meaning it to into a question. He looks at Kim, his eyebrows furrowed, prepared for her to challenge him, to correct him, to laugh in his face. He holds his breath. His face tingles, whether from triumph or terror he isn't sure.

But Kim accepts it gladly. "Nikhil," she says, blowing a thin plume of smoke toward the ceiling. Again she turns to him and smiles. "Nikhil," she repeats. "I've never heard that before. That's a lovely name."

They sit awhile longer, the conversation continuing, Gogol stunned at how easy it is. His mind floats; he only half listens as Kim talks about her classes, about the town in Connecticut where she's from. He feels at once guilty and exhilarated, protected as if by an invisible shield. Because he knows he will never see her again, he is brave that evening, kissing her lightly on the mouth as she is talking to him, his leg pressing gently against her leg on the sofa, briefly running a hand through her hair. It is the first time he's kissed anyone, the first time he's felt a girl's face and body and breath so close to his own. "I can't believe you kissed her, Gogol," his friends exclaim as they drive home from the party. He shakes his head in a daze, as astonished as they are, elation still welling inside him. "It wasn't me," he nearly says. But he doesn't tell them that it hadn't been Gogol who'd kissed Kim. That Gogol had had nothing to do with it.

5.

Plenty of people changed their names: actors, writers, revolutionaries, transvestites. In history class, Gogol has learned that European immigrants had their names changed at Ellis Island, that slaves renamed themselves once they were emancipated. Though Gogol doesn't know it, even Nikolai Gogol renamed himself, simplifying his surname at the age of twenty-two from Gogol-Yanovsky to Gogol upon publication in the *Literary Gazette*. (He had also published under the name Yanov, and once signed his work "OOOO" in honor of the four *o*'s in his full name.)

One day in the summer of 1986, in the frantic weeks before moving away from his family, before his freshman year at Yale is about to begin, Gogol Ganguli does the same. He rides the commuter rail into Boston, switching to the Green Line at North Station, getting out at Lechmere. The area is somewhat familiar: he has been to Lechmere countless times with his family, to buy new televisions and vacuum cleaners, and he has been to the Museum of Science on field trips from school. But he has never been to this neighborhood on his own, and

155

in spite of the directions he's written on a sheet of paper he gets briefly lost on his way to the Middlesex Probate and Family Court. He wears a blue oxford shirt, khakis, a camel-colored corduroy blazer bought for his college interviews that is too warm for the sultry day. Knotted around his neck is his only tie, maroon with yellow stripes on the diagonal. By now Gogol is just shy of six feet tall, his body slender, his thick brown-black hair slightly in need of a cut. His face is lean, intelligent, suddenly handsome, the bones more prominent, the pale gold skin clean-shaven and clear. He has inherited Ashima's eyes, large, penetrating, with bold, elegant brows, and shares with Ashoke the slight bump at the very top of his nose.

The courthouse is an imposing, old, pillared brick building occupying a full city block, but the entrance is off to the side, down a set of steps. Inside, Gogol empties his pockets and steps through a metal detector, as if he were at an airport, about to embark on a journey. He is soothed by the chill of the air-conditioning, by the beautifully carved plaster ceiling, by the voices that echo pleasantly in the marbled interior. He had pictured a setting far less grand. And yet this is a place, he gathers, that people come to seek divorces, dispute wills. A man at the information booth tells him to wait upstairs, in an area filled with round tables, where people sit eating their lunch. Gogol sits impatiently, one long leg jiggling up and down. He has forgotten to bring a book to read and so he picks up a discarded section of the *Globe*, skimming an article in the "Arts" section about Andrew Wyeth's Helga paintings. Eventually he begins to practice his new signature in the margins of the paper. He tries it in various styles, his hand unaccustomed to the angles of the *N*, the dotting of the two *i*'s. He wonders how many times he has written his old name, at the tops of how many tests and quizzes, how many homework assignments, how many yearbook inscriptions to friends. How many times does a person write his name in a lifetime — a million? Two million?

The idea to change his name had first occurred to him a few months ago. He was sitting in the waiting room of his dentist, flipping through an issue of *Reader's Digest*. He'd been turning the pages at random until he came to an article that caused him to stop. The article was called "Second Baptisms." "Can you identify the following famous people?" was written beneath the headline. A list of names followed and, at the bottom of the page, printed in tiny letters upside down, the famous personalities they corresponded to. The only one he guessed correctly was Robert Zimmerman, Bob Dylan's real name. He had no idea that

Molière had been born Jean-Baptiste Poquelin and that Leon Trotsky was born Lev Davidovich Bronstein. That Gerald Ford's name was Leslie Lynch King, Jr., and that Engelbert Humperdinck's was Arnold George Dorsey. They had all renamed themselves, the article said, adding that it was a right belonging to every American citizen. He read that tens of thousands of Americans had their names changed each year. All it took was a legal petition, the article had said. And suddenly he envisioned "Gogol" added to the list of names, "Nikhil" printed in tiny letters upside down.

That night at the dinner table, he brought it up with his parents. It was one thing for Gogol to be the name penned in calligraphy on his high school diploma, and printed below his picture in the yearbook, he'd begun. It was one thing, even, for it to be typed on his applications to five Ivy League colleges, as well as to Stanford and Berkeley. But engraved, four years from now, on a bachelor of arts degree? Written at the top of a résumé? Centered on a business card? It would be the name his parents picked out for him, he assured them, the good name they'd chosen for him when he was five.

"What's done is done," his father had said. "It will be a hassle. Gogol has, in effect, become your good name."

"It's too complicated now," his mother

158

said, agreeing. "You're too old."

"I'm not," he persisted. "I don't get it. Why did you have to give me a pet name in the first place? What's the point?"

"It's our way, Gogol," his mother maintained. "It's what Bengalis do."

"But it's not even a Bengali name."

He told his parents what he'd learned in Mr. Lawson's class, about Gogol's lifelong unhappiness, his mental instability, about how he'd starved himself to death. "Did you know all this stuff about him?" he asked.

"You forgot to mention that he was also a genius," his father said.

"I don't get it. How could you guys name me after someone so strange? No one takes me seriously," Gogol said.

"Who? Who does not take you seriously?" his father wanted to know, lifting his fingers from his plate, looking up at him.

"People," he said, lying to his parents. For his father had a point; the only person who didn't take Gogol seriously, the only person who tormented him, the only person chronically aware of and afflicted by the embarrassment of his name, the only person who constantly questioned it and wished it were otherwise, was Gogol. And yet he'd continued, saying that they should be glad, that his official name would be Bengali, not Russian.

"I don't know, Gogol," his mother had

said, shaking her head. "I really don't know." She got up to clear the dishes. Sonia slinked away, up to her room. Gogol remained at the table with his father. They sat there together, listening to his mother scraping the plates, the water running in the sink.

"Then change it," his father said simply, quietly, after a while.

"Really?"

"In America anything is possible. Do as you wish."

And so he had obtained a Commonwealth of Massachusetts change-of-name form, to submit along with a certified copy of his birth certificate and a check to the Middlesex Probate and Family Court. He'd brought the form to his father, who had glanced at it only briefly before signing his consent, with the same resignation with which he signed a check or a credit card receipt, his eyebrows slightly raised over his glasses, inwardly calculating the loss. He'd filled out the rest of the form in his room, late at night when his family was asleep. The application consisted of a single side of a cream-colored sheet, and yet it had taken him longer to fill out than his applications for college. On the first line he filled out the name he wished to change, and his place and date of birth. He wrote in the new name he wished to adopt, then signed the form with his old signature. Only one part of the form had given him pause: in approximately three lines, he was asked to provide a reason for seeking the change. For nearly an hour he'd sat there, wondering what to write. He'd left it blank in the end.

At the appointed time, his case is called. He enters a room and sits on an empty wooden bench at the back. The judge, a middle-aged, heavyset black woman wearing half-moon glasses, sits opposite, on a dais. The clerk, a thin young woman with bobbed hair, asks for his application, reviewing it before handing it to the judge. There is nothing decorating the room apart from the Massachusetts state and American flags and an oil portrait of a judge. "Gogol Ganguli," the clerk says, motioning for Gogol to approach the dais, and as eager as he is to go through with it, he is aware, with a twinge of sadness, that this is the last time in his life he will hear that name uttered in an official context. In spite of his parents' sanction he feels that he is overstepping them, correcting a mistake they've made.

"What is the reason you wish to change your name, Mr. Ganguli?" the judge asks.

The question catches him off-guard, and for several seconds he has no idea what to say. "Personal reasons," he says eventually.

The judge looks at him, leaning forward, her chin cupped in her hand. "Would you care to be more specific?"

At first he says nothing, unprepared to give

any further explanation. He wonders whether to tell the judge the whole convoluted story, about his great-grandmother's letter that never made it to Cambridge, and about pet names and good names, about what had happened on the first day of kindergarten. But instead he takes a deep breath and tells the people in the courtroom what he has never dared admit to his parents. "I hate the name Gogol," he says. "I've always hated it."

"Very well," the judge says, stamping and signing the form, then returning it to the clerk. He is told that notice of the new name must be given to all other agencies, that it's his responsibility to notify the Registry of Motor Vehicles, banks, schools. He orders three certified copies of the name change decree, two for himself, and one for his parents to keep in their safe-deposit box. No one accompanies him on this legal rite of passage, and when he steps out of the room no one is waiting to commemorate the moment with flowers and Polaroid snapshots and balloons. In fact the procedure is entirely unmomentous, and when he looks at his watch he sees that from the time he'd entered the courtroom it had taken all of ten minutes. He emerges into the muggy afternoon, perspiring, still partly convinced it is a dream. He takes the T across the river to Boston. He walks with his blazer clasped by a finger over his shoulder, across the Common, through the

Public Garden, over the bridges and along the curving paths that rim the lagoon. Thick clouds conceal the sky, which appears only here and there like the small lakes on a map, and the air threatens rain.

He wonders if this is how it feels for an obese person to become thin, for a prisoner to walk free. "I'm Nikhil," he wants to tell the people who are walking their dogs, pushing children in their strollers, throwing bread to the ducks. He wanders up Newbury Street as drops begin to fall. He dashes into Newbury Comics, buys himself *London Calling* and *Talking Heads: 77* with his birthday money, a Che poster for his dorm room. He pockets an application for a student American Express card, grateful that his first credit card will not say Gogol in raised letters at the bottom. "I'm Nikhil," he is tempted to tell the attractive, nose-ringed cashier with dyed black hair and skin as pale as paper. The cashier hands him his change and looks past him to the next customer, but it doesn't matter; instead he thinks of how many more women he can now approach, for the rest of his life, with this same unobjectionable, uninteresting fact. Still, for the next three weeks, even though his new driver's license says "Nikhil," even though he's sliced up the old one with his mother's sewing scissors, even though he's ripped out the pages in front of his favorite books in which he'd written his name until now, there's a snag: everyone he knows in the world still calls him Gogol. He is aware that his parents, and their friends, and the children of their friends, and all his own friends from high school, will never call him anything but Gogol. He will remain Gogol during holidays and in summer; Gogol will revisit him on each of his birthdays. Everyone who comes to his going-away-to-college party writes "Good Luck, Gogol" on the cards.

It isn't until his first day in New Haven, after his father and teary mother and Sonia are heading back up 95 toward Boston, that he begins to introduce himself as Nikhil. The first people to call him by his new name are his suitemates, Brandon and Jonathan, both of whom had been notified by mail over the summer that his name is Gogol. Brandon, lanky and blond, grew up in Massachusetts not far from Gogol, and went to Andover. Jonathan, who is Korean and plays the cello, comes from L.A.

"Is Gogol your first name or your last?" Brandon wants to know.

Normally that question agitates him. But today he has a new answer. "Actually, that's my middle name," Gogol says by way of explanation, sitting with them in the common room to their suite. "Nikhil is my first name. It got left out for some reason."

164

Jonathan nods in acceptance, distracted by the task of setting up his stereo components. Brandon nods, too. "Hey, Nikhil," Brandon says awhile later, after they have arranged the furniture in the common room to their liking. "Want to smoke a bowl?" Since everything else is suddenly so new, going by a new name doesn't feel so terribly strange to Gogol. He lives in a new state, has a new telephone number. He eats his meals off a tray in Commons, shares a bathroom with a floor full of people, showers each morning in a stall. He sleeps in a new bed, which his mother had insisted on making before she left.

He spends the days of orientation rushing around campus, back and forth along the intersecting flagstone path, past the clock tower, and the turreted, crenelated buildings. He is too harried, at first, to sit on the grass in Old Campus as the other students do, perusing their course catalogues, playing Frisbee, getting to know one another among the verdigris-covered statues of robed, seated men. He makes a list of all the places he has to go, circling the buildings on his campus map. When he is alone in his room he types out a written request on his Smith Corona, notifying the registrar's office of his name change, providing examples of his former and current signatures side by side. He gives these documents to a secretary, along with a copy of the change-of-name form. He tells his freshman counselor about his name change; he tells the person in charge of processing his student ID and his library card. He corrects the error in stealth, not bothering to explain to Jonathan and Brandon what he's so busy doing all day, and then suddenly it is over. After so much work it is no work at all. By the time the upperclassmen arrive and classes begin, he's paved the way for a whole university to call him Nikhil: students and professors and TAs and girls at parties. Nikhil registers for his first four classes: Intro to the History of Art, Medieval History, a semester of Spanish, Astronomy to fulfill his hard science requirement. At the last minute he registers for a drawing class in the evenings. He doesn't tell his parents about the drawing class, something they would consider frivolous at this stage of his life, in spite of the fact that his own grandfather was an artist. They are already distressed that he hasn't settled on a major and a profession. Like the rest of their Bengali friends, his parents expect him to be, if not an engineer, then a doctor, a lawyer, an economist at the very least. These were the fields that brought them to America, his father repeatedly reminds him, the professions that have earned them security and respect.

But now that he's Nikhil it's easier to ignore his parents, to tune out their concerns and pleas. With relief, he types his name at the tops of his freshman papers. He reads the telephone messages his suitemates leave for Nikhil on assorted scraps in their rooms. He opens up a checking account, writes his new name into course books. *"Me llamo Nikhil,"* he says in his Spanish class. It is as Nikhil, that first semester, that he grows a goatee, starts smoking Camel Lights at parties and while writing papers and before exams, discovers Brian Eno and Elvis Costello and Charlie Parker. It is as Nikhil that he takes Metro-North into Manhattan one weekend with Jonathan and gets himself a fake ID that allows him to be served liquor in New Haven bars. It is as Nikhil that he loses his virginity at a party at Ezra Stiles, with a girl wearing a plaid woolen skirt and combat boots and mustard tights. By the time he wakes up, hung-over, at three in the morning, she has vanished from the room, and he is unable to recall her name.

There is only one complication: he doesn't feel like Nikhil. Not yet. Part of the problem is that the people who now know him as Nikhil have no idea that he used to be Gogol. They know him only in the present, not at all in the past. But after eighteen years of Gogol, two months of Nikhil feel scant, inconsequential. At times he feels as if he's cast himself in a play, acting the part of twins, indistinguishable to the naked eye yet fundamentally different. At times he still feels his old name, painfully and without warning, the way his front tooth had unbearably throbbed in recent weeks after a filling, threatening for an instant to sever from his gums when he drank coffee, or iced water, and once when he was riding in an elevator. He fears being discovered, having the whole charade somehow unravel, and in nightmares his files are exposed, his original name printed on the front page of the *Yale Daily News*. Once, he signs his old name by mistake on a credit card slip at the college bookstore. Occasionally he has to hear Nikhil three times before he answers.

Even more startling is when those who normally call him Gogol refer to him as Nikhil. For example, when his parents call on Saturday mornings, if Brandon or Jonathan happens to pick up the phone, they ask if Nikhil is there. Though he has asked his parents to do precisely this, the fact of it troubles him, making him feel in that instant that he is not related to them, not their child. "Please come to our home with Nikhil one weekend," Ashima says to his roommates when she and Ashoke visit campus during parents weekend in October, the suite hastily cleared of liquor bottles and ashtrays and Brandon's bong for the occasion. The substitution sounds wrong to Gogol, correct but off-key, the way it sounds when his parents speak English to him instead of Bengali. Stranger still is when one of his parents addresses him, in front of his new friends, as Nikhil directly: "Nikhil, show us the buildings where you have your classes," his father suggests. Later that evening, out to dinner with Jonathan at a restaurant on Chapel Street, Ashima slips, asking, "Gogol, have you decided yet what your major will be?" Though Jonathan, listening to something his father is saying, doesn't hear, Gogol feels helpless, annoyed yet unable to blame his mother, caught in the mess he's made.

During his first semester, obediently but unwillingly, he goes home every other weekend, after his last Friday class. He rides Amtrak to Boston and then switches to a commuter rail, his duffel bag stuffed with course books and dirty laundry. Somewhere along the two-and-a-half-hour journey, Nikhil evaporates and Gogol claims him again. His father comes to the station to fetch him, always calling ahead to check whether the train is on time. Together they drive through the town, along the familiar tree-lined roads, his father asking after his studies. Between Friday night and Sunday afternoon the laundry, thanks to his mother, gets done, but the course books are neglected; in spite of his intentions, Gogol finds himself capable of doing little at his parents' but eat and sleep.

The desk in his room feels too small. He is distracted by the telephone ringing, by his parents and Sonia talking and moving through the house. He misses Sterling Library, where he studies every night after dinner, and the nocturnal schedule of which he is now a part. He misses being in his suite in Farnam, smoking one of Brandon's cigarettes, listening to music with Jonathan, learning how to tell the classical composers apart.

At home he watches MTV with Sonia as she doctors her jeans, cutting inches off the bottoms and inserting zippers at the newly narrowed ankles. One weekend, the washing machine is occupied because Sonia is in the process of dyeing the vast majority of her clothing black. She is in high school now, taking Mr. Lawson's English class, going to the dances Gogol never went to himself, already going to parties at which both boys and girls are present. Her braces have come off her teeth, revealing a confident, frequent, American smile. Her formerly shoulder-length hair has been chopped asymmetrically by one of her friends. Ashima lives in fear that Sonia will color a streak of it blond, as Sonia has threatened on more than one occasion to do, and that she will have additional holes pierced in her earlobes at the mall. They argue violently about such things, Ashima crying, Sonia slamming doors. Some weekends his parents are invited to parties, and they insist that both Gogol and Sonia go with them. The host or hostess shows him to a room where he can study alone while the party thunders below, but he always ends up watching television with Sonia and the other children, just as he has done all his life. "I'm eighteen," he says once to his parents as they drive back from a party, a fact that makes no difference to them. One weekend Gogol makes the mistake of referring to New Haven as home. "Sorry, I left it at home," he says when his father asks if he remembered to buy the Yale decal his parents want to paste to the rear window of their car. Ashima is outraged by the remark, dwelling on it all day. "Only three months, and listen to you," she says, telling him that after twenty years in America, she still cannot bring herself to refer to Pemberton Road as home.

But now it is his room at Yale where Gogol feels most comfortable. He likes its oldness, its persistent grace. He likes that so many students have occupied it before him. He likes the solidity of its plaster walls, its dark wooden floorboards, however battered and stained. He likes the dormer window he sees first thing in the mornings when he opens his eyes and looking at Battell Chapel. He has fallen in love with the Gothic archi-tecture of the campus, always astonished by the physical beauty that surrounds him, that roots him to his environs in a way he had never felt growing up on Pemberton Road. For his drawing class, in which he is required to make half a dozen sketches every week, he is inspired to draw the details of buildings: flying buttresses, pointed archways filled with flowing tracery, thick rounded doorways, squat columns of pale pink stone. In the spring semester he takes an introductory class in architecture. He reads about how the pyramids and Greek temples and Medieval cathedrals were built, studying the plans of churches and palaces in his textbook. He learns the endless terms, the vocabulary that classifies the details of ancient buildings, writing them on separate index cards and making illustrations on the back: architrave, entablature, tympanum, voussoir. Together the words form another language he longs to know. He files these index cards in a shoebox, reviews them before the exam, memorizing far more terms than he needs to, keeping the box of cards even after the exam is done, adding to them in his spare time.

In the autumn of his sophomore year, he boards a particularly crowded train at Union Station. It is the Wednesday before Thanksgiving. He edges through the compartments, his duffel bag heavy with books for his Renaissance architecture class, for which he has to write a paper over the next five days. Passengers have already staked out parts of the vestibule, sitting glumly on their luggage. "Standing room only," the conductor hollers. "I want my money back," a passenger complains. Gogol keeps walking, from one compartment to the next, looking for an uncrowded vestibule in which he might sit. In the very last car of the train he sees an empty seat. A girl is seated next to the window, reading a folded-back issue of *The New Yorker*. Arranged on the seat beside her is a chocolate brown, shearling-lined suede coat, which is what had caused the person in front of Gogol to move on. But something tells Gogol the coat belongs to the girl, and so he stops and says, "Is that yours?"

She lifts up her narrow body and in a single, swift motion arranges the coat beneath her buttocks and legs. It's a face he recognizes from campus, someone he's crossed paths with in the corridors of buildings as he walks to and from class. He remembers that freshman year she'd had hair dyed an emphatic shade of cranberry red, cut to her jaw. She's grown it to her shoulders now, and allowed it to resume what appears to be its natural shade, light brown with bits of blond here and there. It is parted just off-center, a bit crooked at the base. The hair of her eyebrows is darker, lending her otherwise friendly features a serious expression. She wears a pair of nicely faded jeans, brown leather boots with yellow laces and thick rubber soles. A cabled sweater the same flecked gray of her eyes is too large for her, the sleeves coming partway up her hands. A man's billfold bulges prominently from the front pocket of her jeans.

"Hi, I'm Ruth," she says, recognizing him in that same vague way.

"I'm Nikhil." He sits, too exhausted to put his duffel bag away in the luggage rack overhead. He shoves it as best he can under his seat, his long legs bent awkwardly, aware that he is perspiring. He unzips his blue down parka. He massages his fingers, crisscrossed with welts from the leather straps of the bag.

"Sorry," Ruth says, watching him. "I guess I was just trying to put off the inevitable."

Still seated, he pries his arms free of the parka. "What do you mean?"

"Making it look like someone was sitting here. With the coat."

"It's pretty brilliant, actually. Sometimes I pretend to fall asleep for the same reason," he admits. "No one wants to sit next to me if I'm sleeping."

She laughs softly, putting a strand of her hair behind her ear. Her beauty is direct, unassuming. She wears no make-up apart from something glossy on her lips; two small brown moles by her right cheekbone are the only things that distract from the pale peach of her complexion. She has slim, small hands with unpolished nails and ragged cuticles. She leans over to put the magazine away and get a book from the bag at her feet, and he briefly glimpses the skin above her waistband.

"Are you going to Boston?" he asks.

"Maine. That's where my dad lives. I have to switch to a bus at South Station. It's another four hours from there. What college are you in?"

"J.E."

He learns that she is in Silliman, that she is planning to be an English major. Comparing notes of their experiences at college so far, they discover that they had both taken Psychology 110 the previous spring. The book in her hands is a paperback copy of *Timon of Athens*, and though she keeps a finger marking her page she never reads a word of it. Nor does he bother to open up the volume on perspective he's pulled out of his duffel. She tells him she was raised on a commune in Vermont, the child of hippies, educated at home until the seventh grade. Her parents are divorced now. Her father lives with her stepmother, raising llamas on a farm. Her mother, an anthropologist, is doing fieldwork on midwives in Thailand.

He cannot imagine coming from such parents, such a background, and when he describes his own upbringing it feels bland by comparison. But Ruth expresses interest, asking about his visits to Calcutta. She tells

175

him her parents went to India once, to an ashram somewhere, before she was born. She asks what the streets are like, and the houses, and so on the blank back page of his book on perspective Gogol draws a floor plan of his maternal grandparents' flat, navigating Ruth along the verandas and the terrazzo floors, telling her about the chalky blue walls, the narrow stone kitchen, the sitting room with cane furniture that looked as if it belonged on a porch. He draws with confidence, thanks to the drafting course he is taking this term. He shows her the room where he and Sonia sleep when they visit, and describes the view of the tiny lane lined with corrugated tin–roofed businesses. When he is finished, Ruth takes the book from him and looks at the drawing he's made, trailing her finger through the rooms. "I'd love to go," she says, and suddenly he imagines her face and arms tan, a backpack strapped to her shoulders, walking along Chowringhee as other Western tourists do, shopping in New Market, staying at the Grand.

As they are talking a woman across the aisle reprimands them; she's been trying to take a nap, she says. This only goads them into talking further, in lowered voices, their heads leaning in toward each other. Gogol is unaware of which state they are in, which stations they've passed. The train rumbles over a bridge; the setting sun is feverishly beautiful, casting a striking pink glow on the facades of the clapboard houses that dot the water's edge. In minutes these shades fade, replaced by the pallor that precedes dusk. When it is dark he sees that their images are reflected at an angle in the glass, hovering as if outside the train. Their throats are parched from talking and at one point he offers to go to the café car. She asks him to get her a bag of potato chips and a cup of tea with milk. He likes that she doesn't bother to pull the billfold out of her jeans, that she allows him to buy them for her. He returns with a coffee for himself, and the chips and the tea, along with a paper cup of milk the bartender has given him instead of the regulation container of cream. They continue talking, Ruth eating the chips, brushing the salt from around her lips with the back of her hand. She offers some to Gogol, pulling them out for him one by one. He tells her about the meals he'd eaten on Indian trains the time he traveled with his family to Delhi and Agra, the rotis and slightly sour dal ordered at one station and delivered hot at the next, the thick vegetable cutlets served with bread and butter for breakfast. He tells her about the tea, how it was bought through the window from men on the platform who poured it from giant aluminum kettles, the milk and sugar already mixed in, and how it was drunk in crude clay cups that were smashed afterward on the tracks. Her appreciation for these details flatters him; it occurs to him that he has never spoken of his experiences in India to any American friend.

They part suddenly, Gogol working up the nerve to ask for her number at the last minute, writing it into the same book where he'd drawn her the floor plan. He wishes he could wait with her at South Station for her bus to Maine, but he has a commuter train to catch in ten minutes to take him to the suburbs. The days of the holiday feel endless; all he can think of is getting back to New Haven and calling Ruth. He wonders how many times they've crossed paths, how many meals they've unwittingly shared in Commons. He thinks back to Psychology 110, wishing his memory would yield some image of her, taking notes on the other side of the law school auditorium, her head bent over her desk. Most often he thinks of the train, longs to sit beside her again, imagines their faces flushed from the heat of the compartment, their bodies cramped in the same way, her hair shining from the yellow lights overhead. On the ride back he looks for her, combing each and every compartment, but she is nowhere and he ends up sitting next to an elderly nun with a brown habit and prominent white down on her upper lip, who snores all the way.

The following week, back at Yale, Ruth

agrees to meet him for coffee at the Atticus bookshop. She is a few minutes late and dressed in the same jeans and boots and chocolate suede coat she'd worn when they met. Again she asks for tea. At first he senses an awkwardness he hadn't felt on the train. The café feels loud and hectic, the table between them too wide. Ruth is quieter than before, looking down at her cup and playing with the sugar packets, her eyes occasionally wandering to the books that line the walls. But soon enough they are conversing easily, as they had before, exchanging tales of their respective holidays. He tells her about how he and Sonia occupied the kitchen on Pemberton Road for a day, stuffing a turkey and rolling out dough for pies, things his mother did not particularly like to do. "I looked for you on my way back," he admits to her, telling her about the snoring nun. Afterward they walk together through the Center for British Art; there is an exhibit of Renaissance works on paper, which they've both been meaning to see. He walks her back to Silliman, and they arrange to have coffee a few days later. After saying good night, Ruth lingers by the gate, looking down at the books pressed up to her chest, and he wonders if he should kiss her, which is what he's been wanting to do for hours, or whether, in her mind, they are only friends. She starts walking backward toward her entryway, smiling at him, taking an impressive number of steps before giving a final wave and turning away.

He begins to meet her after her classes, remembering her schedule, looking up at the buildings and hovering casually under the archways. She always seems pleased to see him, stepping away from her girlfriends to say hello. "Of course she likes you," Jonathan tells Gogol, patiently listening to a minute account of their acquaintance one night in the dining hall. A few days later, following Ruth back to her room because she's forgotten a book she needs for a class, he places his hand over hers as she reaches for the doorknob. Her roommates are out. He waits for her on the sofa in the common room as she searches for the book. It is the middle of the day, overcast, lightly raining. "Found it," she says, and though they both have classes, they remain in the room, sitting on the sofa and kissing until it is too late to bother going.

Every evening they study together at the library, sitting at either end of a table to keep from whispering. She takes him to her dining hall, and he to hers. He takes her to the sculpture garden. He thinks of her constantly, while leaning over the slanted board in his drafting class, under the strong white lights of the studio, and in the darkened lecture hall of his Renaissance architecture class, as images of Palladian villas flash onto the screen from a slide projector. Within weeks the end of the semester is upon them, and they are besieged by exams and papers and hundreds of pages of reading. Far more than the amount of work he faces, he dreads the month of separation they will have to endure at winter break. One Saturday afternoon, just before exams, she mentions to him in the library that both her roommates will be out all day. They walk together through Cross Campus, back to Silliman, and he sits with her on her unmade bed. The room smells as she does, a powdery floral smell that lacks the acridness of perfume. Postcards of authors are taped to the wall over her desk, Oscar Wilde and Virginia Woolf. Their lips and faces are still numb from the cold, and at first they still keep their coats on. They lie together against the shearling lining of hers, and she guides his hand beneath her bulky sweater. It had not been like this the first time, the only other time, that he'd been with a girl. He recalled nothing from that episode, only being thankful, afterward, that he was no longer a virgin.

But this time he is aware of everything, the warm hollow of Ruth's abdomen, the way her lank hair rests in thick strands on the pillow, the way her features change slightly when she is lying down. "You're great, Nikhil," she whispers as he touches small breasts set wide apart, one pale nipple slightly larger than the other. He kisses them, kisses the moles scattered on her stomach as she arcs gently toward him, feels her hands on his head and then on his shoulders, guiding him between her parted legs. He feels inept, clumsy, as he tastes and smells her there, and yet he hears her whispering his name, telling him it feels wonderful. She knows what to do, unzipping his jeans, standing up at one point and getting a diaphragm case from her bureau drawer.

A week later he is home again, helping Sonia and his mother decorate the tree, shoveling the driveway with his father, going to the mall to buy last-minute gifts. He mopes around the house, restless, pretending to be coming down with a cold. He wishes he could simply borrow his parents' car and drive up to Maine to see Ruth after Christmas, or that she could visit him. He was perfectly welcome, she'd assured him, her father and stepmother wouldn't mind. They'd put him in the guest room, she'd said; at night he'd creep into her bed. He imagines himself in the farmhouse she's described to him, waking up to eggs frying in a skillet, walking with her through snowy, abandoned fields. But such a trip would require telling his parents about Ruth, something he has no desire to do. He has no patience for their surprise, their nervousness, their quiet disappointment, their questions about what Ruth's parents did and whether or not the relationship was serious. As much as he longs to see her, he cannot picture her at the kitchen table on Pemberton Road, in her jeans and her bulky sweater, politely eating his mother's food. He cannot imagine being with her in the house where he is still Gogol.

He speaks to her when his family is asleep, quietly in the empty kitchen, charging the calls to his telephone at school. They arrange to meet one day in Boston and spend the day together in Harvard Square. There is a foot of snow on the ground, and the sky is a piercing blue. They go first to a movie at the Brattle, buying tickets for whatever is about to begin, sitting at the back of the balcony and kissing, causing people to turn back and stare. They have lunch at Café Pamplona, eating pressed ham sandwiches and bowls of garlic soup off in a corner. They exchange presents: she gives him a small used book of drawings by Goya, and he gives her a pair of blue woolen mittens and a mixed tape of his favorite Beatles songs. They discover a store just above the café that sells nothing but architecture books, and he browses the aisles, treating himself to a paperback edition of Le Corbusier's *Journey to the East*, for he is thinking of declaring himself an architecture major in the spring. Afterward they wander hand in hand, kissing now and then against a building, along the very streets he was pushed up and down in his stroller as a child. He shows her the American professor's house where he and his parents once lived, a time before Sonia was born, years that he has no memory of. He's seen the house in pictures, knows from his parents the name of the street. Whoever lives there now appears to be away; the snow hasn't been cleared from the porch steps, and a number of rolled-up newspapers have collected on the doormat. "I wish we could go inside," he says. "I wish we could be alone together." Looking at the house now, with Ruth at his side, her mittened hand in his, he feels strangely helpless. Though he was only an infant at the time, he feels nevertheless betrayed by his inability to know then that one day, years later, he would return to the house under such diffcrent circumstances, and that he would be so happy.

By the following year his parents know vaguely about Ruth. Though he has been to the farmhouse in Maine twice, meeting her father and her stepmother, Sonia, who secretly has a boyfriend these days, is the only person in his family to have met Ruth, during a weekend when Sonia came to New Haven. His parents have expressed no curiosity about his girlfriend. His relationship with her is one accomplishment in his life about which they are not in the least bit proud or pleased. Ruth tells him she doesn't mind his parents' disapproval, that she finds it romantic. But Gogol knows it isn't right. He wishes his parents could simply accept her, as her family accepts him, without pressure of any kind. "You're too young to get involved this way," Ashoke and Ashima tell him. They've even gone so far as to point out examples of Bengali men they know who've married Americans, marriages that have ended in divorce. It only makes things worse when he says that marriage is the last thing on his mind. At times he hangs up on them. He pities his parents when they speak to him this way, for having no experience of being young and in love. He suspects that they are secretly glad when Ruth goes away to Oxford for a semester. She'd mentioned her interest in going there long ago, in the first weeks of their courtship, when the spring of junior year had felt like a remote speck on the horizon. She'd asked him if he minded if she applied, and though the idea of her being so far had made him queasy he'd said no, of course not, that twelve weeks would go like that.

He is lost that spring without her. He spends all his time in the studio, especially the Friday nights and weekends he would normally have been with her, the two of them eating at Naples and going to see movies in the law school auditorium. He listens to the music she loves: Simon and Garfunkel, Neil Young, Cat Stevens, buying himself brand-new copies of the albums she'd inherited from her parents. It sickens him to think of the physical distance between them, to think that when he is asleep at night she is leaning over a sink somewhere, brushing her teeth and washing her face to start the next day. He longs for her as his parents have longed, all these years, for the people they love in India — for the first time in his life, he knows this feeling. But his parents refuse to give him the money to fly to England on his spring break. He spends what little money he has from working in the dining hall on transatlantic phone calls to Ruth twice a week. Twice a day he checks his campus mailbox for letters and postcards stamped with the multicolored profiles of the queen. He carries these letters and postcards wherever he goes, stuck into his books. "My Shakespeare class is the best I've ever taken," she's written in violet-colored ink. "The coffee is undrinkable. Everyone constantly says 'cheers.' I think of you all the time."

One day he attends a panel discussion about Indian novels written in English. He feels obligated to attend; one of the presenters on the panel, Amit, is a distant cousin who lives in Bombay, whom Gogol has never met. His mother has asked him to greet Amit on her behalf. Gogol is bored by

186

the panelists, who keep referring to something called "marginality," as if it were some sort of medical condition. For most of the hour, he sketches portraits of the panelists, who sit hunched over their papers along a rectangular table. "Teleologically speaking, ABCDs are unable to answer the question 'Where are you from?' " the sociologist on the panel declares. Gogol has never heard the term *ABCD*. He eventually gathers that it stands for "American-born confused deshi." In other words, him. He learns that the *C* could also stand for "conflicted." He knows that *deshi*, a generic word for "countryman," means "Indian," knows that his parents and all their friends always refer to India simply as *desh*. But Gogol never thinks of India as desh. He thinks of it as Americans do, as India.

Gogol slouches in his seat and ponders certain awkward truths. For instance, although he can understand his mother tongue, and speak it fluently, he cannot read or write it with even modest proficiency. On trips to India his American-accented English is a source of endless amusement to his relatives, and when he and Sonia speak to each other, aunts and uncles and cousins always shake their heads in disbelief and say, "I didn't understand a word!" Living with a pet name and a good name, in a place where such distinctions do not exist — surely that was emblematic of the greatest confusion of all. He searches the audience for someone he knows, but it isn't his crowd — lots of lit majors with leather satchels and gold-rimmed glasses and fountain pens, lots of people Ruth would have waved to. There are also lots of ABCDs. He has no idea there are this many on campus. He has no ABCD friends at college. He avoids them, for they remind him too much of the way his parents choose to live, befriending people not so much because they like them, but because of a past they happen to share. "Gogol, why aren't you a member of the Indian association here?" Amit asks later when they go for a drink at the Anchor. "I just don't have the time," Gogol says, not telling his well-meaning cousin that he can think of no greater hypocrisy than joining an organization that willingly celebrates occasions his parents forced him, throughout his childhood and adolescence, to attend. "I'm Nikhil now," Gogol says, suddenly depressed by how many more times he will have to say this, asking people to remember, reminding them to forget, feeling as if an errata slip were perpetually pinned to his chest.

Thanksgiving of his senior year he takes the train, alone, up to Boston. He and Ruth are no longer together. Instead of coming back from Oxford after those twelve weeks,

188

she'd stayed on to do a summer course, explaining that a professor she admired would be retiring after that. Gogol had spent the summer on Pemberton Road. He had had an unpaid internship at a small architecture firm in Cambridge, where he'd run errands at Charrette for the designers, been sent to photograph nearby sites, lettered a few drawings. To make money he worked nights washing dishes at an Italian restaurant in his parents' town. Late in August he'd gone to Logan to welcome Ruth home. He had waited for her at the arrival gate, taken her to a hotel for one night, paying for it with the money he'd made at the restaurant. The room overlooked the Public Garden, its walls covered with thickly striped pink-and-cream paper. They'd made love for the first time in a double bed. They'd gone out for their meals, neither of them able to afford the items on the room service menu. They walked up Newbury Street and went to a Greek restaurant with tables on the sidewalk. The day was blazing hot. Ruth looked the same, but her speech was peppered with words and phrases she'd picked up in England, like "I imagine" and "I suppose" and "presumably." She spoke of her semester and how much she'd liked England, the traveling she'd done in Barcelona and Rome. She wanted to go back to England for graduate school, she said. "I imagine they've got good architecture schools," she'd added. "You could come as well." The next morning he'd put her on the bus to Maine. But within days of being together again in New Haven, in an apartment he'd rented on Howe Street with friends, they'd begun fighting, both admitting in the end that something had changed.

They avoid each other now, when they happen to cross paths in the library and on the streets. He's scratched out her phone number and the addresses he'd written down for her at Oxford and in Maine. But boarding the train it is impossible not to think of the afternoon, two years ago, they'd met. As usual the train is incredibly crowded, and this time he sits for half the journey in the vestibule. After Westerly he finds a seat, and settles down with the course selection guide for next semester. But he feels distracted for some reason, gloomy, impatient to be off the train; he does not bother to remove his coat, does not bother to go to the café car for something to drink even though he is thirsty. He puts away the course guide and opens up a library book that might be helpful for his senior thesis project, a comparison between Renaissance Italian and Mughal palace design. But after a few paragraphs he closes this book as well. His stomach growls and he wonders what there will be for dinner at home, what his father has prepared. His mother and Sonia have

190

gone to India for three weeks, to attend a cousin's wedding, and this year Gogol and his father will spend Thanksgiving at the home of friends.

He angles his head against the window and watches the autumnal landscape pass: the spewing pink and purple waters of a dye mill, electrical power stations, a big ball-shaped water tank covered with rust. Abandoned factories, with rows of small square windows partly bashed in, ravaged as if by moths. On the trees the topmost branches are bare, the remaining leaves yellow, paper-thin. The train moves more slowly than usual, and when he looks at his watch he sees that they are running well behind schedule. And then, somewhere outside Providence, in an abandoned, grassy field, the train stops. For over an hour they stand there as a solid, scarlet disk of sun sinks into the tree-lined horizon. The lights turn off, and the air inside the train turns uncomfortably warm. The conductors rush anxiously through the compartments. "Probably a broken wire," the gentleman sitting beside Gogol remarks. Across the aisle a gray-haired woman reads, a coat clutched like a blanket to her chest. Behind him two students discuss the poems of Ben Jonson. Without the sound of the engine Gogol can hear an opera playing faintly on someone's Walkman. Through the window he admires the darkening sapphire sky. He sees spare lengths of rusted rails heaped in piles. It isn't until they start moving again that an announcement is made on the loudspeaker about a medical emergency. But the truth, overheard by one of the passengers from a conductor, quickly circulates: a suicide had been committed, a person had jumped in front of the train.

He is shocked and discomfited by the news, feeling bad about his irritation and impatience, wondering if the victim had been a man or a woman, young or old. He imagines the person consulting the same schedule that's in his backpack, determining exactly when the train would be passing through. The approach of the train's headlights. As a result of the delay he misses his commuter rail connection in Boston, waits another forty minutes for the next one. He puts a call through to his parents' house, but no one answers. He tries his father's department at the university, but there too the phone rings and rings. At the station he sees his father waiting on the darkened platform, wearing sneakers and corduroys, anxiousness in his face. A trench coat is belted around his waist, a scarf knitted by Ashima wrapped at his throat, a tweed cap on his head.

"Sorry I'm late," Gogol says. "How long have you been waiting?"

"Since quarter to six," his father says. Gogol looks at his watch. It is nearly eight.

"There was an accident."

"I know. I called. What happened? Were you hurt?"

Gogol shakes his head. "Someone jumped onto the tracks. Somewhere in Rhode Island. I tried to call you. They had to wait for the police, I think."

"I was worried."

"I hope you haven't been standing out in the cold all this time," Gogol says, and from his father's lack of response he knows that this is exactly what he has done. Gogol wonders what it is like for his father to be without his mother and Sonia. He wonders if he is lonely. But his father is not the type to admit such things, to speak openly of his desires, his moods, his needs. They walk to the parking lot, get into the car, and begin the short drive home.

The night is windy, so much so that the car jostles slightly from time to time, and brown leaves as large as human feet fly across the road in the headlights' glare. Normally on these rides back from the station his father asks questions, about his classes, about his finances, about his plans after graduation. But tonight they are silent, Ashoke concentrating on driving. Gogol fidgets with the radio, switching from the AM news station to NPR.

"I want to tell you something," his father says when the piece ends, once they have already turned onto Pemberton Road.

"What?" Gogol asks.

"It's about your name."

Gogol looks at his father, puzzled. "My name?"

His father shuts off the radio. "Gogol."

These days he is called Gogol so seldom that the sound of it no longer upsets him as it used to. After three years of being Nikhil the vast majority of the time, he no longer minds.

"There is a reason for it, you know," his father continues.

"Right, Baba. Gogol's your favorite author. I know."

"No," his father says. He pulls into the driveway and switches off the engine, then the headlights. He undoes his seat belt, guiding it with his hand as it retracts, back behind his left shoulder. "Another reason."

And as they sit together in the car, his father revisits a field 209 kilometers from Howrah. With his fingers lightly grasping the bottom of the steering wheel, his gaze directed through the windshield at the garage door, he tells Gogol the story of the train he'd ridden twenty-eight years ago, in October 1961, on his way to visit his grandfather in Jamshedpur. He tells him about the night that had nearly taken his life, and the book that had saved him, and about the year afterward, when he'd been unable to move.

Gogol listens, stunned, his eyes fixed on his father's profile. Though there are only inches between them, for an instant his father is a stranger, a man who has kept a secret, has survived a tragedy, a man whose past he does not fully know. A man who is vulnerable, who has suffered in an inconceivable way. He imagines his father, in his twenties as Gogol is now, sitting on a train as Gogol had just been, reading a story, and then suddenly nearly killed. He struggles to picture the West Bengal countryside he has seen on only a few occasions, his father's mangled body, among hundreds of dead ones, being carried on a stretcher, past a twisted length of maroon compartments. Against instinct he tries to imagine life without his father, a world in which his father does not exist.

"Why don't I know this about you?" Gogol says. His voice sounds harsh, accusing, but his eyes well with tears. "Why haven't you told me this until now?"

"It never felt like the right time," his father says.

"But it's like you've lied to me all these years." When his father doesn't respond, he adds, "That's why you have that limp, isn't it?"

"It happened so long ago. I didn't want to upset you."

"It doesn't matter. You should have told me."

"Perhaps," his father concedes, glancing briefly in Gogol's direction. He removes the keys from the ignition. "Come, you must be hungry. The car is getting cold."

But Gogol doesn't move. He sits there, still struggling to absorb the information, feeling awkward, oddly ashamed, at fault. "I'm sorry, Baba."

His father laughs softly. "You had nothing to do with it."

"Does Sonia know?"

His father shakes his head. "Not yet. I'll explain it to her one day. In this country, only your mother knows. And now you. I've always meant for you to know, Gogol."

And suddenly the sound of his pet name, uttered by his father as he has been accustomed to hearing it all his life, means something completely new, bound up with a catastrophe he has unwittingly embodied for years. "Is that what you think of when you think of me?" Gogol asks him. "Do I remind you of that night?"

"Not at all," his father says eventually, one hand going to his ribs, a habitual gesture that has baffled Gogol until now. "You remind me of everything that followed."

6.

He lives in New York now. In May he graduated from the architecture program at Columbia. He's been working since then for a
firm in midtown, with celebrated large-scale
commissions to its name. It's not the sort of
job he'd envisioned for himself as a student;
designing and renovating private residences
was what he'd wanted to do. That might
come later, his advisers have told him; for
now, it was important to apprentice with the
big names. And so, facing the tawny brick
wall of a neighboring building across the air
shaft, he works with a team on designs for
hotels and museums and corporate head-
quarters in cities he's never seen: Brussels,
Buenos Aires, Abu Dhabi, Hong Kong. His
contributions are incidental, and never fully
his own: a stairwell, a skylight, a corridor,
an air-conditioning duct. Still, he knows that
each component of a building, however small,
is nevertheless essential, and he finds it grati-
fying that after all his years of schooling, all
his crits and unbuilt projects, his efforts are
to have some practical end. He typically

works late into his evenings, and on most of his weekends, drawing designs on the computer, drafting plans, writing specifications, building Styrofoam and cardboard models to scale. He goes home to a studio in Morningside Heights, with two windows facing west, on Amsterdam Avenue. The entrance is easy to miss, a scratched-up glass door between a newsstand and a nail salon. It's the first apartment he has to himself, after an evolving chain of roommates all through college and graduate school. There is so much street noise that when he is on the phone and the windows are open, people often ask if he is calling from a pay phone. The kitchen is built into what should have been an entryway, a space so small that the refrigerator stands several feet away, over by the bathroom door. On the stove sits a teakettle he has never filled with water, and on the countertop a toaster he's never plugged in.

His parents are distressed by how little money he makes, and occasionally his father sends him checks in the mail to help him with his rent, his credit card bills. They had been disappointed that he'd gone to Columbia. They'd hoped he would choose MIT, the other architecture program to which he'd been accepted. But after four years in New Haven he didn't want to move back to Massachusetts, to the one city in America his parents know. He didn't want to attend his father's alma mater, and live in an apartment in Central Square as his parents once had, and revisit the streets about which his parents speak nostalgically. He didn't want to go home on the weekends, to go with them to pujos and Bengali parties, to remain unquestionably in their world.

He prefers New York, a place which his parents do not know well, whose beauty they are blind to, which they fear. He'd come to know the city slightly during his years at Yale, on visits with architecture classes. He'd been to a few parties at Columbia. Sometimes he and Ruth would ride in on Metro-North, and they would go to museums, or to the Village, or to browse for books at the Strand. But as a child he'd been to New York only once with his family, a trip that had given him no sense of what the city was like. They had gone one weekend to visit Bengali friends who lived in Queens. The friends had given his family a tour of Manhattan. Gogol had been ten years old, Sonia four. "I want to see Sesame Street," Sonia had said, believing that it was an actual landmark in the city, and she had cried when Gogol had laughed at her, saying it didn't exist. On the tour they were driven past sites like Rockefeller Center and Central Park and the Empire State Building, and Gogol had ducked his head below the car's window to try to see how tall the buildings were. His parents had remarked endlessly at the amount of traffic, the pedestrians, the noise. Calcutta was no worse, they had said. He remembered wanting to get out and go to the top of one of the skyscrapers, the way his father had once taken him to the top of the Prudential Center in Boston when he was little. But they were allowed out of the car only once they got to Lexington Avenue, to eat lunch at an Indian restaurant and then to buy Indian groceries, and polyester saris and 220-volt appliances to give to relatives in Calcutta. This, to his parents, was what one came to Manhattan to do. He remembered wishing that his parents would walk through the park, take him to the Museum of Natural History to see the dinosaurs, ride the subway even. But they had had no interest in such things.

One night, Evan, one of the draftsmen at work with whom he is friendly, talks him into going to a party. Evan tells Gogol that it's an apartment worth seeing, a Tribeca loft that happens to be designed by one of the partners at the firm. The host of the party, Russell, an old friend of Evan, works for the UN and has spent several years in Kenya, and as a result the loft is filled with an impressive collection of African furniture and sculpture and masks. Gogol imagines that it will be a party of hundreds filling up a vast space, the sort of party where he might arrive and leave undetected. But by the time Gogol and Evan get there, the party is nearly over, and there are only a dozen or so people sitting around a low coffee table surrounded by cushions, eating picked-over grapes and cheese. At one point Russell, who is diabetic, raises his shirt and injects himself in the stomach with insulin. Beside Russell is a woman Gogol can't stop looking at. She is kneeling on the floor at Russell's side, spreading a generous amount of brie on a cracker, paying no attention to what Russell is doing. Instead she is arguing with a man on the other side of the coffee table about a movie by Buñuel. "Oh, come on," she keeps saying, "it was brilliant." At once strident and flirtatious, she is a little bit drunk. She has dirty blond hair gathered sloppily into a bun, strands falling randomly, attractively, around her face. Her forehead is high and smooth, her jawbones sloping and unusually long. Her eyes are greenish, the irises encased by thin rings of black. She is dressed in silk capri pants and a sleeveless white shirt that shows off her tan. "What did you think of it?" she asks Gogol, drawing him without warning into the discussion. When he tells her he hasn't seen the film she looks away.

She approaches him again as he is standing idle, looking up at an imposing wooden mask that hangs above a suspended metal staircase, the hollow diamond-shaped eyes and mouth of the mask revealing the white brick wall behind it. "There's an even scarier one in the bedroom," she says, making a face, shuddering. "Imagine opening your eyes and seeing something like that first thing in the morning." The way she says this makes him wonder if she speaks from experience, if she's Russell's lover, or ex-lover, if that is what she is implying.

Her name is Maxine. She asks him about the program at Columbia, mentioning that she'd gone to Barnard for college, majoring in art history. She leans back against a column as she speaks, smiling at him easily, drinking a glass of champagne. At first he assumes she is older than he is, closer to thirty than twenty. He is surprised to learn that she'd graduated from college the year after he started graduate school, that for a year they overlapped at Columbia, living just three blocks away from each other, and that they have in all likelihood crossed paths on Broadway or walking up the steps of Low Library or in Avery. It reminds him of Ruth, of the way they, too, had once lived in such close proximity as strangers. Maxine tells him she works as an assistant editor for a publisher of art books. Her current project is a book on Andrea Mantegna, and he impresses her, remembering correctly that his frescoes are in Mantua, in the Palazzo Ducale. They speak in that slightly strained, silly way that he associates now with flirtation — the exchange feels desperately arbitrary, fleeting. It is the sort of conversation he might have had with anybody, but Maxine has a way of focusing her attention on him completely, her pale, watchful eyes holding his gaze, making him feel, for those brief minutes, the absolute center of her world.

The next morning she calls, waking him; at ten on a Sunday he is still in bed, his head aching from the Scotch and sodas he'd consumed throughout the evening. He answers gruffly, a bit impatiently, expecting it to be his mother calling to ask how his week has been. He has the feeling, from the tone of Maxine's voice, that she's been up for hours, that her breakfast has already been eaten, her *Times* thoroughly read. "It's Maxine. From last night," she says, not bothering to apologize for waking him. She tells him she'd found his number in the phone book, though he doesn't remember telling her his last name. "God, your apartment's noisy," she remarks. Then, without awkwardness or pause, she invites him to dinner at her place. She specifies the evening, a Friday, tells him the address, somewhere in Chelsea. He assumes it will be a dinner party, asks if there's anything he can bring, but she says no, it will be just him.

"I should probably warn you that I live with my parents," she adds.

"Oh." This unexpected piece of information deflates him, confuses him. He asks if her parents will mind his coming over, if perhaps they should meet at a restaurant instead.

But she laughs at this suggestion in a way that makes him feel vaguely foolish. "Why on earth would they mind?"

He takes a cab from his office to her neighborhood, getting out at a liquor store to buy a bottle of wine. It is a cool evening in September, raining steadily, the summer's leaves still plentiful on the trees. He turns onto a remote, tranquil block between Ninth and Tenth Avenues. It is his first date in a long time; with the exception of a few forgettable affairs at Columbia he's been with no one seriously since Ruth. He doesn't know what to make of the whole arrangement with Maxine, but as odd as the terms of the invitation seem he'd been unable to refuse. He is curious about her, attracted, flattered by the boldness of her pursuit.

He is stunned by the house, a Greek Revival, admiring it for several minutes like a tourist before opening the gate. He notes the pedimented window lintels, the Doric pilasters, the bracketed entablature, the black cruciform paneled door. He climbs a low stoop with cast-iron railings. The name below the bell is Ratliff. Several minutes after he

204

presses it, enough to make him double-check the address on the scrap of paper in his jacket pocket, Maxine arrives. She kisses him on the cheek, leaning toward him on one foot, the other leg extended, slightly raised behind her. She is barefoot, wearing flowing black wool pants and a thin beige cardigan. As far as he can tell she wears nothing under the cardigan apart from her bra. Her hair is done up in the same careless way. His raincoat is draped on a coat rack, his folding umbrella dropped into a stand. He glimpses himself quickly in a mirror in the foyer, smoothing his hair and his tie.

She leads him down a flight of stairs to a kitchen that appears to occupy an entire floor of the house, with a large farmhouse table at one end, and beyond that French doors leading to a garden. The walls are adorned with prints of roosters and herbs and an arrangement of copper skillets. Ceramic plates and platters are displayed on open shelves, along with what seem to be hundreds of cookbooks, food encyclopedias, and volumes of essays about eating. A woman stands at a butcher-block island by the appliances, snipping the ends of a pile of green beans with a pair of scissors.

"This is my mother, Lydia," Maxine says. "And this is Silas," she tells him, pointing to a reddish brown cocker spaniel dozing under the table.

Lydia is tall and slender like her daughter, with straight iron-colored hair cut youthfully to frame her face. She is carefully dressed, with gold jewelry at her ears and throat, a navy apron wrapped around her waist, gleaming black leather shoes. Though her face is lined and her complexion a bit splotchy, she is more beautiful even than Maxine, her features more regular, the cheekbones higher, the eyes more elegantly defined.

"Lovely to meet you, Nikhil," she says, smiling brightly, and though she looks at him with interest, she does not pause in her work or offer to shake his hand.

Maxine pours him a glass of wine, not asking if perhaps he might prefer something else. "Come on," she says, "I'll show you the house." She leads him up five flights of uncarpeted stairs that creak noisily beneath their combined weight. The plan of the house is simple, two immense rooms per floor, each of which, he is certain, is larger than his own apartment. Politely he admires the plaster cove moldings, the ceiling medallions, the marble mantelpieces, things he knows how to speak intelligently and at length about. The walls are painted in flamboyant colors: hibiscus pink, lilac, pistachio, and are crowded with clusters of paintings and drawings and photographs. In one room he sees an oil portrait of a small girl he assumes is Maxine, sitting in the lap of a stunning, youthful Lydia, wearing a yellow sleeveless dress. Along the hallways on every floor shelves ascend to the ceiling, crammed with all the novels one should read in a lifetime, biographies, massive monographs of every artist, all the architecture books Gogol has ever coveted. Alongside the clutter there is a starkness about the place that appeals to him: the floors are bare, the woodwork stripped, many of the windows without curtains to highlight their generous proportions.

Maxine has the top floor to herself: a peach-colored bedroom with a sleigh bed at the back, a long black and red bathroom. The shelf above the sink is full of different creams for her neck, her throat, her eyes, her feet, daytime, nighttime, sun and shade. Through the bedroom is a gray sitting room she treats as a closet, her shoes and handbags and clothes scattered across the floor, piled on a fainting couch, spilling over the backs of chairs. These patches of disorder make no difference — it is a house too spectacular to suffer distraction, forgiving of oversight and mess.

"Lovely frieze-band windows," he comments, looking toward the ceiling.

She turns to him, puzzled. "What?"

"That's what those are called," he explains, pointing. "They're fairly common in houses from this period."

She looks up, and then at him, seeming impressed. "I never knew that."

He sits with Maxine on the fainting couch, leafing through a coffee table book she'd helped to edit on eighteenth-century French wallpapers, one side of the book resting on each of their knees. She tells him this is the house she's grown up in, mentioning casually that she'd moved back six months ago after living with a man in Boston, an arrangement that had not worked out. When he asks if she plans to look for a place of her own she says it hasn't occurred to her. "It's such a bother renting a place in the city," she says. "Besides, I love this house. There's really nowhere else I'd rather live." For all her sophistication he finds the fact that she's moved back with her parents after a love affair has soured endearingly old-fashioned; it is something he cannot picture himself doing at this stage in his life.

At dinner he meets her father, a tall, good-looking man with luxuriant white hair, Maxine's pale green-gray eyes, thin rectangular glasses perched halfway down his nose. "How do you do. I'm Gerald," he says, nodding, shaking Gogol's hand. Gerald gives him a bunch of cutlery and cloth napkins and asks him to set the table. Gogol does as he is told, aware that he is touching the everyday possessions of a family he barely knows. "You'll sit here, Nikhil," Gerald says, pointing to a chair once the silverware is laid. Gogol takes his place on one side of the table, across from Maxine. Gerald and Lydia are at either end. Gogol had skipped lunch that day in order to leave the office in time for the date with Maxine, and already the wine, at once heavier and smoother than what he is used to drinking, has gone to his head. He feels a pleasant ache at his temples, and a sudden gratitude for the day and where it has brought him. Maxine lights a pair of candles. Gerald tops off the wine. Lydia serves the food on broad white plates: a thin piece of steak rolled into a bundle and tied with string, sitting in a pool of dark sauce, the green beans boiled so that they are still crisp. A bowl of small, round, roasted red potatoes is passed around, and afterward a salad. They eat appreciatively, commenting on the tenderness of the meat, the freshness of the beans. His own mother would never have served so few dishes to a guest. She would have kept her eyes trained on Maxine's plate, insisting she have seconds and then thirds. The table would have been lined with a row of serving bowls so that people could help themselves. But Lydia pays no attention to Gogol's plate. She makes no announcement indicating that there is more. Silas sits at Lydia's feet as they eat, and at one point Lydia slices off a generous portion of her meat and feeds it to him off of her palm.

The four of them go quickly through two bottles of wine, then move on to a third. The Ratliffs are vociferous at the table, opinionated about things his own parents are indifferent to: movies, exhibits at museums, good restaurants, the design of everyday things. They speak of New York, of stores and neighborhoods and buildings they either despise or love, with an intimacy and ease that make Gogol feel as if he barely knows the city. They speak about the house, which Gerald and Lydia bought back in the seventies, when no one wanted to live in the area, about the history of the neighborhood, and about Clement Clarke Moore, who Gerald explains was a professor of classics at the seminary across the street. "He was the person responsible for local residential zoning," Gerald says. "That and writing ' 'Twas the Night Before Christmas,' of course." Gogol is unaccustomed to this sort of talk at mealtimes, to the indulgent ritual of the lingering meal, and the pleasant aftermath of bottles and crumbs and empty glasses that clutter the table. Something tells him that none of this is for his benefit, that this is the way the Ratliffs eat every night. Gerald is a lawyer. Lydia is a curator of textiles at the Met. They are at once satisfied and intrigued by his background, by his years at Yale and Columbia, his career as an architect, his Mediterranean looks. "You could be

Italian," Lydia remarks at one point during the meal, regarding him in the candle's glow.

Gerald remembers a bar of French chocolate he bought on his way home, and this is unwrapped, broken apart, and passed around the table. Eventually the talk turns to India. Gerald asks questions about the recent rise of Hindu fundamentalism, a topic Gogol knows little about. Lydia talks at length about Indian carpets and miniatures, Maxine about a college class she'd once taken on Buddhist stupas. They have never known a person who has been to Calcutta. Gerald has an Indian colleague at work who just went to India for his honeymoon. He'd brought back spectacular photographs, of a palace built on a lake. Was that in Calcutta?

"That's Udaipur," Gogol tells them. "I've never been there. Calcutta's in the east, closer to Thailand."

Lydia peers into the salad bowl, fishing out a stray piece of lettuce and eating it with her fingers. She seems more relaxed now, quicker to smile, her cheeks rosy from the wine. "What's Calcutta like? Is it beautiful?"

The question surprises him. He is accustomed to people asking about the poverty, about the beggars and the heat. "Parts of it are beautiful," he tells her. "There's a lot of lovely Victorian architecture left over from the British. But most of it's decaying."

211

"That sounds like Venice," Gerald says. "Are there canals?"

"Only during monsoons. That's when the streets flood. I guess that's the closest it comes to resembling Venice."

"I want to go to Calcutta," Maxine says, as if this has been a thing denied to her all her life. She gets up and walks over to the stove. "I feel like tea. Who wants tea?"

But Gerald and Lydia decide against tea tonight; there is an *I, Claudius* video they want to watch before bed. Without tending to the dishes they stand up, Gerald taking their two glasses and the rest of the wine. "Good night, dear," Lydia says, kissing Gogol lightly on the cheek. And then their footsteps creak noisily up the stairs.

"I suppose you've never been subjected to someone's parents on the first date before," Maxine says once they are alone, sipping milky cups of Lapsang Souchong from heavy white mugs.

"I enjoyed meeting them. They're charming."

"That's one way of putting it."

They remain awhile at the table, talking, the sound of the rain echoing quietly in the enclosed space behind the house. The candles shrink to stubs, and specks of wax drip onto the table. Silas, who has been softly pacing on the floor, comes and presses his head against Gogol's leg, looking up at him, wagging his tail. Gogol bends over, pats him tentatively.

"You've never had a dog, have you?" Maxine says, observing him.

"No."

"Didn't you ever want one?"

"When I was a kid. But my parents never wanted the responsibility. Plus we had to go to India every couple of years."

He realizes it's the first time he's mentioned his parents to her, his past. He wonders if perhaps she'll ask him more about these things. Instead she says, "Silas likes you. He's very picky."

He looks at her, watching as she undoes her hair, letting it hang loose for a moment over her shoulders before wrapping it thoughtlessly around her hand. She looks back at him, smiling. Once again he is aware of her nakedness beneath the cardigan.

"I should go," he says. But he is glad that she accepts his offer to help her clean up before leaving. They loiter over the task, loading the dishwasher, wiping down the table and the butcher-block island, washing and drying the pots and pans. They agree to go to the Film Forum on Sunday afternoon, to see the Antonioni double feature that Lydia and Gerald have recently been to and recommended over dinner.

"I'll walk you to the subway," Maxine says when they are finished, putting a leash around Silas. "He needs to go out." They go up to the parlor level, put on their coats. He hears the sound of a television faintly through the ceiling. He pauses at the foot of the stairs. "I forgot to thank your parents," he says.

"For what?"

"For having me over. For dinner."

She links elbows with him. "You can thank them next time."

From the very beginning he feels effortlessly incorporated into their lives. It is a different brand of hospitality from what he is used to; for though the Ratliffs are generous, they are people who do not go out of their way to accommodate others, assured, in his case correctly, that their life will appeal to him. Gerald and Lydia, busy with their own engagements, keep out of the way. Gogol and Maxine come and go as they please, from movies and dinners out. He goes shopping with her on Madison Avenue at stores they must be buzzed into, for cashmere cardigans and outrageously expensive English colognes that Maxine buys without deliberation or guilt. They go to darkened, humble-looking restaurants downtown where the tables are tiny, the bills huge. Almost without fail they wind up back at her parents' place. There is always some delicious cheese or pâté to snack on, always some good wine to drink. It is in her claw-footed tub that they soak together, glasses of wine or single-malt Scotch on the floor. At night he sleeps with her in the room she grew up in, on a soft, sagging mattress, holding her body, as warm as a furnace, through the night, making love to her in a room just above the one in which Gerald and Lydia lie. On nights he has to stay late at work he simply comes over; Maxine keeps dinner waiting for him, and then they go up-stairs to bed. Gerald and Lydia think nothing, in the mornings, when he and Maxine join them downstairs in the kitchen, their hair uncombed, seeking bowls of café au lait and toasted slices of French bread and jam. The first morning he'd slept over he'd been mortified to face them, showering beforehand, putting on his wrinkled shirt and trousers from the day before, but they'd merely smiled, still in their bathrobes, and of-fered him warm sticky buns from their fa-vorite neighborhood bakery and sections of the paper.

Quickly, simultaneously, he falls in love with Maxine, the house, and Gerald and Lydia's manner of living, for to know her and love her is to know and love all of these things. He loves the mess that surrounds Maxine, her hundreds of things always cov-ering her floor and her bedside table, her habit, when they are alone on the fifth floor, of not shutting the door when she goes to the bathroom. Her unkempt ways, a chal-lenge to his increasingly minimalist taste, charm him. He learns to love the food she and her parents eat, the polenta and risotto, the bouillabaisse and osso buco, the meat baked in parchment paper. He comes to expect the weight of their flatware in his hands, and to keep the cloth napkin, still partially folded, on his lap. He learns that one does not grate Parmesan cheese over pasta dishes containing seafood. He learns not to put wooden spoons in the dishwasher, as he had mistakenly done one evening when he was helping to clean up. The nights he spends there, he learns to wake up earlier than he is used to, to the sound of Silas barking downstairs, wanting to be taken for his morning walk. He learns to anticipate, every evening, the sound of a cork emerging from a fresh bottle of wine.

Maxine is open about her past, showing him photographs of her ex-boyfriends in the pages of a marble-papered album, speaking of those relationships without embarrassment or regret. She has the gift of accepting her life; as he comes to know her, he realizes that she has never wished she were anyone other than herself, raised in any other place, in any other way. This, in his opinion, is the biggest difference between them, a thing far more foreign to him than the beautiful house she'd grown up in, her education at private schools. In addition, he is continually amazed by how much Maxine emulates her parents, how much she respects their tastes and their ways. At the dinner table she argues with them about books and paintings and people they know in common the way one might argue with a friend. There is none of the exasperation he feels with his own parents. No sense of obligation. Unlike his parents, they pressure her to do nothing, and yet she lives faithfully, happily, at their side.

She is surprised to hear certain things about his life: that all his parents' friends are Bengali, that they had had an arranged marriage, that his mother cooks Indian food every day, that she wears saris and a bindi. "Really?" she says, not fully believing him. "But you're so different. I would never have thought that." He doesn't feel insulted, but he is aware that a line has been drawn all the same. To him the terms of his parents' marriage are something at once unthinkable and unremarkable; nearly all their friends and relatives had been married in the same way. But their lives bear no resemblance to that of Gerald and Lydia: expensive pieces of jewelry presented on Lydia's birthday, flowers brought home for no reason at all, the two of them kissing openly, going for walks through the city, or to dinner, just as Gogol and Maxine do. Seeing the two of them curled up on the sofa in the evenings, Gerald's head resting on Lydia's shoulder, Gogol is reminded that in all his life he has never witnessed a single moment of physical affection between his parents. Whatever love exists between them is an utterly private, uncelebrated thing. "That's so depressing," Maxine says when he confesses this fact to her, and though it upsets him to hear her reaction, he can't help but agree. One day Maxine asks him if his parents want him to marry an Indian girl. She poses the question out of curiosity, without hoping for a particular response. He feels angry at his parents then, wishing they could be otherwise, knowing in his heart what the answer is. "I don't know," he tells her. "I guess so. It doesn't matter what they want."

She visits him infrequently; she and Gogol are never close to his neighborhood for any reason, and even the absolute privacy they would have had there is of no appeal. Still, some nights when her parents have a dinner party she has no interest in, or simply to be fair, she appears, quickly filling up the small space with her gardenia perfume, her coat, her big brown leather bag, her discarded clothes, and they make love on his futon as the traffic rumbles below. He is nervous to have her in his place, aware that he has put nothing up on his walls, that he has not bothered to buy lamps to replace the dismal glow of the ceiling light. "Oh, Nikhil, it's too awful," she eventually says on one of these occasions, barely three months after they've met. "I won't let you live here." When his mother had said more or less the same thing, the first time his parents had visited the apartment, he'd argued with her, hotly defending the merits of his spartan, solitary existence. But when Maxine says it, adding "you should just stay with me," he is quietly thrilled. By then he knows enough about her to know that she is not one to offer things if she doesn't mean them. Still, he demurs; what would her parents think? She shrugs. "My parents love you," she says matter-of-factly, definitively, just as she says everything else. And so he moves in with her in a way, bringing a few bags of his clothes, nothing else. His futon and his table, his kettle and toaster and television and the rest of his things, remain on Amsterdam Avenue. His answering machine continues to record his messages. He continues to receive his mail there, in a nameless metal box.

Within six months he has the keys to the Ratliffs' house, a set of which Maxine presents to him on a silver Tiffany chain. Like her parents, he has come to call her Max. He drops off his shirts at the dry cleaner around the corner from her place. He keeps a toothbrush and razor on her cluttered pedestal sink. In the mornings a few times a week he gets up early and goes running before work with Gerald along the Hudson, down to Battery Park City and back. He volunteers to take Silas out for walks, holding the leash as the dog sniffs and pokes at trees, and he picks up Silas's warm shit with a plastic bag. He spends entire weekends holed up in the house, reading books from Gerald and Lydia's shelves, admiring the sunlight that filters through the enormous unadorned windows during the course of the day. He comes to prefer certain sofas and chairs to others; when he is not there, he can conjure the paintings and photographs arrayed on the walls. He has to make a point of going to his studio, of resetting the tape on his answering machine, paying his rent check and his bills.

Often, on weekends, he helps to shop and prepare for Gerald and Lydia's dinner parties, peeling apples and deveining shrimp with Lydia, helping to shuck oysters, going down to the cellar with Gerald to bring up the extra chairs, the wine. He has fallen the tiniest bit in love with Lydia and with the understated, unflustered way she entertains. He is always struck by these dinners: only a dozen or so guests sitting around the candlelit table, a carefully selected mix of painters, editors, academics, gallery owners, eating the meal course by course, talking intelligently until the evening's end. How different they are from his own parents' parties, cheerfully unruly evenings to which there were never fewer than thirty people invited, small children in tow. Fish and meat served side by side, so many courses that people had to eat in shifts, the food still in the pans they were cooked in crowding the table. They sat where they could, in the different rooms of the house, half the people having finished before the other half began. Unlike Gerald and Lydia, who preside at the center of their dinners, his parents behaved more like caterers in their own home, solicitous and watchful, waiting until most of their guests' plates were stacked by the sink in order finally to help themselves. At times, as the laughter at Gerald and Lydia's table swells, and another bottle of wine is opened, and Gogol raises his glass to be filled yet again, he is conscious of the fact that his immersion in Maxine's family is a betrayal of his own. It isn't simply the fact that his parents don't know about Maxine, that they have no idea how much time he spends with her and Gerald and Lydia. Instead it is his knowledge that apart from their affluence, Gerald and Lydia are secure in a way his parents will never be. He cannot imagine his parents sitting at Lydia and Gerald's table, enjoying Lydia's cooking, appreciating Gerald's selection of wine. He cannot imagine them contributing to one of their dinner party conversations. And yet here he is, night after night, a welcome addition to the Ratliffs' universe, doing just that.

★ ★ ★

In June, Gerald and Lydia disappear to their lake house in New Hampshire. It is an unquestioned ritual, a yearly migration to the town where Gerald's parents live year-round. For a few days a series of canvas tote bags accumulate in the hallway, cardboard boxes full of liquor, shopping bags full of food, cases of wine. Their departure reminds Gogol of his family's preparations for Calcutta every few years, when the living room would be crowded with suitcases that his parents packed and repacked, fitting in as many gifts as possible for their relatives. In spite of his parents' excitement, there was always a solemnity accompanying these preparations, Ashima and Ashoke at once apprehensive and eager, steeling themselves to find fewer faces at the airport in Calcutta, to confront the deaths of relatives since the last time they were there. No matter how many times they'd been to Calcutta, his father was always anxious about the job of transporting the four of them such a great distance. Gogol was aware of an obligation being fulfilled; that it was, above all else, a sense of duty that drew his parents back. But it is the call of pleasure that summons Gerald and Lydia to New Hampshire. They leave without fanfare, in the middle of the day, when Gogol and Maxine are both at work. In Gerald and Lydia's wake, certain things are missing:

Silas, some of the cookbooks, the food processor, novels and CDs, the fax machine so that Gerald can keep in touch with his clients, the red Volvo station wagon they keep parked on the street. A note is left on the island in the kitchen: "We're off!" Lydia has written, followed by *X*'s and *O*'s.

Suddenly Gogol and Maxine have the house in Chelsea to themselves. They stray to the lower stories, making love on countless pieces of furniture, on the floor, on the island in the kitchen, once even on the pearl gray sheets of Gerald and Lydia's bed. On weekends they wander naked from room to room, up and down the five flights of stairs. They eat in different places according to their moods, spreading an old cotton quilt on the floor, sometimes eating take-out on Gerald and Lydia's finest china, falling asleep at odd hours as the strong summer light of the lengthened days pours through the enormous windows onto their bodies. As the days grow warmer, they stop cooking complicated things. They live off sushi and salads and cold poached salmon. They switch from red wine to white. Now that it is just the two of them it seems to him, more than ever, that they are living together. And yet for some reason it is dependence, not adulthood, he feels. He feels free of expectation, of responsibility, in willing exile from his own life. He is responsible for nothing in the house; in spite of their absence, Gerald and Lydia continue to lord, however blindly, over their days. It is their books he reads, their music he listens to. Their front door he unlocks when he gets back from work. Their telephone messages he takes down.

He learns that the house, for all its beauty, has certain faults in the summer months, so that it makes all the more sense that it is a place Gerald and Lydia annually avoid. It lacks air-conditioning, something Gerald and Lydia have never bothered to install because they are never there when it's hot, and the enormous windows lack screens. As a result, the rooms are sweltering during the day, and at night, because it is necessary to leave the windows wide open, he is ambushed by mosquitoes that shriek in his ears and leave angry, lumpen welts between his toes, on his arms and thighs. He longs for a mosquito net to drape over Maxine's bed, remembers the filmy blue nylon boxes that he and Sonia would sleep inside of on their visits to Calcutta, the corners hooked onto the four posts of the bed, the edges tucked tightly beneath the mattress, creating a temporary, tiny, impenetrable room for the night. There are times when he cannot bear it, turning on the light and standing on the bed, looking for them, a rolled-up magazine or a slipper in his hand, as Maxine, unbothered and unbitten, begs him to get back to sleep. He sees them sometimes against the peach-colored paint on the wall, faint specks engorged with his blood, just inches below the ceiling, always too high up to kill.

With work as an excuse he does not go home to Massachusetts all summer. The firm is entering a competition, submitting designs for a new five-star hotel to be built in Miami. At eleven at night, he is still there, along with most of the other designers on his team, all rushing to finish drawings and models by the month's end. When his phone rings, he hopes it's Maxine, calling to coax him into leaving the office. Instead it's his mother.

"Why are you calling me here so late?" he asks her, distracted, his eyes still focused on the computer screen.

"Because you are not at your apartment," his mother says. "You are never at your apartment, Gogol. In the middle of the night I have called and you are not there."

"I am, Ma," he lies. "I need my sleep. I shut off the phone."

"I cannot imagine why anyone would want to have a phone only to shut it off," his mother says.

"So, is there a reason you're calling me?"

She asks him to visit the following weekend, the Saturday before his birthday.

"I can't," he says. He tells her he has a

deadline at work, but it's not true — that's the day that he and Maxine are leaving for New Hampshire, for two weeks. But his mother insists; his father is leaving for Ohio the following day — doesn't Gogol want to go with them to the airport, to see him off?

He knows vaguely of his father's plans to spend nine months at a small university somewhere outside Cleveland, that he and a colleague have received a grant funded by the colleague's university, to direct research for a corporation there. His father had sent him a clipping about the grant printed in the campus newspaper, with a photograph of his father standing outside the engineering building: "Prestigious grant for Professor Ganguli," the caption read. At first it was assumed that his parents would shut up the house, or rent it out to students, and that his mother would go too. But then his mother had surprised them, pointing out that there would be nothing for her to do in Ohio for nine months, that his father would be busy all day at the lab, and that she preferred to stay in Massachusetts, even if it meant staying in the house alone.

"Why do I have to see him off?" Gogol asks his mother now. He knows that for his parents, the act of travel is never regarded casually, that even the most ordinary of journeys is seen off and greeted at either end. And yet he continues, "Baba and I already live in different states. I'm practically as far from Ohio as I am from Boston."

"That's no way to think," his mother says. "Please, Gogol. You haven't been home since May."

"I have a job, Ma. I'm busy. Besides, Sonia's not coming."

"Sonia lives in California. You are so close."

"Listen, I can't come home that weekend," he says. The truth seeps out of him slowly. He knows it's his only defense at this point. "I'm going on a vacation. I've already made plans."

"Why do you wait to tell us these things at the last minute?" his mother asks. "What sort of vacation? What plans?"

"I'm going to spend a couple of weeks in New Hampshire."

"Oh," his mother says. She sounds at once unimpressed and relieved. "Why do you want to go there, of all places? What's the difference between New Hampshire and here?"

"I'm going with a girl I'm seeing," he tells her. "Her parents have a place there."

Though she says nothing for a while, he knows what his mother is thinking, that he is willing to go on vacation with someone else's parents but not see his own.

"Where is this place, exactly?"

"I don't know. Somewhere in the mountains."

"What's her name?"

"Max."

"That's a boy's name."

He shakes his head. "No, Ma. It's Maxine."

And so, on the way to New Hampshire, they stop off at Pemberton Road for lunch, which is what, in the end, he has agreed to. Maxine doesn't mind, it's on their way, after all, and she is curious by now to meet his parents. They drive up from New York in a rented car, the trunk packed with more supplies that Gerald and Lydia have asked them for on the back of a postcard: wine, bags of a particular imported pasta, a large tin of olive oil, thick wedges of Parmesan and Asiago cheese. When he asks Maxine why these things are necessary, she explains that they are going to the middle of nowhere, that if they were to depend on the general store they would have nothing to live on but potato chips and Wonder bread and Pepsi. On the way to Massachusetts, he tells her things he figures she should know in advance — that they will not be able to touch or kiss each other in front of his parents, that there will be no wine with lunch.

"There's plenty of wine in the trunk of the car," Maxine points out.

"It doesn't matter," he tells her. "My parents don't own a corkscrew."

The restrictions amuse her; she sees them as a single afternoon's challenge, an anomaly never to be repeated. She does not associate him with his parents' habits; she still cannot believe that she is to be the first girlfriend he's ever brought home. He feels no excitement over this prospect, wants simply to be done with it. Once they get off at his parents' exit he senses that the landscape is foreign to her: the shopping plazas, the sprawling brick-faced public high school from which he and Sonia graduated, the shingled houses, uncomfortably close to one another, on their grassy quarter-acre plots. The sign that says CHILDREN AT PLAY. He knows that this sort of life, one which is such a proud accomplishment for his own parents, is of no relevance, no interest, to her, that she loves him in spite of it.

A van from a company that installs security systems blocks his parents' driveway, and so he parks on the street, by the mailbox on the edge of the lawn. He leads Maxine up the flagstone path, ringing the bell because his parents always keep the front door locked. His mother opens the door. He can tell she is nervous, dressed in one of her better saris, wearing lipstick and perfume, in contrast to the khakis and T-shirts and soft leather moccasins Gogol and Maxine both wear.

"Hi, Ma," he says, leaning over, giving his mother a quick kiss. "This is Maxine. Max, this is my mother. Ashima."

"It's so nice to finally meet you, Ashima," Maxine says, leaning over and giving his mother a kiss as well. "These are for you," she says, handing Ashima a cellophane-wrapped basket full of tinned pâtés and jars of cornichons and chutneys that Gogol knows his parents will never open or enjoy. And yet when Maxine had shopped for the things to put in the basket, at Dean and DeLuca, he'd said nothing to dissuade her. He walks in with his shoes on instead of changing into a pair of flip-flops that his parents keep in the hall closet. They follow his mother across the living room and around the corner into the kitchen. His mother returns to the stove, where she is deep-frying a batch of samosas, filling the air with a haze of smoke.

"Nikhil's father is upstairs," his mother says to Maxine, lifting out a samosa with a slotted spatula and putting it on a paper-towel-lined plate. "With the man from the alarm company. Sorry, lunch will be ready in a minute," she adds. "I was not expecting you to arrive for another half an hour."

"Why on earth are we getting a security system?" Gogol wants to know.

"It was your father's idea," his mother says, "now that I will be on my own." She says that there have been two burglaries recently in the neighborhood, both of them in the middle of the afternoon. "Even in good areas like this, these days there are crimes," she says to Maxine, shaking her head.

His mother offers them glasses of frothy

pink lassi, thick and sweet-tasting, flavored with rose water. They sit in the formal living room, where they normally never sit. Maxine sees the school pictures of Sonia and him in front of blue-gray backgrounds arranged on the mantel of the brick fireplace, the family portraits from Olan Mills. She looks at his childhood photo albums with his mother. She admires the material of his mother's sari, mentioning that her mother curates textiles at the Met.

"The Met?"

"The Metropolitan Museum of Art," Maxine explains.

"You've been there, Ma," Gogol says. "It's the big museum on Fifth Avenue. With all the steps. I took you there to see the Egyptian temple, remember?"

"Yes, I remember. My father was an artist," she tells Maxine, pointing to one of his grandfather's watercolors on the wall.

They hear footsteps coming down the stairs, and then his father enters the living room, along with a uniformed man holding a clipboard. Unlike his mother, his father is not dressed up at all. He wears a pair of thin brown cotton pants, an untucked, slightly wrinkled short-sleeved shirt, and flip-flops. His gray hair looks more sparse than the last time Gogol remembers, his potbelly more pronounced. "Here's your copy of the receipt. Any problems, you just call the eight hundred number," the uniformed man says. He and his father shake hands. "Have a nice day," the man calls out before leaving.

"Hi, Baba," Gogol says. "I'd like you to meet Maxine."

"Hello," his father says, putting up a hand, looking as if he is about to take an oath. He does not sit down with them. Instead he asks Maxine, "That is your car outside?"

"It's a rental," she says.

"Better to put it in the driveway," his father tells her.

"It doesn't matter," Gogol says. "It's fine where it is."

"But better to be careful," his father persists. "The neighborhood children, they are not very careful. One time my car was on the road and a baseball went through the window. I can park it for you if you like."

"I'll do it," Gogol says, getting up, irritated by his parents' perpetual fear of disaster. When he returns to the house, the lunch is set out, too rich for the weather. Along with the samosas, there are breaded chicken cutlets, chickpeas with tamarind sauce, lamb biryani, chutney made with tomatoes from the garden. It is a meal he knows it has taken his mother over a day to prepare, and yet the amount of effort embarrasses him. The water glasses are already filled, plates and forks and paper napkins set on the dining room table they use only for special occasions, with uncomfortable high-backed chairs and seats upholstered in gold velvet.

"Go ahead and start," his mother says, still hovering between the dining room and the kitchen, finishing up the last of the samosas.

His parents are diffident around Maxine, at first keeping their distance, not boisterous as they typically are around their Bengali friends. They ask where she went to college, what it is her parents do. But Maxine is immune to their awkwardness, drawing them out, devoting her attention to them fully, and Gogol is reminded of the first time he'd met her, when she'd seduced him in the same way. She asks his father about his research project in Cleveland, his mother about her part-time job at the local public library, which she's recently begun. Gogol is only partly attentive to the conversation. He is overly aware that they are not used to passing things around the table, or to chewing food with their mouths fully closed. They avert their eyes when Maxine accidentally leans over to run her hand through his hair. To his relief she eats generously, asking his mother how she made this and that, telling her it's the best Indian food she's ever tasted, accepting his mother's offer to pack them some extra cutlets and samosas for the road.

When his mother confesses that she is nervous to be in the house alone, Maxine tells her she'd be nervous, too. She mentions a break-in at her parents' once when she was by herself. When she tells them that she lives with her parents, Ashima says, "Really? I thought no one did that in America." When she tells them she was born and raised in Manhattan, his father shakes his head. "New York is too much," he says, "too many cars, too many tall buildings." He tells the story of the time they'd driven in for Gogol's graduation from Columbia, the trunk of the car broken into in just five minutes, their suitcase stolen, having to attend the commencement without a jacket and tie.

"It's a pity you can't stay for dinner," his mother says as the meal comes to an end.

But his father urges them to get going. "Better not to drive in the dark," he says.

Afterward there is tea, and bowls of payesh made in honor of his birthday. He receives a Hallmark card signed by both of his parents, a check for one hundred dollars, a navy blue cotton sweater from Filene's.

"He'll need that where we're going," Maxine says approvingly. "The temperature can really drop at night."

In the driveway there are hugs and kisses good-bye, initiated by Maxine, his parents reciprocating clumsily. His mother invites Maxine to please come again. He is given a piece of paper with his father's new phone number in Ohio, and the date on which it will be activated.

"Have a good trip to Cleveland," he tells his father. "Good luck with the project."

"Okay," his father says. He pats Gogol on the shoulder. "I'll miss you," he says. In Bengali he adds, "Remember to check in on your mother now and again."

"Don't worry, Baba. See you at Thanksgiving."

"Yes, see you," his father says. And then: "Drive safely, Gogol."

At first he's unaware of the slip. But as soon as they're in the car, buckling their seat belts, Maxine says, "What did your dad just call you?"

He shakes his head. "It's nothing. I'll explain it later." He turns on the ignition and begins to back out of the driveway, away from his parents, who stand there, waving, until the last possible moment. "Call to let us know you've arrived there safely," his mother says to Gogol in Bengali. But he waves and drives off, pretending not to hear.

It's a relief to be back in her world, heading north across the state border. For a while it's nothing different, the same expanse of sky, the same strip of highway, large liquor stores and fast-food chains on either side. Maxine knows the way, so there is no need to consult a map. He has been to New Hampshire once or twice with his family, to see the leaves, driving for the day to places one could pull off the road and take pictures of and admire the view. But he's never been so far north. They pass farms, spotted cows grazing in fields, red silos, white wooden churches, barns with rusted tin roofs. Small, scattered towns. The names of the towns mean nothing to him. They leave the highway behind and drive on steep, slender, two-lane ribbons of road, the mountains appearing like enormous milky waves suspended against the sky. Wisps of cloud hang low over the summits, like smoke rising from the trees. Other clouds cast broad shadows across the valley. Eventually there are only a few cars on the road, no signs for tourist facilities or campgrounds, just more farms and woods, the roadsides full of blue and purple flowers. He has no idea where he is, or how far they've traveled. Maxine tells him they aren't far from Canada, that if they're motivated they could drive into Montreal for the day.

They turn down a long dirt road in the middle of a forest, dense with hemlock and birch. There is nothing to mark where they turned, no mailbox or sign. At first there is no house visible, nothing but large lime-colored ferns covering the ground. Small stones spray wildly under the tires and the trees throw patterns of shade onto the hood of the car. They come to a partial clearing, to a humble house covered with bleached brown shingles and surrounded by a low wall of flat stones.

Gerald and Lydia's Volvo is parked on the grass because there is no driveway. Gogol and Maxine step out, and he is led by the hand to the back of the house, his limbs stiff from the hours in the car. Though the sun is beginning to set, its warmth is still palpable, the air lazy and mild. As they approach he sees that after a certain expanse the yard falls away, and then he sees the lake, a blue a thousand times deeper, more brilliant, than the sky and girded by pines. The mountains rise up behind them. The lake is bigger than he'd expected, a distance he cannot imagine swimming across.

"We're here," Maxine calls out, waving, her arms in a V. They walk toward her parents, who are sitting on Adirondack chairs on the grass, their legs and feet bare, drinking cocktails and admiring the view. Silas comes bounding toward them, barking across the lawn. Gerald and Lydia are tanner, leaner, a bit scantily dressed, Lydia in a white tank top and a denim wrap skirt, Gerald in wrinkled blue shorts, a green polo shirt faded with use. Lydia's arms are nearly as dark as his own. Gerald has burned. Discarded books lie at their feet, facedown on the grass. A turquoise dragonfly hovers above them, then darts crookedly away. They turn their heads in greeting, shielding their eyes from the sun's glare. "Welcome to paradise," Gerald says.

It is the opposite of how they live in New York. The house is dark, a bit musty, full of primitive, mismatched furniture. There are exposed pipes in the bathrooms, wires stapled over doorsills, nails protruding from beams. On the walls are clusters of local butterflies, mounted and framed, a map of the region on thin white paper, photographs of the family at the lake over the years. Checkered cotton curtains hang in the windows on thin white rods. Instead of staying with Gerald and Lydia, he and Maxine sleep in an unheated cabin down a path from the main house. No bigger than a cell, the space was originally built for Maxine to play in when she was a girl. There is a small chest of drawers, a crude night table between two twin beds, a lamp with a plaid paper shade, two wooden chests in which extra quilts are stored. The beds are covered with ancient electric blankets. In the corner is a device whose hum is supposed to keep the bats away. Hairy, unfinished logs hold up the roof, and there is a gap between where the floor ends and the wall begins, so that one can see a thin line of grass. There are insect carcasses everywhere, squashed against the windowpanes and walls, languishing in pools of water behind the taps of the sink. "It's sort of like being at camp," Maxine says as they unpack their things, but Gogol has never been to camp, and though he is only three hours away from his parents' house, this is an unknown world to him, a kind of holiday he's never been on.

During the days he sits with Maxine's family on a thin strip of beach, looking out onto the glittering jade lake, surrounded by other homes, overturned canoes. Long docks jut into the water. Tadpoles dart close to shore. He does as they do, sitting on a folding chair, a cotton cap on his head, applying sunblock at intervals to his arms, reading, falling asleep after barely a page. He wades into the water and swims to the dock when his shoulders grow too warm, the sand free of stones or growth, smooth and yielding under his feet. Occasionally they are joined by Maxine's grandparents, Hank and Edith, who live on the lake several houses away. Hank, a retired professor of classical archaeology, always brings a small volume of Greek poetry to read, his long sun-spotted fingers curling over the tops of the pages. At some point he gets up, laboriously removing his shoes and socks, and walks calf-deep into the water, regarding the surroundings with his hands on his hips, his chin thrust pridefully into the air. Edith is small and thin, proportioned like a girl, her white hair cut in a bob and her face deeply wrinkled. They have traveled a bit of the world together, Italy, Greece, Egypt, Iran. "We never got as far as India," Edith tells him. "We would certainly have loved to have seen that."

All day he and Maxine walk about the property barefoot in their bathing suits. Gogol goes for runs around the lake with Gerald, arduous laps along steep hilly dirt roads, so infrequently traveled that they can occupy the dead center. Halfway around is a small private graveyard where members of the Ratliff family lie buried, where Gerald and Gogol always stop to catch their breath. Where Maxine will be buried one day. Gerald spends most of his time in his vegetable garden, his nails permanently blackened from his careful cultivation of lettuce and herbs. One day, Gogol and Maxine swim over to Hank and Edith's for lunch, for egg salad sandwiches and canned tomato soup. Some nights, when it's too warm in the cabin, he and Maxine take a flashlight and walk to the lake in their pajamas to go skinny-dipping. They swim in the dark water, under the moonlight, weeds catching their limbs, out to the neighboring dock. The unfamiliar sensation of the water surrounding his unclothed body arouses Gogol, and when they come back to shore they make love on the grass that is wet from their bodies. He looks up at her, and behind her, at the sky, which holds more stars than he ever has seen at one time, crowded together, a mess of dust and gems.

In spite of the fact that there is nothing in particular to do, the days assume a pattern. There is a certain stringency to life, a willful doing without. In the mornings they wake early to the frenzied chirping of birds, when the eastern sky is streaked with the thinnest of pink clouds. Breakfast is eaten by seven, on the screened-in porch overlooking the lake where they have all their meals, homemade preserves slathered on thick slices of bread. Their news of the world comes from the thin local paper Gerald brings back each day from the general store. In the late afternoons, they shower and dress for dinner. They sit with their drinks on the lawn, eating pieces of the cheese Gogol and Maxine brought from New York, and watch the sun set behind the mountains, bats darting between the pines that soar as tall as ten-story buildings, all the bathing suits hung to dry on a line. Dinners are simple: boiled corn from a farm stand, cold chicken, pasta with pesto, tomatoes from the garden sliced and salted on a plate. Lydia bakes pies and cobblers with berries picked by hand. Occasionally she disappears for the day, to go antiquing in the surrounding towns. There is no television to watch in the evenings, just an old stereo on which they sometimes play a symphony or jazz. On the first rainy day Gerald and Lydia teach him to play cribbage. They are often in bed by nine. The phone, in the main house, seldom rings.

He grows to appreciate being utterly disconnected from the world. He grows used to the quiet, the scent of sun-warmed wood.

The only sounds are the occasional motor-boat cutting across the water, screen doors snapping shut. He presents Gerald and Lydia with a sketch of the main house done one afternoon down at the beach, the first thing he's drawn in years that hasn't been for work. They set it atop the crowded mantel of the stone fireplace, next to piles of books and photographs, promise to have it framed. The family seems to possess every piece of the landscape, not only the house itself but every tree and blade of grass. Nothing is locked, not the main house, or the cabin that he and Maxine sleep in. Anyone could walk in. He thinks of the alarm system now installed in his parents' house, wonders why they cannot relax about their physical surroundings in the same way. The Ratliffs own the moon that floats over the lake, and the sun and the clouds. It is a place that has been good to them, as much a part of them as a member of the family. The idea of returning year after year to a single place appeals to Gogol deeply. Yet he cannot picture his family occupying a house like this, playing board games on rainy afternoons, watching shooting stars at night, all their relatives gathered neatly on a small strip of sand. It is an impulse his parents have never felt, this need to be so far from things. They would have felt lonely in this setting, remarking that they were the only Indians. They would not want to go

242

hiking, as he and Maxine and Gerald and Lydia do almost every day, up the rocky mountain trails, to watch the sun set over the valley. They would not care to cook with the fresh basil that grows rampant in Gerald's garden or to spend a whole day boiling blueberries for jam. His mother would not put on a bathing suit or swim. He feels no nostalgia for the vacations he's spent with his family, and he realizes now that they were never really true vacations at all. Instead they were overwhelming, disorienting expeditions, either going to Calcutta, or sightseeing in places they did not belong to and intended never to see again. Some summers there had been road trips with one or two Bengali families, in rented vans, going to Toronto or Atlanta or Chicago, places where they had other Bengali friends. The fathers would be huddled at the front, taking turns at the wheel, consulting maps highlighted by AAA. All the children would sit in the back with plastic tubs of aloo dum and cold flattened luchis wrapped in foil, fried the day before, which they would stop in state parks to eat on picnic tables. They had stayed in motels, slept whole families to a single room, swum in pools that could be seen from the road.

One day they canoe across the lake. Maxine teaches him how to paddle properly, angling the oar and drawing it back through the still, gray water. She speaks reverently of her summers here. This is her favorite place in the world, she tells him, and he understands that this landscape, the water of this particular lake in which she first learned to swim, is an essential part of her, even more so than the house in Chelsea. This was where she lost her virginity, she confesses, when she was fourteen years old, in a boathouse, with a boy whose family once summered here. He thinks of himself at fourteen, his life nothing like it is now, still called Gogol and nothing else. He remembers Maxine's reaction to his telling her about his other name, as they'd driven up from his parents' house. "That's the cutest thing I've ever heard," she'd said. And then she'd never mentioned it again, this essential fact about his life slipping from her mind as so many others did. He realizes that this is a place that will always be here for her. It makes it easy to imagine her past, and her future, to picture her growing old. He sees her with streaks of gray in her hair, her face still beautiful, her long body slightly widened and slack, sitting on a beach chair with a floppy hat on her head. He sees her returning here, grieving, to bury her parents, teaching her children to swim in the lake, leading them with two hands into the water, showing them how to dive cleanly off the edge of the dock.

It is here that his twenty-seventh birthday is celebrated, the first birthday in his life that he hasn't spent with his own parents, either in Calcutta or on Pemberton Road. Lydia and Maxine plan a special dinner, curling up with cookbooks for days beforehand on the beach. They decide to make a paella, drive to Maine for the mussels and clams. An angel food cake is baked from scratch. They bring the dining table out onto the lawn, a few card tables added on to make room for everyone. In addition to Hank and Edith, a number of friends from around the lake are invited. The women arrive in straw hats and linen dresses. The front lawn fills up with cars, and small children scamper among them. There is talk of the lake, the temperature dropping, the water turning cooler, summer coming to an end. There are complaints about motorboats, gossip about the owner of the general store, whose wife has run off with another man and is seeking a divorce. "Here's the architect Max brought up with her," Gerald says at one point, leading him over to a couple interested in building an addition to their cottage. Gogol speaks to the couple about their plans, promises to come down and have a look at their place before he leaves. At dinner he is asked by his neighbor, a middle-aged woman named Pamela, at what age he moved to America from India.

"I'm from Boston," he says.

It turns out Pamela is from Boston as well, but when he tells her the name of the suburb where his parents live Pamela shakes her head. "I've never heard of that." She goes on, "I once had a girlfriend who went to India."

"Oh? Where did she go?"

"I don't know. All I remember is that she came back thin as a rail, and that I was horribly envious of her." Pamela laughs. "But you must be lucky that way."

"What do you mean?"

"I mean, you must never get sick."

"Actually, that's not true," he says, slightly annoyed. He looks over at Maxine, trying to catch her eye, but she's speaking intently with her neighbor. "We get sick all the time. We have to get shots before we go. My parents devote the better part of a suitcase to medicine."

"But you're Indian," Pamela says, frowning. "I'd think the climate wouldn't affect you, given your heritage."

"Pamela, Nick's American," Lydia says, leaning across the table, rescuing Gogol from the conversation. "He was born here." She turns to him, and he sees from Lydia's expression that after all these months, she herself isn't sure. "Weren't you?"

Champagne is poured with the cake. "To Nikhil," Gerald announces, raising his glass.

Everybody sings "Happy Birthday," this group who has known him for only one evening. Who will forget him the next day. It is in the midst of the laughter of these drunken adults, and the cries of their children running barefoot, chasing fireflies on the lawn, that he remembers that his father left for Cleveland a week ago, that by now he is there, in a new apartment, alone. That his mother is alone on Pemberton Road. He knows he should call to make sure his father has arrived safely, and to find out how his mother is faring on her own. But such concerns make no sense here among Maxine and her family. That night, lying in the cabin beside Maxine, he is woken by the sound of the phone ringing persistently in the main house. He gets out of bed, convinced that it's his parents calling to wish him a happy birthday, mortified that it will wake Gerald and Lydia from sleep. He stumbles onto the lawn, but when his bare feet strike the cold grass there is silence, and he realizes the ringing he'd heard had been a dream. He returns to bed, squeezing in beside Maxine's warm, sleeping body, and drapes his arm around her narrow waist, fits his knees behind hers. Through the window he sees that dawn is creeping into the sky, only a handful of stars still visible, the shapes of the surrounding pines and cabins growing distinct. A bird begins to call. And then he remembers that his parents can't possibly reach him: he has not given them the number, and the Ratliffs are unlisted. That here at Maxine's side, in this cloistered wilderness, he is free.

7.

Ashima sits at the kitchen table on Pemberton Road, addressing Christmas cards. A cup of Lipton tea grows slowly cold by her hand. Three different address books are open before her, along with some calligraphy pens she's found in the desk drawer in Gogol's room, and the stack of cards, and a bit of dampened sponge to seal the envelopes with. The oldest of the address books, bought twenty-eight years ago at a stationery store in Harvard Square, has a pebbly black cover and blue pages, bound together by a rubber band. The other two are larger, prettier, the alphabetical tabs still intact. One has a padded dark green cover and pages edged in gilt. Her favorite, a birthday gift from Gogol, features paintings that hang in the Museum of Modern Art. On the endpapers of all these books are phone numbers corresponding to no one, and the 800 numbers of all the airlines they've flown back and forth to Calcutta, and reservation numbers, and her ballpoint doodles as she was kept on hold.

Having three separate address books makes her current task a bit complicated. But

Ashima does not believe in crossing out names, or consolidating them into a single book. She prides herself on each entry in each volume, for together they form a record of all the Bengalis she and Ashoke have known over the years, all the people she has had the fortune to share rice with in a foreign land. She remembers the day she bought the oldest book, soon after arriving in America, one of her first trips out of the apartment without Ashoke at her side, the five-dollar bill in her purse feeling like a fortune. She remembers selecting the smallest and cheapest style, saying "I would like to buy this one, please" as she placed the item on the counter, her heart pounding for fear that she would not be understood. The salesperson had not even glanced at her, had said nothing other than the price. She had come back to the apartment and written into the book's blank blue pages her parents' address in Calcutta, on Amherst Street, and then her in-laws' in Alipore, and finally her own, the apartment in Central Square, so that she would remember it. She had written in Ashoke's extension at MIT, conscious of writing his name for the first time in her life, writing his last name as well. That had been her world.

She has made her own Christmas cards this year, an idea she picked up from a book in the crafts section of the library. Normally she buys boxes of cards, marked fifty percent off at department stores in January, always forgetting, by the following winter, exactly where in the house she's put them. She is careful to choose ones that say "Happy Holidays" or "Season's Greetings" as opposed to "Merry Christmas," to avoid angels or nativity scenes in favor of what she considers firmly secular images — a sleigh being pulled through a snow-covered field, or skaters on a pond. This year's card is a drawing she has done herself, of an elephant decked with red and green jewels, glued onto silver paper. The elephant is a replica of a drawing her father had done for Gogol over twenty-seven years ago, in the margins of an aerogramme. She has saved her dead parents' letters on the top shelf of her closet, in a large white purse she used to carry in the seventies until the strap broke. Once a year she dumps the letters onto her bed and goes through them, devoting an entire day to her parents' words, allowing herself a good cry. She revisits their affection and concern, conveyed weekly, faithfully, across continents — all the bits of news that had had nothing to do with her life in Cambridge but which had sustained her in those days nevertheless. Her ability to reproduce the elephant has surprised her. She has not drawn a thing since she was a child, has assumed she'd long forgotten what her father had once taught her, and what her son has inherited, about holding the pen with confidence and making bold, swift strokes. She spent a whole day redoing the drawing on different sheets of paper, coloring it in, trimming it to size, taking it to the university copy center. For an entire evening she had driven herself to different stationery stores in the town, looking for red envelopes that the cards would fit into.

She has time to do things like this now that she is alone. Now that there is no one to feed or entertain or talk to for weeks at a time. At forty-eight she has come to experience the solitude that her husband and son and daughter already know, and which they claim not to mind. "It's not such a big deal," her children tell her. "Everyone should live on their own at some point." But Ashima feels too old to learn such a skill. She hates returning in the evenings to a dark, empty house, going to sleep on one side of the bed and waking up on another. At first she was wildly industrious, cleaning out closets and scrubbing the insides of kitchen cupboards and scraping the shelves of the refrigerator, rinsing out the vegetable bins. In spite of the security system she would sit up startled in the middle of the night by a sound somewhere in the house, or the rapid taps that traveled through the baseboards when heat flowed through the pipes. For nights on end, she would double-check all the window locks, making sure that they were fastened tightly. There was the night she'd been roused by a repetitive banging outside the front door and called Ashoke in Ohio. With the cordless phone pressed to her ear, she'd gone downstairs and looked through the peephole, and when she'd finally opened the door she saw that it was only the screen door, which she'd forgotten to latch, swinging wildly in the wind.

Now she does the laundry once a month. She no longer dusts, or notices dust, for that matter. She eats on the sofa, in front of the television, simple meals of buttered toast and dal, a single pot lasting her a week and an omelette to go with it if she has energy to bother. Sometimes she eats the way Gogol and Sonia do when they visit, standing in front of the refrigerator, not bothering to heat up the food in the oven or to put it on a plate. Her hair is thinning, graying, still parted in the middle, worn in a bun instead of a braid. She's been fitted for bifocals recently, and they hang against the folds of her sari on a chain around her neck. Three afternoons a week and two Saturdays a month, she works at the public library, just as Sonia had done when she was in high school. It is Ashima's first job in America, the first since before she was married. She signs her small paychecks over to Ashoke, and he deposits them for her at the bank into their account.

She works at the library to pass the time — she has been going regularly for years, taking her children to story hour when they were young and checking out magazines and books of knitting patterns for herself, and one day Mrs. Buxton, the head librarian, asked if she would be interested in a part-time position. At first her responsibilities were the same as those of the high school girls, shelving the books that people returned, making sure that sections of shelves were in precise alphabetical order, sometimes running a feather duster along the spines. She mended old books, put protective covers on new arrivals, organized monthly displays on subjects such as gardening, presidential biographies, poetry, African-American history. Lately she's begun to work at the main desk, greeting the regular patrons by name as they walk through the doors, filling out forms for interlibrary loans. She is friendly with the other women who work at the library, most of them also with grown children. A number of them live alone, as Ashima does now, because they are divorced. They are the first American friends she has made in her life. Over tea in the staff room, they gossip about the patrons, about the perils of dating in middle age. On occasion she has her library friends over to the house for lunch, goes shopping with them on weekends to outlet stores in Maine.

Every three weekends her husband comes

home. He arrives by taxi — though she is willing to drive herself around their town, she is not willing to get on the highway and drive to Logan. When her husband is in the house, she shops and cooks as she used to. If there is a dinner invitation at friends', they go together, driving along the highway without the children, sadly aware that Gogol and Sonia, now both grown, will never sit with them in the back seat again. During his visits, Ashoke keeps his clothes in his suitcase, his shaving things in a bag by the sink. He does the things she still doesn't know how to do. He pays all the bills, and rakes the leaves on the lawn, and puts gas from the self-service station into her car. His visits are too short to make a difference, and, within hours it seems, Sunday comes, and she is on her own again. When they are apart, they speak by phone every night, at eight o'clock. Sometimes, not knowing what to do with herself after dinner, she is already in bed by then, in her nightgown, watching the small black-and-white television they've owned for decades that lives on her side of the bed, the picture gradually disappearing, a rim of black perpetually framing the screen. If there is nothing decent on television she leafs through books she takes out of the library, books that occupy the space Ashoke normally does on the bed.

Now it is three in the afternoon, the sun's strength already draining from the sky. It is

255

the sort of day that seems to end minutes after it begins, defeating Ashima's intentions to spend it fruitfully, the inevitability of nightfall distracting her. The sort of day when Ashima craves her dinner by five. It's one of the things she's always hated about life here: these chilly, abbreviated days of early winter, darkness descending mere hours after noon. She expects nothing of days such as this, simply waits for them to end. She is resigned to warming dinner for herself in a little while, changing into her nightgown, switching on the electric blanket on her bed. She takes a sip of her tea, now stone cold. She gets up to refill the kettle, make another cup. The petunias in her window box, planted Memorial Day weekend, the last time Gogol and Sonia were home together, have withered to shuddering brown stalks that she's been meaning, for weeks, to root from the soil. Ashoke will do it, she thinks to herself, and when the phone rings, and her husband says hello, this is the first thing she tells him. She hears noises in the background, people speaking. "Are you watching television?" she asks him.

"I'm in the hospital," he tells her.

"What's happened?" She turns off the whistling kettle, startled, her chest tightening, terrified that he's been in some sort of accident.

"My stomach's been bothering me since

256

morning." He tells Ashima it's probably something he's eaten, that he'd been invited the previous evening to the home of some Bengali students he'd met in Cleveland who are still teaching themselves to cook, where he was subjected to a suspicious-looking chicken biryani.

She exhales audibly, relieved that it's nothing serious. "So take an Alka-Seltzer."

"I did. It didn't help. I just came to the emergency room because all the doctors' offices are closed today."

"You're working too hard. You're no longer a student, you know. I hope you're not getting an ulcer," she says.

"No. I hope not."

"Who drove you there?"

"No one. I'm here on my own. Really, it's not that bad."

Nevertheless she feels a wave of sympathy for him, at the thought of him driving to the hospital alone. She misses him suddenly, remembering afternoons years ago when they'd first moved to this town, when he would surprise her and come home from the university in the middle of the day. They would indulge in a proper Bengali lunch instead of the sandwiches they'd gotten used to by then, boiling rice and warming the previous night's leftovers, filling their stomachs, sitting and talking at the table, sleepy and sated, as their palms turned yellow and dry.

"What does the doctor say?" she asks Ashoke now.

"I'm waiting to see him. It's a rather long wait. Do me one thing."

"What?"

"Call Dr. Sandler tomorrow. I'm due for a physical anyway. Make an appointment for me next Saturday, if he has an opening."

"All right."

"Don't worry. I'm feeling better already. I'll call you when I get home."

"All right." She hangs up the phone, prepares her tea, returns to the table. She writes "Call Dr. Sandler" on one of the red envelopes, propping it up against the salt and pepper shakers. She takes a sip of tea and winces, detecting a faint film of dishwashing liquid on this section of the rim, chiding herself for being careless about rinsing. She wonders if she ought to call Gogol and Sonia, to tell them that their father is in the hospital. But quickly she reminds herself that he is not technically in the hospital, that if this were any other day but Sunday he'd be at a doctor's office having an ordinary checkup. He had spoken to her normally, sounding a bit tired, perhaps, but not in great pain.

And so she returns to her project. At the bottom of the cards, over and over, she signs their names: her husband's name, which she has never once uttered in his presence, followed by her own, and then the names of her children, Gogol and Sonia. She refuses to write Nikhil, even though she knows that's what he would prefer. No parent ever called a child by his good name. Good names had no place within a family. She writes the names one below the other, in order of age, Ashoke Ashima Gogol Sonia. She decides to send a card to each of them, shifting the respective name to the top of the card: to her husband's apartment in Cleveland, to Gogol in New York, adding Maxine's name, too. Though she'd been polite enough the one time Gogol had brought Maxine to the house, Ashima doesn't want her for a daughter-in-law. She'd been startled that Maxine had addressed her as Ashima, and her husband as Ashoke. And yet Gogol has been dating her for over a year now. By now Ashima knows that Gogol spends his nights with Maxine, sleeping under the same roof as her parents, a thing Ashima refuses to admit to her Bengali friends. She even has his number there; she'd called it once, listening to the voice of the woman who must be Maxine's mother, not leaving any message. She knows the relationship is something she must be willing to accept. Sonia has told her this, and so have her American friends at the library. She addresses a card to Sonia and the two girlfriends she lives with in San Francisco. Ashima looks forward to Christmas, the four of them being together. It still bothers her that neither Gogol nor Sonia had come home for Thanksgiving this year. Sonia, who is working for an environmental agency and studying for her LSAT, had said it was too far to travel. Gogol, who had to work the following day because of a project at his firm, had spent the holiday with Maxine's family in New York. Having been deprived of the company of her own parents upon moving to America, her children's independence, their need to keep their distance from her, is something she will never understand. Still, she had not argued with them. This, too, she is beginning to learn. She had complained to her friends at the library, and they had told her it was inevitable, that eventually parents had to stop assuming that their children would return faithfully for the holidays. And so she and Ashoke had spent Thanksgiving together, not bothering, for the first time in years, to buy a turkey. "Love, Ma," she writes now at the bottom of the cards to her children. And at the bottom of the one for Ashoke, simply, "Ashima."

She passes over two pages filled only with the addresses of her daughter, and then her son. She has given birth to vagabonds. She is the keeper of all these names and numbers now, numbers she once knew by heart, numbers and addresses her children no longer remember. She thinks of all the dark, hot apartments Gogol has inhabited over the years, beginning with his first dorm room in New Haven, and now the apartment in Manhattan with the peeling radiator and cracks in the walls. Sonia has done the same as her brother, a new room every year ever since she was eighteen, new roommates Ashima must keep track of when she calls. She thinks of her husband's apartment in Cleveland, which she had helped him settle into one weekend when she visited. She'd bought him inexpensive pots and plates, the kind she used back in Cambridge, as opposed to the gleaming ones from Williams-Sonoma her children buy for her these days as gifts. Sheets and towels, some sheer curtains for the windows, a big sack of rice. In her own life Ashima has lived in only five houses: her parents' flat in Calcutta, her in-laws' house for one month, the house they rented in Cambridge, living below the Montgomerys, the faculty apartment on campus, and, lastly, the one they own now. One hand, five homes. A lifetime in a fist.

From time to time, she looks out the window, at the lilac sky of early evening, vividly tinged with two parallel stripes of pink. She looks up at the phone on the wall, wishing it would ring. She will buy her husband a cell phone for Christmas, she decides. She continues to work in the silent house, in the waning light, not bothering to rest, though her wrist has begun to ache, not bothering to get up and turn on the lamp over the table, or the lights on the lawn or in any of the other rooms, until the telephone rings. She answers after half a ring, but it's only a telemarketer, some poor soul on weekend duty, asking reluctantly if a Mrs., um —

"Ganguli," Ashima replies tartly before hanging up.

At twilight the sky turns a pale but intense blue, and the trees on the lawn and the shapes of the neighboring houses become silhouettes, solidly black. At five o'clock her husband still hasn't called. She calls his apartment and gets no answer. She calls ten minutes later, then ten minutes after that. It is her own voice on the answering machine, reciting the number and asking the caller to leave a message. Each time she calls she listens to the tone, but she doesn't leave a message. She considers the places he may have stopped on his way home — the pharmacy to pick up a prescription, the supermarket for food. By six o'clock she can no longer distract herself by sealing and stamping the envelopes she's spent all day addressing. She calls directory assistance, asking for an operator in Cleveland, then calls the number of the hospital he told her he'd gone to. She asks for the emergency room, is connected to one part of the hospital after another. "He's just there for an examination," she tells the people who answer and tell her to hold. She spells the last name as she has hundreds of thousands of times by now, "G like green," "N like napkin." She holds the line until she is tempted to hang up, wondering all the while if her husband is trying to reach her from home, regretting not having call waiting. She is disconnected, calls again. "Ganguli," she says. Again she is told to hold. Then a person comes on the line, a young woman's voice, no older than Sonia probably. "Yes. I do apologize for the wait. To whom am I speaking?"

"Ashima Ganguli," Ashima says. "Ashoke Ganguli's wife. To whom am I speaking, please?"

"I see. I'm sorry, ma'am. I'm the intern who first examined your husband."

"I've been holding on for nearly half an hour. Is my husband still there or has he gone?"

"I'm very sorry, ma'am," the young woman repeats. "We've been trying to reach you."

And then the young woman tells her that the patient, Ashoke Ganguli, her husband, has expired.

Expired. A word used for library cards, for magazine subscriptions. A word which, for several seconds, has no effect whatsoever on Ashima.

"No, no, it must be a mistake," Ashima says calmly, shaking her head, a small laugh escaping from her throat. "My husband is not there for an emergency. Only for a stomachache."

"I'm sorry, Mrs. . . . Ganguli, is it?"

She listens to something about a heart attack, that it had been massive, that all attempts to revive him had failed. Did she wish to have any of her husband's organs donated? she is asked. And then, is there anyone in the Cleveland area to identify and claim the body? Instead of answering, Ashima hangs up the phone as the woman is still speaking, pressing down the receiver as hard as she can into the cradle, keeping her hand there for a full minute, as if to smother the words she's just heard. She stares at her empty teacup, and then at the kettle on the stove, which she'd had to turn off in order to hear her husband's voice just a few hours ago. She begins to shiver violently, the house instantly feeling twenty degrees colder. She pulls her sari tightly around her shoulders, like a shawl. She gets up and walks systematically through the rooms of the house, turning on all the light switches, turning on the lamppost on the lawn and the floodlight over the garage, as if she and Ashoke are expecting company. She returns to the kitchen and stares at the pile of cards on the table, in the red envelopes it had pleased her so much to buy, most of them ready to be dropped in the mailbox. Her husband's name is on all of them. She opens her address book, suddenly unable to remember her son's phone number, a thing she can normally dial in her sleep. There is no answer at his office or at his apartment and so she tries the number she has written down for Maxine. It's listed, along with the other numbers, under *G*, both for *Ganguli* and for *Gogol*.

Sonia flies back from San Francisco to be with Ashima. Gogol flies from LaGuardia to Cleveland alone. He leaves early the next morning, boarding the first flight he can get. On the plane he stares through the window at the land below, at the snow-covered patches of the Midwest and at curving rivers that seem covered with tinfoil glinting under the sun. The plane's shape darkens a shifting length of ground. The flight is more than half empty, men and a few women in business suits, people used to such flights and to traveling at such hours, typing on laptops or reading the news of the day. He is unaccustomed to the banality of domestic flights, the narrow cabin, the single bag he's packed, small enough to stow overhead. Maxine has offered to go with him, but he has told her no. He doesn't want to be with someone who barely knew his father, who's met him only once. She walked him to Ninth Avenue, stood with him at dawn, her hair uncombed, her face still thick with sleep, her coat and a pair of boots slipped on over her pajamas. He withdrew cash from an ATM, hailed a cab. Most of the city, including Gerald and Lydia, were still asleep in their beds.

He and Maxine had been at a book party for one of Maxine's writer friends the night before. Afterward they'd gone out to dinner with a small group. At about ten o'clock they returned to her parents' house as usual, tired as if it were much later, pausing on their way upstairs to say good night to Gerald and Lydia, who were sitting under a blanket on the sofa, watching a French film on video, sipping glasses of after-dinner wine. The lights had been turned off, but from the glow of the television screen Gogol could see that Lydia was resting her head on Gerald's shoulder, that they both had their feet propped against the edge of the coffee table. "Oh, Nick. Your mother called," Gerald had said, glancing up from the screen. "Twice," Lydia added. He felt a sting of embarrassment. No, she hadn't left any message, they said. His mother called him more often these days, now that she was living on her own. Every day, it seemed, she needed to hear the voices of her children. But she had never called him at Maxine's parents'. She called him at work, or left messages at his apartment that he would receive days later. He decided that whatever it was could wait until morning. "Thanks, Gerald," he'd said, his arm around Maxine's waist, turning to leave the room. But then the phone had rung again. "Hello," Gerald had said, and then to Gogol, "It's your sister this time."

He takes a cab from the airport to the hospital, shocked by how much colder it is in Ohio than in New York, by the thick layer of snow that cakes the ground. The hospital is a compound of beige stone buildings situated on the crest of a softly sloping hill. He enters the same emergency room his father had entered the day before. After giving his name, he is told to take the elevator to the sixth floor, and then to wait in an empty room, the walls painted a rich dark blue. He watches the clock on the wall, donated, along with the rest of the furnishings in the room, by the loving family of someone named Eugene Arthur. There are no magazines in the waiting room, no television, only a collection of matching wing chairs lined up against the walls and a water fountain at one end. Through the glass door he sees a white hallway, a few empty hospital beds. There is little commotion, no doctors or nurses scurrying down the halls. He keeps his eyes on the elevator, half expecting his father to walk out and fetch him, to indicate, with a slight tilt of the head, that it is time to go. When the elevator doors eventually open, he sees a cart stacked with breakfast trays, most of their contents hidden under domes, and tiny cartons of milk. He feels hungry all of a sudden, wishes he'd thought to save the bagel the stewardess had handed him on the plane. His last meal had been at the restaurant the night before, a bright, bustling place in Chinatown. They had waited nearly an hour on the sidewalk for their table and then feasted on flowering chives and salted squid and the clams in black bean sauce that Maxine loved best. They were already drunk from the book party, lazily sipping their beers, their cold cups of jasmine tea. All that time, his father was in the hospital, already dead.

The door opens and a short, pleasant-looking, middle-aged man with a salt-and-pepper beard steps into the room. He wears a white knee-length coat over his clothing and carries a clipboard. "Hello," he says, smiling kindly at Gogol.

"Are you — were you my father's doctor?"

"No. I'm Mr. Davenport. I'll be taking you downstairs."

Mr. Davenport escorts Gogol in an elevator reserved for patients and doctors, to the subbasement of the hospital. He stands with Gogol in the morgue as a sheet is pulled back to show his father's face. The face is yellow and waxy, a thickened, oddly bloated image. The lips, nearly colorless, are set in an expression of uncharacteristic haughtiness. Below the sheet, Gogol realizes, his father is unclothed. The fact shames him, causes him to turn briefly away. When he looks again he studies the face more closely, still thinking that perhaps it's a mistake, that a tap on his father's shoulder will wake him. The only thing that feels familiar is the mustache, the excess hair on his cheeks and chin shaved less than twenty-four hours ago.

"His glasses are missing," Gogol says, looking up at Mr. Davenport.

Mr. Davenport does not reply. After a few minutes he says, "Mr. Ganguli, are you able to positively identify the body? Is this your father?"

"Yes, that's him," Gogol hears himself saying. After a few moments he realizes that a chair has been brought for him to sit in, that Mr. Davenport has stepped aside. Gogol sits down. He wonders if he should touch his father's face, lay a hand on his forehead as his father used to do to Gogol when he was unwell, to see if he had a fever. And yet he feels terrified to do so, unable to move. Eventually, with his index finger, he grazes his father's mustache, an eyebrow, a bit of the hair on his head, those parts of him, he knows, that are still quietly living.

Mr. Davenport asks Gogol if he's ready, and then the sheet is replaced, and he is led from the room. A resident arrives, explaining exactly how and when the heart attack happened, why there was nothing the doctors could do. Gogol is given the clothes his father had been wearing, navy slacks, a white shirt with brown stripes, a gray L.L.Bean sweater vest that Gogol and Sonia had gotten him for Christmas one year. Dark brown socks, light brown shoes. His glasses. A trench coat and a scarf. The items brim to the top of a large paper shopping bag. There is a book in the pocket of the trench coat, a copy of *The Comedians* by Graham Greene, with yellow pages and tiny print. Opening the cover, he sees that the book had been bought used, a stranger's name, Roy Goodwin, is written inside. In a separate envelope he is given his father's wallet, his car keys. He tells the hospital that no religious services are necessary, is told that the ashes would be ready in a few days. He could pick them up personally, at the funeral home the hospital suggests, or have them sent, along with the death certificate, directly to Pemberton Road. Before leaving he asks to see the exact place in the emergency room his father was last alive. The bed number is looked up on a chart; a young man with his arm in a sling lies in it now, otherwise in good spirits, talking on the telephone. Gogol glimpses the curtains that had partly girded his father when life left him, green and gray flowers with a section of white mesh at the top; metal hooks hang from the ceiling, traveling on a white U-shaped rail.

His father's leased car, described to him by his mother on the telephone last night, is still parked in the visitors' parking lot. AM news fills his ears as soon as he turns on the ignition, startling him; his father had always been particular about turning off the radio at the end of a drive. In fact, there is no sign of his father in the car. No maps or scraps of paper, no empty cups or loose change or receipts. All he finds in the glove compartment is the registration and the owner's manual. He spends a few minutes reading through the manual, comparing the features of the dashboard to the illustration in the book. He turns the wipers on and off and tests the headlights even though it's still daylight. He shuts off the radio, drives in silence through the cold, bleak afternoon, through the flat, charmless town he will never visit again. He follows directions a nurse at the hospital gave him to the apartment where his father had lived, wondering if this route is the same one his father had taken when he drove himself to the hospital. Each time he passes a restaurant he considers turning off the road, but then he finds himself in a residential section, blocks of Victorian mansions on snow-covered lawns, sidewalks covered with lacy patches of ice.

His father's apartment is part of a complex called Baron's Court. Beyond the gate, oversized silver mailboxes, spacious enough to hold a month's worth of mail, stand in a row. A man outside the first of the buildings, marked RENTAL OFFICE, nods to him as he drives past, seeming to recognize the car. Has he mistaken him for his father? Gogol wonders, the thought comforting. The only thing to distinguish each building is a number and a name; to either side of it are more units, absolutely identical, each three stories tall, arranged around a vast looping road. Tudor facades, tiny metal balconies, wood chips under the stairs. The relentless uniformity of it upsets him profoundly, more so than even the hospital, and the sight of his father's face. Thinking of his father living here alone these past three months, he feels the first threat of tears, but he knows that his father did not mind, that he was not offended by such things. He parks in front of his father's building, remaining long enough in the car to see an elderly, sprightly couple emerge with tennis rackets. He remembers his father telling him that the residents are mostly retired, or divorced. There are paths for walking, a small exercise complex, a man-made pond surrounded by benches and willow trees.

His father's apartment is on the second floor. He unlocks the door, takes off his shoes, puts them on the plastic runner that his father must have placed there to protect the plush off-white wall-to-wall carpeting. He sees a pair of his father's sneakers, and a pair of flip-flops for wearing around the house. The door opens onto a spacious living room, with a sliding glass door to the right, a kitchen to the left. Nothing hangs on the freshly painted ivory walls. The kitchen is separated on one side by a half wall, one of the things his mother always wanted in their own house, so that it would be possible to cook and still see and speak to people in another room. Against the refrigerator is a picture of himself and his mother and Sonia, behind a magnet from a local bank. They are standing at Fatehpur Sikri with cloths tied over their feet to protect them from the hot stone surface. He was a freshman in high school, thin and glum, Sonia just a girl, his mother in a salwar kameeze, something she was too shy to wear in front of their relatives in Calcutta, who always expected her to be in a sari. He opens the cupboards, first the ones above the countertop, then the ones below. Most of them are empty. He finds four plates, two mugs, four glasses. In a drawer he finds one knife and two forks, a pattern recognizable from home. In another cupboard are a box of tea bags, Peek Freans shortbread biscuits, a five-pound bag of sugar that has not been poured into a bowl, a tin of evaporated milk. There are several small bags of yellow split peas and a large plastic bag of rice. A rice cooker sits mindfully unplugged on the counter. The ledge of the stove is lined with a few spice jars, labeled in his mother's hand. Below the sink he finds a bottle of Windex, a box of trash bags, a single sponge.

He walks through the rest of the apartment. Behind the living room is a small bedroom with nothing in it but a bed, and across from it a windowless bathroom. A jar of Pond's cold cream, his father's lifelong answer to after-shave, sits at the side of the sink. He goes to work immediately, going through the room and putting things into garbage bags: the spices, the cold cream, the issue of *Time* magazine by his father's bed. "Don't bring anything back," his mother had told him on the phone. "It's not our way." He lingers over nothing at first, but in the kitchen he pauses. He feels guilty throwing out the food; were it his father in his place, he would have packed the spare rice and tea bags into his suitcase. His father had abhorred waste of any kind, to the point where he complained to Ashima if a kettle had been filled with too much water.

On his first trip to the basement, Gogol sees a table on which other tenants have left things up for grabs: books, videotapes, a white casserole with a clear glass lid. Soon the table is filled with his father's hand-held vacuum, the rice cooker, the tape player, the television, the curtains still attached to their collapsible plastic rods. From the bag he'd brought back from the hospital, he saves his father's wallet, containing forty dollars, three credit cards, a wad of receipts, photographs of Gogol and Sonia when they were babies. He saves the photograph on the fridge.

Everything takes much longer than he expects. The task of emptying three rooms, practically empty to begin with, leaves him exhausted. He is surprised to see how many garbage bags he's managed to fill up, how many trips up and down the stairs he's had to make. By the time he is finished, it is already beginning to get dark. He has a list with him of the people he has to call before the business day is over: Call rental office. Call university. Cancel utilities. "We're so very sorry," he is told by a series of people he's never met. "We just saw him Friday," one of his father's colleagues says. "What a shock it must be." The rental office tells him not to worry, that they will send someone by to remove the couch and the bed. When he finishes, he drives through town to the dealer who leased his father the car, and then he takes a cab back to Baron's Court. In the lobby he notices a menu for pizza delivery. He orders a pizza, calls home as he waits for it to arrive. For an hour the line is busy; by the time he gets through, his mother and Sonia are both asleep, a friend of the family informs him. The house is filled with noise, and it is only then that he realizes how quiet it is on his end. He considers going back down to the basement to get the tape player or the television. Instead he calls Maxine, describing the details of his day, amazed to think she'd been with him at the beginning of it, that it was in her arms, in her bed, that he'd woken.

"I should have come with you," she says. "I could still make it out there by morning."

"I'm finished. There's nothing else to do. I'm taking the first flight back tomorrow."

"You're not going to spend the night there, are you, Nick?" she asks him.

"I have to. There aren't any other flights tonight."

"In that apartment, I mean."

He feels defensive; after all his efforts, he feels protective of the three empty rooms. "I don't know anyone here."

"For God's sake, get out of there. Check yourself into a hotel."

"Okay," he says. He thinks of the last time he'd seen his father, three months ago: the image of him waving good-bye as he and Maxine pulled out of the driveway on their way to New Hampshire. He cannot remember the last time he and his father had spoken. Two weeks ago? Four? His father was not one to make frequent phone calls the way his mother does.

"You were with me," he tells her.

"What?"

"The last time I saw my father. You were there."

"I know. I'm so sorry, Nick. Just promise me you'll go to a hotel."

"Yeah. I promise." He hangs up and opens the phone book, looking at his choices of places to stay. He is accustomed to obeying her, to taking her advice. He dials one of the numbers. "Good evening, may I help you?" a voice inquires. He asks if there are any rooms available for the night, but while he is on hold he hangs up. He doesn't want to inhabit an anonymous room. As long as he is here, he doesn't want to leave his father's apartment empty. He lies on the couch in the dark, in his clothes, his body covered by his jacket, preferring that to the stripped mattress in the bedroom. For hours he lies in the dark, falling in and out of sleep. He thinks of his father, in the apartment just yesterday morning. What had he been doing when he'd begun to feel badly? Was he at the stove making tea? Sitting on the sofa, where Gogol sits now? Gogol imagines his father by the door, bending over to tie his shoelaces for the last time. Putting on his coat and scarf and driving to the hospital. Stopping at a traffic light, listening to the weather report on the radio, the thought of death absent from his mind. Eventually Gogol is aware of bluish light creeping into the room. He feels strangely vigilant, as if, were he to pay close enough attention, some sign of his father might manifest itself, putting a stop to the events of the day. He watches the sky whiten, listens as the perfect silence is replaced by the faintest hum of distant traffic, until suddenly he succumbs, for a few hours, to the deepest sleep possible, his mind blank and undisturbed, his limbs motionless, weighted down.

It is nearly ten in the morning when he wakes up again, unobstructed sunlight brightening the room. A dull, steady ache persists on the right side of his head, emanating from deep inside his skull. He opens the sliding glass door to the balcony and stands outside. His eyes burn from fatigue. He gazes at the man-made pond, which, his father had told Gogol during a phone conversation, he walked around twenty times each evening before eating his dinner, that it equaled a distance of two miles. A few people are out there now, walking their dogs, couples exercising side by side, swinging their arms, thick fleece bands covering their ears. Gogol puts on his coat, goes outside and attempts to walk around the pond once. At first he welcomes the cold air on his face, but the chill turns brutal, unforgiving, slicing through his body and pressing the backs of his pants against his legs, and so he returns to the apartment. He takes a shower, changing into the same clothes he'd worn the day before. He calls himself a cab and goes to the basement one last time to throw away the towel he'd used to dry off, the gray push-button phone. He is taken to the airport, boards a flight to Boston. Sonia and his mother will be there, along with a few friends of the family, waiting for him at the arrival gate. He wishes it could be otherwise. Wishes he could simply get into another cab, and ride along another highway, deferring the moment he must face them. He is terrified to see his mother, more than he had been to see his father's body in the morgue. He knows now the guilt that his parents carried inside, at being able to do nothing when their parents had died in India, of arriving weeks, sometimes months later, when there was nothing left to do.

On the way to Cleveland, the journey had felt endless, but this time, staring out the plane window, seeing nothing, all too quickly he feels the plane's descent in his chest. Just before landing he goes into the bathroom, wretches into the tiny metal basin. He rinses his face and looks at himself in the mirror. Apart from a day's growth on his face, he looks exactly the same. He remembers when his paternal grandfather died, sometime in the seventies, remembers his mother screaming when she walked in on his father, who was shaving off all his hair with a disposable razor. In the process his scalp had bled in numerous places, and for weeks he had worn a cap to work to hide the scabs. "Stop it, you're hurting yourself," his mother had said. His father had shut the door, and locked it, and emerged shrunken and bald. Years later Gogol had learned the significance, that it was a Bengali son's duty to shave his head in the wake of a parent's death. But at the time Gogol was too young to understand; when the bathroom door opened he had laughed at the sight of his hairless, grief-stricken father, and Sonia, just a baby, had cried.

For the first week they are never alone. No longer a family of four, they become a household of ten, sometimes twenty, friends coming by to sit with them quietly in the living room, their heads bent, drinking cups of tea, a cluster of people attempting to make up for his father's loss. His mother has shampooed the vermilion from her part. She has taken off her iron wedding bracelet, forcing it from her hand with cold cream, along with all the other bracelets she's always worn. Cards and flowers come continually to the house, from his father's colleagues at the university, from the women who work with his mother at the library, from neighbors who normally do little but wave from their lawns. People call from the West Coast, from Texas, from Michigan and D.C. All the people in his mother's address books, always added to, never crossed out, all of them are stricken by the news. Who had forsaken everything to come to this country, to make a better life, only to die here? The phone rings constantly, and their ears ache from speaking to all these people, their throats turning weak from explaining again and again. No he wasn't ill, they say; yes, it was completely unexpected. A short obituary runs in the town paper, citing the names of Ashima and Gogol and Sonia, mentioning that the children had been educated at the local schools. In the middle of the night, they call their relatives in India. For the first time in their lives, it's they who have bad news to bear.

For ten days following his father's death, he and his mother and Sonia eat a mourner's diet, forgoing meat and fish. They eat only rice and dal and vegetables, plainly prepared. Gogol remembers having to do the same thing when he was younger, when his grandparents died, his mother yelling at him when he forgot one day and had a hamburger at school. He remembers, back then, being bored by it, annoyed at having to observe a ritual no one else he knew followed, in honor of people he had seen only a few times in his life. He remembers his father sitting unshaven on a chair, staring through them, speaking to no one. He remembers those meals eaten in complete silence, the television turned off. Now, sitting together at the kitchen table at six-thirty every evening, the hour feeling more like midnight through the window, his father's chair empty, this meatless meal is the only thing that seems to make sense. There is no question of skipping this meal; on the contrary, for ten evenings the three of them are strangely hungry, eager to taste the blandness on their plates. It is the one thing that structures their days: the sound of the food being warmed in the microwave, three plates lowered from the cupboard, three glasses filled. The rest of it — the calls, the flowers that are everywhere, the visitors, the hours they spend sitting together in the living room unable to say a word, mean nothing. Without articulating it to one another, they draw comfort from the fact that it is the only time in the day that they are alone, isolated, as a family; even if there are visitors lingering in the house, only the three of them partake of this meal. And only for its duration is their grief slightly abated, the enforced absence of certain foods on their plates conjuring his father's presence somehow.

On the eleventh day they invite their friends to mark the end of the mourning period. There is a religious ceremony conducted on the floor in one corner of the living room; Gogol is asked to sit in front of a picture of his father, as a priest chants verses in Sanskrit. Before the ceremony they had spent a whole day looking for a picture to frame, going through albums. But there are almost no pictures of his father alone, his father who was forever behind the lens. They decide to crop one, of him and Ashima standing together years ago in front of the sea. He is dressed like a New Englander, in a parka and a scarf. Sonia takes it to CVS to have it enlarged. They prepare an elaborate meal, fish and meat bought one bitterly cold morning at Chinatown and Haymarket, cooked as his father liked them best, with extra potatoes and fresh coriander leaves. When they shut their eyes, it's as if it is just another party, the house smelling of food. All those years of entertaining have prepared them somehow. Ashima frets that there will not be enough rice; Gogol and Sonia take people's coats and put them upstairs, on the guest room bed. The friends his parents have collected for almost thirty years are in attendance, to pay their respects, cars from six different states lining the whole of Pemberton Road.

Maxine drives up from New York, bringing Gogol the clothes he normally keeps at her house, his laptop, his mail. His bosses have given him a month off from work. It's a bit of a shock to see Maxine, to introduce her to Sonia. This time he doesn't care how the house, how the pile of guests' shoes heaped by the doorway, might appear to her eyes. He can tell that she feels useless, a bit excluded in this house full of Bengalis. And yet he doesn't bother to translate what people are saying, to introduce her to everyone, to stay close by her side. "I'm so sorry," he hears her say to his mother, aware that his father's death does not affect Maxine in the least. "You guys can't stay with your mother forever," Maxine says when they are alone for a moment after the ceremony, upstairs in his room, sitting side by side on the edge of the bed. "You know that." She says it gently, puts her hand to his cheek. He stares at her, takes her hand and puts it back in her lap.

"I miss you, Nikhil."

He nods.

"What about New Year's Eve?" she says.

"What about it?"

"Do you still want to try to go up to New Hampshire?" For they had talked of this, going away together, just the two of them, Maxine picking him up after Christmas, staying at the lake house. Maxine was going to teach him how to ski.

"I don't think so."

"It might do you good," she says, tilting her head to one side. She glances around the room. "To get away from all this."

"I don't want to get away."

In the weeks that follow, as their neighbors' hedges and windows are decorated with strings of colored lights, as piles of Christmas cards arrive at the house, each of them assumes a task his father normally had done. In the mornings his mother goes to the mailbox and brings in the paper. Sonia drives into town and does the weekly grocery shopping. Gogol pays the bills, shovels the driveway when it snows. Instead of arranging the Christmas cards on the fireplace mantel, Ashima glances at the return addresses and then, without opening the envelopes, she throws them away.

Each small event seems like an enormous accomplishment. His mother spends hours on the phone and has all the names changed on the bank account, the mortgage, the bills. She is unable to stem the tide of junk mail that will continue to arrive for years, addressed to her dead husband. In the wan, dreary afternoons Gogol goes running. Sometimes he drives to the university, parking behind his father's department, running along the campus roads, through the confined, picturesque universe that had been his father's world for most of the past twenty-five years. Eventually, on weekends, they begin to visit the homes of their parents' friends who live in surrounding suburbs. Gogol drives one way, Sonia the other. Ashima sits in the back seat. At the homes of their friends, his mother tells the story of calling the hospital. "He went in for a stomachache," she says each time, reciting the details of the afternoon, the pink streaks that had been in the sky, the pile of cards, the cup of tea at her side, reciting it in a way that Gogol cannot bear to have repeated, a way he quickly comes to dread. Friends suggest she go to India, see her brother and her cousins for a while. But for the first time in her life, Ashima has no desire to escape to Calcutta, not now. She refuses to be so far from the place where her husband made his life, the country in which he died. "Now I know why he went to Cleveland," she tells people, refusing, even in death, to utter her husband's name. "He was teaching me how to live alone."

Early in January, after holidays they don't celebrate, in the first days of a year that his father does not live to see, Gogol boards a train and goes back to New York. Sonia is staying on with Ashima, thinking of getting an apartment in Boston or Cambridge so that she will be nearby. They come to the station to see him off, standing on the platform in the cold, his diminished family, straining but failing to see Gogol, who waves at them through the tinted glass. He remembers them all coming to see him off each time, in his first year of college, he would head back to Yale. And though, over the years, his departures had become mundane, his father would always stand on the platform until the moment the train was out of sight. Now Gogol raps his knuckles on the window, but the train begins to move as his mother and Sonia are still struggling to spot him.

The train rattles forward, jostles from side to side, its engine making a sound like the propeller of a plane. The whistle blares intermittently in a minor key. He sits on the left side of the train, the winter sunlight strong on his face. Instructions for removing the window in the event of an emergency, in three steps, are pasted to the glass. Snow covers the straw-colored ground. Trees stand like spears, dried copper leaves from the previous season still clinging to a few of the branches. He sees the backs of houses made of brick and wood. Small snowy lawns. A solid shelf of winter clouds stops just short of the horizon. More snow, possibly heavy, is expected by evening. He hears a young woman somewhere in the compartment, talking to her boyfriend on a cell phone, softly laughing. She talks about where they should meet for dinner once she gets into the city. "I'm so bored," she complains. Gogol will arrive in New York in time for dinner as well. Maxine will be there to greet him at Penn Station, something she has never bothered to do in the past, waiting for him under the arrivals-and-departures board.

The landscape jerks forward, falls away, the

train casting a passing shadow on an expanse of nondescript buildings. The tracks resemble endless ladders that stretch ahead rather than upward, rooted to the ground. Between Westerly and Mystic, the tracks are at an angle, embedded into the sloping land, so that the whole train threatens, ever so slightly, to topple over. Though the other passengers seldom comment on this, the way they do, for example, when the engine changes at New Haven from diesel to electric with a sudden jolt, this momentary shift never fails to rouse Gogol from his nap, or the book he is reading, or the conversation he is engaged in, or the thought that has gathered in his head. The train tilts to the left heading south to New York, to the right on the way to Boston. In that brief period of suggested peril, he thinks, always, of that other train he has never seen, the one that had nearly killed his father. Of the disaster that has given him his name.

The train rights itself, the angle falls behind. Again he feels its motion at the small of his back. For several miles the tracks hug the ocean, which is close enough to touch. The shallowest waves lap against mere inches of shore. He sees a stone bridge, scattered islands the size of rooms, gracious gray and white homes with pleasant views. Boxy houses built on stilts. Lone herons and cormorants perch on bleached wooden posts.

Boats with naked masts crowd the marina. It is a view his father would have appreciated, and Gogol is reminded of the many times he had driven with his family, on cold Sunday afternoons, to the sea. There were times when it had been so cold that they had simply sat in the car, in the parking lot, looking at the water, his parents sharing tea from a thermos in the front seat, the engine running to keep them warm. Once they had gone to Cape Cod, driving along that curving piece of land until they could drive no farther. He and his father had walked to the very tip, across the breakwater, a string of giant gray slanted stones, and then on the narrow, final inward crescent of sand. His mother had stopped after a few stones and waited with Sonia, too young to go with them, at her side. "Don't go too far," his mother had warned, "don't go so that I can't see you." His legs began to ache halfway there, but his father marched ahead, stopping at times to lend Gogol an arm, his body slightly tilted when he rested on a rock. While on these rocks, some far apart enough to make them pause and consider the best way to reach the next one, water had surrounded them on both sides. It was early winter. Ducks swam in the tide pools. The waves flowed in two directions. "He's too little," his mother had called out. "Are you listening? He's too little to go so far." Gogol had stopped then, thinking that perhaps his father would agree. "What do you say?" his father had said instead. "Are you too little? No, I didn't think so."

At the end of the breakwater, there was a field of yellow reeds to the right, and dunes beyond, and the ocean behind it all. He had expected his father to turn back, but still they had continued, stepping onto the sand. They walked along the water to the left, heading toward the lighthouse, past rusted boat frames, fish spines as thick as pipes attached to yellow skulls, a dead gull whose feathery white breast was freshly stained with blood. They began to pick up small, faded black stones with white stripes running around them, stuffing them into their pockets so that they drooped on either side. He remembers his father's footprints in the sand; because of his limp, the right toe of his shoe was always turned outward, the left straight ahead. Their shadows that day were unnaturally slender and long, leaning in toward each other, the late afternoon sun at their backs. They paused to regard a cracked wooden buoy painted blue and white, shaped like an old parasol. The surface was wrapped with thin brown strands of seaweed and encrusted with barnacles. His father lifted and inspected it, pointing to a live mussel underneath. Finally they stood by the lighthouse, exhausted, surrounded by water on three sides, pale green in the harbor, azure behind. Overheated from the exertion, they unzipped their coats. His father stepped away to urinate. He heard his father cry out — they had left the camera with his mother. "All this way, and no picture," he'd said, shaking his head. He reached into his pocket and began to throw the striped stones into the water. "We will have to remember it, then." They looked around, at the gray and white town that glowed across the harbor. Then they started back again, for a while trying not to make an extra set of footsteps, inserting their shoes into the ones they had just made. A wind had picked up, so strong that it forced them to stop now and then.

"Will you remember this day, Gogol?" his father had asked, turning back to look at him, his hands pressed like earmuffs to either side of his head.

"How long do I have to remember it?"

Over the rise and fall of the wind, he could hear his father's laughter. He was standing there, waiting for Gogol to catch up, putting out a hand as Gogol drew near.

"Try to remember it always," he said once Gogol had reached him, leading him slowly back across the breakwater, to where his mother and Sonia stood waiting. "Remember that you and I made this journey, that we went together to a place where there was nowhere left to go."

8.

A year has passed since his father's death. He still lives in New York, rents the apartment on Amsterdam Avenue. He works for the same firm. The only significant difference in his life, apart from the permanent absence of his father, is the additional absence of Maxine. At first she'd been patient with him, and for a while he'd allowed himself to fall back into her life, going home after work to her parents' house, to their world in which nothing had changed. Initially she'd tolerated his silences at the dinner table, his indifference in bed, his need to speak to his mother and Sonia every evening, and to visit them, on weekends, without her. But she had not understood being excluded from the family's plans to travel to Calcutta that summer to see their relatives and scatter Ashoke's ashes in the Ganges. Quickly they began to argue about this, and about other things, Maxine going so far one day as to admit that she felt jealous of his mother and sister, an accusation that struck Gogol as so absurd that he had no energy to argue anymore. And so, a few months after his father's death, he stepped out of Maxine's life for good. Recently, bumping into Gerald and Lydia in a gallery, he learned of their daughter's engagement to another man.

On weekends he takes the train to Massachusetts, to the house in which his father's photograph, the one used during the funeral, hangs in a frame on a wall in the upstairs hallway. On the anniversary of his father's death, and on his father's birthday, a day they never celebrated when his father was alive, they stand together in front of the photograph and drape a garland of rose petals around the frame and anoint his father's forehead with sandalwood paste through the glass. It is the photograph more than anything that draws Gogol back to the house again and again, and one day, stepping out of the bathroom on his way to bed and glancing at his father's smiling face, he realizes that this is the closest thing his father has to a grave.

His visits home are different now; often it's Sonia who does the cooking. Sonia is still living there with his mother, settled back into the room she had occupied as a girl. Four days a week she leaves the house at five-thirty in the morning, takes a bus to a train that takes her to downtown Boston. She works as a paralegal, is applying to law schools nearby. It is she who drives his mother to weekend parties, and to Haymarket on Saturday mornings. Their mother has become thinner, her hair gray. The white column of her part, the sight of her bare wrists, pains Gogol when he first catches sight of her. From Sonia he learns of how their mother spends her evenings, alone in her bed, unable to sleep, watching television without sound. One weekend he suggests going to one of the beaches where his father had liked to walk. At first his mother agrees, cheered by the prospect, but as soon as they step out into the windy parking lot she gets back into the car, saying she will wait.

He is preparing to take his registration exam, the two-day ordeal that will enable him to become a licensed architect, to stamp drawings and design things under his own name. He studies in his apartment, and occasionally up at one of the libraries at Columbia, learning about the matter-of-fact aspects of his profession: electricity, materials, lateral forces. He enrolls in a review class to help him prepare for the exam. The class meets twice a week in the evenings, after work. He enjoys the passivity of sitting in a classroom again, listening to an instructor, being told what to do. He is reminded of being a student, of a time when his father was still alive. It's a small class, and afterward several of them soon begin going out for drinks. Though he is invited to join them, he always says no. Then one day, as they are all filing out of the classroom, one of the women approaches him, and says, "So what's your excuse?" and because he has none, that night he tags along. The woman's name is Bridget, and at the bar she sits beside him. She is starkly attractive, with brown hair cut extremely short, the sort of style that would have looked disastrous on most women. She speaks slowly, deliberately, her speech un-hurried. She was raised in the south, in New Orleans. She tells him that she works for a small firm, a husband-and-wife team who operate out of a brownstone in Brooklyn Heights. For a while they talk about the projects they are working on, the architects they both admire: Gropius, van der Rohe, Saarinen. She is his age, married. She sees her husband on weekends; he is a professor at a college in Boston. He thinks of his par-ents then, living apart for the final months of his father's life. "That must be difficult," he tells her. "It can be," she says. "But it was either that or adjuncting in New York." She tells him about the house her husband rents in Brookline, a sprawling Victorian that costs less than half of their one-bedroom apart-ment in Murray Hill. She says that her hus-band had insisted on putting her name on the mailbox, her voice on the answering ma-chine. He had even insisted on hanging a few items of her clothing in the closet, putting a tube of her lipstick in the medicine cabinet. She tells Gogol that her husband delights in illusions like these, is consoled by them, whereas she finds them simply to be reminders of what is missing.

That night they share a cab back to his apartment. Bridget excuses herself to use the bathroom and when she emerges her wedding ring is absent from her finger. When they are together, he is ravenous; it has been a long time since he's made love. And yet he never thinks about seeing her at any other time. The day he sets out with his *AIA Guide to New York City* to explore Roosevelt Island, it doesn't occur to him to ask her to come along. Only twice a week, the nights the review class meets, does he look forward to her company. They do not have each other's phone numbers. He does not know exactly where she lives. She always goes with him to his apartment. She never spends the night. He likes the limitations. He has never been in a situation with a woman in which so little of him is involved, so little expected. He does not know, nor does he want to know, her husband's name. Then one weekend, when he is on the train to Massachusetts to see his mother and Sonia, a southbound train slices by, and he wonders if perhaps the husband is on the other train, on his way to see Bridget. Suddenly he imagines the house where Bridget's husband lives alone, longing for her, with his unfaithful wife's name on the mailbox, her lipstick beside his shaving things. Only then does he feel guilty.

‪★ ★ ★‬

From time to time his mother asks him if he has a new girlfriend. In the past she broached the topic defensively, but now she is hopeful, quietly concerned. She even asks once whether it is possible to patch things up with Maxine. When he points out to her that she had disliked Maxine, his mother says that that isn't the point, the point is for him to move on with his life. He works to remain calm during these conversations, not to accuse her of meddling, as he once would have done. When he tells her that he isn't even thirty, she tells him that by that age she had already celebrated her tenth wedding anniversary. He is aware, without having to be told, that his father's death has accelerated certain expectations, that by now his mother wants him settled. The fact that he is single doesn't worry him, and yet he is conscious of the degree to which it troubles his mother. She makes a point of mentioning the engagements and weddings of the Bengali children he's grown up with in Massachusetts, and his cousins in India. She mentions grandchildren being born.

One day when he is speaking to her on the phone, she asks him if he might be willing to call someone. He had known her as a girl, his mother explains. Her name is Moushumi Mazoomdar. He remembers her vaguely. She was the daughter of friends of his parents who had lived for a while in Massachusetts, then moved to New Jersey when he was in high school. She had a British accent. Always with a book in her hand at parties. This is all he remembers about her — details neither appealing nor unappealing. His mother tells him that she is a year younger than he is, that she has a much younger brother, that her father is a renowned chemist with a patent to his name. That he called her mother Rina Mashi, her father Shubir Mesho. Her parents had driven up for his father's funeral, his mother says, from New Jersey, but Gogol has no memory of them there. Moushumi lives in New York City these days, is a graduate student at NYU. She was supposed to have been married a year ago, a wedding that he and his mother and Sonia had been invited to, but her fiancé, an American, had backed out of the engagement, well after the hotel had been booked, the invitations sent, the gift registry selected. Her parents are a bit worried about her. She could use a friend, his mother says. Why doesn't he give her a call?

When his mother asks if he has a pen to take down the number he lies, telling her yes, not listening as she recites it to him. He has no intention of calling Moushumi; his exam is coming up, besides which, as much as he wants to make his mother happy, he refuses to let her set him up with someone. He refuses to go that far. The next time he is home for the weekend, his mother brings it up again. This time, because he is in the same room with her, he writes down the number, still with no intention of calling. But his mother persists, reminding him, the next time they speak, that her parents had come to his father's funeral, that it was the least he could do. A cup of tea, a conversation — did he have no time for that?

They meet at a bar in the East Village, a place Moushumi had suggested when they'd spoken on the phone. It's a small, dark, silent space, a single square room with just three booths against one wall. She's there, sitting at the bar reading a paperback book, when he arrives, and when she looks up from its pages, though it is she who is waiting for him, he has the feeling that he is interrupting her. She has a slender face, pleasingly feline features, spare, straight brows. Her eyes are heavy-lidded and boldly lined on the top lids, in the manner of 1960s movie stars. Her hair is middle-parted, gathered into a chignon, and she wears stylishly narrow tortoiseshell glasses. A gray wool skirt and a thin blue sweater cling suggestively to her sides. Opaque black tights cover her calves. A collection of white shopping bags lie at the base of her stool. On the phone, he hadn't bothered to ask what she looked like, assuming he'd recognize her, but now he is no longer sure.

"Moushumi?" he says, approaching her.

"Hey there," she says, closing the cover of the book and kissing him casually on both sides of his face. The book has a plain ivory cover, a title written in French. Her British accent, one of the few things he clearly remembers about her, is gone; she sounds as American as he does, with the low, gravelly voice that had surprised him on the phone. She has ordered herself a martini with olives. Beside it is a blue packet of Dunhills.

"Nikhil," she says as he sits down on the stool beside her, and orders a single malt.

"Yes."

"As opposed to Gogol."

"Yes." It had annoyed him, when he'd called her, that she hadn't recognized him as Nikhil. This is the first time he's been out with a woman who'd once known him by that other name. On the phone, she'd sounded guarded, faintly suspicious, as he had. The conversation had been brief and thoroughly awkward. "I hope you don't mind my calling," he'd begun, after explaining to her that he'd changed his name. "Let me check my book," she'd told him when he'd asked if she was free Sunday evening for a drink, and then he'd listened to her footsteps clicking across a bare wooden floor.

She studies him for a moment, playfully

twisting her lips. "As I recall, given that you're a year older than me, I was taught by my parents to call you Gogol Dada."

He is aware of the bartender glancing at them briefly, assessing their potential. He can smell Moushumi's perfume, something slightly overpowering that makes him think of wet moss and prunes. The silence and the intimacy of the room disconcerts him. "Let's not dwell on that."

She laughs. "I'll drink to that," she says, lifting her glass.

"I never did, of course," she adds.

"Did what?"

"Call you Gogol Dada. I don't remember our ever talking, really."

He sips his drink. "Neither do I."

"So, I've never done this before," she says after a pause. She speaks matter-of-factly, but nevertheless she averts her gaze.

He knows what she is referring to. In spite of this he asks, "Done what?"

"Gone out on a blind date that's been engineered by my mom."

"Well, it's not a blind date, exactly," he says.

"No?"

"We already know each other, in a way."

She shrugs and gives a quick smile, as if she has yet to be convinced. Her teeth are crowded together, not entirely straight. "I guess. I guess we do."

Together they watch as the bartender puts a CD into the player mounted to the wall. Some jazz. He is thankful for the distraction.

"I was sorry to hear about your father," she says.

Though she sounds genuinely sympathetic, he wonders whether she even remembers his father. He is tempted to ask her, but instead he nods. "Thanks," he says, all he can ever think to say.

"How is your mother getting along?"

"All right, I guess."

"Is she okay on her own?"

"Sonia's living with her now."

"Oh. That's good. That must be a relief to you." She reaches for the Dunhills, opening the box and peeling back the gold foil. After offering one to him, she reaches for the book of matches that lies in an ashtray on the bar and lights a cigarette for herself. "Do you guys still live in that same house I used to visit?" she asks.

"Yeah."

"I remember it."

"Do you?"

"I remember that the driveway was to the right of the house as you faced it. There was a flagstone path cut into the lawn."

The fact that she can recall these details so precisely is at once startling and endearing to him. "Wow. I'm impressed."

"I also remember watching lots of television in a room covered with really thick brownish gold carpeting."

He groans. "It still is."

She apologizes for not being at the funeral, she'd been in Paris at the time. It was where she'd lived after graduating from Brown, she explains. Now she is a candidate for a Ph.D. in French literature at NYU. She's been living in the city for almost two years. She's spent the past summer temping, working for two months in the business office of an expensive midtown hotel. Her job was to review and file all the exit surveys left by the guests, make copies, distribute them to the appropriate people. This simple task had taken up her day. She'd been amazed by the energy people put into the surveys. They complained about the pillows being too hard or too soft, or that there wasn't enough space around the sinks for their toiletries, or that the bedskirt had a loose thread. Most of the people didn't even pay for the rooms themselves. They were at conventions, everything expensed. One person had complained that an architectural print above the desk had a visible speck of dust under the glass.

The anecdote amuses him. "That might have been me," he speculates.

She laughs.

"Why did you leave Paris for New York?" he asks. "I'd think you'd rather study French literature in France."

"I moved here for love," she says. Her frankness surprises him. "Surely you know about my prenuptial disaster."

"Not really," he lies.

"Well, you ought to." She shakes her head. "Every other Bengali living on the East Coast does." She speaks of it lightly, but he detects a bitterness in her voice. "In fact, I'm pretty sure you and your family were invited to the wedding."

"When was the last time we saw each other?" he says, in an effort to change the subject.

"Correct me if I'm wrong, but I think it was your high school graduation party."

His mind goes back to a brightly lit space in the basement of a church his parents and their friends sometimes rented for especially large parties. It was where Sunday school classes were normally held. In the hallways were felt hangings, mottoes about Jesus. He remembers the big, long folding tables that he'd helped his father to set up, chalkboards on the walls, Sonia standing up on a chair, writing "Congratulations."

"You were there?"

She nods. "It was right before we moved to New Jersey. You sat with your American friends from high school. A few of your teachers were there. You seemed a little embarrassed by it all."

He shakes his head. "I don't remember you

there. Did I speak to you?"

"You ignored me thoroughly. But it doesn't matter." She smiles. "I'm sure I brought a book with me."

They have a second round of drinks. The bar is beginning to fill up, small groups occupying each of the booths, people sitting on either side of them. A large party enters, and now there are patrons standing behind them to order drinks. When he'd arrived, he'd been bothered by the lack of people, of sounds, feeling on display, but now the crowd bothers him even more.

"It's getting pretty crazy in here," he says.

"It's not usually like this on a Sunday. Should we leave?"

He considers. "Maybe."

They ask for the bill, step out together into the cool October evening. Glancing at his watch, he sees that not even an hour has passed.

"Where are you headed?" she asks in a way that makes him realize that she assumes the date is over.

He hadn't planned to take her to dinner. He had intended to go back to his apartment after the drink, and study, and order in some Chinese food. But now he finds himself saying that he is thinking of getting something to eat, did she want to join him?

"I'd like that," she says.

Neither can think of a place to go and so

they decide to walk a bit. He offers to carry her shopping bags, and though they weigh nothing at all she allows him to, telling him she'd been to a sample sale in SoHo just before they'd met. They stop in front of a small place that looks as if it has just opened. They study the handwritten menu taped to the window, the review that was printed a few days ago in the *Times*. He is distracted by her reflection in the glass, a more severe version of herself, for some reason more stunning.

"Shall we try it?" he asks, stepping away and reaching for the door. Inside, the walls are painted red. They are surrounded by old posters advertising wine, and street signs and photographs of Paris arranged above the picture rails.

"This place must seem silly to you," he acknowledges, watching her gaze up at the walls.

She shakes her head. "It's pretty authentic, actually."

She asks for a glass of champagne and looks carefully at the wine list. He asks for another single malt, but is told that there is only beer and wine.

"Shall we have a bottle?" she says, handing him the list.

"You choose."

She orders a salad and the bouillabaisse and a bottle of Sancerre. He orders the cassoulet. She doesn't speak French to the waiter, who is French himself, but the way she pronounces the items on the menu makes it clear that she is fluent. It impresses him. Apart from Bengali, he has never bothered to master another language. The meal passes quickly. He speaks of his work, the projects he is involved in, his upcoming exam. They comment on each other's dishes, trading tastes on their bread plates. They order espresso and share a crème brûlée, their two teaspoons cracking the hard amber surface from either side.

She offers to pay her share when the bill comes, as she'd done in the bar, but this time he insists on treating. He walks her to her apartment, which is on a run-down but pretty residential block, close to the bar where they'd met. Her building has a crumbling stoop, a terra cotta–colored facade with a gaudy green cornice. She thanks him for the dinner, says she's had a great time. Again she kisses him on both cheeks, then begins to search for the keys in her purse.

"Don't forget these." He gives her the shopping bags, watches as she loops them over her wrist. Now that he is no longer carrying them he feels awkward, unsure of what to do with his hands. He is parched from the alcohol he has consumed. "So, should we make our parents happy and see each other again?"

She looks at him, studying his face intently. "Maybe." Her eyes stray to a passing car on the street, the headlights briefly shining on their bodies, but then her gaze returns to his face. She smiles at him, nodding. "Give me a call."

He watches as she ascends quickly up the stoop with her shopping bags, her heels suspended over the treads in a way that looks precarious. She turns briefly to wave at him and then she goes through a second glass door, not waiting to see him waving back. For a minute longer he stands there, watching as the door opens again and a tenant emerges to deposit something into one of the trash cans below the stoop. Gogol looks up at the building, wondering which of the apartments is hers, waiting to see if a light will turn on in one of the windows.

He had not expected to enjoy himself, to be attracted to her in the least. It strikes him that there is no term for what they once were to each other. Their parents were friends, not they. She is a family acquaintance but she is not family. Their contact until tonight has been artificial, imposed, something like his relationship to his cousins in India but lacking even the justification of blood ties. Until they'd met tonight, he had never seen her outside the context of her family, or she his. He decides that it is her very familiarity that makes him curious about her, and as he begins to walk west, to the subway, he wonders when he might see her again. When he reaches Broadway he changes his mind and hails a cab. The decision feels indulgent, as it is not particularly late, or cold, or raining, and he is in no great rush to be home. But he has the urge to be alone all of a sudden, to be thoroughly passive, to revisit the evening in solitude. The driver of the cab is a Bangladeshi; the name on the registration card pasted to the plexiglass behind the front seat says Mustafa Sayeed. He is talking in Bengali on his cell phone, complaining of traffic on the FDR, of difficult passengers, as they sail uptown, past the shuttered shops and restaurants on Eighth Avenue. If his parents were in the cab they would have struck up a conversation with the driver, asking what part of Bangladesh he was from, how long he'd been in this country, whether his wife and children lived here or there. Gogol sits silently, as if he were any other passenger, lost in his own thoughts, thinking of Moushumi. But as they near his apartment, he leans toward the plexiglass and says to the driver, in Bengali, "It's that one, up on the right."

The driver turns around, surprised, smiling. "I didn't realize," he says.

"That's okay," Gogol says, reaching for his wallet. He tips the driver excessively and steps out of the car.

In the days that follow, he begins to remember things about Moushumi, images that
come to him without warning while he is sitting
at his desk at work, or during a meeting, or
drifting off to sleep, or standing in the mornings
under the shower. They are scenes he has carried within him, buried but intact, scenes he
has never thought about or had reason to conjure up until now. He is grateful that his mind
has retained these images of her, pleased with
himself, as if he has just discovered an innate
talent for a sport or a game he's never played.
He remembers her mainly at the pujos he had
attended every year, twice a year, with his
family, where she would be dressed in a sari
carefully pinned to the top of her shoulder.
Sonia would have to do the same, but she
would always take off her sari after an hour or
two and put on her jeans, stuffing the sari into
a plastic bag and telling Gogol or their father to
put it away for her in the car. He does not remember Moushumi ever accompanying the
other teenagers to the McDonald's that was
across the street from the building in Water-
town where the pujos often were, or eventually
sitting in someone's car in the parking lot, listening to the radio and drinking beer from a
can. He struggles but fails to recall her presence at Pemberton Road; still, he is secretly
pleased that she has seen those rooms, tasted
his mother's cooking, washed her hands in the

bathroom, however long ago.

He remembers once going to a Christmas party at her parents' home. He and Sonia had not wanted to go; Christmas was supposed to be spent with just family. But their parents had replied that in America, Bengali friends were the closest thing they had to family, and so they had gone to Bedford, where the Mazoomdars lived. Her mother, Rina Mashi, had served cold pound cake and warmed-up frozen doughnuts that deflated at the touch. Her brother, Samrat, now a senior in high school, had been a boy of four, obsessed with Spider-Man. Rina Mashi had gone to a great deal of trouble to organize an anonymous gift exchange. Each family was asked to bring as many gifts as there were members, so that there would be something for everyone to open. Gogol had been asked to write numbers on squares of paper, one set to tape onto the gifts and another to pass around, folded up in a drawstring pouch, to the guests. Everyone gathered in a single room, cramming through the two doorways. He remembers sitting in their living room, listening with all the other guests to Moushumi play something on the piano. On the wall above her was a framed reproduction of Renoir's girl with a green watering can. After great deliberation, just as people were beginning to fidget, she had played a short piece by Mozart, adapted for children, but the guests wanted her to play "Jingle Bells." She shook her head no, but her mother said, "Oh, Moushumi's just being shy, she knows very well how to play 'Jingle Bells.' " For an instant she had glared at her mother, but then she'd played the song, again and again, as the numbers were called out and people claimed their gifts, sitting with her back to the room.

A week later they meet for lunch. It is the middle of the week and she has offered to meet him someplace near his office, so he's told her to come to the building where he works. When the receptionist tells him she is waiting in the lobby he feels the anticipation rise in his chest; all morning he'd been unable to concentrate on the elevation he was working on. He spends a few minutes showing her around, pointing out photographs of projects he's worked on, introducing her to one of the principal designers, showing her the room where the partners meet. His coworkers in the drafting room look up from their desks as she passes by. It is early November, a day on which the temperature has suddenly dropped, bringing the first true cold of the year. Outside, unprepared pedestrians scurry past unhappily, arms folded across their chests. Fallen leaves, battered and bleached, scuttle in swirls on the pavement. Gogol has no hat or gloves, and as they walk he puts his hands into the pockets of his jacket. Moushumi, in contrast, seems enviably protected, at ease in the cold. She wears a navy wool coat, a black wool scarf at her throat, long black leather boots that zip up the sides.

He takes her to an Italian restaurant where he goes from time to time with people at work, to celebrate birthdays and promotions and projects well done. The entrance is a few steps below street level, the windows shielded with panels of lace. The waiter recognizes him, smiles. They are led to a small table at the back as opposed to the long one in the center that he normally sits at. Underneath the coat he sees that she is wearing a nubbly gray suit, with large buttons on the jacket and a bell-shaped skirt that stops short of her knees.

"I taught today," she explains, aware that he is looking at her — she preferred to wear a suit when she taught, she says, given that her students were only a decade younger than she was. Otherwise she feels no sense of authority. He envies her students suddenly, seeing her without fail, three times a week, pictures them gathered together around a table, staring at her continuously as she writes on the board.

"The pastas are usually pretty good here," he says as the waiter hands them menus.

"Join me for a glass of wine," she says. "I'm done for the day."

"Lucky you. I have a stressful meeting to go to after this."

She looks at him, closing the menu. "All the more reason for a drink," she points out cheerfully.

"True," he concedes.

"Two glasses of the merlot," he says when the waiter returns. She orders what he does, porcini ravioli and a salad of arugula and pears. He's nervous that she'll be disappointed by the choice, but when the food arrives she eyes it approvingly, and she eats heartily, quickly, sopping up the leftover sauce on her plate with bread. As they drink their wine and eat their meal, he admires the light on her face, the faint pale hairs that shine against the contours of her cheek. She speaks of her students, the topic for the dissertation she plans to write, about twentieth-century francophone poets from Algeria. He tells her about his memory of the Christmas party, of her being forced to play "Jingle Bells."

"Do you remember that night?" he asks, hopeful that she will.

"No. My mother was always forcing me to do things like that."

"Do you still play?"

She shakes her head. "I never wanted to learn in the first place. My mother had this fantasy. One of many. I think my mother's taking lessons now."

The room is quiet again, the lunch crowd

has come and gone. He looks around for the waiter, signals for the check, dismayed that their plates are empty, that the hour has passed.

"She is your sister, *signore?*" the waiter asks as he sets the check between them, glancing at Moushumi and then back at Gogol.

"Oh, no," Gogol says, shaking his head, laughing, at once insulted and oddly aroused. In a way, he realizes, it's true — they share the same coloring, the straight eyebrows, the long, slender bodies, the high cheekbones and dark hair.

"You are sure?" the waiter persists.

"Quite sure," Gogol says.

"But you could be," the waiter says. "*Sì, sì,* there is quite a resemblance."

"You think so?" Moushumi says. She appears to be at ease with the comparison, looking comically askance at Gogol. And yet he notices that some color has risen to her cheeks, whether from the wine or from self-consciousness he doesn't know.

"It's funny he should say that," she says, once they have stepped out into the cold.

"What do you mean?"

"Well, it's just funny to think that all our lives our parents raised us according to the illusion that we were cousins, that we were all part of some makeshift extended Bengali family, and now here we are, years later, and someone actually thinks we're related."

He does not know what to say. The waiter's comment has discomfited him, making his attraction to Moushumi feel mildly illicit.

"You're not dressed warmly enough," she observes, twisting the woolen scarf securely around her neck.

"It's so damn hot in my apartment all the time," he says. "The heat just got turned on. For some reason I can never get my mind around the fact that it won't be the same temperature outside."

"Don't you check the paper?"

"I get it on my way to work."

"I always check the weather by phone when I leave the house," Moushumi says.

"You're joking." He stares at her, surprised that she should actually be the type to go to such lengths. "Please tell me you're joking."

She laughs. "I don't admit that to just anyone, you know." She finishes arranging her scarf, and then, without removing her hands from it, she says, "Why don't you borrow this?" and begins to untie it again.

"Please, I'm fine." He puts a hand to his throat, against the knot of his tie.

"Sure?"

He nods, half tempted to say yes, to feel her scarf against his skin.

"Well, at the very least you need a hat," she tells him. "I know a place nearby. Do you need to be back at work right away?"

She leads him to a little boutique on Madison. The window is crowded with women's hats perched on gray, featureless heads, with sloping necks nearly a foot long.

"They have men's stuff in the back," she says. The shop is crowded with women. The back is relatively tranquil, stacks of fedoras and berets arrayed on curved wooden shelves. He picks up a fur hat, a top hat, trying them on as a joke. The glass of wine has made him tipsy. Moushumi begins rummaging through a basket.

"This will be warm," she says, placing her fingers inside a thick navy cap with yellow stripes on the brim. She stretches the hat with her fingers. "What do you think?" She puts it on his head, touching his hair, his scalp. She smiles, pointing to the mirror. She watches as he studies himself.

He is aware that she is looking at him rather than at his reflection. He wonders what her face looks like without her glasses, when her hair is loose. He wonders what it might be like to kiss her on the mouth. "I like it," he says. "I'll take it."

She pulls it off his head quickly, spoiling his hair.

"What are you doing?"

"I want to buy it for you."

"You don't have to do that."

"I want to," she says, already heading to-ward the register. "It was my idea, anyway. You were perfectly happy freezing to death."

At the register the cashier notices Moushumi eyeing a brown wool and velvet hat decorated with feathers. "It's an exquisite piece," the cashier says, carefully lifting it off the bust. "Handmade by a woman in Spain. No two are alike. Would you like to try it?"

Moushumi places it on her head. A customer compliments her. So does the cashier. "Not many women can pull off a hat like that," the cashier says.

Moushumi blushes, glances at the price tag dangling from a thread on one side of her face. "I'm afraid it's out of my budget for today," she says.

The cashier replaces the hat on the shelf. "Well, now you know what to get her for her birthday," she says, looking at Gogol.

He puts on the new cap and they step out of the store. He is late for his meeting. If it weren't for that, he would be tempted to stay with her, to walk through the streets beside her, or disappear with her into the dark of a movie theater. The day has turned even colder, the wind more forceful, the sun a faint white patch. She walks him back to his office. For the rest of the day, throughout his meeting and as he struggles, afterward, to get back to work, he thinks of her. When he leaves the office, instead of walking to the subway, he retraces the steps they'd taken together earlier, past the restaurant where people are now having their dinners, and finds his way to the hat store, the sight of it lifting his spirits. It is nearly eight o'clock, dark outside. He assumes the store will be closed, is surprised to see the lights still on inside, the grate only partly lowered. He studies the items in the window, and his reflection in the glass, wearing the cap she'd bought for him. Eventually he walks in. He is the only customer; he can hear the sound of a vacuum cleaner running at the rear of the store.

"I knew you'd be back," the saleswoman says as he walks through the door. She takes the brown velvet hat off the Styrofoam head without his having to ask. "He was here earlier today with his girlfriend," she explains to her assistant. "Shall I wrap it for you?"

"That would be great." It excites him to hear himself referred to that way. He watches as the hat is placed in a round chocolate-colored box, tied with a thick, creamy ribbon. He realizes that he has not asked the price, but without a thought he signs the receipt for two hundred dollars. He takes the hat back to his apartment, hiding it at the back of his closet even though Moushumi has never been there. He would give it to her on her birthday, in spite of the fact that he has no idea when her birthday is.

And yet he has the feeling that he has been to a few of her birthdays, and she to his.

That weekend, at his parents' house, he confirms this; at night, after his mother and Sonia have gone up to bed, he hunts for her in the photo albums that his mother has assembled over the years. Moushumi is there, lined up behind a blazing cake in his parents' dining room. She is looking away, a pointed paper hat on her head. He stares straight at the lens, the knife in his hand, poised, for the camera's benefit, over the cake, his face shining with impending adolescence. He tries to peel the image from the sticky yellow backing, to show her the next time he sees her, but it clings stubbornly, refusing to detach cleanly from the past.

The following weekend she invites him over for dinner at her place. She has to come downstairs in order to let him into the building; the buzzer is broken, she'd warned him when they'd made their plans.

"Nice cap," she says. She wears a sleeveless black dress tied loosely at the back. Her legs are bare, her feet slim, her toenails, exposed at the tops of her sandals, painted maroon. Strands of hair have come loose from her chignon. She holds half a cigarette between her fingers, but just before she leans forward to kiss him on the cheeks she lets it drop and crushes it with the toe of her sandal. She leads him up the steps to an apartment on the third floor. She's left the door open. The apartment smells strongly of cooking; on the stove, a few large pieces of chicken are browning in a pan full of oil. Music is playing, a man singing songs in French. Gogol gives her a bunch of sunflowers whose massive stems are heavier in his arms than the bottle of wine he's also brought. She does not know where to put the flowers; the countertops, limited to begin with, are crammed with evidence of the meal she is preparing, onions and mushrooms, flour, a stick of butter rapidly softening in the heat, a glass of wine she is in the process of drinking, plastic grocery bags she has not had time to put away.

"I should have brought something more manageable," he says as she looks around the kitchen, the flowers resting against her shoulder, as if expecting a surface to miraculously clear.

"I've been meaning for weeks to buy myself some sunflowers," she says. She glances quickly at the pan on the stove and takes him through the kitchen and into the living room. She unwraps the flowers. "There's a vase up there," she says, pointing to the top of a bookcase. "Would you mind getting it down?"

She carries the vase into the bathroom, and he can hear water running in the tub. He takes the opportunity to remove his coat and cap, drape them over the back of the sofa.

He has dressed with care, a blue-and-white-striped Italian shirt that Sonia had bought for him at Filene's Basement, a pair of black jeans. She returns and fills the vase with the flowers, putting it on the coffee table. The place is nicer than he expected from the grimy look of the lobby. The floors have been redone, the walls freshly painted, the ceiling dotted with track lights. The living room has a square dining table in one corner, and a desk and file cabinets set up in another. Three particleboard bookcases line one wall. On the dining table, there is a pepper mill, a saltcellar, bright, clear-skinned clementines arranged in a bowl. He recognizes versions of things he knows from home: a Kashmiri crewelwork carpet on the floor, Rajasthani silk pillows on the sofa, a cast-iron Natraj on one of the bookcases.

Back in the kitchen she sets out some olives and some goat cheese coated with ash. She hands him a corkscrew and asks him to open the bottle he's brought, to pour himself a glass. She dredges more of the chicken on a plate of flour. The pan is sputtering loudly and has showered the wall behind the stove with oil. He stands there as she refers to a cookbook by Julia Child. He is overwhelmed by the production taking place for his benefit. In spite of the meals they've already shared, he is nervous about eating with her.

"When would you like to eat?" she says. "Are you hungry?"

"Whenever. What are you making?"

She looks at him doubtfully. "Coq au vin. I haven't made it before. I just found out that you're supposed to cook it twenty-four hours in advance. I'm afraid I'm running a bit behind."

He shrugs. "It already smells great. I'll help you." He rolls up his sleeves. "What can I do?"

"Let's see," she says, reading. "Oh. Okay. You can take those onions, and make X's in the bottom with a knife, and drop them into that pan."

"In with the chicken?"

"No. Shoot." She kneels down and retrieves a pot from one of the lower cupboards. "In here. They need to boil for a minute and then you take them out."

He does as he is told, filling the pan with water and turning on the flame. He finds a knife and scores the onions, as he had once been taught to do with Brussels sprouts in the Ratliffs' kitchen. He watches her measure wine and tomato paste into the pan containing the chicken. She searches in a cupboard for a stainless-steel spice caddy and throws in a bay leaf.

"Of course, my mother is appalled that I'm not making you Indian food," she says, studying the contents of the pan.

"You told her I was coming over?"

"She happened to call today." Then she asks him, "What about you? Have you been giving your mother updates?"

"I haven't gone out of my way. But she probably suspects something given that it's a Saturday and I'm not at home with her and Sonia."

Moushumi leans over the pan, watching the contents come to a simmer, prodding the pieces of chicken with a wooden spoon. She glances back at the recipe. "I think I need to add more liquid," she says, pouring water from a teakettle into the pan, causing her glasses to steam. "I can't see." She laughs, stepping away so that she stands a bit closer to him. The CD has ended and the apartment is silent apart from the sounds on the stove. She turns to him, still laughing, her eyes still obscured. She holds up her hands, messy from cooking, coated with flour and chicken fat. "Would you mind taking these off for me?"

With both hands he pries the glasses from her face, clasping the frames where they meet her temples. He puts them on the counter. And then he leans over and kisses her. He touches his fingers to her bare arms, cool in spite of the warmth of the kitchen. He presses her close, a hand at the small of her back, against the knot of her dress, tasting the warm, slightly sour tang of her mouth.

They make their way through the living room, to the bedroom. He sees a box spring and mattress without a frame. He unties the knot at the back of her dress with difficulty, then swiftly undoes the long zipper, leaving a small black pool at her feet. In the light cast from the living room, he glimpses black mesh underwear and a matching bra. She is curvier than she appears clothed, her breasts fuller, her hips generously flared. They make love on top of the covers, quickly, efficiently, as if they've known each other's bodies for years. But when they are finished she switches on the lamp by her bed and they examine each other, quietly discovering moles and marks and ribs.

"Who would have thought," she says, her voice tired, satisfied. She is smiling, her eyes partly closed.

He looks down at her face. "You're beautiful."

"And you."

"Can you even see me without those glasses?"

"Only if you stay close," she says.

"Then I'd better not move."

"Don't."

They peel back the covers and lie together, sticky and spent, in each other's arms. He begins to kiss her again, and she wraps her legs around him. But the smell of something burning causes them to bolt naked from the bed, rushing comically to the kitchen, laughing. The sauce has evaporated and the chicken is irreparably scorched, so much so that the pan itself has to be thrown away. By then they are starving and because they lack the energy either to go out or to prepare another meal they end up ordering in, feeding each other tart, tiny wedges of clementines as they wait for Chinese food to arrive.

Within three months they have clothes and toothbrushes at each other's apartments. He sees her for entire weekends without make-up, sees her with gray shadows under her eyes as she types papers at her desk, and when he kisses her head he tastes the oil that accumulates on her scalp between shampoos. He sees the hair that grows on her legs between waxings, the black roots that emerge between appointments at the salon, and in these moments, these glimpses, he believes he has known no greater intimacy. He learns that she sleeps, always, with her left leg straight and her right leg bent, ankle over knee, in the shape of a 4. He learns that she is prone to snoring, ever so faintly, sounding like a lawn mower that will not start, and to gnashing her jaws, which he massages for her as she sleeps. At restaurants and bars, they sometimes slip Bengali phrases into their conversation in order to comment with impunity on another diner's unfortunate hair or shoes.

They talk endlessly about how they know and do not know each other. In a way there is little to explain. There had been the same parties to attend when they were growing up, the same episodes of *The Love Boat* and *Fantasy Island* the children watched as the parents feasted in another part of the house, the same meals served to them on paper plates, the carpets lined with newspapers when the hosts happened to be particularly fastidious. He can imagine her life, even after she and her family moved away to New Jersey, easily. He can imagine the large suburban house her family owned; the china cabinet in the dining room, her mother's prized possession; the large public high school in which she had excelled but that she had miserably attended. There had been the same frequent trips to Calcutta, being plucked out of their American lives for months at a time. They calculate the many months that they were in that distant city together, on trips that had overlapped by weeks and once by months, unaware of each other's presence. They talk about how they are both routinely assumed to be Greek, Egyptian, Mexican — even in this misrendering they are joined.

She speaks with nostalgia of the years her family had spent in England, living at first in London, which she barely remembers, and then in a brick semidetached house in Croydon, with rosebushes in front. She describes the narrow house, the gas fireplaces, the dank odor of the bathrooms, eating Weetabix and hot milk for breakfast, wearing a uniform to school. She tells him that she had hated moving to America, that she had held on to her British accent for as long as she could. For some reason, her parents feared America much more than England, perhaps because of its vastness, or perhaps because in their minds it had less of a link to India. A few months before their arrival in Massachusetts, a child had disappeared while playing in his yard and was never found; for a long time afterward there were posters in the supermarket. She remembers always having to call her mother every time she and her friends moved to another house in the neighborhood, a house visible from her own, to play with another girl's toys, to have another family's cookies and punch. She would have to excuse herself upon entering and ask for the telephone. The American mothers were at once charmed and perplexed by her sense of duty. "I'm at Anna's house," she would report to her mother in English. "I'm at Sue's."

He does not feel insulted when she tells him that for most of her life he was exactly the sort of person she had sought to avoid. If anything it flatters him. From earliest girlhood, she says, she had been determined not to allow her parents to have a hand in her marriage. She had always been admonished not to marry an American, as had he, but he gathers that in her case these warnings had been relentless, and had therefore plagued her far more than they had him. When she was only five years old, she was asked by her relatives if she planned to get married in a red sari or a white gown. Though she had refused to indulge them, she knew, even then, what the correct response was. By the time she was twelve she had made a pact, with two other Bengali girls she knew, never to marry a Bengali man. They had written a statement vowing never to do so, and spit on it at the same time, and buried it somewhere in her parents' backyard.

From the onset of adolescence she'd been subjected to a series of unsuccessful schemes; every so often a small group of unmarried Bengali men materialized in the house, young colleagues of her father's. She never spoke to them; she strutted upstairs with the excuse of homework and did not come downstairs to say good-bye. During summer visits to Calcutta, strange men mysteriously appeared in the sitting room of her grandparents' flat. Once on a train to Durgapur to visit an uncle, a couple had been bold enough to ask her parents if she was engaged; they had a son doing his surgical residency in Michigan. "Aren't you going to arrange a wedding for her?" relatives would ask her parents. Their inquiries had filled her with a cold dread. She hated the way they would talk of the details of her wedding, the menu and the different colors of saris she would wear for the different ceremonies, as if it were a fixed certainty in her life. She hated when her grandmother would unlock her almari, showing her which jewels would be hers when the day came.

The shameful truth was that she was not involved, was in fact desperately lonely. She had rebuffed the Indian men she wasn't interested in, and she had been forbidden as a teenager to date. In college she had harbored lengthy infatuations, with students with whom she never spoke, with professors and TAs. In her mind she would have relationships with these men, structuring her days around chance meetings in the library, or a conversation during office hours, or the one class she and a fellow student shared, so that even now she associated a particular year of college with the man or boy she had silently, faithfully, absurdly, desired. Occasionally one of her infatuations would culminate in a lunch or coffee date, an encounter on which she would pin all her hopes but which would lead to nothing. In reality there had been no one, so that toward the end of college, as graduation loomed, she was convinced in her bones that there would be no one at all. Sometimes she wondered if it was her horror of being married to someone she didn't love that had caused her, subconsciously, to shut herself off. She shakes her head as she speaks, irritated with having revisited this aspect of her past. Even now she regrets herself as a teenager. She regrets her obedience, her long, unstyled hair, her piano lessons and lace-collared shirts. She regrets her mortifying lack of confidence, the extra ten pounds she carried on her frame during puberty. "No wonder you never talked to me back then," she says. He feels tenderness toward her when she disparages herself this way. And though he had witnessed that stage of her himself, he can no longer picture it; those vague recollections of her he's carried with him all his life have been wiped clean, replaced by the woman he knows now.

At Brown her rebellion had been academic. At her parents' insistence, she'd majored in chemistry, for they were hopeful she would follow in her father's footsteps. Without telling them, she'd pursued a double major in French. Immersing herself in a third language, a third culture, had been her refuge — she approached French, unlike things American or Indian, without guilt, or misgiving, or expectation of any kind. It was easier to turn her back on the two countries that could claim her in favor of one that had no claim whatsoever. Her four years of secret study had prepared her, at the end of college, to escape as far as possible. She told her parents she had no intention of being a chemist and, deaf to their protests, she'd scraped together all the money she had and moved to Paris, with no specific plans.

Suddenly it was easy, and after years of being convinced she would never have a lover she began to fall effortlessly into affairs. With no hesitation, she had allowed men to seduce her in cafés, in parks, while she gazed at paintings in museums. She gave herself openly, completely, not caring about the consequences. She was exactly the same person, looked and behaved the same way, and yet suddenly, in that new city, she was transformed into the kind of girl she had once envied, had believed she would never become. She allowed the men to buy her drinks, dinners, later to take her in taxis to their apartments, in neighborhoods she had not yet discovered on her own. In retrospect she saw that her sudden lack of inhibition had intoxicated her more than any of the men had. Some of them had been married, far older, fathers to children in secondary school. The men had been French for the most part, but also German, Persian, Italian, Lebanese. There were days she slept with one man after lunch, another after dinner. They were a bit excessive, she tells Gogol with a roll of her eyes, the type to lavish her with perfume and jewels.

She found a job working for an agency, helping American businesspeople learn conversational French, and French businesspeople learn conversational English. She would meet with them in cafés, or speak with them by phone, asking questions about their families, their backgrounds, their favorite books and foods. She began to socialize with other American expatriates. Her fiancé was part of that crowd. He was an investment banker from New York, living in Paris for a year. His name was Graham. She had fallen in love and very quickly moved in with him. It was for Graham that she'd applied to NYU. They took a place together on York Avenue. They lived there in secret, with two telephone lines so that her parents would never know. When her parents came to the city, he'd disappear to a hotel, removing all traces of himself from the apartment. It had been exciting at first, maintaining such an elaborate lie. But then it had gotten tiresome, impossible. She brought him home to New Jersey, prepared herself for battle, but in fact, to her enormous surprise, her parents were relieved. By then she was old enough so that it didn't matter to them that he was an American. Enough of their friends' children had married Americans, had produced pale, dark-haired, half-American grandchildren, and none of it was as terrible as they had feared. And so her parents did their best to accept him. They told their Bengali friends that Graham was well behaved, Ivy educated, earned an impressive salary. They learned to overlook the fact that his parents were divorced, that his father had remarried not once but twice, that his second wife was only ten years older than Moushumi.

One night, in a taxi stuck in midtown traffic, she had impulsively asked him to marry her. Looking back on it, she supposed it was all those years of people attempting to claim her, choose her, of feeling an invisible net cast around her, that had led her to this proposal. Graham had accepted, gave her his grandmother's diamond. He had agreed to fly with her and her parents to Calcutta, to meet her extended family and ask for her grandparents' blessing. He had charmed them all, learned to sit on the floor and eat with his fingers, take the dust from her grandparents' feet. He had visited the homes of dozens of her relatives, eaten the plates full of syrupy mishti, patiently posed for countless photographs on rooftops, surrounded by her cousins. He had agreed to a Hindu wedding, and so she and her mother had gone shopping in Gariahat and New Market, selected a dozen saris, gold jewelry in red cases with purple velvet linings, a dhoti and a topor for Graham that her mother carried by hand on the plane ride back. The wedding was planned for summer in New Jersey, an engagement party thrown, a few gifts already received. Her mother had typed up an explanation of Bengali wedding rituals on the computer and mailed it to all the Americans on the guest list. A photograph of the two of them was taken for the local paper in her parents' town.

A few weeks before the wedding, they were out to dinner with friends, getting happily drunk, and she heard Graham talking about their time in Calcutta. To her surprise, he was complaining about it, commenting that he found it taxing, found the culture repressed. All they did was visit her relatives, he said. Though he thought the city was fascinating, the society, in his opinion, was somewhat provincial. People tended to stay at home most of the time. There was nothing to drink. "Imagine dealing with fifty in-laws without alcohol. I couldn't even hold her hand on the street without attracting stares," he had said. She had listened to him, partly sympathetic, partly horrified. For it was one thing for her to reject her background, to be critical of her family's heritage, another to hear it from him. She realized that he had fooled everyone, including her. On their walk home from the restaurant, she brought it up, saying that his comments had upset her, why hadn't he told her these things? Was he only pretending to enjoy himself all that time? They'd begun to argue, a chasm opening up between them, swallowing them, and suddenly, in a rage, she had removed his grand-mother's ring from her finger and tossed it into the street, into oncoming traffic, and then Graham had struck her on the face as pedestrians watched. By the end of the week, he had moved out of the apartment they shared. She stopped going to school, filed for incompletes in all her classes. She swallowed half a bottle of pills, was forced to drink charcoal in an emergency room. She was given a referral to a therapist. She called her adviser at NYU, told him she'd had a nervous breakdown, took off the rest of the semester. The wedding was canceled, hundreds of phone calls made. They lost the deposit they'd paid to Shah Jahan caterers, as well as to their honeymoon destination, Palace on Wheels. The gold was taken to a bank vault, the saris and blouses and petticoats put away in a mothproof box.

Her first impulse was to move back to Paris. But she was in school, too invested to drop out, and besides, she had no money for that. She fled the apartment on York Avenue, unable to afford it on her own. She refused to go home to her parents. Some friends in Brooklyn took her in. It was painful, she told him, living with a couple at that particular time, listening to them shower together in the mornings, watching them kiss and shut the door to their bedroom at the end of each night, but in the beginning she could not face being alone. She started temping. By the time she'd saved enough to move to her own place in the East Village, she was thankful to be alone. All summer she went to movies by herself, sometimes as many as three a day. She bought *TV Guide* every week and read it from cover to cover, planning her nights around her favorite shows. She began to subsist on a diet of raita and Triscuits. She grew thinner than she'd ever been in her life, so that in the few pictures taken of her in that period her face is faintly unrecognizable. She went to end-of-summer sales and bought everything in a size four; six months later she would be forced to donate it all to a thrift shop. When autumn came, she threw herself into her studies, catching up on all the work she had abandoned that spring, began every now and then to date. And then one day her mother called, asking if she remembered a boy named Gogol.

9.

They marry within a year, at a DoubleTree hotel in New Jersey, close to the suburb where her parents live. It's not the type of wedding either of them really wants. They would have preferred the sorts of venues their American friends choose, the Brooklyn Botanic Gardens or the Metropolitan Club or the Boat House in Central Park. They would have preferred a sit-down dinner, jazz played during the reception, black-and-white photographs, keeping things small. But their parents insist on inviting close to three hundred people, and serving Indian food, and providing easy parking for all the guests. Gogol and Moushumi agree that it's better to give in to these expectations than to put up a fight. It's what they deserve, they joke, for having listened to their mothers, and for getting together in the first place, and the fact that they are united in their resignation makes the consequences somewhat bearable. Within weeks of announcing their engagement, the date is settled, the hotel booked, the menu decided, and though for a while there are nightly phone calls, her mother asking if they prefer a sheet cake or layers,

338

sage- or rose-colored napkins, Chardonnay or Chablis, there is little for either Gogol or Moushumi to do other than listen and say yes, whichever seems best, it all sounds fine. "Consider yourselves lucky," Gogol's co-workers tell him. Planning a wedding is incredibly stressful, the first real trial of a marriage, they say. Still, it feels a little strange to be so uninvolved in his own wedding, and he is reminded of the many other celebrations in his life, all the birthdays and graduation parties his parents had thrown when he was growing up, in his honor, attended by his parents' friends, occasions from which he had always felt at a slight remove.

The Saturday of the wedding they pack suitcases, rent a car, and drive down to New Jersey, separating only when they get to the hotel, where they are claimed one last time by their respective families. Starting tomorrow, he realizes with a shock, he and Moushumi will be regarded as a family of their own. They have not seen the hotel beforehand. Its most memorable feature is a glass elevator that rises and falls ceaselessly at its center, much to the amusement of children and adults alike. The rooms are gathered around successive elliptical balconies that can be seen from the lobby, reminding Gogol of a parking garage. He has a room to himself, on a floor with his mother and Sonia and a few of the Gangulis' closest family friends. Moushumi stays chastely on the floor above, next door to her parents, though by now she and Gogol are practically living together at her place. His mother has brought him the things he is to wear, a parchment-colored Punjabi top that had once belonged to his father, a prepleated dhoti with a drawstring waist, a pair of nagrai slippers with curling toes. His father had never worn the punjabi, and Gogol has to hang it in the bathroom, hot water running in the shower, to get the creases out. "His blessings are always with you," his mother says, reaching up and placing both her hands for a moment on his head. For the first time since his father's death, she is dressed with care, wearing a pretty pale green sari, a pearl necklace at her throat, has agreed to let Sonia put some lipstick on her lips. "Is it too much?" his mother worries, regarding herself in the mirror. Still, he has not seen her looking this lovely, this happy, this excited, in years. Sonia wears a sari, too, fuchsia with silver embroidery, a red rose stuck into her hair. She gives him a box wrapped in tissue.

"What's this?" he asks.

"You didn't think I forgot your thirtieth birthday, did you?"

It had been a few days ago, a weeknight he and Moushumi had both been too busy to celebrate properly. Even his mother, preoccupied with last-minute wedding details, had for-

340

gotten to call him first thing in the morning, as she normally did.

"I think I'm officially at the age when I want people to forget my birthday," he says, accepting the gift.

"Poor Goggles."

Inside he finds a small bottle of bourbon and a red leather flask. "I had it engraved," she says, and when he turns the flask over he sees the letters NG. He remembers poking his head into Sonia's room years ago, telling her about his decision to change his name to Nikhil. She'd been thirteen or so, doing her homework on her bed. "You can't do that," she'd told him then, shaking her head, and when he'd asked her why not she'd simply said, "Because you can't. Because you're Gogol." He watches her now, applying her make-up in his room, pulling at the skin next to her eye and painting a thin black line on the lid, and he recalls photographs of his mother at her own wedding.

"You're next, you know," he says.

"Don't remind me." She grimaces, then laughs. Their shared giddiness, the excitement of the preparations, saddens him, all of it reminding him that his father is dead. He imagines his father wearing an outfit similar to his own, a shawl draped over one shoulder, as he used to during pujo. The ensemble he fears looks silly on himself would have looked dignified, elegant, befitting his father in a way he knows it does not him. The nagrais are a size too large and need to be stuffed with tissues. Unlike Moushumi, who is having her hair and make-up professionally styled and applied, Gogol is ready in a matter of minutes. He regrets not having brought his running shoes along; he could have done a few miles on the treadmill before preparing himself for the event.

There is an hour-long watered-down Hindu ceremony on a platform covered with sheets. Gogol and Moushumi sit cross-legged, first opposite each other, then side by side. The guests sit facing them in folding metal chairs; the accordion wall between two windowless banquet rooms, with dropped ceilings, has been opened up to expand the space. A video camera and hand-held white lights hover above their faces. Shenai music plays on a boom box. Nothing has been rehearsed or explained to them beforehand. A cluster of mashis and meshos surround them, telling them continually what to do, when to speak or stand or throw flowers at a small brass urn. The priest is a friend of Moushumi's parents, an anesthesiologist who happens to be a Brahmin. Offerings are made to pictures of their grandparents and his father, rice poured into a pyre that they are forbidden by the management of the hotel to ignite. He thinks of his parents, strangers until this moment, two people who had not spoken until after they were actually wed. Suddenly, sitting next to Moushumi, he realizes what it means, and he is astonished by his parents' courage, the obedience that must have been involved in doing such a thing.

It's the first time he's seen Moushumi in a sari, apart from all those pujos years ago, which she had suffered through silently. She has about twenty pounds of gold on her — at one point, when they are sitting face to face, their hands wrapped up together in a checkered cloth, he counts eleven necklaces. Two enormous paisleys have been painted in red and white on her cheeks. Until now, he has continued to call Moushumi's father Shubir Mesho, and her mother Rina Mashi, as he always has, as if they were still his uncle and aunt, as if Moushumi were still a sort of cousin. But by the end of the night he will become their son-in-law and so be expected to address them as his second set of parents, an alternative Baba and Ma.

For the reception he changes into a suit, she into a red Banarasi gown with spaghetti straps, something she'd designed herself and had made by a seamstress friend. She wears the gown in spite of her mother's protests — what was wrong with a salwar kameeze, she'd wanted to know — and when Moushumi happens to forget her shawl on a chair and bares her slim, bronze shoulders, which quietly sparkle from a special powder she's applied to them, her mother manages, in the midst of that great crowd, to shoot her reproachful glances, which Moushumi ignores. Countless people come to congratulate Gogol, saying they had seen him when he was so little, asking him to pose for photographs, to wrap his arms around families and smile. He is numbly drunk through it all, thanks to the open bar her parents have sprung for. Moushumi is horrified, in the banquet room, to see the tables wreathed with tulle, the ivy and baby's breath twisted around the columns. They bump into each other on her way out of the ladies' room and exchange a quick kiss, the smoke on her breath faintly masked by the mint she is chewing. He imagines her smoking in the stall, the lid of the toilet seat down. They've barely said a word to each other all evening; throughout the ceremony she'd kept her eyes lowered, and during the reception, each time he'd looked at her, she'd been deep in conversation with people he didn't know. He wants to be alone with her suddenly, wishes they could sneak off to her room or his, ignore the rest of the party as he would when he was a boy. "Come on," he urges, motioning toward the glass elevator, "fifteen minutes. No one will notice." But the dinner has begun, and table numbers are being called one by one on the loudspeaker. "I'd need someone to redo my hair," she says.

The heated silver chafing dishes are labeled for the American guests. It's typical north Indian fare, mounds of hot pink tandoori, aloo gobi in thick orange sauce. He overhears someone in the line saying the chickpeas have gone bad. They sit at the head table in the center of the room, with his mother and Sonia, her parents and a handful of her relatives visiting from Calcutta, and her brother, Samrat, who is missing out on his orientation at the University of Chicago in order to attend the wedding. There are awkward champagne toasts and speeches by their families, their parents' friends. Her father stands up, smiling nervously, forgets to raise his glass, and says, "Thank you very much for coming," then turns to Gogol and Moushumi: "Okay, be happy." Forks are tapped against glasses by giggling, sari-clad mashis, instructing them when to kiss. Each time he obliges them and kisses his bride tamely on the cheek.

A cake is wheeled out, "Nikhil Weds Moushumi" piped across its surface. Moushumi smiles as she always smiles for a camera, her mouth closed, her head tilted slightly downward and to the left. He is aware that together he and Moushumi are fulfilling a collective, deep-seated desire — because they're both Bengali, everyone can let his hair down a bit. At times, looking out at the guests, he can't help but think that two years ago he might have been sitting in the sea of round tables that now surround him, watching her marry another man. The thought crashes over him like an unexpected wave, but quickly he reminds himself that he is the one sitting beside her. The red Banarasi wedding sari and the gold had been bought two years ago, for her wedding to Graham. This time all her parents have had to do is bring down the boxes from a closet shelf, retrieve the jewels from the safety deposit box, find the itemized list for the caterer. The new invitation, designed by Ashima, the English translation lettered by Gogol, is the only thing that isn't a leftover.

Since Moushumi has to teach a class three days after the wedding, they have to postpone the honeymoon. The closest they come is a night alone in the DoubleTree, which they are both dying to leave. But their parents have gone to great trouble and expense to book the newlywed suite. "I have got to take a shower," she says as soon as they are finally alone, and disappears into the bathroom. He knows she is exhausted, as he is — the night had ended with a long session of dancing to Abba songs. He examines the room, opening drawers and pulling out the stationery, opening the minibar, reading the contents of the room service menu, though he is not at all hungry. If anything, he feels slightly ill, from the combination of the bourbon and the two large pieces of cake he'd had because he had not had any dinner. He sprawls on the king-sized bed. The bedspread has been strewn with flower petals, a final gesture before their families withdrew. He waits for her, flipping through the channels on the television. Beside him is a bottle of champagne in a bucket, heart-shaped chocolates on a lace-covered plate. He takes a bite out of one of the chocolates. The inside is an unyielding toffee, requiring more chewing than he expects.

He fidgets with the gold ring she'd placed on his finger after they'd cut the cake, identical to the one he'd placed on hers. He'd proposed to her on her birthday, giving her a diamond solitaire in addition to the hat he'd bought for her after their second date. He'd made a production out of it, using her birthday as an excuse to take her to a country inn for the weekend, in a town upstate on the banks of the Hudson, the first trip they'd taken together that wasn't to her parents' place in New Jersey, or to Pemberton Road. It was springtime, the velvet hat out of season by then. She'd been overwhelmed that he'd remembered it all this time. "I can't believe the store still had it," she said. He didn't tell her the truth about when he'd bought the hat. He'd presented it to her downstairs, in the dining room, after a Châteaubriand that had been carved for them at the table. Strangers turned to admire

Moushumi when the hat was on her head. After trying it on, she'd put the box away under her chair, not noticing the smaller box lost among the tissue. "There's something else in there," he'd been forced to say. In retrospect he decided that she had been more shocked by the hat than by his proposal. For while the former was a true surprise, the latter was something expected — from the very beginning it was safely assumed by their families, and soon enough by themselves, that as long as they liked each other their courtship would not lag and they would surely wed. "Yes," she'd told him, grinning, looking up from the hatbox before he'd even had to ask.

She emerges now in the snow-white terrycloth hotel robe. She has taken off her makeup and her jewels; the vermilion with which he'd stained her part at the end of the ceremony has been rinsed from her hair. Her feet are free of the three-inch heels she'd worn as soon as the religious part of the wedding was over, causing her to tower over almost everyone. This is the way he still finds her most ravishing, unadorned, aware that it is a way she is willing to look for no one but him. She sits on the edge of the mattress, applies some blue cream from a tube to her calves and the bottoms of her feet. She'd massaged the cream onto his own feet once, the day they'd walked across the Brooklyn

Bridge, causing them to tingle and go cold. And then she lies against the pillows, and looks at him, and puts out a hand. Underneath the robe he expects to find some racy lingerie — back in New York he'd glimpsed the pile of things she'd received for her shower in the corner of her bedroom. But she is naked, her skin smelling, a little too intensely, of some sort of berry. He kisses the dark hair on her forearms, the prominent collarbone, which she had once confessed to him is her favorite part of her body. They make love in spite of their exhaustion, her damp hair limp and cool against his face, the rose petals sticking to their elbows and shoulders and calves. He breathes in the scent of her skin, still unable to fathom that they are husband and wife. When would it sink in? Even then he does not feel fully alone with her, half waiting for someone to knock on the door and tell them how to go about things. And though he desires her as much as ever, he is relieved when they are through, lying naked side by side, knowing that nothing else is expected of them, that finally they can relax.

Afterward they open up the champagne and sit together on the bed, going through a large shopping bag full of cards with personal checks inside them. The checks have been given to them by their parents' hundreds of friends. She had not wanted to register for gifts. She told Gogol it was because she didn't have the time, but he sensed that it was something she couldn't bring herself to face the second time around. It's fine with him, not to have their apartment crammed with a dozen crystal vases and platters and matching pots and pans. There is no calculator, and so they add up the figures on numerous sheets of the hotel stationery. Most of the checks have been written out to Mr. and Mrs. Nikhil and Moushumi Ganguli. Several are written to Gogol and Moushumi Ganguli. The amounts are for one hundred and one dollars, two hundred and one dollars, occasionally three hundred and one dollars, as Bengalis consider it inauspicious to give round figures. Gogol adds up the subtotals on each page.

"Seven thousand thirty-five," he announces.

"Not bad, Mr. Ganguli."

"I'd say we've made a killing, Mrs. Ganguli."

Only she is not Mrs. Ganguli. Moushumi has kept her last name. She doesn't adopt Ganguli, not even with a hyphen. Her own last name, Mazoomdar, is already a mouthful. With a hyphenated surname, she would no longer fit into the window of a business envelope. Besides, by now she has begun to publish under Moushumi Mazoomdar, the name printed at the top of footnoted articles on French feminist theory in a number of prestigious academic journals that always manage

350

to give Gogol a paper cut when he tries to read them. Though he hasn't admitted this to her, he'd hoped, the day they'd filled out the application for their marriage license, that she might consider otherwise, as a tribute to his father if nothing else. But the thought of changing her last name to Ganguli has never crossed Moushumi's mind. When relatives from India continue to address letters and cards to "Mrs. Moushumi Ganguli," she will shake her head and sigh.

They put the money toward a security deposit for a one-bedroom apartment in the Twenties, off Third Avenue. It's slightly more than they can comfortably afford, but they are won over by the maroon awning, the part-time doorman, the lobby paved with pumpkin-colored tiles. The apartment itself is small but luxurious, with built-in mahogany bookcases rising to the ceiling and dark, oily, wide-planked floors. There is a living room with a skylight, a kitchen with expensive stainless-steel appliances, a bathroom with a marble floor and walls. There is a Juliet balcony off the bedroom, in one corner of which Moushumi sets up her desk, her computer and printer, her files. They are on the top floor, and if one leans far enough to the left outside the bathroom window it's possible to see the Empire State Building. They spend a few weekends taking the shuttle bus to Ikea and filling up the rooms: imitation Noguchi lamps, a black sectional sofa, kilim and flokati carpets, a blond wood platform bed. Both her parents and Ashima are at once impressed and puzzled when they come to visit for the first time. Isn't it a bit small, now that they are married? But Gogol and Moushumi aren't thinking of children at the moment, certainly not until Moushumi finishes her dissertation. On Saturdays they shop together for food at the farmers' market in Union Square, with canvas bags over their shoulders. They buy things they are not certain how to prepare, leeks and fresh fava beans and fiddleheads, looking up recipes in the cookbooks they've received for their wedding. From time to time when they cook they set off the fire alarm, which is overly sensitive, and they bang it into silence with the handle of a broom.

They entertain together on occasion, throwing the sorts of parties their parents never had, mixing martinis in a stainless-steel shaker for a few of the architects at Gogol's work or Moushumi's graduate student friends at NYU. They play bossa nova and serve bread and salami and cheese. He transfers the money in his bank account over to hers, and they have pale green checks with both their names printed in the corner. The pass code they decide on for their ATM card, Lulu, is the name of the French restaurant where they had their first meal together. They eat most nights side by side on the stools at the kitchen counter or at the coffee table, watching TV. They make Indian food infrequently — usually it's pasta or broiled fish or take-out from the Thai restaurant down the block. But sometimes, on a Sunday, both craving the food they'd grown up eating, they ride the train out to Queens and have brunch at Jackson Diner, piling their plates with tandoori chicken and pakoras and kabobs, and shop afterward for basmati rice and the spices that need replenishing. Or they go to one of the hole-in-the-wall tea shops and drink tea in paper cups with heavy cream, asking the waitress in Bengali to bring them bowls of sweet yogurt and haleem. He calls every evening before leaving the office to say he is on his way home, asks if he needs to pick up lettuce or a loaf of bread. After dinner they watch television, as Moushumi writes out thank-you cards to all their parents' friends, for the checks they had needed twenty different slips to deposit. These are the things that make him feel married. Otherwise it's the same, only now they're always together. At night she sleeps beside him, always rolling onto her stomach, waking up every morning with a pillow pressed over her head.

Occasionally, in the apartment, he finds odd remnants of her life before he'd appeared in it, her life with Graham — the inscription to the two of them in a book of poems, a postcard from Provence stuffed into the back of a dictionary, addressed to the apartment they'd secretly shared. Once, unable to stop himself, he'd walked to this address during his lunch break, wondering what her life had been like back then. He imagined her walking along the sidewalk, carrying grocery bags from the supermarket that was on the next corner, in love with another man. He doesn't feel jealous of her past per se. It's only that sometimes Gogol wonders whether he represents some sort of capitulation or defeat. He doesn't feel this always, just enough to nag at him, settling over his thoughts like a web. But then he looks around the apartment for reassurance, reminding himself of the life they've set up together and share. He looks at the photograph taken at their wedding, in which matching garlands hang from their necks. It sits in a tasteful leather frame on top of the television set. He wanders into the bedroom, where she's working, kissing her on the shoulder, drawing her to bed. But in the closet they now share is a garment bag containing a white dress he knows she would have worn a month after the Indian ceremony that had been planned for her and Graham, a second ceremony before a justice of the peace on Graham's father's lawn in Pennsylvania. She had told him about it. A patch of the dress is visible through a plastic window in the garment bag. He'd unzipped it once, glimpsed something sleeveless, to the knee, with a plain round neck, reminding him of a tennis dress. One day he asks her why she still keeps it. "Oh that," she says with a shrug. "I keep meaning to have it dyed."

In March they go to Paris. Moushumi is invited to give a paper at a conference at the Sorbonne, and they decide to make a vacation out of it, Gogol arranging to take the week off from work. Instead of staying in a hotel, they stay in an apartment in the Bastille which belongs to a friend of Moushumi's, a male friend named Emanuel, a journalist, who is on holiday in Greece. The apartment is barely heated, minuscule, at the top of six steep flights of stairs, with a bathroom the size of a phone booth. There is a loft bed just inches from the ceiling, so that sex is a serious hazard. An espresso pot nearly fills the narrow two-burner stove. Apart from two chairs at the dining table, there is no place to sit. The weather is raw, cheerless, the sky white, the sun perpetually hidden from view. Paris is famous for such weather, Moushumi tells him. He feels hidden himself; men on the streets stare at Moushumi constantly, their glances lingering plainly, in spite of the fact that Gogol is at her side.

It is his first time in Europe. The first time he sees the sort of architecture he has read about for so many years, admired only in the pages of books and slides. For some reason, in Moushumi's company, he feels more apologetic than excited. Though they journey together one day to Chartres, and another to Versailles, he has the feeling she'd rather be meeting friends for coffee, attending panels at the conference, eating at her favorite bistros, shopping at her favorite stores. From the beginning he feels useless. Moushumi makes all the decisions, does all the talking. He is mute in the brasseries where they eat their lunches, mute in the shops where he gazes at beautiful belts, ties, paper, pens; mute on the rainy afternoon they spend together at the d'Orsay. He is particularly mute when he and Moushumi get together for dinners with groups of her French friends, drinking Pernods and feasting on couscous or choucroute, smoking and arguing around paper-covered tables. He struggles to grasp the topic of conversation — the euro, Monica Lewinsky, Y2K — but everything else is a blur, indistinguishable from the clatter of plates, the drone of echoing, laughing voices. He watches them in the giant gilt-framed mirrors on the walls, their dark heads leaning close.

Part of him knows this is a privilege, to be here with a person who knows the city so well, but the other part of him wants simply to be a tourist, fumbling with a phrase book, looking at all the buildings on his list, getting lost. When he confesses his wish to Moushumi one night as they are walking back to the apartment, she says, "Why didn't you tell me that in the first place?" and the next morning she instructs him to walk to the Métro station, have his photo taken in a booth, get a Carte Orange. And so Gogol goes sightseeing, alone, while Moushumi is off at her conference, or as she sits at the table in the apartment and puts the final touches on her paper. His only companion is Moushumi's *Plan de Paris*, a small red guide to the arrondissements, with a folded map attached to the back cover. On the last page, Moushumi writes in a few phrases for his benefit: *"Je voudrais un café, s'il vous plaît."* *"Où sont les toilettes?"* And she warns as he's walking out the door, "Avoid ordering a café crème unless it's morning. The French never do that."

Though the day is bright for a change, it is particularly cold, brisk air stinging his ears. He remembers his first lunch with Moushumi, the afternoon she'd dragged him to the hat store. He remembers the two of them crying out in unison as the wind blasted their faces, a time too soon for them to cling to each other for warmth. He walks now to the corner, decides to get another croissant at the boulangerie where he and Moushumi go every morning to buy breakfast. He sees a young couple standing in a patch of sunlight on the sidewalk, feeding each other pastries from a bag. Suddenly he wants to go back to the apartment, climb into the loft bed and forget about sightseeing, hold Moushumi in his arms. He wants to lie with her for hours, as they did at the beginning, skipping meals, then wandering the streets at odd hours, desperate for something to eat. But she must present her paper at the end of the week, and he knows she will not be roused from her task of reading it aloud, timing its duration, making small marks in the margin. He consults his map and for the next few days he follows the routes she has charted for him with a pencil. He wanders for miles along the famous boulevards, through the Marais, arriving after many wrong turns at the Picasso Museum. He sits on a bench and sketches the town houses in the Place des Vosges, walks along the desolate gravel paths in the Luxembourg Gardens. Outside the Academie des Beaux-Arts he wanders for hours through the shops selling prints, eventually buying a drawing of the Hôtel de Lauzun. He photographs the narrow sidewalks, the dark cobblestone streets, the mansard roofs, the ancient, shuttered buildings of pale beige stone. All of it he finds beautiful beyond description, and yet at the same time it depresses him that none of it is new to Moushumi, that she has seen it all hundreds of times. He understands why she lived here for as long as she did, away from her family, away from anyone she knew. Her French friends adore her. Waiters and shopkeepers adore her. She both fits in perfectly yet remains slightly novel. Here Moushumi had reinvented herself, without misgivings, without guilt. He admires her, even resents her a little, for having moved to another country and made a separate life. He realizes that this is what their parents had done in America. What he, in all likelihood, will never do.

On their last day, in the morning, he shops for gifts for his in-laws, his mother, Sonia. It is the day Moushumi is presenting her paper. He had offered to go with her, to sit in the audience and listen to her speak. But she told him that was silly, why sit in the middle of a roomful of people speaking a language he doesn't understand when there was still more of the city he could see? And so, after shopping, he sets off, alone, for the Louvre, a destination he's put off until now. At the end of the day he meets her at a café in the Latin Quarter. She is there waiting for him behind a glassed-in partition on the sidewalk, wearing a dark red lipstick, sipping a glass of wine.

He sits down, orders a coffee. "How was it? How did it go?"

She lights a cigarette. "Okay. Over with, at any rate."

She looks more regretful than relieved, her eyes lingering over the small round table between them, the veins in the marble bluish, like those in cheese.

Normally she wants a full account of his adventures, but today they sit silently, watching the passers-by. He shows her the things he's bought, a tie for his father-in-law, soaps for their mothers, a shirt for Samrat, a silk scarf for Sonia, sketchbooks for himself, bottles of ink, a pen. She admires the drawings he's done. It is a café they've been to before, and he feels the slight nostalgia it is sometimes possible to feel at the end of an extended stay in a foreign place, taking in the details that will soon evaporate from his mind: the surly waiter who has served them both times, the view of the shops across the street, the green and yellow straw chairs.

"Are you sad to be leaving?" he asks, stirring sugar into his coffee, drinking it back in one gulp.

"A little. I guess a little part of me wishes I'd never left Paris, you know?"

He leans over, takes both her hands in his. "But then we would never have met," he says, with more confidence than he feels.

"True," she acknowledges. And then: "Maybe we'll move here one day."

He nods. "Maybe."

She looks beautiful to him, tired, the concentrated light of the dying day on her face, infusing it with an amber-pink glow. He watches the smoke drift away from her. He wants to remember this moment, the two of them together, here. This is how he wants to remember Paris. He takes out his camera, focusing it on her face.

"Nikhil, please, don't," she says, laughing, shaking her head. "I look awful." She shields her face with the back of her hand.

He still holds up the camera. "Oh, come on, Mo. You're beautiful. You look great."

But she refuses to indulge him, moving her chair out of view with a scrape on the pavement; she doesn't want to be mistaken for a tourist in this city, she says.

A Saturday evening in May. A dinner party in Brooklyn. A dozen people are gathered around a long, scratched-up dining table, smoking cigarettes, drinking Chianti from juice glasses, sitting on a series of backless wooden stools. The room is dark apart from a domed metal lamp hanging from a long cord, which casts a concentrated pool of light on the table's center. An opera plays on a battered boom box on the floor. A joint is being passed around. Gogol takes a hit, but as he sits there, holding his breath, he regrets it — he is already starved. Though it's close to ten o'clock, dinner has yet to be served.

Apart from the Chianti, the only offerings so far are a loaf of bread and a small bowl of olives. A blizzard of crumbs and pointy violet olive pits litter the tabletop. The bread, like a hard, dusty cushion, is full of prune-sized holes and has a crust that hurts the roof of Gogol's mouth when he chews.

They are at the home of Moushumi's friends Astrid and Donald. It's a brownstone under renovation; Astrid and Donald, expecting their first child, are in the process of expanding their domain from a single floor of the house to the top three. Thick plastic sheets hang from rafters, creating transparent, temporary corridors. Behind them, a wall is missing. Even at this hour, guests continue to arrive. They enter complaining of the cold that has persisted this far into spring, of the stinging, bothersome wind that tosses the treetops outside. They remove their coats, introduce themselves, pour themselves Chianti. If it happens to be their first time in the house they eventually drift from the table and troop up the stairs, to admire the pocket doors, the original tin ceilings, the vast space that will eventually become the nursery, the distant, sparkling view of Manhattan visible from the top floor.

Gogol has been to the house before, a bit too frequently in his opinion. Astrid is a friend of Moushumi's from Brown. The first time he'd met Donald and Astrid had been at his wedding. At least that's what Moushumi says; he doesn't remember them. They were living in Rome the first year that Gogol and Moushumi were together, on a Guggenheim that Astrid had gotten. But they've since moved back to New York, where Astrid has begun teaching film theory at the New School. Donald is a moderately talented painter of small still lifes of single, everyday objects: an egg, a cup, a comb, suspended against brightly colored backgrounds. Donald's rendition of a spool of thread, a wedding present to Gogol and Moushumi, hangs in their bedroom. Donald and Astrid are a languidly confident couple, a model, Gogol guesses, for how Moushumi would like their own lives to be. They reach out to people, hosting dinner parties, bequeathing little bits of themselves to their friends. They are passionate spokespeople for their brand of life, giving Gogol and Moushumi a steady, unquestionable stream of advice about quotidian things. They swear by a certain bakery on Sullivan Street, a certain butcher on Mott, a certain style of coffeemaker, a certain Florentine designer of sheets for their bed. Their decrees drive Gogol crazy. But Moushumi is loyal. She regularly goes out of her way, and thus out of their budget, to buy bread at that bakery, meat at that butcher.

He recognizes a few familiar faces tonight: Edith and Colin, who teach sociology at

Princeton and Yale, respectively, and Louise and Blake, both Ph.D. candidates, like Moushumi, at NYU. Oliver is an editor at an art magazine; his wife, Sally, works as a pastry chef. The rest are painter friends of Donald's, poets, documentary filmmakers. They are all married. Even now, a fact as ordinary, as obvious, as this astonishes him. All married! But this is life now, the weekend sometimes more tiring than the workweek, an endless stream of dinner parties, cocktail parties, occasional after-eleven parties with dancing and drugs to remind them that they are still young, followed by Sunday brunches full of unlimited Bloody Marys and overpriced eggs.

They are an intelligent, attractive, well-dressed crowd. Also a bit incestuous. The vast majority of them know each other from Brown, and Gogol can't ever shake the feeling that half the people in the room have slept with one another. There is the usual academic talk around the table, versions of the same conversation he can't participate in, concerning conferences, job listings, ungrateful undergraduates, proposal deadlines. At one end of the table, a woman with short red hair and cat's-eye glasses is talking about a Brecht play she'd once acted in in San Francisco, performed fully in the nude. At the other end, Sally is putting the finishing touches on a dessert she's brought, intently

364

assembling layers and covering them with glistening white meringue that shoots up like a dense thicket of flames. Astrid is showing a few people paint chips, which she's lined up in front of her like tarot cards, versions of an apple green she and Donald are considering for the front hallway. She wears glasses that might have belonged to Malcolm X. She eyes the paint chips with precision; though she seeks the advice of her guests, she has already made up her mind about which permutation of the shade she will choose. To Gogol's left, Edith is discussing her reasons for not eating bread. "I just have so much more energy if I stay off wheat," she maintains.

Gogol has nothing to say to these people. He doesn't care about their dissertation topics, or their dietary restrictions, or the color of their walls. In the beginning these occasions hadn't been quite so excruciating. When Moushumi had first introduced him to her crowd he and she would sit with their arms around each other, their fellow guests a footnote to their own ongoing conversation. Once, at a party at Sally and Oliver's, they'd wandered off to make quick, giddy love in Sally's walk-in closet, piles of her sweaters looming over them. He knows that that sort of insular passion can't be sustained. Still, Moushumi's devotion to these people puzzles him. He looks at her now. She is lighting a

Dunhill. Her smoking hadn't bothered him initially. He liked it, after sex, when she'd lean over the bedside table and strike a match, and he would lie beside her, listening to her exhale in the quiet, watching the smoke drift up over their heads. But these days the stale smell of it, in her hair and on her fingertips, and in the bedroom where she sits typing, slightly disgusts him, and from time to time he can't help but have a fleeting vision of himself, tragically abandoned as a result of her mild but persistent addiction. When he'd admitted his fear to her one day, she'd laughed. "Oh, Nikhil," she'd said, "you can't be serious."

She is laughing now, nodding intently at something Blake is saying. She seems animated in a way he doesn't remember her having been in a while. He looks at her straight, smooth hair, which she's had cut recently so that it flips up at the ends. The glasses that only emphasize her beauty. Her pale, pretty mouth. He knows that the approval of these people means something to her, though what exactly he isn't sure. And yet, as much as Moushumi enjoys seeing Astrid and Donald, Gogol has recently begun to notice that she is gloomy in the aftermath, as if seeing them serves only to remind her that their own lives will never match up. The last time they'd gone home after one of Astrid and Donald's dinner parties, she'd picked a fight with him as soon as they'd walked in the door, complaining about the noise on Third Avenue, about the sliding doors on the closets that always fall off the rails, about the fact that it's impossible to use the bathroom without being deafened by the exhaust fan. He tells himself that it's the stress — she's been studying for her orals, holed up in her carrel at the library until nine o'clock most nights. He remembers how it was studying for his licensing exam, which he failed twice before passing. He remembers the sustained isolation it had demanded, speaking to no one for days at a time, and so he doesn't say anything. Tonight he'd held out the hope that she'd use her orals as a reason to decline the invitation to Astrid and Donald's. But by now he's learned that there is never a question of saying no when it comes to them.

It was through Astrid and Donald that Moushumi had met her former fiancé, Graham; Donald had gone to prep school with him, and he had given Moushumi's number to Graham when he'd moved to Paris. Gogol doesn't like to think about the fact that Moushumi's connection to Graham persists through Astrid and Donald, that through them Moushumi has learned that Graham lives in Toronto now, is married and a father of twins. Back when Moushumi and Graham were together they'd made a foursome with Donald and Astrid, renting cottages together in Vermont, time-shares in the Hamptons. They try to incorporate Gogol into similar plans; this summer, for example, they are thinking of renting a house on the coast of Brittany. Though Astrid and Donald have welcomed Gogol heartily into their lives, sometimes he has the feeling they still think she's with Graham. Once Astrid even called him Graham by mistake. No one had noticed except Gogol. They had all been a little drunk, but he knew he'd heard correctly, toward the end of an evening much like this one. "Mo, why don't you and Graham take some of this pork loin home," Astrid had said as they'd been clearing the dishes. "It's great for sandwiches."

At the moment, the guests are united in a single topic of conversation, talking about names for the baby. "What we want is something totally unique," Astrid is saying. Lately Gogol has started to notice a trend: now that they inhabit this world of couples, dinner party small talk gravitates to the naming of children. If a woman at the table happens to be pregnant, as Astrid is now, the subject is inevitable.

"I always liked the names of popes," Blake says.

"You mean John and Paul?" Louise asks.

"More like Innocent and Clement."

There are nonsensical names, like Jet and

Tipper. These elicit groans. Someone claims to have once known a girl named Anna Graham — "Get it? Anagram!" — and everyone laughs.

Moushumi argues that a name like hers is a curse, complains that no one can say it properly, that the kids at school pronounced it Moosoomi and shortened it to Moose. "I hated being the only Moushumi I knew," she says.

"See now, I'd have loved that," Oliver tells her.

Gogol pours himself another juice glass of Chianti. He hates contributing to these conversations, hates listening. A number of name books are passed around the table: *Finding the Perfect Name, Alternative Baby Names, The Idiot's Guide to Naming Your Baby.* One is called *What Not to Name Your Baby.* Pages are folded down, some with stars and checks in the margins. Someone suggests Zachary. Someone else says she once had a dog named Zachary. Everyone wants to look up his or her own name to see what it means, is by turns pleased and disappointed. Both Gogol and Moushumi are absent from these books, and for the first time all evening he feels a hint of that odd bond that had first drawn them together. He goes over to where she's sitting, takes one of her hands, which have been resting flat on the surface of the table, her arms extended. She turns to look at him.

"Hey there," she says. She smiles at him, temporarily leaning her head on his shoulder, and he realizes that she's drunk.

"What *does* Moushumi mean?" Oliver asks on the other side of her.

"A damp southwesterly breeze," she says, shaking her head, rolling her eyes.

"Sort of like the one outside?"

"I always knew you were a force of nature," Astrid says, laughing.

Gogol turns to Moushumi. "Really?" he says. He realizes that it's something he'd never thought to ask about her, something he hadn't known.

"You never told me that," he says.

She shakes her head, confused. "I haven't?"

It bothers him, though he's not quite sure why. But it's not the time to dwell on it. Not in the middle of all this. He gets up to go to the bathroom. When he is finished, instead of returning to the dining room, he walks up a flight of stairs, to check out the renovations. He pauses at the doors to a series of whitewashed rooms with nothing but ladders in them. Others are filled with boxes, stacked six or seven deep. He stops to inspect some blueprints spread out on the floor. He remembers that when he and Moushumi were first dating they'd spent an entire afternoon, in a bar, drawing a plan of the ideal house. He'd argued for something modernist, full of glass and light, but she'd wanted a brownstone like this one. In the end they'd designed something implausible, a town house of poured concrete with a glass facade. It was before they'd slept together, and he remembers how they'd both grown embarrassed when deciding where the bedroom should go.

He ends up in the kitchen, where Donald is only now beginning to prepare spaghetti alle vongole. It's an old kitchen from one of the former rental units, which they're using until their new one is ready. Dingy linoleum and appliances lining a single wall remind Gogol of his former place on Amsterdam Avenue. On the stove is an empty, gleaming stainless-steel stockpot so large that it covers two burners. Salad leaves are in a bowl covered with dampened paper towels. A heap of tiny pale green clams no larger than quarters soak in the deep porcelain sink.

Donald is tall, wearing jeans and flip-flops and a paprika-colored shirt whose sleeves are rolled up to just above his elbows. He is handsome, with patrician features and swept-back, slightly greasy, light brown hair. He wears an apron over his clothes, and is busily plucking leaves from an excessively large bunch of parsley.

"Hey there," Gogol says. "Need any help?"

"Nikhil. Welcome." Donald hands over the parsley. "Be my guest."

Gogol is grateful for something to do, to

be occupied and productive, even in the role of sous-chef to Donald.

"So, how are the renovations going?"

"Don't ask," Donald says. "We just fired our contractor. At this rate our kid will already have moved out by the time the nursery's ready."

Gogol watches as Donald begins to remove the clams from their bath, scrubbing the shells with something that looks like a tiny toilet bowl brush, then tossing them one by one into the stockpot. Gogol pokes his head into the pot and sees the vongole, their shells uniformly parted in a quietly foaming broth.

"So when are you guys moving out to this neighborhood?" Donald asks.

Gogol shrugs. He has no interest in moving to Brooklyn, not in such proximity to Donald and Astrid, anyway. "I haven't really considered it. I prefer Manhattan. Moushumi does too."

Donald shakes his head. "You're wrong. Moushumi adores Brooklyn. We practically had to kick her out after the whole Graham thing."

The mention of the name pricks him, deflates him as it always does.

"She stayed here with you?"

"Right down the hall. She was here for a couple of months. She was a real mess. I've never seen anyone so devastated."

He nods. This was something else she'd

372

never told him. He wonders why. He hates the house suddenly, aware that it was here, with Donald and Astrid, that she spent her darkest hour. That it was here she'd mourned for another man.

"But you're much better for her," Donald concludes.

Gogol looks up, surprised.

"Don't get me wrong, Graham's a great guy. But they were too alike somehow, too intense together."

Gogol does not find this observation particularly reassuring. He finishes plucking the last of the parsley leaves, watches as Donald grabs a knife and chops them, expertly and swiftly, a hand held flat over the top of the blade.

Gogol feels incompetent all of a sudden. "I've never quite figured out how to do that," he says.

"All you need is a really good knife," Donald tells him. "I swear by these."

Gogol is sent off with a stack of plates, a bunch of forks and knives. On his way he pokes his head into the room down the hall where Moushumi had stayed. It's empty now, a drop cloth on the floor, a tangle of wires poking out of the center of the ceiling. He imagines her in a bed in the corner, sullen, emaciated, a cloud of smoke over her head. Downstairs, he takes his place beside Moushumi. She kisses his earlobe. "Where did you wander off to?"

"Just keeping Donald company."

The name conversation is still going full force. Colin says he likes names that signify a virtue: Patience, Faith, Chastity. He says his great-grandmother was named Silence, something nobody wants to believe.

"What about Prudence? Isn't Prudence one of the virtues?" Donald says, coming down the stairs with a platter of spaghetti. The platter is lowered onto the table to scattered applause. The pasta is served, the plates passed around.

"It just feels like such a huge responsibility to name a baby. What if he hates it," Astrid frets.

"So he'll change it," Louise says. "By the way. Remember Joe Chapman from college? I heard he's a Joanne now."

"God, I would never change my name," Edith says. "It's my grandmother's."

"Nikhil changed his," Moushumi blurts out suddenly, and for the first time all evening, with the exception of the opera singers, the room goes completely quiet.

He stares at her, stunned. He has never told her not to tell anyone. He simply assumed she never would. His expression is lost on her; she smiles back at him, unaware of what she's done. The dinner guests regard him, their mouths hanging open in confused smiles.

"What do you mean he changed his

374

name?" Blake asks slowly.

"Nikhil. It wasn't the name he was born with." She nods, her mouth full, tossing a clamshell onto the table. "Not his name when we were kids."

"What name were you born with?" Astrid says, looking at him suspiciously, her eyebrows furrowed for effect.

For a few seconds he says nothing. "Gogol," he says finally. It has been years since he's been Gogol to anyone other than his family, their friends. It sounds as it always does, simple, impossible, absurd. He stares at Moushumi as he says it, but she's too drunk to absorb his reproach.

"As in 'The Overcoat'?" Sally asks.

"I get it," Oliver says. "Nick-olai Gogol."

"I can't believe you've kept this from us, Nick," Astrid chides.

"What in the world made your parents choose that name?" Donald wants to know.

He thinks back to the story he cannot bring himself to tell these people, at once as vivid and as elusive as it's always been: the capsized train in the middle of the night, his father's arm sticking through a window, the crumpled page of a book clutched in his fist. It's a story he'd told Moushumi, in the months after they'd first met. He'd told her of the accident, and then he'd told her about the night his father had told him, in the driveway at Pemberton Road. He'd confessed to her that he still felt guilty at times for changing his name, more so now that his father was dead. And she'd assured him that it was understandable, that anyone in his place would have done the same. But now it's become a joke to her. Suddenly he regrets having ever told Moushumi; he wonders whether she'll proclaim the story of his father's accident to the table as well. By morning, half the people in the room will have forgotten. It will be a tiny, odd fact about him, an anecdote, perhaps, for a future dinner party. This is what upsets him most.

"My father was a fan," he says finally.

"Then maybe we should call the baby Verdi," Donald muses, just as the opera surges to its closing bars, and the tape ends with a click.

"You're not helping," Astrid says, petulant, kissing Donald on the nose. Gogol watches them, knowing that it's all in jest — they're not the type to do something so impulsive, so naive, to blunder, as his own parents had done.

"Relax," Edith says. "The perfect name will come to you in time."

Which is when Gogol announces, "There's no such thing."

"No such thing as what?" Astrid says.

"There's no such thing as a perfect name. I think that human beings should be allowed to name themselves when they turn eighteen," he adds. "Until then, pronouns."

People shake their heads dismissively. Moushumi shoots him a look that he ignores. The salad is served. The conversation takes a new turn, carries on without him. And yet he can't help but recall a novel he'd once picked up from the pile on Moushumi's side of the bed, an English translation of something French, in which the main characters were simply referred to, for hundreds of pages, as He and She. He had read it in a matter of hours, oddly relieved that the names of the characters were never revealed. It had been an unhappy love story. If only his own life were so simple.

10.

1999

On the morning of their first anniversary, Moushumi's parents call, waking them, wishing them a happy anniversary before they've had the chance to say it to each other. In addition to their anniversary, there is something else to celebrate: Moushumi successfully passed her orals the week before, is now officially ABD. There's a third thing worth celebrating but which she hasn't mentioned — she's been awarded a research fellowship to work on her dissertation in France for the year. She'd applied for the grant secretly, just before the wedding, simply curious to see if she'd get it. It was always good practice, she'd reasoned, to strive for such things. Two years ago she would have said yes on the spot. But it's no longer possible to fly off to France for the year, now that she has a husband, a marriage, to consider. So when the good news came she decided it was easier to decline the fellowship quietly, to file away the letter, not to bring it up.

She's taken the initiative for the evening, making reservations at a place in midtown, which Donald and Astrid have recommended. She feels a bit guilty for all these months of studying, aware that with her exams as an excuse, she has ignored Nikhil perhaps more than necessary. There were nights that she told him she was at her carrel in the library when really she'd met Astrid and her baby, Esme, in SoHo, or gone for a walk by herself. Sometimes she would sit at a restaurant alone, at the bar, ordering sushi or a sandwich and a glass of wine, simply to remind herself that she was still capable of being on her own. This assurance is important to her; along with the Sanskrit vows she'd repeated at her wedding, she'd privately vowed that she'd never grow fully dependent on her husband, as her mother has. For even after thirty-two years abroad, in England and now in America, her mother does not know how to drive, does not have a job, does not know the difference between a checking and a savings account. And yet she is a perfectly intelligent woman, was an honors student in philology at Presidency College before she was married off at twenty-two.

They've both dressed up for the occasion — when she emerges from the bathroom she sees that he is wearing the shirt she's given him, moss-colored with a velvet Nehru collar of slightly darker green. It was only after the salesman had wrapped it that she'd remembered the rule about giving paper on the first anniversary. She considered saving the shirt for Christmas, going to Rizzoli and buying him an architecture book instead. But there hasn't been the time. She is wearing the black dress she'd worn the first time he'd come to dinner, the first time they'd slept together, and over it, a lilac pashmina shawl, Nikhil's anniversary present to her. She still remembers their very first date, liking the slightly untamed look of his hair as he'd approached her at the bar, the dark pine stubble on his cheeks, the shirt he'd worn with green stripes and thinner stripes of lavender, the collar beginning to fray. She still remembers her bewilderment, looking up from her book and seeing him, her heart skipping, feeling the attraction instantly, powerfully, in her chest. For she had been expecting an older version of the boy she remembered, distant, quiet, in corduroy jeans and a sweatshirt, a few pimples dotting his chin. The day before the date, she'd had lunch with Astrid. "I just don't see you with some Indian guy," Astrid had said dismissively over salads at City Bakery. At the time Moushumi had not protested, maintaining apologetically that it was just one date. She'd been deeply skeptical herself — apart from the young Shashi Kapoor and a cousin in India, she had never until then found herself attracted to an Indian man. But she'd genuinely liked Nikhil. She'd liked that he was neither a doctor nor an engineer. She'd liked that he'd changed his name from Gogol to Nikhil; though she'd known him all those years, it was a thing that made him somehow new, not the person her mother had mentioned.

They decide to walk to the restaurant, thirty blocks north of their apartment, four blocks west. Though it's dark already, the evening is pleasantly warm, so much so that she hesitates under the awning of their building, wondering if the pashmina is necessary. She has nowhere to put it, her evening bag is too small. She lets the shawl drop from her shoulders, gathers it up in her hands.

"Maybe I should leave this upstairs."

"What if we want to walk back?" he says. "You'll probably need it then."

"I guess."

"It looks nice on you, by the way."

"Do you remember this dress?"

He shakes his head. She's disappointed but not surprised. By now she's learned that his architect's mind for detail fails when it comes to everyday things. For example, he had not bothered to hide the receipt for the shawl, leaving it, along with change emptied from his pocket, on top of the bureau they share. She can't really blame him for not remembering. She herself can no longer remember the exact date of that evening. It had been a

Saturday in November. But now those landmarks in their courtship have faded, have given way to the occasion they are now celebrating.

They walk up Fifth Avenue, past the stores that sell Oriental carpets, unfurled in illuminated windows. Past the public library. Instead of proceeding to the restaurant, they decide to wander up the sidewalk for a while; there are still twenty minutes before their reservation. Fifth Avenue is eerily uncluttered, only a handful of people and cabs in a neighborhood usually choked with shoppers and tourists. She comes here seldom, only to buy make-up at Bendel's, or to see the odd movie at the Paris, and once, with Graham and his father and stepmother, to have drinks at the Plaza. They walk past the windows of closed shops displaying watches, luggage, trench coats. A pair of turquoise sandals causes Moushumi to stop. The shoes are arranged on a Lucite pedestal, glowing under a spotlight, the gladiator-style straps festooned with rhinestones.

"Ugly or beautiful?" she asks him. It is a question she poses to him often, as they leaf together through apartments featured in *Architectural Digest* or the design section of the *Times* magazine. Often his answers surprise her, convincing her to appreciate an object she would have otherwise dismissed.

"I'm pretty certain they're ugly. But I would have to see them on."

"I agree. Guess how much they cost," she says.

"Two hundred dollars."

"Five. Can you believe it? I saw them featured in *Vogue*."

She begins to walk away. After a few paces she turns back and sees that he's still standing there, bent down to see if there's a price tag on the bottom of the shoe. There is something at once innocent and irreverent about the gesture, and she is reminded, forcefully, of why she still loves him. It reminds her of how grateful she'd felt when he'd reappeared in her life. By the time she'd met him she'd begun to fear that she was retreating into her former self, before Paris — untouched, bookish, alone. She recalled the panic she'd felt, all her friends married. She'd even considered placing a personal ad. But he had accepted her, had obliterated her former disgrace. She believed that he would be incapable of hurting her as Graham had. After years of clandestine relationships, it felt refreshing to court in a fishbowl, to have the support of her parents from the very start, the inevitability of an unquestioned future, of marriage, drawing them along. And yet the familiarity that had once drawn her to him has begun to keep her at bay. Though she knows it's not his fault, she can't help but associate him, at times, with a sense of resignation, with the very life she had resisted, had struggled so mightily to leave behind. He was not who she saw herself ending up with, he had never been that person. Perhaps for those very reasons, in those early months, being with him, falling in love with him, doing precisely what had been expected of her for her entire life, had felt forbidden, wildly transgressive, a breach of her own instinctive will.

They can't find the restaurant at first. Though they have the exact address, written on a slip of folded paper in Moushumi's evening bag, it leads them only to a suite of offices in a town house. They press the buzzer, peer through the glass door into the empty, carpeted foyer, at a big vase of flowers at the foot of the stairs.

"It can't be this," she says, putting her hands up to the glass, shielding either side of her face in order to block out the glare.

"Are you sure you wrote down the address right?" Gogol asks.

They wander partway up and down the block, look on the other side. They return to the town house, looking up at the darkened windows for signs of life.

"There it is," he says, noticing a couple emerging from a basement door below the steps. There, in an entryway lit by a single sconce, they find a plaque nailed discreetly into the facade of the building bearing the restaurant's name, Antonia. A small fleet gathers to welcome them, to tick their names off a list at a podium, to lead them to their table. The fuss feels unwarranted as they step into a stark, sunken dining room. The atmosphere is somber, vaguely abandoned, as the streets had been. There is a family eating after the theater, she guesses, the two small daughters in absurdly fancy dresses with petticoats and large lacy collars. There are a few wealthy-looking middle-aged couples in suits. A well-dressed elderly gentleman is dining alone. She finds it suspicious that there are so many empty tables, that no music plays. She'd been hoping for something more bustling, warmer. Given that it's subterranean, the place seems surprisingly vast, the ceilings high. The air-conditioning is too strong, chilling her bare legs and arms. She wraps the pashmina tightly around her shoulders.

"I'm freezing. Do you think they'd turn down the AC if I asked?"

"I doubt that. Would you like my jacket?" Nikhil offers.

"No, it's okay." She smiles at him. And yet she feels uncomfortable, depressed. She is depressed by the pair of teenaged Bangladeshi busboys who wear tapestry waistcoats and black trousers, serving them warm bread with silver tongs. It annoys her that the waiter, perfectly attentive, looks neither of them in the eye as he describes the menu, speaking instead to the bottle of mineral water positioned between them. She knows it's too late to change their plans now. But even after they place their order, a part of her has a nagging urge, feels like standing up, leaving. She had done something similar a few weeks ago, sitting in the chair of an expensive hair salon, walking out after the apron had been tied behind her neck, while the stylist had gone to check on another client, simply because something about the stylist's manner, the bored expression on her face as she'd lifted a lock of Moushumi's hair and studied it in the mirror, had felt insulting. She wonders what Donald and Astrid like about this place, decides it must be the food. But when it arrives, it too disappoints her. The meal, served on square white plates, is fussily arranged, the portions microscopically small. As usual they trade plates partway through the meal, but this time she doesn't like the taste of his so she sticks to her own. She finishes her entree of scallops too quickly, sits for a very long time, it seems, watching Nikhil work his way through his quail.

"We shouldn't have come here," she says suddenly, frowning.

"Why not?" He looks approvingly around the room. "It's nice enough."

"I don't know. It's not what I thought it would be."

"Let's just enjoy ourselves."

But she is not able to enjoy herself. As

they near the end of the meal, it occurs to her that she is neither very drunk nor full. In spite of two cocktails and the bottle of wine they'd shared she feels distressingly sober. She looks at the hair-thin quail bones Nikhil has discarded on his plate and is faintly repulsed, wishing he'd finish so that she could light her after-dinner cigarette.

"Madam, your shawl," one of the busboys says, picking it up from the floor and handing it to her.

"Sorry," she says, feeling clumsy, unkempt. Then she notices that her black dress is coated with lilac fibers. She brushes at the material, but the fibers cling stubbornly, like cat hair.

"What's the matter?" Nikhil asks, looking up from his plate.

"Nothing," she says, not wanting to hurt his feelings, to find fault with his costly gift.

They are the last of the diners to leave. It's been wildly expensive, far more than they'd expected. They put down a credit card. Watching Nikhil sign the receipt, she feels cheap all of a sudden, irritated that they have to leave such a generous tip though there had been no real reason to fault the waiter's performance. She notices that a number of tables have already been cleared, chairs placed upside down on their surfaces.

"I can't believe they're already stripping the tables."

He shrugs. "It's late. They probably close early on Sundays."

"You'd think they could wait for us to leave," she says. She feels a lump form in her throat, tears filming her eyes.

"Moushumi, what's wrong? Is there something you want to talk about?"

She shakes her head. She doesn't feel like explaining. She wants to be home, crawl into bed, put the evening behind her. Outside, she's relieved that it's drizzling, so that instead of walking back to the apartment as they'd planned they can hail a cab.

"Are you sure nothing's wrong?" he says as they are riding home. He's beginning to lose patience with her, she can tell.

"I'm still hungry," she says, looking out the window, at the restaurants still open at this hour — brashly lit diners with specials scrawled on paper plates, cheap calzone places with sawdust-coated floors, the type of restaurants she would never think to enter normally but which look suddenly enticing. "I could eat a pizza."

Two days later, a new semester begins. It's Moushumi's eighth semester at NYU. She is finished with classes, will never in her life take a class again. Never again will she sit for an exam. This fact delights her — finally, a formal emancipation from studenthood. Though she still has a dissertation to write, still has an adviser to monitor her progress, she feels un-moored already, somehow beyond the world that has defined and structured and limited her for so long. This is the third time she's taught the class. Beginning French, Mondays, Wednesdays, and Fridays, a total of three hours a week. All she's had to do is look ahead in her calendar and change the date of the class meetings. Her biggest effort will be to learn her students' names. She is always flattered when they assume she herself is French, or half-French. She enjoys their looks of disbelief when she tells them she is from New Jersey, born to Bengali parents.

Moushumi's been given an eight a.m. section, something that had annoyed her at first. But now that she's up, showered, dressed, walking down the street, a latte from the deli on their block in one hand, she's invigorated. Being out at this hour already feels like an accomplishment. When she'd left the apartment, Nikhil had still been asleep, undisturbed by the persistent beeping of the alarm. The night before, she'd laid out her clothes, her papers, something she had not done since she was a girl preparing for school. She likes walking through the streets so early, had liked rising by herself in semidarkness, liked the sense of promise it lent the day. It's a pleasant change from their usual routine — Nikhil showered, in his suit, flying out the door as she's just pouring herself a first cup of coffee. She's thankful not to have to face her desk in the corner of their bedroom first thing, surrounded as it is by sacks full of dirty clothes they keep meaning to drop off at the laundry but get around to only once a month, when buying new socks and underwear becomes necessary. Moushumi wonders how long she will live her life with the trappings of studenthood in spite of the fact that she is a married woman, that she's as far along in her studies as she is, that Nikhil has a respectable if not terribly lucrative job. It would have been different with Graham — he'd made more than enough money for the both of them. And yet that, too, had been frustrating, causing her to fear that her career was somehow an indulgence, unnecessary. Once she has a job, a real full-time tenure-track job, she reminds herself, things will be different. She imagines where that first job might take her, assumes it will be in some far-flung town in the middle of nowhere. Sometimes she jokes with Nikhil about their having to pick up and move, in a few years, to Iowa, to Kalamazoo. But they both know it's out of the question for him to leave New York, that she will be the one to fly back and forth on weekends. There is something appealing to her about this prospect, to make a clean start in a place where no one knows her, as she had done in Paris. It's the one thing about her parents' lives she truly admires — their ability, for better or for worse, to turn their back on their homes.

As she approaches the department she sees that something is wrong. An ambulance is parked on the sidewalk, the doors at the back flung open. Static crackles from a paramedic's walkie-talkie. She peeks into the ambulance as she crosses the street, sees the resuscitative equipment but no people. The sight causes her to shudder nevertheless. Upstairs, the hallway is crowded. She wonders who's hurt, whether it's a student or a professor. She recognizes no one, only a group of bewildered-looking freshmen bearing add-drop forms. "I think someone fainted," people are saying. "I have no idea." A door opens and they are told to make way. She expects to see someone in a wheelchair, is startled to see a body covered by a sheet, being carried out on a stretcher. A number of onlookers cry out in alarm. Moushumi's hand goes to her mouth. Half the crowd is looking down, away, shaking their heads. From the splayed feet at one end of the stretcher, wearing a pair of beige flat-heeled shoes, she can tell that it's a woman. From a professor, she learns what happened: Alice, the administrative assistant, had fallen suddenly by the mailboxes. One minute she was sorting campus mail, the next minute she was out cold. By the time the paramedics had arrived she was dead from an aneurysm. She was in her thirties, unmarried, perpetually sipping herbal tea. Moushumi had never been particularly fond of her. There had been a brittle quality to her, something unyielding, a young person who carried about her a premonition of old age.

Moushumi feels sick at the thought of it, of a death so sudden, of a woman so marginal and yet so central to her world. She enters the office she shares with the other TAs, empty now. She calls Nikhil at home, at work. No answer. She looks at her watch, realizes he must be on the subway, on his way to work. Suddenly she's glad he's unreachable — she's reminded of the way Nikhil's father had died, instantly, without warning. Surely this would remind him of that. She has the urge to leave campus, return to the apartment. But she has a class to teach in half an hour. She goes back to the Xerox room to copy her syllabus and a short passage from Flaubert to translate in class. She pushes the button to collate the syllabus but forgets to push the button for staples. She searches in the supply closet for a stapler, and when she fails to find one, goes instinctively to Alice's desk. The phone is ringing. A cardigan is draped over the back of the chair. She opens up Alice's drawer, afraid to touch anything. She finds a stapler behind paper clips and Sweet'N Low packets in the drawer. ALICE is written on masking tape stuck to the top. The faculty mailboxes are still half-empty, the mail piled in a bin.

Moushumi goes to her mailbox to look for her class roster. Her box is empty, so she roots through the bin for her mail. As she picks up each piece of mail, addressed to this or that faculty member or TA, she begins putting it into the appropriate box, matching name to name. Even after she's found her roster, she continues, completing the task Alice left undone. The mindlessness soothes her nerves. As a child she always had a knack for organization; she would take it upon herself to neaten closets and drawers, not only her own but her parents' as well. She had organized the cutlery drawer, the refrigerator. These self-appointed tasks would occupy her during quiet, hot days of her summer vacation, and her mother would look on in disbelief, sipping watermelon sherbet in front of the fan. There are just a handful of items left in the bin. She bends over to pick them up. And then another name, a sender's name typed in the upper left-hand corner of a business-sized envelope, catches her eye.

She takes the stapler and the letter and the rest of her things into her office. She shuts the door, sits at her desk. The envelope is addressed to a professor of Comparative Literature who teaches German as well as French. She opens the envelope. Inside she finds a cover letter and a résumé. For a minute she simply stares at the name centered at the top of the résumé, laser-printed in an elegant font. She remembers the name, of course. The name alone, when she'd first learned it, had been enough to seduce her. Dimitri Desjardins. He pronounced Desjardins the English way, the *s*'s intact, and in spite of her training in French this is how she still thinks of it. Underneath the name is an address on West 164th Street. He is looking for an adjunct position, teaching German part-time. She reads through the résumé, learns exactly where he's been and what he's done for the past decade. Travels in Europe. A job working with the BBC. Articles and reviews published in *Der Spiegel*, *Critical Inquiry*. A Ph.D. in German literature from the University of Heidelberg.

She had met him years ago, in her final months of high school. It was a period in which she and two of her friends, in their eagerness to be college students, in desperation over the fact that no one their own age was interested in dating them, would drive to Princeton, loiter on the campus, browse in the college bookstore, do their homework in buildings they could enter without an ID. Her parents had encouraged these expeditions, believing she was at the library, or attending lectures — they hoped she would go to Princeton for college, live with them at home. One day, as she and her friends were sitting on the grass, they were invited to join a student coalition from the university, a coalition protesting apartheid in South Africa. The group was planning a march on Washington, calling for sanctions.

They took a chartered overnight bus to D.C. in order to be at the rally by early morning. Each of them had lied to their parents, claiming to be sleeping over at one another's homes. Everyone on the bus was smoking pot and listening to the same Crosby, Stills, and Nash album continuously, on a tape player running on batteries. Moushumi had been facing backward, leaning over and talking to her friends, who were in the two seats behind her, and when she turned back around he was in the neighboring seat. He seemed aloof from the rest of the group, not an actual member of the coalition, somehow dismissive of it all. He was wiry, slight, with small, downward-sloping eyes and an intellectual, ravaged-looking face that she found sexy though not handsome. His hairline was already receding, his hair curly and fair. He needed a shave; his fingernails needed paring. He was wearing a white button-down shirt, faded Levi's with threadbare knees, pliable gold-framed spectacles that wrapped around his ears. Without introducing himself he began talking to her, as if they were already acquainted. He was twenty-seven, had gone to Williams College, was a student of European history. He was taking a German course at Princeton now, living with his parents, both of whom taught at the university, and he was going out of his mind. He had spent the years after college traveling around Asia, Latin America. He told her he probably wanted to get a Ph.D., eventually. The randomness of all this had appealed to her. He asked her what her name was and when she told him he had leaned toward her, cupping his ear, even though she knew he had heard it perfectly well. "How in the world do you spell that?" he'd asked, and when she told him, he mispronounced it, as most people did. She corrected him, saying that "Mou" rhymed with "toe," but he shook his head and said, "I'll just call you Mouse."

The nickname had irritated and pleased her at the same time. It made her feel foolish, but she was aware that in renaming her he had claimed her somehow, already made her his own. As the bus grew quiet, as everyone began to fall asleep, she had let him lean his head against her shoulder. Dimitri was asleep, or so she thought. And so she pretended to fall asleep too. After a while she felt his hand on her leg, on top of the white denim skirt she was wearing. And then slowly, he began to unbutton the skirt. Several minutes passed between his undoing of one button and the next, his eyes closed all the while, his head still on her shoulder, as the bus hurtled down the empty, dark highway. It was the first time in her life a man had touched her. She held herself perfectly still. She was desperate to touch him too, but she was terrified. Finally Dimitri opened his eyes. She felt his mouth near her ear, and she turned to him, prepared to be kissed, at seventeen, for the very first time. But he had not kissed her. He had only looked at her, and said, "You're going to break hearts, you know." And then he leaned back, in his own seat this time, removed his hand from her lap, and closed his eyes once again. She had stared at him in disbelief, angry that he assumed she hadn't broken any hearts yet, and at the same time flattered. For the rest of the journey she kept her skirt unbuttoned, hoping he would return to the task. But he didn't touch her after that, and in the morning there was no acknowledgment of what had passed between them. At the demonstration he had wandered off, paid her no attention. On the way back they had sat apart.

Afterward she returned to the university every day to try to run into him. After some weeks she saw him striding across campus, alone, holding a copy of *The Man Without Qualities*. They shared some coffee and sat on a bench outside. He had asked her to see a movie, Goddard's *Alphaville*, and to have

Chinese food. She had worn an outfit that still causes her to wince, an old blazer of her father's that was too long for her, over jeans, the sleeves of the blazer rolled up as if it were a shirt, to reveal the striped lining inside. It had been the first date of her life, strategically planned on an evening her parents were at a party. She recalled nothing of the movie, had eaten nothing at the restaurant, part of a small shopping complex off Route 1. And then, after watching Dimitri eat both of their fortune cookies without reading either prediction, she had made her error: she had asked him to be her date to her senior prom. He had declined, driven her home, kissed her lightly on her cheek in the driveway, and then he never called her again. The evening had humiliated her; he had treated her like a child. Sometime over the summer she bumped into him at the movies. He was with a date, a tall freckled girl with hair to her waist. Moushumi had wanted to flee, but he'd made a point of introducing her to the girl. "This is Moushumi," Dimitri had said deliberately, as if he'd been waiting for the opportunity to say her name for weeks. He told her he was going to Europe for a while, and from the look on the date's face she realized that she was going with him. Moushumi told him she'd been accepted at Brown. "You look great," he told her when the date wasn't listening.

While she was at Brown, postcards would arrive from time to time, envelopes plastered with colorful, oversized stamps. His handwriting was minuscule but sloppy, always causing her eyes to strain. There was never a return address. For a time she carried these letters in her book bag, to her classes, thickening her agenda. Periodically he sent her books he'd read and thought she might like. A few times he called in the middle of the night, waking her, and she spoke to him for hours in the dark, lying in bed in her dorm room, then sleeping through her morning classes. A single call kept her sailing for weeks. "I'll come visit you. I'll take you to dinner," he told her. He never did. Eventually the letters tapered off. His last communication had been a box of books, along with several postcards he'd written to her in Greece and Turkey but not managed to send at the time. And then she'd moved to Paris.

She reads Dimitri's résumé again, then the cover letter. The letter reveals nothing other than earnest pedagogical intent, mentions a panel Dimitri and the professor to whom it's addressed attended some years ago. Practically the same letter exists in a file on her computer. His third sentence is missing a period, which she now carefully inserts with her finest-nibbed fountain pen. She can't bring herself to write down his address, though she doesn't want to forget it. In the Xerox room,

399

she makes a copy of the résumé. She sticks it in the bottom of her bag. Then she types up a new envelope and puts the original in the professor's mailbox. As she returns to her office, she realizes there's no stamp or postmark on the new envelope, worries that the professor will suspect something. But she reassures herself that Dimitri could easily have delivered the letter personally; the idea of him standing in the department, occupying the same space she occupies now, fills her with the same combination of desperation and lust he's always provoked.

The hardest part is deciding where to write down the phone number, in what part of her agenda. She wishes she had a code of some sort. In Paris she had briefly dated an Iranian professor of philosophy who would write the names of his students in Persian on the backs of index cards, along with some small, cruel detail to help him distinguish among them. Once he read the cards to Moushumi. Bad skin, one said. Thick ankles, said another. Moushumi can't resort to such trickery, can't write in Bengali. She barely remembers how to write her own name, something her grandmother had once taught her. Finally she writes it on the *D* page, but she doesn't include his name beside it. Just the numbers, disembodied, don't feel like a betrayal. They could be anybody's. She looks outside. As she sits down at her desk, her eye travels upward; the window in the office reaches the top of the wall, so that the rooftop of the building across the street stretches across the bottom edge of the sill. The view induces the opposite of vertigo, a lurching feeling inspired not by gravity's pull to earth, but by the infinite reaches of heaven.

At home that night, after dinner, Moushumi hunts among the shelves in the living room she and Nikhil share. Their books have merged since they've gotten married, Nikhil had unpacked them all, and nothing is where she expects it to be. Her eyes pass over stacks of Nikhil's design magazines, thick books on Gropius and Le Corbusier. Nikhil, bent over a blueprint at the dining table, asks what she's looking for.

"Stendhal," she tells him. It's not a lie. An old Modern Library edition of *The Red and the Black* in English, inscribed to Mouse. Love Dimitri, he'd written. It was the one book he'd inscribed to her. Back then it was the closest thing she'd ever had to a love letter; for months she had slept with the book under her pillow, and later, slipped it between her mattress and box spring. Somehow she managed to hold on to it for years; it's moved with her from Providence to Paris to New York, a secret talisman on her shelves that she would glance at now and again, still faintly flattered by his peculiar pursuit of her, and always faintly curious as to what had become of him. But now that she's desperate to locate the book she's convinced that it won't be in the apartment, that maybe Graham had taken it by mistake when he'd moved out of their place on York Avenue, or that it's in the basement of her parents' house, in one of the boxes she'd shipped there a few years ago, when her shelves were getting too full. She doesn't remember packing it from her old apartment, doesn't remember unpacking it when she and Nikhil moved in together. She wishes she could ask Nikhil if he's seen it — a small green clothbound book missing its dust jacket, the title embossed in a rectangle of black on the spine. And then suddenly she sees it herself, sitting in plain view, on a shelf she'd scanned a minute ago. She opens the book, sees the Modern Library emblem, the dashing, naked, torch-bearing figure. She sees the inscription, the force of the ballpoint pen he'd used slightly crimping the other side of the page. She'd abandoned the novel after the second chapter. Her place is still marked by a yellowing receipt for shampoo. By now she's read the book in French three times. She finishes Scott-Moncrieff's English translation within days, reading it at her desk in the department, and in her carrel in the library. In the evenings, at home, she reads it in bed until Nikhil comes in to join her —

then she puts it away and opens something else.

She calls him the following week. By then she's dug up the postcards, saved in an unsealed, unmarked manila envelope in the box where she keeps her tax returns, and read them, too, amazed that his words, the sight of his handwriting, still manage to discombobulate her. She tells herself she's calling an old friend. She tells herself the coincidence of finding his résumé, of stumbling upon him in this way, is too great, that anyone in her position would pick up the phone and call. She tells herself he could very well be married, as she is. Perhaps all four of them will go out to dinner, become great friends. Still, she doesn't tell Nikhil about the résumé. One night in her office, after seven o'clock when only a janitor roams the halls, after a few sips from the small bottle of Maker's Mark she has stashed at the back of her file cabinet, she calls. A night Nikhil thinks she's working on revisions for an article for *PMLA*.

She dials the number, listens as it rings four times. She wonders if he'll even remember her. Her heart races. Her finger moves to the cradle, ready to press down.

"Hello?"

It's his voice. "Hi. Dimitri?"

"Speaking. Who's this?"

She pauses. She can still hang up if she wants. "It's Mouse."

They begin seeing each other Mondays and Wednesdays, after she teaches her class. She takes the train uptown and they meet at his apartment, where lunch is waiting. The meals are ambitious: poached fish; creamy potato gratins; golden, puffed chickens roasted with whole lemons in their cavities. There is always a bottle of wine. They sit at a table with his books and papers and laptop pushed to one side. They listen to WQXR, drink coffee and cognac and smoke a cigarette afterward. Only then does he touch her. Sunlight streams through large dirty windows into the shabby prewar apartment. There are two spacious rooms, flaking plaster walls, scuffed parquet floors, towering stacks of boxes he has not yet bothered to unpack. The bed, a brand-new mattress and box spring on wheels, is never made. After sex they are always amazed to discover that the bed has moved several inches away from the wall, pushing up against the bureau on the other side of the room. She likes the way he looks at her when their limbs are still tangled together, out of breath as if he'd been chasing her, his expression anxious before relaxing into a smile. Some gray has come into Dimitri's hair and chest, some lines around the mouth and eyes. He's heavier than before, his stomach undeniably wide, so that his thin legs appear slightly comic. He recently turned thirty-nine. He has not been married. He does not seem very desperate to be employed. He spends his days cooking meals, reading, listening to classical music. She gathers that he has inherited some money from his grandmother.

The first time they met, the day after she called him, at the bar of a crowded Italian restaurant near NYU, they had not been able to stop staring at each other, not been able to stop talking about the résumé, and the uncanny way it had fallen into Moushumi's hands. He had moved to New York only a month ago, had tried to look her up but the phone is listed under Nikhil's last name. It didn't matter, they agreed. It was better this way. They drank glasses of prosecco. She agreed to an early dinner with Dimitri that night, sitting at the bar of the restaurant, for the prosecco had gone quickly to their heads. He had ordered a salad topped with warm lambs' tongue, a poached egg, and pecorino cheese, something she swore she would not touch but ended up eating the better part of. Afterward she'd gone into Balducci's to buy the pasta and ready-made vodka sauce she would have at home with Nikhil.

On Mondays and Wednesdays no one knows where she is. There are no Bengali fruit sellers to greet her on the walk from

Dimitri's subway stop, no neighbors to recognize her once she turns onto Dimitri's block. It reminds her of living in Paris — for a few hours at Dimitri's she is inaccessible, anonymous. Dimitri is not terribly curious about Nikhil, does not ask her his name. He expresses no jealousy. When she told him in the Italian restaurant that she was married, his expression had not changed. He regards their time together as perfectly normal, as destined, and she begins to see how easy it is. Moushumi refers to Nikhil in conversation as "my husband": "My husband and I have a dinner to go to next Thursday." "My husband's given me this cold."

At home, Nikhil suspects nothing. As usual they have dinner, talk of their days. They clean up the kitchen together, then sit on the sofa and watch television while she corrects her students' quizzes and exercises. During the eleven o'clock news, they have bowls of Ben and Jerry's, then brush their teeth. As usual they get into bed, kiss, then slowly they turn away from each other in order to stretch comfortably into sleep. Only Moushumi stays awake. Each Monday and Wednesday night, she fears that he will sense something, that he will put his arms around her and instantly know. She stays awake for hours after they've turned out the lights, prepared to answer him, prepared to lie to his face. She had gone shopping, she would tell him if he were to ask, for in fact she had done this on her way home that first Monday, halting her journey back from Dimitri's in midstream, getting out of the subway at 72nd Street before continuing downtown, stopping in a store she'd never been in, buying a pair of the most ordinary-looking black shoes.

One night it's worse than usual. It's three o'clock, then four. Construction work has been taking place for the past few nights on their street, giant bins of rubble and concrete are moved and crushed, and Moushumi feels angry at Nikhil for being able to sleep through it. She's tempted to get up, pour herself a drink, take a bath, anything. But fatigue keeps her in bed. She watches the shadows that the passing traffic throws onto their ceiling, listens to a truck wailing in the distance like a solitary, nocturnal beast. She is convinced she will be up to see the sun rise. But somehow she falls asleep again. She is woken just after dawn by the sound of rain beating against the bedroom window, pelting it with such ferocity that she almost expects the glass to shatter. She has a splitting headache. She gets out of bed and parts the curtains, then returns to bed and shakes Nikhil awake. "Look," she says, pointing at the rain, as if it were something truly extraordinary. Nikhil obliges, fully asleep, sits upright, then closes his eyes again.

At seven-thirty she gets out of bed. The morning sky is clear. She walks out of the bedroom and sees that rain has leaked through the roof, left an unsightly yellow patch on the ceiling and puddles in the apartment: one in the bathroom, another in the front hall. The sill of a window left open in the living room is soaked, streaked with mud, as are the bills and books and papers piled on it. The sight of it makes her weep. At the same time she's thankful that there's something tangible for her to be upset about.

"Why are you crying?" Nikhil asks, squinting at her in his pajamas.

"There are cracks in the ceiling," she says.

Nikhil looks up. "They're not too bad. I'll call the super."

"The rainwater came right through the roof."

"What rain?"

"Don't you remember? It was pouring rain at dawn. It was incredible. I woke you."

But Nikhil doesn't remember a thing.

A month of Mondays and Wednesdays passes. She begins to see him on Fridays as well. One Friday she finds herself alone in Dimitri's apartment; he goes out as soon as she arrives, to buy a stick of butter for a white sauce he is making to pour over trout. Bartók plays on the stereo, expensive components scattered on the floor. She watches him from the window, walking down the block, a small, balding, unemployed middle-aged man, who is enabling her to wreck her marriage. She wonders if she is the only woman in her family ever to have betrayed her husband, to have been unfaithful. This is what upsets her most to admit: that the affair causes her to feel strangely at peace, the complication of it calming her, structuring her day. After the first time, washing up in the bathroom, she'd been horrified by what she'd done, at the sight of her clothes scattered throughout the two rooms. Before leaving, she'd combed her hair in the bathroom mirror, the only one in the apartment. She'd kept her head bent low, glancing up only briefly at the end. When she did she saw that it was one of those mirrors that was for some reason particularly flattering, due to some trick of the light or the quality of the glass, causing her skin to glow.

There is nothing on Dimitri's walls. He is still living out of a series of mammoth duffel bags. She is glad not to be able to picture his life in all its detail, its mess. The only things he's set up are the kitchen, the stereo components, and some of his books. Each time she visits, there are modest signs of progress. She wanders around his living room, looks at the books he is beginning to organize on his plywood shelves. Apart from all the German, their personal libraries are similar. There is the same lime green spine of *The Princeton Encyclopedia of Poetry and Poetics.* The same edition of *Mimesis.* The same boxed set of Proust. She pulls out an oversized volume of photographs of Paris, by Atget. She sits on an armchair, Dimitri's only piece of living room furniture. It was here that she'd sat the first time she'd visited, and he'd stood behind her, massaging a spot on her shoulder, arousing her, until she stood up, and they'd walked together to the bed.

She opens up the book to regard the streets and the landmarks she once knew. She thinks of her wasted fellowship. A large square of sunlight appears on the floor. The sun is directly behind her, and the shadow of her head spreads across the thick, silken pages, a few strands of her hair strangely magnified, quivering, as if viewed through a microscope. She leans back her head, closes her eyes. When she opens them a moment later the sun has slipped away, a lone sliver of it now diminishing into the floorboards, like the gradual closing of a curtain, causing the stark white pages of the book to turn gray. She hears Dimitri's footsteps on the stairs, then the clean sound of his key in the lock, slicing sharply into the apartment. She gets up to put the book away, searching for the gap in which it had stood.

11.

Gogol wakes up late on a Sunday morning, alone, from a bad dream he cannot recall. He looks over at Moushumi's side of the bed, at the untidy pile of her books and magazines on the end table, the bottle of lavender room spray she likes to squirt sometimes on their pillows, the tortoiseshell barrette with strands of her hair caught in its clasp. She's at another conference this weekend, in Palm Beach. By tonight she'll be home. She claimed she'd told him about the conference months ago, but he doesn't remember. "Don't worry," she'd said as she was packing, "I won't be there long enough to get a tan." But when he'd seen her bathing suit on top of the clothing on the bed, a strange panic had welled up inside of him as he thought of her lying without him by a hotel pool, her eyes closed, a book at her side. At least one of us isn't cold, he thinks to himself now, crossing his arms tightly in front of his chest. Since yesterday afternoon the building's boiler has been broken, turning the apartment into an icebox. Last night he'd had to turn the oven on in order to tolerate being in the living room, and he'd worn his old Yale sweatpants, a thick sweater over a T-shirt, and a pair of rag-wool socks to bed. He throws back the comforter and the extra blanket he'd placed on top of it in the middle of the night. He couldn't find the blanket at first, nearly called Moushumi at the hotel to ask where she kept it. But by then it was nearly three in the morning, and so, eventually, he'd hunted it down himself, found it wedged on the top shelf of the hall closet, an unused wedding gift still in its zippered plastic case.

He gets out of bed, brushes his teeth with freezing-cold water from the tap, decides to skip shaving. He pulls on jeans and an extra sweater, and Moushumi's bathrobe over that, not caring how ridiculous he looks. He makes a pot of coffee, toasts some bread to eat with butter and jam. He opens the front door and retrieves the *Times*, removing the blue wrapper, putting it on the coffee table to read later. There is a drawing for work he must complete by tomorrow, a cross section for a high school auditorium in Chicago. He unrolls the plan from its tube and spreads it out on the dining table, securing the corners with paperback books he grabs off the bookcase. He puts on his *Abbey Road* CD, skipping ahead to the songs that would have been on side 2 of the album, and tries to work on the drawing, making sure his measurements correspond to the principal designer's notes. But his fingers are stiff and so he rolls up the plan, leaves a note for Moushumi on the kitchen counter, and goes in to the office.

He's glad to have an excuse to be out of the apartment, instead of waiting for her, at some point this evening, to return. It feels milder outside, the air pleasantly damp, and instead of taking the train he walks the thirty blocks, up Park Avenue and over to Madison. He is the only person at the office. He sits in the darkened drafting room, surrounded by the desks of his coworkers, some piled with drawings and models, others as neat as a pin. He crouches over his table, a single pool of light from a swinging metal lamp illuminating the large sheet of paper. Tacked to the wall over his desk is a tiny calendar showing the entire year, which is coming once again to a close. At the end of the week, it will be the fourth anniversary of his father's death. Circled dates indicate all his deadlines, past and future. Meetings, site visits, conferences with clients. A lunch with an architect who's interested, possibly, in hiring him. He's eager to move to a smaller firm, to have some domestic commissions, to work with fewer people. Next to the calendar there is a postcard of a Duchamp painting he has always loved, of a chocolate grinder that reminds him of a set of drums, suspended against a gray background. Several Post-it notes. The photograph of his mother and Sonia and himself at Fatehpur Sikri, salvaged from his father's refrigerator door in Cleveland. And next to this, a picture of Moushumi, an old passport photo he'd found and asked to keep. She is in her early twenties, her hair loose, her heavy-lidded eyes slightly lowered, looking to one side. It was taken before he'd begun to date her, when she was living in Paris. A time in her life in which he was still Gogol to her, a remnant from her past with little likelihood of appearing in her future. And yet they had met; after all her adventures, it was he whom she had married. He with whom she shared her life.

Last weekend was Thanksgiving. His mother and Sonia and Sonia's new boyfriend, Ben, had come, along with Moushumi's parents and brother, and they had all celebrated the holiday together in New York, crowded together in Gogol and Moushumi's apartment. It was the first time he had not gone either to his parents' or to his in-laws' for a holiday. It felt strange to be hosting, to assume the center of responsibility. They had ordered a fresh turkey in advance from the farmers' market, planned the menu out of *Food & Wine*, bought folding chairs so that everyone would have a place to sit. Moushumi had gone out and bought a rolling pin, made an apple pie for the first time in her life. For Ben's sake they had all spoken in English. Ben is half-

Jewish, half-Chinese, raised in Newton, close to where Gogol and Sonia grew up. He is an editor at the *Globe*. He and Sonia met by chance, at a café on Newbury Street. Seeing them together, sneaking into the hallway so that they could kiss freely, holding hands discreetly as they sat at the table, Gogol had been oddly envious, and as they all sat eating their turkey and roasted sweet potatoes and cornbread stuffing, and the spiced cranberry chutney his mother had made, he looked at Moushumi and wondered what was wrong. They didn't argue, they still had sex, and yet he wondered. Did he still make her happy? She accused him of nothing, but more and more he sensed her distance, her dissatisfaction, her distraction. But there had been no time to dwell on this worry. The weekend had been exhausting, getting their various family members to the apartments of nearby friends who were away and had given them keys. The day after Thanksgiving they had all gone to Jackson Heights, to the halal butcher so that both their mothers could stock up on goat meat, and then to brunch. And on Saturday there had been a concert of classical Indian music up at Columbia. Part of him wants to bring it up with her. "Are you happy you married me?" he would ask. But the fact that he is even thinking of this question makes him afraid.

He finishes up the drawing, leaves it

pinned on his desk to be reviewed in the morning. He's worked through lunch, and when he steps out of his office building it is colder, the light fading rapidly from the sky. He buys a cup of coffee and a falafel sandwich at the Egyptian restaurant on the corner and walks south as he eats, toward the Flatiron and lower Fifth Avenue, the twin towers of the World Trade Center looming in the distance, sparkling at the island's end. The falafel, wrapped in foil, is warm and messy in his hands. The stores are full, the windows decorated, the sidewalks crammed with shoppers. The thought of Christmas overwhelms him. Last year they went to Moushumi's parents' house. This year they'll go to Pemberton Road. He no longer looks forward to the holiday; he wants only to be on the other side of the season. His impatience makes him feel that he is, incontrovertibly, finally, an adult. He wanders absently into a perfume store, a clothing store, a store that sells only bags. He has no idea what to get Moushumi for Christmas. Normally she drops hints, showing him catalogues, but he has no clue as to what she's coveting this season, if it's a new pair of gloves or a wallet or new pajamas she'd like. In the maze of stalls in Union Square that sell candles and shawls and handmade jewelry, nothing inspires him.

He decides to try the Barnes and Noble at the northern edge of the square. But staring at the immense wall of new titles on display he realizes he has read none of these books, and what was the point of giving her something he hadn't read? On his way out of the store he pauses by a table devoted to travel guides. He picks up one for Italy, full of illustrations of the architecture he had studied so carefully as a student, has admired only in photographs, has always meant to see. It angers him, yet there is no one to blame but himself. What was stopping him? A trip together, to a place neither of them has been — maybe that's what he and Moushumi need. He could plan it all himself, select the cities they would visit, the hotels. It could be his Christmas gift to her, two airplane tickets tucked into the back of the guide. He was due for another vacation; he could plan it for her spring break. Inspired by the thought, he goes to the register, waits in a long line, and pays for the book.

He walks across the park toward home, thumbing through the book, anxious to see her now. He decides to stop off at the new gourmet grocery that's opened on Irving Place, to buy some of the things she likes: blood oranges, a wedge of cheese from the Pyrenees, slices of soppresata, a loaf of peasant bread. For she will be hungry — they serve nothing on planes these days. He looks up from the book, at the sky, at the darkness gathering, the clouds a deep, beautiful gold, and is momentarily stopped by a flock of pigeons flying dangerously close. Suddenly terrified, he ducks his head, feeling foolish afterward. None of the other pedestrians has reacted. He stops and watches as the birds shoot up, then land simultaneously on two neighboring bare-branched trees. He is unsettled by the sight. He has seen these graceless birds on windowsills and sidewalks, but never in trees. It looks almost unnatural. And yet, what could be more ordinary? He thinks of Italy, of Venice, the trip he will begin to plan. Maybe it's a sign that they are meant to go there. Wasn't the Piazza San Marco famous for its pigeons?

The lobby of the apartment is warm when he enters, the building's heat restored. "She just got back," the doorman tells Gogol with a wink as he walks past, and his heart leaps, unburdened of its malaise, grateful for her simple act of returning to him. He imagines her puttering around the apartment, drawing a bath, pouring herself a glass of wine, her bags in the hallway. He slips the book he will give her for Christmas into the pocket of his coat, making sure it's well concealed, and calls the elevator to take him upstairs.

12.

2000

It is the day before Christmas. Ashima Ganguli sits at her kitchen table, making mincemeat croquettes for a party she is throwing that evening. They are one of her specialties, something her guests have come to expect, handed to them on small plates within minutes of their arrival. Alone, she manages an assembly line of preparation. First she forces warm boiled potatoes through a ricer. Carefully she shapes a bit of the potato around a spoonful of cooked ground lamb, as uniformly as the white of a hard-boiled egg encases its yolk. She dips each of the croquettes, about the size and shape of a billiard ball, into a bowl of beaten eggs, then coats them on a plate of bread crumbs, shaking off the excess in her cupped palms. Finally she stacks the croquettes on a large circular tray, a sheet of wax paper between each layer. She stops to count how many she's made so far. She estimates three for each adult, one or two for each of the children. Counting the lines on the backs of her fingers, she reviews, once more, the exact number of her guests. Another dozen to be safe, she decides. She pours a fresh heap of bread crumbs on the plate, their color and texture reminding her of sand on a beach. She remembers making the first batches in her kitchen in Cambridge, for her very first parties, her husband at the stove in white drawstring pajamas and a T-shirt, frying the croquettes two at a time in a small blackened saucepan. She remembers Gogol and Sonia helping her when they were small, Gogol's hand wrapped around the can of crumbs, Sonia always wanting to eat the croquettes before they'd been breaded and fried.

This will be the last party Ashima will host at Pemberton Road. The first since her husband's funeral. The house in which she has lived for the past twenty-seven years, which she has occupied longer than any other in her life, has been recently sold, a Realtor's sign stuck into the lawn. The buyers are an American family, the Walkers, a young professor new to the university where her husband used to work, and a wife and daughter. The Walkers are planning renovations. They will knock down the wall between the living and dining rooms, put an island in the kitchen, track lights overhead. They want to pull up the wall-to-wall carpeting, convert the sun deck into a den. Listening to their plans, Ashima had felt a moment's panic, a protective instinct, wanting to retract her offer, wanting the house to remain as it's always been, as her husband had last seen it. But this had been sentimentality speaking. It is foolish for her to hope that the golden letters spelling GANGULI on the mailbox will not be peeled off, replaced. That Sonia's name, written in Magic Marker on the inside of her bedroom door, will not be sanded, restained. That the pencil markings on the wall by the linen closet, where Ashoke used to record his children's height on their birthdays, will not be painted over.

Ashima has decided to spend six months of her life in India, six months in the States. It is a solitary, somewhat premature version of the future she and her husband had planned when he was alive. In Calcutta, Ashima will live with her younger brother, Rana, and his wife, and their two grown, as yet unmarried daughters, in a spacious flat in Salt Lake. There she will have a room, the first in her life intended for her exclusive use. In spring and summer she will return to the Northeast, dividing her time among her son, her daughter, and her close Bengali friends. True to the meaning of her name, she will be without borders, without a home of her own, a resident everywhere and nowhere. But it's no longer possible for her to live here now that Sonia's going to be married. The wedding will be in Calcutta, a little over a year from now, on an auspicious January day, just as she and her husband were married nearly thirty-four years ago. Something tells her Sonia will be happy with this boy — quickly she corrects herself — this young man. He has brought happiness to her daughter, in a way Moushumi had never brought it to her son. That it was she who had encouraged Gogol to meet Moushumi will be something for which Ashima will always feel guilty. How could she have known? But fortunately they have not considered it their duty to stay married, as the Bengalis of Ashoke and Ashima's generation do. They are not willing to accept, to adjust, to settle for something less than their ideal of happiness. That pressure has given way, in the case of the subsequent generation, to American common sense.

For a few final hours she is alone in the house. Sonia has gone with Ben to pick up Gogol at the train station. It occurs to Ashima that the next time she will be by herself, she will be traveling, sitting on the plane. For the first time since her flight to meet her husband in Cambridge, in the winter of 1967, she will make the journey entirely on her own. The prospect no longer terrifies her. She has learned to do things on her own, and though she still wears saris, still puts her long hair in a bun, she is not the same Ashima who had once lived in Calcutta. She will return to India with an American passport. In her wallet will remain her Massachusetts driver's license, her social security card. She will return to a world where she will not single-handedly throw parties for dozens of people. She will not have to go to the trouble of making yogurt from half-and-half and sandesh from ricotta cheese. She will not have to make her own croquettes. They will be available to her from restaurants, brought up to the flat by servants, bearing a taste that after all these years she has still not quite managed, to her entire satisfaction, to replicate.

She finishes breading the final croquette, then glances at her wristwatch. She is slightly ahead of schedule. She sets the platter on the counter next to the stove. She takes a pan out of the cupboard and pours in the oil, several cupfuls, to be heated in the minutes before her guests are expected. From a crock she selects the slotted spatula she will use. For now, there is nothing left to be done. The rest of the food has been prepared, sitting in long CorningWare pans on the dining room table: dal coated with a thick skin that will rupture as soon as the first of it is served, a roasted cauliflower dish, eggplant, a korma of lamb. Sweet yogurt and pantuas for dessert sit on the sideboard. She eyes everything with anticipation. Normally cooking for parties leaves her without an appetite, but tonight she looks forward to serving herself, sitting among her guests. With Sonia's help the house has been cleaned one last time. Ashima has always loved these hours before a party, the carpets vacuumed, the coffee table wiped with Pledge, her dimmed, blurry reflection visible in the wood just as the old television commercial used to promise.

She roots through her kitchen drawer for a packet of incense. She lights a stick by the flame of the stove and walks from room to room. It's gratified her to go to all this effort — to make a final, celebratory meal for her children, her friends. To decide on a menu, to make a list and shop in the supermarket and fill the refrigerator shelves with food. It's a pleasant change of pace, something finite in contrast to her current, overwhelming, ongoing task: to prepare for her departure, picking the bones of the house clean. For the past month, she has been dismantling her household piece by piece. Each evening she has tackled a drawer, a closet, a set of shelves. Though Sonia offers to help, Ashima prefers to do this alone. She has made piles of things to give to Gogol and Sonia, things to give to friends, things to take with her, things to donate to charities, things to put into trash bags and drive to the dump. The task both saddens and satisfies her at the same time. There is a thrill to whittling down her possessions to little more than what she'd come with, to those three rooms in Cam-

424

bridge in the middle of a winter's night. To-night she will invite friends to take whatever might be useful, lamps, plants, platters, pots and pans. Sonia and Ben will rent a truck and take whatever furniture they have room for.

She goes upstairs to shower and change. The walls now remind her of the house when they'd first moved in, bare except for the photograph of her husband, which will be the last thing she will remove. She pauses for a moment, waving the remains of the incense in front of Ashoke's image before throwing the stick away. She lets the water run in the shower, turns up the thermostat to compen-sate for the terrible moment when she will have to step onto the mat on the bathroom floor, unclothed. She gets into her beige bathtub, behind the crackled sliding glass doors. She is exhausted from two days of cooking, from her morning of cleaning, from these weeks of packing and dealing with the sale of the house. Her feet feel heavy against the fiberglass floor of the tub. For a while she simply stands there before tending to the shampooing of her hair, the soaping of her softening, slightly shrinking fifty-three-year-old body, which she must fortify each morning with calcium pills. When she is fin-ished, she wipes the steam off the bathroom mirror and studies her face. A widow's face. But for most of her life, she reminds herself, a wife. And perhaps, one day, a grandmother, arriving in America laden with hand-knit sweaters and gifts, leaving, a month or two later, inconsolable, in tears.

Ashima feels lonely suddenly, horribly, permanently alone, and briefly, turned away from the mirror, she sobs for her husband. She feels overwhelmed by the thought of the move she is about to make, to the city that was once home and is now in its own way foreign. She feels both impatience and indifference for all the days she still must live, for something tells her she will not go quickly as her husband did. For thirty-three years she missed her life in India. Now she will miss her job at the library, the women with whom she's worked. She will miss throwing parties. She will miss living with her daughter, the surprising companionship they have formed, going into Cambridge together to see old movies at the Brattle, teaching her to cook the food Sonia had complained of eating as a child. She will miss the opportunity to drive, as she sometimes does on her way home from the library, to the university, past the engineering building where her husband once worked. She will miss the country in which she had grown to know and love her husband. Though his ashes have been scattered into the Ganges, it is here, in this house and in this town, that he will continue to dwell in her mind.

She takes a deep breath. In a moment she will hear the beeps of the security system, the garage door opening, car doors closing, her children's voices in the house. She applies lotion to her arms and legs, reaches for a peach-colored terry-cloth robe that hangs from a hook on the door. Her husband had given her the robe years ago, for a Christmas now long forgotten. This too she will have to give away, will have no use for where she is going. In such a humid climate it would take days for such a thick material to dry. She makes a note to herself, to wash it well and donate it to the thrift shop. She does not remember the year she'd gotten the robe, does not remember opening it, or her reaction. She knows only that it had been either Gogol or Sonia who had picked it out at one of the department stores at the mall, had wrapped it, even. That all her husband had done was to write his name and hers on the to-and-from tag. She does not fault him for this. Such omissions of devotion, of affection, she knows now, do not matter in the end. She no longer wonders what it might have been like to do what her children have done, to fall in love first rather than years later, to deliberate over a period of months or years and not a single afternoon, which was the time it had taken for her and Ashoke to agree to wed. It is the image of their two names on the tag that she thinks of, a tag she had not bothered to save. It reminds her of their life together, of the unexpected life he, in choosing to marry her, had given her here, which she had refused for so many years to accept. And though she still does not feel fully at home within these walls on Pemberton Road she knows that this is home nevertheless — the world for which she is responsible, which she has created, which is everywhere around her, needing to be packed up, given away, thrown out bit by bit. She slips her damp arms into the sleeves of the robe, ties the belt around her waist. It's always been a bit short on her, a size too small. Its warmth is a comfort all the same.

There is no one to greet Gogol on the platform when he gets off the train. He wonders if he's early, looks at his watch. Instead of going into the station house he waits on a bench outside. The last of the passengers board, the train doors slide to a close. The conductors wave their signals to one another, the wheels roll slowly away, the compartments glide forward one by one. He watches his fellow passengers being greeted by family members, lovers reunited with entangled arms, without a word. College students burdened by backpacks, returning for Christmas break. After a few minutes the platform is empty, as is the space the train had occupied. Now Gogol looks onto a field, some spindly trees against a cobalt twilight sky. He thinks of calling home but decides he is content to sit and wait awhile longer. The cool air is pleasant on his face after his hours on the train. He'd slept most of the journey to Boston, the conductor poking him awake once they'd reached South Station, and he was the only person left in the compartment, the last to get off. He had slept soundly, curled up on two seats, his book unread, using his overcoat as a blanket, pulled up to his chin.

He feels groggy still, a bit lightheaded from having skipped his lunch. At his feet are a duffel bag containing clothes, a shopping bag from Macy's with gifts bought earlier that morning, before catching his train at Penn Station. His choices are uninspired — a pair of fourteen-karat gold earrings for his mother, sweaters for Sonia and Ben. They have agreed to keep things simple this year. He has a week of vacation. There is work to do at the house, his mother has warned him. His room must be emptied, every last scrap either taken back with him to New York or tossed. He must help his mother pack her things, settle her accounts. They will drive her to Logan and see her off as far as airport security will allow. And then the house will be occupied by strangers, and there will be no trace that they were ever there, no house to enter, no name in the telephone directory.

Nothing to signify the years his family has lived here, no evidence of the effort, the achievement it had been. It's hard to believe that his mother is really going, that for months she will be so far. He wonders how his parents had done it, leaving their respective families behind, seeing them so seldom, dwelling unconnected, in a perpetual state of expectation, of longing. All those trips to Calcutta he'd once resented — how could they have been enough? They were not enough. Gogol knows now that his parents had lived their lives in America in spite of what was missing, with a stamina he fears he does not possess himself. He had spent years maintaining distance from his origins; his parents, in bridging that distance as best they could. And yet, for all his aloofness toward his family in the past, his years at college and then in New York, he has always hovered close to this quiet, ordinary town that had remained, for his mother and father, stubbornly exotic. He had not traveled to France as Moushumi had, or even to California as Sonia had done. Only for three months was he separated by more than a few small states from his father, a distance that had not troubled Gogol in the least, until it was too late. Apart from those months, for most of his adult life he has never been more than a four-hour train ride away. And there was nothing, apart from his family, to draw him home, to make this train journey, again and again.

It had been on the train, exactly a year ago, that he'd learned of Moushumi's affair. They were on their way up to spend Christmas with his mother and Sonia. They had left the city late, and outside the windows it had been dark, the disturbing pitch-black of early winter evenings. They were in the middle of a conversation about how to spend the coming summer, whether to rent a house in Siena with Donald and Astrid, an idea Gogol was resisting, when she'd said, "Dimitri says Siena is something out of a fairy tale." Immediately a hand had gone to her mouth, accompanied by a small intake of breath. And then, silence. "Who's Dimitri?" he'd asked. And then: "Are you having an affair?" The question had sprung out of him, something he had not consciously put together in his mind until that moment. It felt almost comic to him, burning in his throat. But as soon as he asked it, he knew. He felt the chill of her secrecy, numbing him, like a poison spreading quickly through his veins. He'd felt this way on only one other occasion, the night he had sat in the car with his father and learned the reason for his name. That night he'd experienced the same bewilderment, was sickened in the same way. But he felt none of the tenderness that he had felt for his father, only the anger, the humiliation of having been deceived. And yet, at the same time, he was strangely calm — in the moment that his marriage was effectively severed he was on solid ground with her for the first time in months. He remembered a night weeks ago; looking through her bag for her wallet, to pay the Chinese food delivery man, he'd pulled out her diaphragm case. She told him she'd gone to the doctor that afternoon to have it refitted, and so he'd put it out of his mind.

His first impulse had been to get out at the next station, to be as physically far from her as possible. But they were bound together, by the train, by the fact that his mother and Sonia were expecting them, and so somehow they had suffered through the rest of the journey, and then through the weekend, telling no one, pretending that nothing was wrong. Lying in his parents' house, in the middle of the night, she told him the whole story, about meeting Dimitri on a bus, finding his résumé in the bin. She confessed that Dimitri had gone with her to Palm Beach. One by one he stored the pieces of information in his mind, unwelcome, unforgivable. And for the first time in his life, another man's name upset Gogol more than his own.

The day after Christmas she left Pemberton Road, with the excuse to his mother and Sonia that a last-minute interview had fallen into place at the MLA. But really the job was a ruse; she and Gogol had decided that it was best for her to return to New York alone. By the time he arrived at the apartment, her clothes were gone, and her make-up and her bathroom things. It was as if she were away on another trip. But this time she didn't come back. She wanted nothing of the brief life they'd had together; when she appeared one last time at his office a few months later, so that he could sign the divorce papers, she told him she was moving back to Paris. And so, systematically, as he had done for his dead father, he removed her possessions from the apartment, putting her books into boxes on the sidewalk in the middle of the night for people to take, throwing out the rest. In the spring he went to Venice alone for a week, the trip he'd planned for the two of them, saturating himself in its ancient, melancholy beauty. He lost himself among the darkened narrow streets, crossing countless tiny bridges, discovering deserted squares, where he sat with a Campari or a coffee, sketching the facades of pink and green palaces and churches, unable ever to retrace his steps.

And then he returned to New York, to the apartment they'd inhabited together that was now all his. A year later, the shock has worn off, but a sense of failure and shame persists, deep and abiding. There are nights he still falls asleep on the sofa, without deliberation, waking up at three a.m. with the television still on. It is as if a building he'd been responsible for designing has collapsed for all to see. And yet he can't really blame her. They had both acted on the same impulse, that was their mistake. They had both sought comfort in each other, and in their shared world, perhaps for the sake of novelty, or out of the fear that that world was slowly dying. Still, he wonders how he's arrived at all this: that he is thirty-two years old, and already married and divorced. His time with her seems like a permanent part of him that no longer has any relevance, or currency. As if that time were a name he'd ceased to use.

He hears the familiar beep of his mother's car, spots it pulling into the parking lot. Sonia is sitting in the driver's seat, waving. Ben is next to her. This is the first time he's seeing Sonia since she and Ben have announced their engagement. He decides that he will ask her to stop off at a liquor store so he can buy some champagne. She steps out of the car, walking toward him. She is an attorney now, working in an office in the Hancock building. Her hair is cut to her jaw. She's wearing an old blue down jacket that Gogol had worn back in high school. And yet there is a new maturity in her face; he can easily imagine her, a few years from now, with two children in the back seat. She gives him a hug. For a moment they stand there with their arms around each other in the cold. "Welcome home, Goggles," she says.

For the last time, they assemble the artificial seven-foot tree, the branches color-coded at their base. Gogol brings up the box from the basement. For decades the instructions have been missing; each year they have to figure out the order in which the branches must be inserted, the longest ones at the bottom, the smallest at the top. Sonia holds the pole, and Gogol and Ben insert the branches. The orange go first, then the yellow, then the red and finally blue, the uppermost piece slightly bent under the white speckled ceiling. They place the tree in front of the window, drawing apart the curtains so that people passing by the house can see, as excited as they were when they were children. They decorate it with ornaments made by Sonia and Gogol in elementary school: construction paper candlesticks, Popsicle-stick god's-eyes, glitter-covered pinecones. A torn Banarasi sari of Ashima's is wrapped around the base. At the top they put what they always do, a small plastic bird covered with turquoise velvet, with brown wire claws.

Stockings are hung on nails from the mantel, the one put up for Moushumi last year now put up for Ben. They drink the champagne out of Styrofoam cups, forcing

Ashima to have some, too, and they play the Perry Como Christmas tape his father always liked. They tease Sonia, telling Ben about the year she had refused her gifts after taking a Hinduism class in college, coming home and protesting that they weren't Christian. Early in the morning, his mother, faithful to the rules of Christmas her children had taught her when they were little, will wake up and fill the stockings, with gift certificates to record stores, candy canes, mesh bags of chocolate coins. He can still remember the very first time his parents had had a tree in the house, at his insistence, a plastic thing no larger than a table lamp, displayed on top of the fireplace mantel. And yet its presence had felt colossal. How it had thrilled him. He had begged them to buy it from the drugstore. He remembers decorating it clumsily with garlands and tinsel and a string of lights that made his father nervous. In the evenings, until his father came in and pulled out the plug, causing the tiny tree to go dark, Gogol would sit there. He remembers the single wrapped gift that he had received, a toy that he'd picked out himself, his mother asking him to stand by the greeting cards while she paid for it. "Remember when we used to put on those awful flashing colored lights?" his mother says now when they are done, shaking her head. "I didn't know a thing back then."

★ ★ ★

At seven-thirty the bell rings, and the front door is left open as people and cold air stream into the house. Guests are speaking in Bengali, hollering, arguing, talking on top of one another, the sound of their laughter filling the already crowded rooms. The croquettes are fried in crackling oil and arranged with a red onion salad on plates. Sonia serves them with paper napkins. Ben, the jamai-to-be, is introduced to each of the guests. "I'll never keep all these names straight," he says at one point to Gogol. "Don't worry, you'll never need to," Gogol says. These people, these honorary aunts and uncles of a dozen different surnames, have seen Gogol grow, have surrounded him at his wedding, his father's funeral. He promises to keep in touch with them now that his mother is leaving, not to forget them. Sonia shows off her ring, six tiny diamonds surrounding an emerald, to the mashis, who wear their red and green saris. "You will have to grow your hair for the wedding," they tell Sonia. One of the meshos is sporting a Santa hat. They sit in the living room, on the furniture and on the floor. Children drift down into the basement, the older ones to rooms upstairs. He recognizes his old Monopoly game being played, the board in two pieces, the racecar missing ever since Sonia dropped it into the baseboard heater when she was little. Gogol does

437

not know to whom these children belong —
half the guests are people his mother has befriended in recent years, people who were at
his wedding but whom he does not recognize. People talk of how much they've come
to love Ashima's Christmas Eve parties, that
they've missed them these past few years,
that it won't be the same without her. They
have come to rely on her, Gogol realizes, to
collect them together, to organize the holiday,
to convert it, to introduce the tradition to
those who are new. It has always felt adopted
to him, an accident of circumstance, a celebration not really meant to be. And yet it
was for him, for Sonia, that his parents had
gone to the trouble of learning these customs. It was for their sake that it had come
to all this.

In so many ways, his family's life feels like
a string of accidents, unforeseen, unintended,
one incident begetting another. It had started
with his father's train wreck, paralyzing him
at first, later inspiring him to move as far as
possible, to make a new life on the other side
of the world. There was the disappearance of
the name Gogol's great-grandmother had
chosen for him, lost in the mail somewhere
between Calcutta and Cambridge. This had
led, in turn, to the accident of his being
named Gogol, defining and distressing him
for so many years. He had tried to correct
that randomness, that error. And yet it had

not been possible to reinvent himself fully, to break from that mismatched name. His marriage had been something of a misstep as well. And the way his father had slipped away from them, that had been the worst accident of all, as if the preparatory work of death had been done long ago, the night he was nearly killed, and all that was left for him was one day, quietly, to go. And yet these events have formed Gogol, shaped him, determined who he is. They were things for which it was impossible to prepare but which one spent a lifetime looking back at, trying to accept, interpret, comprehend. Things that should never have happened, that seemed out of place and wrong, these were what prevailed, what endured, in the end.

"Gogol, the camera," his mother calls out over the crowd. "Take some pictures tonight, please? I want to remember this Christmas. Next year at this time I'll be so far away." He goes upstairs to get his father's Nikon, still sitting on the top shelf of Ashoke's closet. There is practically nothing else there. No clothes hang from the rod. The emptiness upsets him, but the weight of the camera is solid, reassuring in his hands. He takes the camera into his room to load a fresh battery, a new roll of film. Last year he and Moushumi slept in the guest room, on the double bed, with its folded towels and a fresh bar of soap on top of the dresser, what his mother always left out for guests. But now that Sonia is here with Ben, the guest room is theirs, and Gogol is back in his room, with a bed he's never shared with Moushumi, or with anyone.

The bed is narrow, covered by a solid brown quilt. He can reach up and touch the frosted white light fixture suspended from the ceiling, filled with dead moths. The stains of Scotch tape once attached to his posters are visible on the walls. His desk was the folding square card table in the corner. Here he had done his homework under the dusty black gooseneck lamp. There is a thin, peacock blue carpet on the floor, slightly too large so that one side curls up against the wall. The shelves and drawers are mostly empty. Unwanted, miscellaneous things are in boxes already: essays written in high school, under the name Gogol. A report done in elementary school on Greek and Roman architecture, Corinthian and Ionic and Doric columns copied from an encyclopedia onto tracing paper. Cross pen-and-pencil sets, records listened to twice and then abandoned, clothes that were too large, too small — that never seemed worth transporting to the increasingly cramped apartments he inhabited over the years. All his old books, the ones he read by flashlight under the covers, and the ones required for college, only half-read, some with yellow USED stickers on the spines. His mother is going to donate them all to the library where she works, for their annual book sale in the spring. She has told him to go through them, make sure there's nothing he wants for himself. He pokes through the box. *The Swiss Family Robinson. On the Road. The Communist Manifesto. How to Get into an Ivy League School.*

And then another book, never read, long forgotten, catches his eye. The jacket is missing, the title on the spine practically faded. It's a thick clothbound volume topped with decades-old dust. The ivory pages are heavy, slightly sour, silken to the touch. The spine cracks faintly when he opens it to the title page. *The Short Stories of Nikolai Gogol.* "For Gogol Ganguli," it says on the front endpaper in his father's tranquil hand, in red ballpoint ink, the letters rising gradually, optimistically, on the diagonal toward the upper right-hand corner of the page. "The man who gave you his name, from the man who gave you your name" is written within quotation marks. Underneath the inscription, which he has never before seen, is his birthday, and the year, 1982. His father had stood in the doorway, just there, an arm's reach from where he sits now. He had left him to discover the inscription on his own, never again asking Gogol what he'd thought of the book, never mentioning the book at all. The handwriting reminds him of the checks his father used to give him all through college, and for years afterward, to help him along, to put down a security deposit, to buy his first suit, sometimes for no reason at all. The name he had so detested, here hidden and preserved — that was the first thing his father had given him.

The givers and keepers of Gogol's name are far from him now. One dead. Another, a widow, on the verge of a different sort of departure, in order to dwell, as his father does, in a separate world. She will call him, once a week, on the phone. She will learn to send e-mail, she says. Once or twice a week, he will hear "Gogol" over the wires, see it typed on a screen. As for all the people in the house, all the mashis and meshos to whom he is still, and will always be, Gogol — now that his mother is moving away, how often will he see them? Without people in the world to call him Gogol, no matter how long he himself lives, Gogol Ganguli will, once and for all, vanish from the lips of loved ones, and so, cease to exist. Yet the thought of this eventual demise provides no sense of victory, no solace. It provides no solace at all.

Gogol gets up, shuts the door to his room, muffling the noise of the party that swells below him, the laughter of the children playing down the hall. He sits cross-legged on the bed. He opens the book, glances at an illustration of Nikolai Gogol, and then at the chronology of the author's life on the facing page. Born March 20, 1809. The death of his father, 1825. Publishes his first story, 1830. Travels to Rome, 1837. Dies 1852, one month before his forty-third birthday. In another ten years, Gogol Ganguli will be that age. He wonders if he will be married again one day, if he will ever have a child to name. A month from now, he will begin a new job at a smaller architectural practice, producing his own designs. There is a possibility, eventually, of becoming an associate, of the firm incorporating his name. And in that case Nikhil will live on, publicly celebrated, unlike Gogol, purposely hidden, legally diminished, now all but lost.

He turns to the first story. "The Overcoat." In a few minutes his mother will come upstairs to find him. "Gogol," she will say, opening the door without knocking, "where is the camera? What's taking so long? This is no time for books," she will scold, hastily noting the volume open against the covers, unaware, as her son has been all these years, that her husband dwells discreetly, silently, patiently, within its pages. "There is a party downstairs, people to talk to, food to be taken out of the oven, thirty glasses of water to fill and line up on the sideboard. To think that we will never again all be here together. If only your father could have stayed with us a bit longer," she will add, her eyes growing momentarily damp. "But come, see the children under the tree."

He will apologize, put the book aside, a small corner of a page turned over to mark his place. He will walk downstairs with his mother, join the crowded party, photographing the people in his parents' life, in this house, one last time, huddled on the sofas, plates held in their laps, eating with their hands. Eventually, at his mother's insistence, he will eat as well, seated cross-legged on the floor, and speak to his parents' friends, about his new job, about New York, about his mother, about Sonia and Ben's wedding. After dinner he will help Sonia and Ben scrape bay leaves and lamb bones and cinnamon sticks from plates, pile them on the counters and two burners of the stove. He will watch his mother do what his father used to do toward the end of every party, spooning fine-leaf Lopchu tea into two kettles. He will watch her give away leftovers in the cooking pots themselves. As the hours of the evening pass he will grow distracted, anxious to return to his room, to be alone, to read the book he had once forsaken, has abandoned until now. Until moments ago it was destined to disappear from his life altogether, but he has salvaged it by chance, as his father was pulled from a crushed train forty years ago. He leans back against the headboard, adjusting a pillow behind his back. In a few minutes he will go downstairs, join the party, his family. But for now his mother is distracted, laughing at a story a friend is telling her, unaware of her son's absence. For now, he starts to read.

The employees of Thorndike Press hope you have enjoyed this Large Print book. All our Thorndike and Wheeler Large Print titles are designed for easy reading, and all our books are made to last. Other Thorndike Press Large Print books are available at your library, through selected bookstores, or directly from us.

For information about titles, please call:

(800) 223-1244

or visit our Web site at:

www.gale.com/thorndike
www.gale.com/wheeler

To share your comments, please write:

Publisher
Thorndike Press
295 Kennedy Memorial Drive
Waterville, ME   04901